unshed tears

Edit
Hofman

unshed
tears

a novel..

but not a fiction

Unshed Tears
by Edith Hofmann

Published in Great Britain by
Quill Press
P.O. Box 2002,
Newark, Nottinghamshire. NG22 9ZG

British Library Catalogue in Publication Data
A catalogue record for this book is available from the British
Library

ISBN 0-9536280-3-5

Printed and bound by
Omnia Books Ltd, Glasgow.

To my parents

and all the children of Prague

who did not return

Author's Acknowledgement

*With special thanks to Stephen Smith
and all those involved in bringing this book to publication*

Introduction

When Edith Hofmann sat down to write this book, she was a 19-year-old coming to terms with the fact of her own survival. It is a story which describes a struggle; the struggle to come to terms with a haunting past, the struggle to survive, and the struggle to unburden a broken heart. It also embodies a struggle to form, in language, that which at times all but defies linguistic form. When Hofmann started writing this book she had only been speaking English for two years, and yet she wanted to convey her experiences, in English, to those with whom she had made her home.

The cruel reality was that no one really wanted to hear. She poured out her soul, only to be told that 'no one was interested in the war any more'. This was 1950. Some fifty years later she brought the manuscript to me, wondering whether such a text would have any value. For fifty years her text had lain in her drawer, waiting to be read. Her story is a novel, but it certainly is not a fiction. Scared for her own safety, Hofmann chose to write in the third person rather than pen a memoir. Every page is bound up with the intricate details of her life, those whom she loved, and those whom she lost; the echoes of those terrible years, and the memory they imposed. In compiling this text, we decided neither to change it, by removing discrepancies or updating anything which Hofmann wrote in the late 1940s, nor to improve her English, but rather to leave it as a raw and indelible testimony not only to her survival but to her bid to survive survival. You will be moved; not only by what she has written, but by the fact that she wrote at all.

Stephen Smith, January 2001

I

The place was Prague. The time was five o'clock in the morning on a misty October day in the year of 1941. The streets were quiet, the city still asleep. The capital's picturesque buildings and its hundred spires rearing up proudly towards the sky, were surrounded by peace and darkness, unaware of the thousand souls for whom this hour meant the beginning of a journey into the unknown. Even the Germans who have changed the gay and prosperous city into a place of fear and hatred, were still tucked under their heavy feather beds, dreaming of a greater Reich.

The winter had come in exceptionally early and the north wind that had been blowing all through the night was bringing with it gusts of sleet and snow. A bird rising to great height could have perceived a thousand little specks weighed down by heavy loads, struggling against the weather and darkness, making their way from all corners of the city to a strange meeting place.

Among them were three silent figures: a man, a woman and a young girl. Their steps were heavy, their backs bent under huge rucksacks. From time to time they halted, leant their rucksacks against the wall of a house in an effort to gather new strength, wiped the slush off their faces, and resumed their journey. They passed the Old Town with its narrow streets, churches and antique shops, and crossed the river Vltava by a bridge that linked this historic part of the capital with the spacious modern one. On the bridge they paused for a moment and looked left where the silhouette of the castle, high upon a hill overlooking the river and the ancient quarters of the town, stood majestically as it had stood there for several hundred years, watching history go by.

This was Prague - the river, the fairy-tale-like castle, ancient but picturesque buildings. It had seen victories, great kings, glory and also defeats.

This was the time of submission, of defeat, but also of quiet fight, resolution and hope....

At last the man beckoned them to continue their journey. Time was passing and they must not be late. A little reluctantly they detached themselves from the parapet on which they had been leaning and directed their steps towards the embankment on the other side of the river.

They turned right and for about ten minutes made their way along the embankment, bordered on one side by the river, on the other by the wooded hill whose wet autumn-coloured leaves were gradually covering the ground, leaving the twisted branches dark and naked. The first tram, almost empty, lighted by small blue lamps, hummed by and disappeared in the distance. The three people gave it a glance, and a look of wrath crept into their faces. For them there were no trams. They were different - a yellow star that was fastened onto their coats told of their creed - they were Jewish, and Jews had long since been deprived of all luxuries.

Chapter I

They plodded on and at last entered the wider streets of Letna. For the following ten minutes the man led them through a labyrinth of side streets and then suddenly they were there. Their steps slowed down and eventually they stopped, gazing with slightly troubled eyes at the scene across the road.

On the pavement in front of the huge, famous Exhibition Hall, a bewildered crowd was being whipped into lines by tall, self-possessed men in the grey-green uniform of the German military police. From all directions dark figures were approaching and looking uncertainly around them, slowly, hesitantly adding themselves to the murmuring crowd.

"This is the end," the woman of about forty said, quietly. She stared in front of her with a pale and clouded face.

Judith, a girl of almost fourteen, slipped her hand into her father's. He was tall, well-built and had an air of culture, intelligence and self-confidence. He pressed her small hand reassuringly, then lifted his wife's chin, forced an easy smile into his face, looked into her eyes and said confidently, gently, "We must have faith and courage, and above all we mustn't show them that we are afraid."

Suddenly the girl's face brightened and an optimistic gleam appeared in her gaze.

"Don't worry Mummy, you never know what good may come of it all. Here we have to be so careful and afraid all the time, the Germans threaten us on every corner. Perhaps they will send us to a town where all the Jews will live together and nobody will bully us. Maybe there will even be a school. It could not be much worse than it is here, anyway, could it?" Judith looked up at her mother, anxious to see her sad look vanish. As if to emphasise her argument she added: "What can we lose, tell me?"

Unshed Tears

The woman, who had a very beautiful and kindly face, stroked her hair tenderly and said softly, "Perhaps you are right."

Then a little smile won its way through the worried mask.

Mr. Baron, who was five years older than his wife, put his arms around her and Judith, and declared determinedly: "Whatever happens, we must stick together. As long as we are together everything will be alright." He kissed them both on the forehead and then decided: "We shall have to go now."

Taking them firmly by the arm he led them across the road. Silently they stood at the end of the line.

The clock on the nearby church struck six. The huge gate of the Exhibition Hall was flung open and the queue began to move forward - very, very slowly.

The bitter crying of children pierced the air. They were uncomfortable and cold and scared of the German officers who were marching stiffly up and down the line, securing order by waving their whips in front of people's eyes, and bellowing in their faces every time anything occurred that did not fall in with their pattern of discipline.

Very few people spoke, and if they uttered something it was only a remark about wet feet, cold hands or a guess about the future.

A number of children, perplexed by their surroundings, persistently questioned their parents, making them nervous, so that they snapped at them impatiently. There were people, however, who held their heads high, determined not to let anything break them, facing the situation with an optimistic air, while others looked indifferent.

Most of the older boys and girls were imbued with an

Chapter I

adventurous spirit, and an eager gleam, mixed with curiosity, shone forth from their eyes. They were going to see the world! Their excitement, innocence and good humour brought tears to the eyes of many mothers whose hearts were charged with foreboding.

Step by step the thousand people moved slowly down the gentle slope towards the big gate - towards a future which all of them were to share. It was the third transport from Prague - the so-called 'intelligentsia transport', because most family men had academic backgrounds. The transport before them, in whose footsteps they were following, now bore the reputation of being the 'millionaires', just as the first transport that had left Prague a fortnight earlier, comprised one thousand of the poorer Jews who had settled in the young nation's capital.

It was in the middle of the night three days before that thunderous knocks shook the doors of hundreds of homes, arousing their inhabitants. With trembling hands they accepted the summons which they had known would come one day and deprive them of their homes and send them away into the unknown with only fifty kilograms of luggage, but which they had hoped would avoid them for a long time to come, and thus allow them the comfort of their hearth during the approaching winter months.

They were Jews - and Jews were not a people like all others: they had to be removed. Forty-seven thousand more, living in Prague, were still waiting anxiously for the hand of the night-messenger to strike at their doors and present them silently with the pink card which announced the beginning of a new chapter in their lives. Other towns would soon follow suit. The German organisers had it all worked out.

Unshed Tears

Once the inhabitants, whose identity cards were marked with a 'J', realised that they were all destined for the same fate, the hustle and bustle began. They had to become practical, seeing their future in the right perspective. The winter lay ahead of them. They sorted out their belongings, filling their cases with their most useful possessions. It was mainly a question of clothes. Money and jewels they had long since handed over to the Nazis, and food was not allowed to exceed the ration for five days. Some made a rush effort to hide part of their property with their Christian friends, while others made arrangements with them for secret codes in case correspondence was to be allowed to pass between them.

Knowing the German mentality, they all decided on one thing: what they had on them was what they were most likely to be able to keep. For the rest - no one knew what was going to happen to it. Who could be sure that the well-selected luggage would still be theirs after they had entered the 'Gate'? Therefore they clad themselves in layers of underwear, pullovers, skiing suits because they were warm and weatherproof, boots and woollen socks over their stockings. They wore their warmest coats and mackintoshes. Women tied scarves around their heads.

As the first rays of light were breaking through the darkness, a lonely figure appeared on the other side of the street. She had no luggage, nor was she dressed in any special outfit. She stopped on the pavement, her eyes searching up and down the line. Then she moved on up the street and again her eyes were sweeping the masses of people opposite her, trying to single out the one person she had come to see. Suddenly a hand raised itself above the crowd and a soft voice of recognition called out: "Eva!"

Chapter I

Eva, a girl of fourteen, was Judith's best friend. She had come to say her last farewell. They had seen each other on the previous night, but as Eva came over, breathless with excitement, she explained, "I didn't have the patience to stay in bed. I had to come and see you off."

For a little while they looked at each other happily, glad to have another few moments together.

" Is there anything I can do for you - give a message to someone, go somewhere, or be helpful in any sort of way?"

Eva's keen, enquiring gaze skipped from Judith to her parents and back again.

"It's very nice of you to have come," Mrs. Baron said, "but I don't think there is really anything you could do for us just now."

"I wish we could go today as well," Eva uttered, a little bitterly. "We shall have to go anyway, so at least we could have been together."

"Perhaps they will send us all to the same place. We might meet again very soon."

For a while they tried to ease the situation by carefree chatter and then suddenly they found themselves quite near the entrance to the hall. Eva's hand plunged into her pocket, recovered a solid penknife and handed it to Judith.

"I have brought you something. It is only a small gift, but it may come in handy one day."

She shook hands with Mr. and Mrs. Baron and lastly with Judith. They made an effort to smile cheerfully as they said their final good bye. Then Eva's lonely figure clad in a blue coat trimmed with grey fur, strolled away. Her hands were in her pockets, her head was bowed. Her brown curls, weighed down by moisture, clung to her head. At the corner she turned once more and her thoughtful face lit up as she waved for the last time.

Then Judith and her parents entered the gate - the gate into another world.

* * * * *

Behind the huge double doors in a wide but short corridor stood a large table. On one side of it were seated three well-fed, self-satisfied, stern-looking German police officers. With superiority in their eyes they lifted their double chins and examined the Baron family from underneath the shields of their tall caps.

"Documents!" one of them ejaculated, in an arrogant voice.

Mr. Baron passed him the family's documents. The giant looked through them in a most official manner, aware of his self-importance, and stamped each one with the words: EVACUATED ON THE 26TH OF OCTOBER 1941. Then he returned them to Mr. Baron.

"Have you any gold or silver, or any precious jewels?" enquired the same man in a voice filled with superiority and threats.

"No, sir," Mr. Baron answered, calmly.

"Any fur coats?"

"No, sir."

"From now on you can forget your names and call yourselves 118, 119, and 120. Remember that! Your places and your luggage will be marked likewise. Is that clear?"

"Yes, sir."

"Now buzz off!... Next one!"

Chapter I

Silently they walked through the short corridor. At the end of it was a wide opening. As they reached it, a huge hall opened up in front of them. It was dimly lit and swarming with people. The floor was covered with mattresses and in the little passages between them the bewildered newcomers were searching for their places. Each mattress was to be the living space for one person for the following few days.

Men, women and children were nervously pushing their way past each other. A new sensation had taken possession of them. They were a mass of people behind locked doors. A shade of hostility crept into a few faces; their owners blamed everyone and everything for their misfortune. From the very first moment they laid aside the etiquette of society and pursued their natural instincts.

The Baron family stepped inside and began to search for their places. They shouldered their way along the winding passages, looking left and right, longing to throw off their luggage, sit down and gather themselves together. Eventually this moment arrived. They dropped down on their mattresses that had fortunately been placed near the wall at the far end of the hall, rid themselves of their rucksacks and stretched out their feet, thankful for the opportunity. Many more people were pouring into the hall. Those whose numbers exceeded five hundred were guided through a door into a hall adjacent to the first one. Several women became hysterical, had crying fits or fainted. Gradually, things began to sort themselves out. By ten o'clock in the morning almost everyone seemed calmer. The excitement and chaos of the first moments had vanished; somehow, in this place, surrounded by four walls and cut off from the outer world, people began to grasp the situation for the first time, and resolutions formed in their minds. They soon realised that there were only two ways of carrying on: one was to consider the battle as lost from the very start and behave accordingly; the other was to reconcile oneself to the truth and fight it in the appropriate manner. The latter required courage, though the persons who chose the former were the more unfortunate ones. They gave up from the beginning and there did not seem anything left to them to fight for. They were surrounded by gloom and wrapped in self-pity.

Two or three women attempted suicide during their stay at the hall: one succeeded. The majority, however, decided to face up to everything, and many even managed to do so with jokes on their lips and an encouraging twinkle in their eyes, a sense of humour seeming doubtlessly the most valuable gift anyone could have been endowed with.

A member of the transport had been appointed by the Germans as the leader and he had four men to help him to keep things in order. He was a man of about forty, well-built, capable and sharp-witted, but not without conceit and a desire to display his importance. He fussed about and certainly made his presence felt.

About eleven o'clock the huge gates closed and all Germans disappeared. The transport leader, who had received full instructions how the place was to be run, his helpers and a permanent Jewish staff, were responsible for law and order inside the building. Outside, the German guards kept watch.

Towards midday the prisoners realised that there was no other way but to get settled in their new surroundings and make themselves 'at home'. They began to spread out sheets and blankets or sleeping bags, which most of them had brought

Chapter I

along rolled up on their rucksacks, on top of their mattresses, found their towels, toothbrushes and other articles and placed them near at hand. Then some began to explore their surroundings. With assumed cheerfulness they wandered along the passages from one hall to the other in order to exchange visits with friends.

Exclamations of surprise and shouts such as "You are here, too?", "Well I never!" were heard all over the place. People shook hands, chatted for a few minutes, reviewed the situation, told each other 'where they lived' and promised to exchange visits later. Some preferred to stay in their places and relax, while others sat on their mattresses and ate. The rest sat, brooded, grumbled, or fainted. Neighbouring little children were making their first moves towards getting acquainted. The older boys and girls, quite excited by the adventure, were roaming about in search of friends.

Judith Baron made her bed, ate a sandwich and wandered away from her corner. She strolled along the passages, her eyes wide open, her mind eager to take in everything that was going on around her. She greeted a few of her parents' friends and enthusiastically acknowledged the presence of boys and girls she knew.

It was quite fun to have so many friends close at hand all the time. The prospect of being able to be with them and have practically nothing else to do but spend her time playing with them, pleased her. The whole situation was promising a lot of excitement, adventure and surprises. Like most schoolchildren, she was enjoying the excitement.

At one end of the hall she discovered an open door that led into a small courtyard which was surrounded on all sides by high walls. On one side were long troughs with cold water taps attached to them; on the other were most primitive latrines. People with towels over their shoulders or arms and soap in their hands were making their way to and from the yard.

They had meat and barley for dinner. It was brought into the hall in huge bins and given out by the cooks in white aprons and tall hats. The people lined up with little pots or tin plates, took the food to their places and ate it with a spoon.

The three days before their departure passed fairly peacefully. They had three meals a day; breakfast that consisted of coffee and rolls, a main meal and a snack in the evening.

People got to know each other; faces became familiar, and the whole place took on a more friendly shape.

As time passed, the tenseness of the first few hours was giving way to an atmosphere in which everyone felt more at home and became part of the place. Some were filling in the time by making social calls, playing cards or chess, chatting about the good old times, telling jokes, or reading. The older children gathered in various corners, played games, sang lively songs, or told stories.

Mr. and Mrs. Baron had many friends among the thousand people. Mr. Alexander, who was one of them, was a frequent visitor to their place. Although he was only about thirty-four, he had held quite an important position in Prague. He was tall, dignified, calm and self-confident. He had dark hair, slightly grey at the temples, and dark eyes that showed intelligence, understanding and a sense of humour. He played chess with Mr. Baron for many hours a day. The rest of the time he spent reading or walking among the people, of whom he knew quite

Chapter I

a fair proportion, talking to his friends, cheering up those who needed it. He was good at cheering up people and more than once he talked Mrs. Baron out of an attack of depression. Judith sat by and watched, and was very grateful to him.

Surprisingly, people slept well during the nights, and the silence was broken only by snores, some of them very violent, and here and there by a crying child.

★ ★ ★ ★ ★

It was about two hours before dawn on the 26th of October 1941, the date marked in the documents of members of the third transport as the day of evacuation. The big gate leading into the hall suddenly flew open and a noisy group of German Schu-Po men stormed in. With rough movements they switched on all the lights and, waving their canes, invaded all the passages between the mattresses, shouting hoarsely, "Aufstehen! Aufstehen!"

The aroused inhabitants at once propped themselves up on their elbows and, realizing the meaning of this early disturbance, got up quickly.

"Everyone is to be ready in an hour's time!" the Germans shouted. Then, still waving their canes, they made for the gate and left, bolting it carefully from the outside.

The appointed Jewish staff got busy hurrying the people on. The latter dressed quickly and began to pack. They gathered all their belongings and filled their rucksacks. Then they rolled up their blankets and tied them on top with pieces of string or leather straps. Having done that, they began to search around, looking under the mattresses, for anything they might have left behind.

Every mattress was a busy area of its own. The whole place was humming with excitement and apprehension. Streams of people with towels over their shoulders were struggling along through the hall strewn with mattresses, luggage, active men and women and reckless children, on their way to and from the little courtyard.

Steaming coffee was brought in in huge cans and the prisoners, carrying mugs, or saucepans, lined up for it. They returned to their places, clutching the vessels between their cold fingers, their bodies eager to receive the hot drink.

The calmer ones seated themselves on their mattresses and, having fished in their rucksacks for some food, settled down to a few minutes' meal. Mothers fed their children, who had received hot milk instead of coffee. By the end of a busy and active hour, most prisoners were sitting by their luggage - some nervous, restless, distressed; others calm and composed.

In exactly an hour's time, the big double doors flew open, and once more the sound of marching feet travelled through the air. At once a hush spread across the hall and a thousand pairs of eyes glued themselves on the officer who climbed onto the table in the front, and raised his hand, asking for full attention. It was the man who, from the beginning, appeared to be in charge of the transport.

Aware of his importance, he now began to shout in a coarse voice: "When I tell you, you will start to line up in fives according to your numbers, outside this building. You are to leave your big bags behind, as they would hinder you in marching in an orderly fashion. Twenty strong men from this transport will collect them and carry them out onto the lorries waiting outside. This luggage, as well as that collected from

Chapter I

your homes a few days ago, will go by the same train as you. Make sure it's carefully marked with your number. You will receive it all on your arrival...."

"I have a feeling that we shall never see our luggage again," Mrs. Baron remarked, bitterly.

"You are always so pessimistic. What would have been the point of them asking us to pack it? They could have just as well told us to leave it behind in our flats. There probably isn't enough room in the carriages and, as he said, we couldn't march very quickly with our rucksacks on."

"They have a reason for everything. They know what they are doing."

"We mustn't worry now, not now before we know for certain...." He paused for a moment, his glance brushed Judith's smaller rucksack, and travelled back to his family who at once suspected the plan in his mind.

"Just in case -" he said in an undertone, "- something saved may be better than nothing."

He picked up Judith's rucksack which, compared with his broad shoulders, looked fairly small in size. They all tied their satchels round their waists and silently followed the crowd into the street.

The air was dry and frosty; the dark blue sky was blurred by slight mist.

Within a quarter of an hour the thousand people were ready, lined up in fives on the wide pavement. A line of German Schu-Po men stood on either side of the ranks like a guard of honour. There was one to every ten prisoners, who stood still, waiting for further orders. A few officers were marching up and down the pavement, counting the fives, making sure that the numbers were not short of one. A signal set the two police officers in the lead in motion. The ranks of prisoners followed.

No one spoke. The file of guards on each side proceeded alongside them. They all left the pavement and marched through the middle of the deserted street like a regiment of tired soldiers. Only the clatter of heavy shoes and boots broke the silence.

Most people guessed to which railway station they were being led. The tall houses on both sides were covered in darkness. The day had not yet begun for the majority of Prague's population. The prisoners could not help feeling that the sound they produced with their feet brought many spectators to the windows to peer at them curiously from behind the black-out curtains.

The procession moved down a hill, by the side of a park, and then along the railway track itself to the station.

A special train stood waiting for them. The thousand people were divided into groups of fifty and then, with a guard in the lead, were marched off to their appointed places. Fifty to a waggon, and every place was marked by the prisoner's number. On each seat lay a little parcel containing a bun, a piece of cheese and dried prunes. The seats were wooden, the windows were bordered by black-out curtains.

After a quarter of an hour's commotion the locks of the doors clicked from outside, and then everything was still. For a whole hour the train stood waiting in the station.

Mr. Baron put his arm gently round his wife and smiled. "Reserved seats with food provided, no luggage to worry about, nothing to carry, service provided and all without cost. What else can we wish for?"

Chapter I

With a little sadness in her eyes, Mrs. Baron smiled back at him: "I wouldn't know, I'm sure."

She placed her head on his shoulder and her gaze wandered off into the space above the rooftops of the wakening city.

II

The sun was rising and its rays penetrated the slight morning mist, greeting the wakening city. A thousand pairs of eyes were gazing longingly, sadly, across the roof-tops, past the towers, towards the castle, whose spires gleamed in this shower of rays the sun was offering them. It was silent in the train that was taking the people across the railway bridge and away from Prague that was theirs no more. Each of them was saying a quiet farewell to the city that in his heart was the most precious place in the world - home. Thoughts and questions were passing through their minds - thoughts that were mostly memories, questions that had no answers to them. Would they ever see this sight again? How long would it all last? Tears were filling many eyes, blurring the view with which they were so reluctant to part.

Suddenly the silence was broken by an old man's voice singing the slow patriotic song known to everyone:

"Prague is so beautiful
at any time of the day or year ..."

Another voice followed, and then all the thousand voices became one. Loyalty and love filled every note and the people felt close to each other, united in their sorrow, fear and courage.

Then everything was over.

The last house drifted out of sight and the unknown future crept upon them, leaving them guessing and tongue-tied for a long while to come.

There were no compartments in the train; each carriage housed fifty people. Barren fields and meadows and little picturesque villages were rushing by. The train was heading north.

One hour followed another, and gradually the mood in the carriages began to take on another aspect. Sentiment was left behind as people realized they had to face the future. It was a future that demanded courage, a strong will and a sense of humour.

From time to time cheerful songs rang through the air, lifting the heaviness of the atmosphere. As time passed, people filled it by sleeping, reading, arguing or telling jokes.

Prague - Dresden - Breslau -

The train was taking them through Germany towards the Polish border. Night set in and everything was blacked out. The darkness was almost impenetrable. The countryside was flat. Everything around was silent; only the roar of the engine indicating some life.

About midnight the train slowed down and stopped with a jerk. People who had been dozing lifted their heads unwillingly, rubbed their eyes, trying to bring themselves to full consciousness. Instinctively they peered out of the window. There, not far away, big furnaces were blazing, clouds of sparks were bursting in the blackness of the night. They were outside Katowitz, in Poland.

Chapter 2

The general stillness of that dark flat countryside was shattered by the sound of steam being released from the engine's outlets, feet running on the gravel along the track, German voices, and the bangs and jolts of carriages being joined together. It was a peculiar mixture of sounds which no-one dared to interrupt.

They stood there for endless hours, for no apparent reason at all. Time crept by, many heads drooped drowsily again, while others kept erect, attuning their ears to every sound, alert to everything that was going on.

At last the final command came, the train jerked once more and set into motion.... A grey dawn found them well within the boundaries of Poland. They were rushing through muddy fields: there was no hill or forest to break the monotony of the flat countryside. Rain mingled with wet snowflakes came pelting against the windowpanes of the train as, from time to time, a strong wind raced past them.

As life began to return in the compartments, Judith drowsily lifted her head and peered through the weatherbeaten windows at the miserable world outside. Then, realising that most of the people around her were preoccupied with inventing a breakfast of some sort, she reached for her knapsack on the rack and, placing it on her knees, began to rummage through its contents in the hope of discovering something that might have got there by a miracle, without her knowing about it. Not in the least surprised, her hand emerged with a solitary bun, a single remnant of yesterday's food package. Discontentedly she gazed at it, nibbled at its edge and put it back in the knapsack. She had never liked dry buns.

Mrs. Baron, with a worried look on her face, shared out to her family some food brought from home. The remainder was frighteningly small, but they had to be fed.

About eleven o'clock the train stopped once more in the middle of the countryside. Reluctantly, not wishing to be taken notice of, Judith recovered a black exercise book from her knapsack and huddling into the corner, began to enter into it the events of the last thirty hours.

In a short while, however, they were on their way again, and the jerks prevented Judith from writing. Resignedly she closed her fountain pen and placed it in the side pocket of her satchel. Involuntarily her fingers began to ramble through the pages of her diary and then, for the following two hours, she was lost in a dreamland and for a long time the surroundings ceased to exist for her.

She read the first lines which she had written on the last day of the year 1937.

"I am having the most wonderful holiday anyone can have. The sun is shining, the snow is perfect and tonight I am going to skate at the open air New Year's Eve Ball...." There was no need for her to read on. The events of that first winter holiday she had away from home came back to her mind, and she found herself able to recapture every minute of that exhilarating time.

She was a small girl of eleven when all this had happened. She was in her first year at grammar school when her teachers organised this trip to the Tatra mountains. There were about a hundred of them altogether, boys and girls between eleven and nineteen. She was the youngest. They lived in two chalets high up on a mountain overlooking the most gorgeous countryside. They were pretty chalets, brown with red roofs and green shutters. Inside, they were quite modern with hot water taps in the rooms.

Chapter 2

What a carefree time they had, skiing, skating, sleighing and snowballing in the glittering sunshine. The year 1938 was on the doorstep, but who among the happy crowd cared what was going on in the world, and in which direction the steps of fate were taking them?

David was there, too. David was more than a year older, and had been her best friend ever since they were quite small. He lived in the same apartment house, just one floor beneath the Barons, and he had never insulted her by calling her a girl. He had said it was her bad luck to have been born one, but he was prepared to forget it and treat her exactly like the other boys. That was ever since, at the age of seven, he had scornfully proclaimed that he wasn't going to play with girls any more, and she, instead of bursting into tears, had put out her fists and proved that she could match any boy where strength and fighting were concerned. Anyway, she could run faster than anyone of her age in the whole street or school, including the boys. Ever since then he had never offended her by calling her a girl, and he even went so far as to explain his theory to the other boys who were of a different opinion. But gradually she had been accepted in their midst, which included playing ice hockey and Red Indians with them.

Judith's mind lingered over this subject. Did she really want to be like a boy or was it only that it was the only way to stay in David's favour? She knew that in his company she had more excitement and fun than when playing with girls, and she was very fond of David. That's what it was - she didn't want their friendship to break up. Often she would dress up in her prettiest dress, hoping that David would secretly notice it....

Anyway, David had gone to England, after which she kept

the company of girls, and gradually woke up to the true meaning of her own sex. She knew she wanted to grow up into a gentle, kind and graceful woman like her mother....

It was on the 18th of April 1938 that she described the episode of the History Master and the sneezing powder, and on the same day they were given a composition to write about "The person I should most like to be." She fixed her eyes upon the sentence, which read: "I wrote that I would not like to be anybody else because I am the happiest person in the world."

That was three years ago.

"I should not like to be anybody else in the whole world because I think I am the happiest person on earth. I would not change my parents for anyone I can think of ... not that I want to be tied to my mother's apron. No. I want to be independent, but it is a good feeling to know that they are here when I want them, that they understand me and see my point of view...."

Judith transferred her gaze from the book to her grey surroundings and let it linger on her mother who was quietly looking out of the window, and then on to her father who was discussing politics with a friend, his hands taking part in the lively conversation.

Everything around was drab and cheerless as if all joy had disappeared from the world and hidden in an unreachable hiding-place.

Instinctively she knew her mother's thoughts, and a feeling of tightness gripped her heart. Where were they going?... For the first time a strange fear of the unknown took possession of her and her mind tried desperately to find a favourable solution to her problems.

With the contents of her composition still in her thoughts,

Chapter 2

she wondered how true these words would sound today. Was she still the happiest child on earth? She thought for a long time, but before she finished thinking, she knew that she wouldn't change places with anybody. Although there might be happier girls somewhere, she wouldn't give up her people for all the freedom and riches in the world....

As she looked back upon her earlier years now, she realized that she never had everything she wanted; presents came only once a year - on her birthday. They were good presents, but in between there was nothing. She never had things her own way if her parents considered them not right, and there was nothing she could do about it. Perhaps it was just that - the knowledge that they did what they, with their wisdom knew was right - that gave her the warm feeling of security....

She had burned those exercise books on the last day at home, for she realized that she had a long way to go yet before she could produce something worth keeping, and she wouldn't leave them behind for strange people to find....

What was to become of all her dreams? What had the future in store for her? Where was it they were going? The sleet was beating against the windowpane....

It was on a dark day like this that she and David sat in their little cubby-hole, he, as usual, confident, sure of everything he was saying. They were having their tea, and over thick slices of rye bread and butter he was putting over his lesson:

"It doesn't really matter whether you were born a girl or a boy as long as you have the mind of a gentleman. That's what counts most of all."

Meeting her eager and willing gaze, he continued: "A real gentleman is always honest and never tells lies. He is not afraid of anything, and faces difficulties with courage. And lastly, he helps others and tries to make himself useful...."

That oath they had drawn up verifying their desire to conform to these rules, and signed with blots of their own blood squeezed out of pin-pricks from their thumbs, lay still buried in a tin box in their secret hiding-place, under a bush in the park. Would they ever recover it, or was someone going to find it many years from now and wonder where it came from?

She hadn't thought about all this for a long, long time. The diary said it happened on the 17th of May 1938. It seemed as though the days of carefree childhood were far in the past and only memories and a part of David's mind remained. They were at present the only connection with all her ambitions....

Slowly Judith was turning the pages of her diary. She read about her mother's birthday, her success in athletics, people talking a great deal about politics, and the glorious summer holiday that followed. And then came autumn, an autumn that made her grow suddenly five years older and opened her eyes to a hundred new things.

Heavy clouds assembled over Czechoslovakia: the atmosphere was getting close. Laughter disappeared from people's faces and anxiety crept silently in its place. Little knots of people gathered on street corners, arguing, talking, reviewing the gravity of the situation. Her parents became tense; she did not dare bother them with anything. And then it really happened.

The Germans occupied the Sudetenland; Jews from Germany, Austria and the occupied part of Bohemia came pouring into Prague, seeking shelter from the Nazis. A family came to live with them before they found a home of their own, which meant mattresses on the floor, beds made between two chairs, suitcases all over the place and the peace of their home gone. Still, they were grateful to have one of their own.

President Beneš spoke to the nation over the radio, said farewell, and left for England. In a strange way people drew closer together, old, petty hostilities ceased; they sang patriotic songs, recited well-known poems and waited anxiously for coming events.

Sirens howled over Prague in readiness for emergency. Black-out practices followed, and the whole nation lived in a state of expectancy. This lasted for several weeks, after which the population began to recover from the first shock. They resumed their normal life; everyday things began to matter again, and one after another they lifted their heads and sang parodies on Hitler and the German Reich. With faith and optimism they looked toward the West....

Then came Munich, and with that, all hopes for freedom were shattered....

March 15, 1939. "Today for the first time I saw what they are really like - pompous, self-confident, arrogant and bad. They came in, marching and singing, and so obviously pleased with themselves - pleased that they had taken our freedom away. Prague is full of uniforms. They have invaded our shops and bought up all the best things...."

That day would always linger in her memory; somehow on that 15th of March the world took on a different aspect. The first she knew about them was when through the haze of sleepiness she became aware of a rhythmic thumping under her bedroom window. It was early morning and she wasn't quite awake yet, though her mind had taken note of a certain strangeness filling the atmosphere.

Unshed Tears

With the first notes of singing she gained full consciousness and, propping herself up to a sitting position, listened to the goings-on. She soon realised that the regular thumping down below came from feet marching on the cobbled street, and the song that had taken on a victorious air, was not one of the Czech soldiers.

Rapidly she jumped up and ran, barefooted, towards the window. Something inside her shrank as she saw the uniformed troops triumphantly marching through the street which had been her home for the past eleven years. Quivering with anxiety she ran into the living-room. At the door she stopped. Her parents were at the window, silently watching the scene below. Quietly she crossed the room and stood between them.

Without saying anything her mother began to stroke her head and Judith had a dreadful feeling that there were tears in her eyes. She had never seen her mother cry before, and a sensation of desperate helplessness swept over her.

Seeing her trembling, her father took her hand and pressed it firmly.

Then the last row of booted heels turned the corner and the street lay deserted under the morning sky. But it wasn't the same street she had known for so many years, any more. The cosy homeliness had gone, the air was filled with the icy stare and hostile spirit of the invader. Heads turned sadly from the windows; the people's nightmare had become reality. There was no time for pranks at school on that day. It was as though they had all suddenly grown up together.

On the following day there was no school. The soldiers had turned it into dormitories for themselves, like many other

Chapter 2

schools, and the rooms that had until now been used to the frolics of lively young people, suddenly became filled with harsh German voices, and the clatter of heavy boots against the floorboards. There were no lessons for many weeks. Then at last it was arranged for them to use another school building in the afternoons.

At first, everything seemed upside down, but gradually people resumed their daily life, and went about their business adapting themselves to the new circumstances. They knew this state of affairs could not last for ever - something was bound to happen sooner or later, and meanwhile they had to make the most of what there was. Their minds searched for opportunities to laugh and be happy, and once the first grimness had been coped with, hope and a desire for revenge helped them to stand on their feet again....

During the months that followed, Judith felt for the first time that to be Jewish meant to be different from others. Notices prohibiting Jews from entering certain places sprang up all over the city, and streaks of anti-semitism wormed their way through the Czech population....

It was on August 20th, though, that her heart received its first great blow. Against his will, David was leaving for England.

It was a hot, oppressive day. They stood on the scorching pavement, waiting for the taxi which was to take him and his parents to the station. At last they separated themselves from the little group of relatives and friends that had gathered outside the house, and walked silently to the corner of the street. They found it hard to speak.

"Judith, I will miss you very much," he said at last, his voice quiet and serious.

"I will miss you too," she said; then, overcome by emotion, she whispered half-desperately: "David. I can't believe all this ... it can't be true."

He tried hard to encourage her, but it was difficult for him to fight his own feelings. He did not sound very convincing.

"Judith, we have to be strong, like real gentlemen. Everything will be all right. You will see."

For a long while she stood silently, the realization of the whole situation descending upon her. What would life without David be like? She attempted to say something, but the lump in her throat was growing. David was fighting away his tears. Then their eyes met and they both made an effort to smile.

"We shall always be the best of friends, Judith. It will all be over soon, then I shall come back and it will be like old times again," he said, more cheerfully.

"Promise that you will write often," she whispered through her tears. "I am sorry, David," she apologized for her weakness.

Then the taxi appeared at the corner.

"Goodbye, Judith, be brave." He smiled.

"I will - I promise," she said, as they shook hands.

They looked at each other and then he had to go.

There was a bustle around the taxi, a lot of farewells which she watched from afar. A while later the car set into motion. She stood on the pavement and with flooded eyes followed it until it disappeared in the distance....

Life was very empty without David at first. She felt that he was bound to be around somewhere, and at times she couldn't comprehend that he was gone. To ease her loneliness she taught herself a game in which she could bring out David's

Chapter 2

presence at will. In her indignation he became a frequent companion and for hours on end they played, walked and talked together.... But time is a great healer and somehow she gradually picked up new threads of life, awakened to new activities into which she threw herself with her customary enthusiasm, and though she had not forgotten David, she got used to life without him. There was Eva who lived in the same road and who shared the double desk in school with her. She was a good sport and they became close friends....

In the autumn, war broke out and new hope surged through the nation. At last things were moving; the horrible, silent inactivity was over. Everyone was sure it couldn't last very long. Great powers were fighting against one country. A few months perhaps, a year, and then everything would be all right again. With that in mind the Jews put up with the growing hardships, submitting to the rules without complaining, contemptuous toward the Germans but with a sense of humour guarding their sanity.

Some of them gave up, though. Eva's grandmother had gassed herself; Mr. Loevy who lived round the corner had taken an overdose of sleeping tablets, and others, losing heart, decided to put an end to it all.

Judith couldn't understand why people should want to take their lives. What kind of premonition was guiding their steps?

On November 15th of the same year, Judith and her parents stood in the doorway of their empty flat, and with sad hearts looked at the place which had been their home for so many years, and which they were leaving now. A German company had bought the apartment house and all Jews had to go. It was as though a new era in her life had begun when they moved into the new flat.

Unshed Tears

It was very tiny but quite modern, sunny and cheerful, and they soon took to it. They brought their best furniture and trinkets and arranged them so that their two rooms and a dingy kitchen became the cosiest little place to come to. The flat was on the sixth floor and there was a verandah overlooking a park, and in the summer that followed they sat there until late at night in the cool breeze, resting after a scorching day.

In the window boxes which her father made, Judith planted beans and peas which wound round the rails of the veranda, and as they were not allowed to go into parks or be in the street after eight o'clock in the evening, the "garden" became their favourite retreat.

"Good old Hitler," her father used to say, jokingly. "Without him we would never have moved into this luxurious place. Central heating, hot water, built-in cupboards, white tiles in the bathroom - what else can one ask for?"

That was two years ago....

Three months later, Mr. Baron, like all Jews, had to give up his job. From the money that was in the bank he was allowed to draw only a very small amount and every little coin took on a different meaning. Every now and again they took a part of their belongings and made a journey with it to the collecting place, where the Germans were waiting to take possession of it. First the radio, then the telephone, jewellery, fur coat and other luxuries. More and more signs prohibiting Jews from entering certain places sprang up all over the town. The yellow star of David gleamed on their clothes and a large 'J' on their identity cards told of their creed.

People, who once used to be their friends, passed them in the street without a sign of recognition; they couldn't risk being

Chapter 2

accused of being friendly with the Jews. Some showed their hatred quite openly, and even Vera had nothing more to do with Judith. She could remember how, the first time her friend had not answered her greeting, she had stood broken-hearted on the pavement, looking behind her with tearful eyes. At twelve years she found it hard to understand. Where had all that rottenness which was gnawing at the decencies of people, come from?...

Judith looked up from her book and with dreamy eyes watched the rain pelting against the windowpane. Voices were humming around her but she paid no attention to them. Her mind picked up singular incidents which at the time seemed so painful to her, and which at an early age undermined her faith in mankind. How could people behave in such a way? How could they lose their sense of honour for a few miserly coins or a sensation of superiority? She still couldn't understand it. She had learned to steel herself to the circumstances which had brought so much unhappiness and frustration to her at first, but she knew she could never forget or forgive those who so shamelessly betrayed the spirit of the country. They were not true Czechs, and one day justice would catch up with them....

The spring of 1940 came with all its splendour, showering the trees and flower beds in the parks with new blossoms. The beauty of it was rationed to gentiles only. Judith and Eva were restricted to the street where they often had to put up with the abuse and attacks of German children. The district was full of them, and even the little children learned to recognise the yellow star as a target for throwing stones, or its bearer as someone to spit at. It was the big boys, however, who were the greatest menace of all. Half grown-up, and full of curiosity and sadistic amusement, they pestered them by trying to touch their breasts, lifting their skirts and otherwise making a nuisance of themselves.

With the warmer weather, they brought chairs and a table onto the verandah, did their homework there, read books, did some play-acting and amused themselves in a hundred different ways.

She was lucky to have her father and mother, who always helped to sort things out for her.

"We must not show them that we are upset by what they are doing to us. After all, there are people who are more unfortunate than we are. They know they will never be happy again. We are strong and healthy, we have a home, we have each other, and one day we will make up for everything. Think of those whose homes are being destroyed by bombs, of the thousands who are being crippled every day and have nowhere to go...."

For several months it looked as though things couldn't get much worse. Then, on an August morning, one of the biggest blows fell among the Jewish youth. It was toward the end of the summer holidays that the daily papers brought the sudden news that Jewish children would not be admitted to any schools, dating as from the new academic year. Enraged, Judith stuffed her breakfast into her, angry thoughts chasing each other in her mind. After a long silence, unable to keep her temper any longer, she burst out: "I am not going to stay stupid!"

"We shall think of something, Judith," her father said, gently.

"I hate the Germans. I hate them, I hate them!"

Chapter 2

Feeling tears coming to her eyes, she left the room and went out onto the balcony. She looked across the rooftops at the town in the distance, then impatiently she returned indoors. Why did the Germans always have to invent something new? Why did they have to make her waste her best years? Why did they want her to be uneducated and stupid? Why? Why? Why? What had she done? What had any of the Jews done? Why did God watch all this without doing anything about it? Flushed and angry she paced up and down the room. Then suddenly she decided: "They can't stop me from learning."

She crossed over to the bookcase and with a determined look ran her eyes along the backs of the volumes whose contents ranged from easy novels to science and philosophy. At last she came to the "History of the World."

"I am going to start straight away, Mother," she said, grimly, and without the slightest hesitation, settled herself upon the divan, examining her new conquest with a challenging air....

However, her method of self-education had not proved very successful. It was about a week later that she learned from one of her friends that several Jewish children were forming a private class under the tuition of a Jewish teacher. She was invited to join them, but the fees, which were comparatively moderate, presented a new problem. Could she dare ask her parents to make that sacrifice for her? She was aware that some of the parents indulged in black market transactions and were able to provide their families with a little extra income, but her father was involved in no such business, and their budget was very tight. To keep his mind active, her father had got himself a voluntary job at the Jewish Welfare Centre in the old ghetto of Prague, and spent several hours there every day. There was no material reward for that.

She spent the afternoon strolling through the streets, wondering how she could solve her problem. She had to study, she knew that. She was not going to be left behind the other children in the country, where knowledge was concerned. What was she to do? She so much wanted to join that class. She wandered aimlessly along the pavement, turning over the ideas which kept coming to her mind. Even if she took a job as an apprentice somewhere, she would have to work the whole day and the pocket money that would come to her would only be a drop in the ocean. She needed fifty crowns a week!

Then, toward the evening, a miracle happened. It was one of those coincidences which leave one gasping and wondering what course life would have taken without it. She met Robert, a Christian boy, who, unafraid, came up to her and seeing the depressed look in her eyes, enquired what was wrong. He was eighteen, a former pupil of their school. They turned into a narrow side street and walking slowly side by side, Judith made the situation clear to him. A silence followed, then Robert gave her an encouraging smile and said quite plainly: "Don't worry, I know what we can do."

After that, everything was all right. They climbed up the stairs to a studio which belonged to a friend of his and she received her first job. With a parcel under her arm she hurried home, a new warmth surging through her veins. She was going to make it after all, and with her own earnings, too! They were nursery pictures outlined in black; she had to provide the colouring. She knew she could do it. Two crowns for each. It was too good to be true! But it was true - she was earning her own money, she was paying for her studies.

Chapter 2

The time that followed was a very busy one - lessons in the morning, homework in the afternoon, work in the evening and weekends; but her zest for carrying on was inexhaustible. Everything else was forgotten. There were big gaps in her diary; there was no time for writing. Only now and again did she record with a sentence or two the most outstanding happenings.

"The conditions in the Protectorate are not so good for Aryans either. Martial law has been proclaimed and people walk about like ghosts for fear they might say something wrong and be overheard by the Nazis."

On another occasion: "Miriam's father was sent to a concentration camp, nobody knows why. It must be a terrible place to be in. Miriam was very upset, but how could we console her?"

It was several months later that his ashes and his belongings had been sent to his wife. Soon afterwards, two or three other Jewish men she knew had met the same fate. The newspapers reported daily on men and women who had been sentenced to death on grounds of treason. People ceased to trust each other; danger threatened on every corner.

Shops had less and less to offer. Coupons came into existence and all traces of the former well-being vanished....

On June 8th, 1941, Judith and her parents once more packed their cases and furniture and said goodbye to the little flat which had grown on them so much. The district had to be cleared of all Jews.

Most of them had begun to live in lodgings in the Old Town, where old relics told the story of a ghetto of long ago. There was an ancient, narrow cobbled street with old-

fashioned houses on either side. Their black walls looked
grimly down at this part of the world where horse-carriages
still took the place of lorries, where life had not yet caught up
with the modern world.

One of them, number twelve, which stood opposite the
local blacksmith was four storeys high and had a large door,
rounded on top, which led into a cold corridor whose floor was
covered with tiles and at the end of which was a dark staircase
leading up to the various floors.

It was in a flat on the second floor that a room had been
vacated for them by an elderly Jewish couple, and there they
established their new home. They had made it into a cosy
place and the two families lived amiably together. They shared
the kitchen, ate there, and showed good will toward each other.
Although there was little space, they learned not to grumble
and to be content with the happiness that was left to them.
Judith went on having lessons and painting, and soon her new
life was in full swing.

That lasted for three months. With the arrival of autumn,
new rumours swept the city - all Jews were going to be
evacuated. They didn't believe it. After all, they were only
rumours. Then one day she came home from classes and found
her relations there, her aunt and uncle, flustered and
aggravated. It was her six-year-old cousin Peter who met her
with the news. "We are going away on Sunday, far away, and
we are not coming back till after the war."

So that was it. It was true after all - the evacuation.

At first there was panic; then people began to be governed
by reason. They made preparations, reckoning with the worst,
waiting for their turn to come. Classes ceased. The first

Chapter 2

transport with her relations left for the unknown. All the Jews
of Prague were roused to a perpetual state of being unsettled,
talking and thinking of nothing else. Who would be next?

The second transport was summoned, and then one night,
the third. It was then that they received the little card ordering
them to appear at the gathering place. A lorry arrived to collect
their luggage. Four days ago, in the cold dark morning, they
put on their rucksacks and made their way across the city to the
place which was the first stage of their strange journey. Some
people were saying their destination might be Siberia. Who
knew?

Judith shut the diary and put it back into the satchel.
Mrs. Baron shared out some food to her family. There wasn't
much left and they didn't know when they would get anything
to eat again.

After she had finished her hard-boiled egg and a piece of
bread, her stomach still felt empty, but she said nothing about
it. The rocking of the train made her tired and she fell asleep.

The engine, dragging the little waggons behind her, wound
its way through the rainy countryside, moving forward, always
widening the gap between them and home they had left
behind.

III

It was about four o'clock in the afternoon when the train began to circle a large town. All eyes were at attention. Hundreds of factory chimneys pierced the mist, and the smoke, prevented from rising by the slight drizzle, formed a dark blanket over the drab rooftops. Everything looked cheerless and grey - the town, the sky and the air.

The rhythm of the train's engine slowed down. Having encircled the town on three sides it suddenly came to a standstill. It had stopped on a side-rail in the middle of a field. The last rows of suburban houses were about four miles in front of them. A small hut from which emerged two or three guards, was the only indication of life around them. There was an exchange of shouts between the guards and some Germans whose carriage was the last one of the train. Eventually there came the sound of heavy boots walking on gravel, and then everything was still again. Inside the carriages, people were busy guessing and discussing the situation.

Two or three hours went by. It was getting quite dark. There was no sign of life anywhere around them. A hush hung over the muddy fields. There was no light in the compartments and with the black evening drawing near, the life inside them subsided. The conversation had been exhausted and everyone was waiting a little nervously for things to happen.

Suddenly the silence was broken by approaching lorries and in a moment the 'station' was alive with a hundred voices spreading along the length of the train. The atmosphere inside it became tense. Locks clicked and doors flung open.

Coarse voices ordered: "Heraus! Heraus! - Out!"

A commotion followed as people of all ages began to struggle out of the doors. Men in uniform, each holding a small whip, were hurrying them along. Surprisingly, the uniform was not a German one, and the men inside them were not Germans. They wore dark suits, each with a yellow and orange ribbon around the sleeve above the elbow. A cap that bore some resemblance to that of a French policeman's, topped each one's head and had the same yellow and orange ribbon around the cylindrical part of it. They shouted in German, but their accent was bad. There was no doubt, however, that they had adopted the mannerisms and the harsh commanding tone of the Nazis, and although no one knew who they were, everyone felt it was wiser to obey their commands.

Old men and women and children were given a helping hand. Everything was very bewildering. The whole procedure of emptying the train was accompanied by noise, confusion and excitement. The large snowflakes that were falling now, melted immediately they touched the ground, making the muddy earth quite slippery. The main concern of everyone was not to become separated from his or her family, which was quite easy in this sudden, unexpected chaos.

By the side of the railway track stood a row of cabs. The

Chapter 3

carriages were shabby, the horses lean. Above the thousand voices that filled the air came shouts: "Children and old people into the cabs, children and old people into the cabs!" These cries only brought about more confusion as in many cases it meant splitting up families. Excitedly they were making up their minds and it was only after repeated, rather impatient reassurings that they would meet again, that some people detached themselves from their families, staggered up the steps, and nervously settled on a seat. Mothers with babies were granted the same privilege and after long hesitation most of them accepted it. Some older children got into groups and fearlessly climbed to their seats, excited about the prospect of a ride, watched by their parents' anxious eyes. What was this all about? Where were they going? Who were these people who were ordering them about?

Judith chose to stay with her mother and father. They stood together in the slush, a little group of their own, waiting to see what the next minutes would bring. They had only their knapsacks to carry, except for Mr. Baron, who had Judith's small rucksack. Everything seemed like a dream. A strange atmosphere surrounded them all.

"When shall we get our rucksacks?" Mr. Baron asked, when one of the men in uniform passed them.

"No luggage came by this train," was the morose answer.

"No luggage!" repeated Mrs. Baron, her voice shaking a little. "We shall never see it again. Our most valuable things. One never knows how to do things the best way."

"It may still arrive with the luggage they fetched from our house," Mr. Baron tried to comfort her.

"That luggage is lost," Mrs. Baron said, resignedly. The

cabs moved off. Their passengers, huddled in the seats, spoke little. They moved forward, along an invisible path and one by one disappeared into the darkness of the night. A little while later the remaining crowd of about eight hundred was herded into a long procession. They were directed to move along the slippery ground, unaware of their destination. The men who drove them forward with their small whips were very energetic. They moved forward and backward along the lines, nagging at the people, hurrying them on. They shouted at each other in Yiddish and their manner was obviously Jewish, though it had acquired a lot of German arrogance. There were however a few of them who treated the newcomers with more respect, and it must have been those that set the rumour in motion. It spread astonishingly quickly. They were going to a ghetto. The town was Lodz, the Germans called it Litzmanstadt.

"Dad, what is a ghetto?" asked a boy who was walking in front of the Barons.

"A ghetto? It is a part of a town put aside for the Jews. Only Jews live there and as a rule are not allowed to leave it."

"Oh, I see. Have you ever been to a ghetto?"

"No, not a real one. But the old synagogue where we used to go, and where Uncle Otto's shop used to be, is in a part of Prague where there was once a ghetto. There were ghettos in Russia, Poland, Spain, and other parts of the world."

"Do you think it is a nice ghetto we are going to?" the boy enquired.

"I don't know, dear. We shall soon find out."

"And who are these men, Dad?"

"They are Jewish policemen. They keep order in the ghetto."

"They are horrible. I do not like them."

Chapter 3

Through the dark muddy fields, step by step, the procession moved slowly forward. Although they had been sitting in the train for so many hours, they felt tired. In spite of the fact that they had a vague idea about their destination the future lay mysteriously in front of them. Everyone's mind was filled with innumerable questions. Hardly anyone spoke. The fields seemed endless. They walked and walked and walked. Everything was shrouded in darkness and there was no sign of life in sight.

"How much longer?" an exhausted woman would ask one of the guards, but the answer would be an unkind one.

Some children began to whimper. Their feet were sore, they were frightened by the gloomy strangeness of their surroundings. The time came when a great number of people stopped worrying about where they were going. Their one wish was to stretch out their legs and rest. The wind was against them, beating the wet snow into their faces. Their shoes, covered in mud, were heavier now, and the moisture penetrated through the soles.

It was late in the evening when the silhouettes of some buildings appeared in the distance. They had no particular shape and some looked more like ruins than actual houses. The people looked in front of themselves with a new and hopeful gleam in their eyes. Mothers comforted their children, telling them that it would not be long now, and that they would be able to sit down and dry their feet.

It took them another fifteen minutes to reach the outskirts of the ghetto. They entered a muddy street and found themselves in another world, a world far divorced from all they had known. It did not take them long to discover that this place was ruled by poverty and tragedy.

Unshed Tears

The sound of footsteps and humming of voices brought the inhabitants into the streets. They came out of the small houses, or what was left of them, wrapped in shawls and blankets. Mothers carried their babies or held their children by the hand. They stood silently, watching the procession go past, eagerly observing the strangely human-looking beings dressed in coats and boots instead of blankets, clogs or bandages on their feet. Had they really been in touch with the normal world until now? What was it like? There must have been a queer mixture of thoughts passing through the minds of these wretched beings who gazed at them with envy and wonderment.

A desperate forlornness entered Judith's heart and with distressed eyes she looked about her as they now plodded along the uneven cobbles of the streets. What strange world was this? What kind of people? How could they live in half destroyed houses with panes missing for so many windows, and rusty pumps giving them their water? Their large dark eyes looked hungrily from faces that had hollows instead of cheeks and temples; women's ruffled hair hung untidily from underneath the blankets or shawls covering their heads and bodies. Their bony hands trembled. The little ragged, dirty-faced children who had been born into this wretchedness, and had never seen anything else, looked at them with bewilderment. The gypsies Judith had come across several times wandering through the forests, had a more human appearance than these hostile figures who had greed, tragedy and shrewdness written in their eyes.

Appalled and anguished, Judith held on to her mother's sleeve. Not in her wildest dreams had she come across poverty of this kind.

Chapter 3

"Who are these people? Are they Poles?" she asked her mother, her voice trembling a little.

"Yes, they must be Polish Jews. Poor people." Mrs. Baron answered quietly.

"Do you think they ever looked like civilised human beings?"

"Yes, I am sure. They must have been here for a long time."

"I can't imagine it. They look like animals, like thieves."

"This place must have done it to them," Mrs. Baron explained, gently.

"Do you think we shall ever look like them?" Her voice was filled with anxiety.

"It's difficult to say. We shall certainly try to stay civilized as long as we can. Perhaps we won't have to stay here long enough to sink to their level."

"But Mummy, we shall never be like them - we mustn't! I can't imagine us ever looking so wicked, whatever happens."

"No, we won't. We shall fight it. Whatever happens, we shall always try to stay as we are," Mrs. Baron decided calmly.

"I shouldn't worry so much. Next winter we shall probably be skiing in the mountains," Mr. Baron said quite cheerfully, and his wife wondered whether he really meant it. It had its effect on Judith and for a moment a bright spark entered her eyes. The white mountains, her friends, skating, stirring music - all crossed her mind. Then the nightmare was back. There was no real escape from it.

It was later on that they entered a wider street that at one time must have been the main street in the district. The houses there were taller. They looked ugly with their straight dark grey walls, and life there seemed to be hidden behind the black-out of the little windows. Tram rails cut the cobbles, but at the moment there was no traffic about, and except for the tired, quiet procession, the street was deserted. They were walking now along a pavement, dragging their feet behind them. They had hardly any energy left to think. What good did thinking do, anyway?

And then suddenly they were there. The policemen stopped the first row and one by one the stragglers caught up and stopped, too.

On their left was a fairly decent looking building. It had two storeys. Once it had been a school. The front was straight and very plain: the little windows made long rows, leaving equal gaps between them.

The children and old people who had come by cabs emerged from the building and joined their relations in their rows. For a considerable time they all stood shivering in the cold while the guards exchanged information and opinions, accompanied by wild gesticulation, with a few men who seemed to have some authority over the place. They argued for a long time.

Eventually, the policemen in charge returned to the transport and, starting at the front row, counted three hundred and made a gap between them and the rest. They counted and re-counted, and at last, separating the group from the rest, led them towards the building.

The Barons were among them. They were thankful that they had come to the journey's end. They wiped their faces, shook the snow off their coats and boots and followed the men inside.

They were ordered up the stairs to the first floor. No one

Chapter 3

else was around. The corridor was long and narrow and badly lit.

"Two, four, six, eight -" the policeman in charge counted up to thirty, and then Judith and her parents and another twenty-seven people found themselves inside a room.

It was small and square, and quite bare. The four walls closed upon them, underneath them the floor, above, not far above, the ceiling.

The thirty people looked around them, but they perceived nothing. It was no good searching for anything. They began to understand that this small space enclosed by bare walls was to be their home - for the time being anyway. There wasn't much to be said. Exhausted, they began to rid themselves of their baggage and wet coats and settled on the floor, leaning against the wall.

Fatigue numbed their brains and they all had one main wish - to stretch their limbs and sleep.

Then a man came in who spoke in Czech.

"Everybody all right? Tomorrow morning you will receive some coffee and bread. You will also be given some information about this place. The w.c. is at the end of the corridor on the left. Now try to get some sleep. You will soon get used to this life and it won't seem quite so bad then."

There seemed to be nothing to wait for. They began to take off their wet shoes, to make a bed for themselves in the best way they could. There were some who were lucky enough to have rescued sleeping bags or blankets from the Germans. The floor was hard and too small. How could thirty people find a space for themselves here, they asked themselves. Somehow they managed it. Like a jig-saw puzzle their bodies fitted into the empty places, making use of every square centimetre. It was exhaustion that saved them from panicking although the settling-down for the night did not exactly run smoothly.

At last the lights went out.

"Now we know what sardines feel like in a tin," an elderly man grumbled in a jovial manner.

Judith and her parents lay on the one blanket they possessed, covered with coats. Although she was so tired, Judith lay awake on her back, her eyes staring into the darkness. A strange fear gripped her heart. With all the people in the room she felt uneasy. The whole world suddenly seemed to have lost its colour. If only her mother hadn't been so unhappy and sad she would have borne it all much better. Not far away from her two women were quarrelling for space.

"There is no need to spread yourself out like this."

"Just look who is talking! Who is doing the spreading out?"

With all the people in one room the air soon became dense. Someone got up and stumbling over people directed his steps towards the window, which, on reaching it at long last, he opened.

It had stopped raining and the moon was gliding behind the web of clouds. Every time it came out it made a pattern on the ceiling. Judith watched it. A woman in the opposite corner sobbed. It must be Mrs. Smidt, she thought. She is here all alone. Something made Judith tremble. It wasn't the cold, for the heat of thirty breathing bodies had soon warmed the air. For the first time in her life the grim fingers of tragedy touched her and made her shiver.

She remembered all the hungry looking people in the street, the merciless greed in their eyes, the dreary greyness of the streets and houses, the broken windows ... was it really all true?

Chapter 3

Her mother wasn't asleep yet; her father was whispering something to her which her ear could not catch. Then the moon came out again.

Judith sat up in her place and looked towards the sky. Suddenly a feeling of relief came over her. She stopped shivering. There it was, the moon, the same moon that looked upon her world - the world she had known. And all her friends and people who lived in that normal world of hers could see the very same moon.

As she thought of it, something calmed her nerves and she stopped being afraid. She lay back on the floor and began to argue with herself. "After all, it is there - somewhere - and one day I will go back to it. I am young and I am not alone. I have my parents. Poor Mrs. Smidt, she is old and hasn't anybody. When all this is over, and it won't be long with almost the whole world fighting against the Germans, we shall go back. They will have to provide us with a home, and return everything they have taken away from us. It won't be long, and then I will be together with my friends again and we will go skiing and skating, and later dancing to the gay tunes of waltzes and tangoes, and I will study and fulfil my ambitions." Gradually colour came back to the drab world. Her heart felt lighter. She turned on her side to face her mother. She groped for her hand, and then feeling the contact she felt safe and relaxed.

Five minutes later she was asleep.

IV

The Germans, even Hitler, were unable to keep the sun out of the ghetto. When life began to stir in room number twelve on the first floor, its rays filled every corner of it, making its inhabitants wonder whether everything was as bad as they had believed it to be on the previous night.

Slowly they came to their senses, arose, rolled up their belongings, secured a place by the wall. The silence was gradually replaced by a humming of voices and eventually the room filled with life.

New hopes entered the prisoners' minds; new resolutions filled their thoughts. Most of them succeeded in pushing aside their distress and anxiety, to make way for an optimism which proved to be a good and useful friend.

Mothers tidied up their children and took them to the toilet where a huge queue was forming. They fed them with remnants they found in their knapsacks and let them play in the little space in the centre of the room.

Women combed their hair, washed their faces with eau-de-cologne or cold cream, powdered their noses and applied lipstick to their mouths. Although their surroundings had changed, they were resolved to stay the same.

Unshed Tears

Judith, who sat under the window, got up and leant over the sill. The air was fresh and dry. The sun hung from a clear blue sky. Her eyes swept the scenery from left to right, eager to summarise the situation. Then they slowly looked from place to place, taking in all the oddities in turn.

A few more people followed Judith's example and pressed towards the window, curious to see the neighbourhood and the different kind of life passing beneath them.

The main street stretched into the distance on both sides, bordered by the same dull houses they had passed on the previous night. Opposite the school was a half-destroyed wall and behind it the mere shell of a bombed building. The street underneath was humming with life. Men and women of all ages were hurrying to and fro, their clogs beating against the stony pavement. Their starved bodies were drooping, wrapped in shawls or blankets. Some had bare feet, the skin hard and black. Little dirty-faced, keen-eyed urchins clad in rags were sliding through the crowd at a greater speed than the rest. Many were barefooted, too. Old bearded men in long black caftans, leaning on sticks, were making their way forward, stopping from time to time to take a new breath.

A little shaken, Judith stepped back into the room. Restlessness had seized its occupants. Many were standing, others dared to go and look around in order to see for themselves what the place was like.

A noise was coming from the corridor and the adjoining rooms. Curiosity had set the people in motion. They went to look at their surroundings and the possibilities. They discovered that the whole of the second transport from Prague was housed on the second floor. Friends met, greeted each other, asked inevitable questions and parted.

Chapter 4

"You get used to it," was the phrase echoing through the corridors and staircase. "But then, you can even get used to the gallows."

Judith was pleased to see that all the members of the second transport had retained their human appearance. She felt relieved, for in waves of anxiety, a picture of her family and herself appeared before her eyes. In it, her mother and father, clad in rags and blankets, looked at the world with greedy, wild eyes, all humanity gone from them. She wondered where her uncle and aunt were, and what they looked like.

Following the example of the others, Judith and her parents picked up their towels and descended the stairs to the ground floor. A stream of people was moving in either direction. As they passed each other they were careful not to miss anyone they knew.

Through a brown door that stood ajar the Barons stepped into a courtyard that, at one time, must have been the school playground. A faulty wooden fence about a metre high, separated it from the rest of the town. The ground of hardened sand, was uneven, with stones sticking out of its fairly smooth surface.

On one side a long queue was forming by the wooden shed where the latrines were. Approximately in the centre of the yard stood a pump, around which gathered a swarm of impatient people. The queue for it was four or five deep and moved forward in slow motion. This pump was the only source from which water could be drawn.

"You mustn't drink it," Judith heard someone say.

"There are typhoid germs in it," came from the other side.

The people of the second transport could easily be

distinguished from the rest, for their movements were filled with confidence, and they looked knowledgeably about themselves. Some were even the proud possessors of bowls. When their turn came, they filled them with water and moved to another part of the yard where they could go about their business in peace. Many men stripped to the waist and had a brisk wash in the freezing water.

"It's not advisable to brush your teeth with this water. We do it with the coffee we get here," someone said.

Judith washed her hands and face under the icy running water, while her father worked the handle of the pump. Then they changed places. When all three of them finished, they took a quick look round the yard, searching for possible friends. They spotted some in the crowd, among them three or four boys and girls Judith had known from school.

They exchanged a few hurried sentences and passed on, for it was time for coffee.

Then Judith discovered her former headmaster. She looked at him from a distance. He stood there alone, poor, hungry and cold. Was this the same man she had known - dignified, strict, self-confident? Something stirred inside her, and it was then that Judith realised for the first time that he was a human being like all the others. There was no authority in him now. He was just a Jew, a prisoner, nothing more and nothing less. He felt the hunger and the cold like everyone else, and he even slept on the bare floor with twenty-nine people in the same room.

* * * * *

Chapter 4

It worried Judith for a long time afterwards, and she wondered whether all people were equal, once the mark of their profession was cast aside. Was status all that mattered, that made a man a man, that gave him respectability? Was it right? Surely there must be something else that gave a person dignity, not just a title.

* * * * *

Judith and her father walked hand in hand along the main street of the ghetto. Mrs Baron chose to stay behind and talk to a friend who had come by the second transport.

They had had breakfast in their room. It had been brought up by two young men. From the following day onwards, two persons from their room would be allotted the task of carrying the heavy coffee can, and then on the day afterwards, it would be two different people.

The unsweetened coffee had the colour of lemon tea. The slice of bread was dark and coarse, but tasted better than any slice of bread had tasted to them before. Most people had their ration of coffee poured into little saucepans which they had been advised to bring from home. It was not sweetened and tasted neither like tea nor coffee. Mrs. Baron gave each member of her family a cube of sugar which they put into their mouth, thus sweetening the repulsive drink as it passed through it.

Judith's stomach was rumbling, but she made no remark. Her mother must have guessed, for she looked at her with tender eyes, but found it useless to comment. This might have been the reason for her staying behind to talk the situation over with someone who had been in the ghetto for almost a week.

It was good to see the sun and breathe the fresh air. They were free to go anywhere within the boundaries of the ghetto.

"We have been to several countries, but we never had the pleasure of setting our eyes on Poland," Mr. Baron said, good-humouredly.

"There is nothing like sight-seeing," Judith grinned, trying to fall in with her father's attempt to overcome the grim situation with a sense of humour.

He pressed her hand and they walked forward through the hideous crowd, a quiet understanding between them.

At the corner they met a former colleague of Mr. Baron, a small, rather stout man with a jovial countenance.

"Hullo, hullo," he shouted, shaking Mr. Baron's hand heartily.

"Hullo," Mr. Baron replied cheerfully.

"When did you have the pleasure of setting foot on this sacred soil?"

"Only yesterday," Mr. Baron laughed glad to see someone unbeaten by circumstance. Then he added, "We are on our way to explore the place. I was told we are allowed to go about freely within the wire fencing."

"That is absolutely correct," the little man grinned. He pinched Judith's cheek and glancing from one to the other, announced:

"There is good news today. You can rely on me, as my name is Sam. In a year from now we shall be settled in nice flats again, or skiing in the Bohemian mountains."

"It's good to hear that," Mr. Baron said, not without a dubious note in his voice.

Chapter 4

"The Germans can't possibly stand the cold winter in Russia. They will start retreating and then we shall be liberated."

Mr. Baron was anxious to hear something about the conditions that confronted him at the present.

"On what do you live here? Do you get enough to eat? What about work? What does one do the whole day here?"

"Well, to be quite honest, you live mostly on hope here. It's the one thing left to us. But by Jove, it's worth a lot! Do you want to know the greatest advantage of it?" He lifted Judith's chin and grinned into her eyes. "Nobody can take it away from us. Ha! ha! ha! Did you say work? There are no jobs for us foreigners yet, but it's hard enough work to look after your property, what's left of it, I mean, and see to it that the lice don't get at you. You have to walk about with hands on pockets here - makes your arms ache. Even the little blighters are as shrewd as highly trained thieves. However, by and by you will penetrate into the secrets of the ghetto. In a week's time or so you will be pounds wiser. You will have learned the tricks of the trade. You sell here, you buy, you keep going somehow. It's only on the first day that you feel silly among the savage crowd. Ha! ... ha!"

"I must say it does one good to see someone so cheerful," Mr. Baron smiled.

The little man dropped his hand on Mr. Baron's shoulder and shouted, "Don't worry, don't worry, everything will be O.K. Just keep smiling. So long now.... If you want to look me up, I am with the first transport, second floor, room fifteen.... So long!" He pinched the girl's cheek once more, raised his hat and rushed away.

Judith and her father walked on silently. Both their minds

were filled with thoughts mingled and intermingled. Judith had always been able to see the funny side of things, but finding herself in a world that was frighteningly ugly and strange, made her inner feelings incompatible with those that she forced on herself at all costs. It was true that last night's arguing with herself, and today's witnessing of an unconquerable spirit in her father's friend had unburdened her mind to a great extent, but as she now walked amidst the ragged, inhuman, savage crowd that had the tragedy of a thousand years written upon its brow, through the streets devoid of all civilization, where the filth of the town ran through its gutter, the smell of it, mixed with that of bad oil and garlic slapped at her face, she found herself incapable of countering the oppression that was gradually settling upon her heart again.

Hygiene and running water appeared non-existent. The houses dark and ancient were crammed tightly together, tiny and large ones standing side by side. Massive gates sometimes opened into dark passages through which one could walk into little courtyards. A picturesque ugliness lay about the place.

Even at this hour of the day the streets were alive with people of all kinds. Besides the prevailing influence of indescribable poverty that had made its mark on their faces, there was written in their eyes something that spoke of sadness and a deep-rooted wisdom. They had in greater part lost their self-respect, which showed in their bearing, expression and speech.

The newly arrived prisoners could be singled out at once. Their clothes were good, their cheeks full, their skin fresh, their backs straight and their eyes calm, although a little

Chapter 4

disturbed at the moment. They had come from various German and Austrian towns, as well as from Prague.

There was no set fashion in the ghetto. Every garment was accepted as a matter of course. It made no difference whether a person was covered in rags, blankets or pieces of clothes that would have been wildly out of place in any other European town or village. Mothers had their babies tied to their backs with shawls or strips of material, the way women do it in the East.

There was hardly any traffic about. The odd lorry or special tram laden with coal or some vegetable, was confined to the main street. Several bombs had left their scars, diminishing the buildings to bare ruins. Little smelly restaurants which only a few could afford to patronize, and dingy shops that sold goods nobody cared to buy, broke the monotony of the drab streets. But behind the doors of these shops, business went on which only a selected few were acquainted with.

The newcomers had obviously become the objects of prey to the cunning bloodsuckers, who did not stop at getting the last drop from their victims. Knowing that they were in possession of good clothes and many other valuable things, and that they were in want of food, they did not hesitate to come up to them anywhere in the street, proposing bargains, slyly drawing the inexperienced victims into their trap. Where the ghetto Jews got the food from, no one knew.

Besides the dingy places selling trinkets, there were grim shops displaying odd bits of furniture probably stolen from the dead, household utensils; there were jewellers' shops whose owners bought precious watches for loaves of bread or less.

Everything that happened behind the counter was covered by a blanket of dark secrecy.

Judith, holding onto her father, was looking around her with wide open eyes. In a way, the swift, dark-eyed, bare-footed children intrigued her. Those who weren't rushing about, stood in groups on the corners, selling saccharin. This was quite a trade on its own.

"Saccharin! Five for one mark! Saccharin!" they chanted.

They could be seen everywhere, clutching little jars with the tiny pills in their hands. They had special miniature spoons with which they took out the saccharins from the jars. Their eyes were filled with business spirit, as they dodged about trying to make people buy.

Just as Judith and Mr. Baron were trying to make up their minds which way to turn, a cry of "Germans!" pierced the air. Within a few seconds the corner was clear of the little pests. A horse-drawn cab drove past, carrying a passenger in uniform who was obviously aware of his own importance. No sooner had it disappeared from sight than the passers-by were once more pestered by the insistent little saccharin sellers.

An old man with a long beard was making his way slowly forward towards this particular corner. The long black traditional caftan and skull cap helped to show up some of the remaining dignity of its religious, mournful bearer. He was humming a tune to himself that was monotonous and sad. Mr. Baron took a few steps forward and addressed him in German.

"Could you tell me where this place is?" he asked, showing him a slip of paper with the address of the first transport.

The man whose mother tongue was Yiddish, made an

Chapter 4

attempt to speak in German. Yiddish was the prevailing language in the ghetto. Polish came second. With his stick, he pointed in various directions, trying to make himself understood. His small black eyes were sharp and bright. He displayed an amount of friendliness which encouraged Mr. Baron to involve himself in a conversation with him. The man was eager to satisfy his curiosity, and for a short time information poured out of him, some of which Mr. Baron guessed had to be taken with a pinch of salt.

"We have been here two and a half years, yes, two and a half years," the man lamented, in half-Yiddish, half-German. "They didn't give us time to pack our things. Within a few hours we had to leave our beautiful home. Some people were lucky, they brought their furniture and money, but not us - we came with nothing, I and my wife and four children. One kid died last year, and another lies in bed at home with consumption, God help us. Some Jews lived here already, they didn't have to move, they kept everything.

"That life I had before the war! Oh God, oh God!" He beat his breast. "I had a large factory with three hundred workers. I had servants in my house, and my children went to the best schools. God be my witness, this is true!"

It was only later that Mr. Baron learned that every Polish inhabitant of the ghetto used to own a large house and a huge factory and all that goes with it.

"It's getting very bad here now. With a thousand new people pouring into the ghetto every day, the housing and food situation is growing grimmer and grimmer."

Judith was eyeing him with great curiosity. It was the first time that she had heard Yiddish spoken, and although she knew German well, she found it hard to follow. It seemed a distorted sort of mixture of words she would have recognized had they not been twisted into unfamiliar shapes. "He must have been one of those orthodox people," Judith thought. To her knowledge she had never before come face to face with an Eastern orthodox person, though she had seen a number of them in pictures.

Bushy eyebrows hung over his piercing eyes. His beard had streaks of grey in it. Judith looked him up and down and then her gaze became fixed on a pale grey louse taking a stroll up and down the black coat. A shudder passed through her, and a feeling of terror and disgust overwhelmed her. She made an attempt to conceal these feelings. It was the first time she had seen a real louse. Once, a long time ago, during a hygiene lesson at school, they had been shown an enlarged picture of this gruesome creature. How it had horrified her! For the rest of the conversation she did not let the crawling object out of her sight.

"Whenever you are hungry and have something to sell, come to me. I am an honest man," the man was saying.

Mr. Baron wrote down his address and they parted. They resumed their journey. The noise as of a far-distant monkey house grew louder and louder with every step.

"What is it?" Judith looked up, a little troubled.

"I don't know. We shall soon see."

A mixture of twittering, yelling, lamenting, shouting and cackling, filled the air. It was an unearthly din. Judith slowed her pace, for something held her back from the corner which would give her a view which, for some reason, she was not too anxious to perceive. When at last they reached the spot which

Chapter 4

opened up a new vista, Judith held her breath and shrank into herself.

There, across the road, not far away, a mob of tattered women and men were attacking a shop from which, from time to time, emerged a person clutching a loaf of bread to his breast.

It was bread-ration day for the Polish occupants of the ghetto. Something like a queue four or five deep, was standing by the wall, but order seemed to have little meaning for the majority of the wildly starved crowd. They were pushing, nudging, fighting, quarrelling and screaming in a savage manner.

"Let's go away from here," Judith pleaded silently, pulling Mr. Baron by the sleeve.

But they didn't escape that sight for long, for it was "bread day", and they repeatedly walked into another scene of the same kind.

"I can't understand it," Judith said meekly.

"One day you will understand."

"But why? Why, why? Why do we have to go through all this?"

★ ★ ★ ★ ★

The first transport was housed in a large building, a former school. A bunch of children were playing football in a forecourt, shouting with excitement.

When Peter spotted his uncle and cousin, he detached himself from the group and with a yell ran towards them. Eagerly he led them into the building, up the wide stony staircase and along a corridor to number eight. He opened the door.

"This is where we live," he announced, pointing his finger at a bunk by the right wall where his father lay outstretched reading. Perceiving his visitors, he jumped up, let himself down with an acquired ease, and approached them with a bewildered smile.

"Well I never!" he said. "You too."

"Yes, we too," he nodded.

"You are welcome," Judith's uncle said, half-jokingly, shaking them by the hand.

Mr. Baron looked around with inquiring eyes: "I say, these wooden beds are quite a luxury. It must keep all those people in their places."

"I expect you will be getting bunks one day. They are quite an advantage."

The room was full of people who were yapping, dozing, resting, playing cards or chess, or mending.

"What is this horrible smell?" Judith asked Peter.

"Guess! It's our dinner. Soup! Soup! Soup all the time! Either red beetroot or turnip soup. It's red beetroot today, by the smell of it."

The door opened, and Aunt Martha entered, carrying something wrapped in a blanket. She gave them a smile of surprise, and said, "Well, it's waiting for all of us."

They exchanged a few sentences, after which she rather impatiently climbed up to their place. Judith followed her movements with visible curiosity. Peter, having lost interest in everything around, went after her, concentrating on the procedure.

Chapter 4

She unwrapped the object in the blanket which turned out to be a huge saucepan. A delicious smell filled the immediate surroundings, and Judith became conscious of a gnawing pain in her stomach.

Aunt Martha took three little saucepans from the rear of the bunk, placed them in front of her and began to share out the potatoes and onions into them. She passed one to her husband, one to the boy, and took one herself, placing it between her knees and began to gulp hungrily. Suddenly she lifted her head and said, a little embarrassed, "We have not eaten anything since last night."

Peter was greedily swallowing his potatoes. Judith remained silent. Mr. Baron took hold of her hand and pressed it encouragingly. Aunt Martha went on, "I gave a whole silk dress for these spuds yesterday. Those dried onions and a bit of flour I brought from home. One has to keep going somehow."

"Yes ... yes, I suppose so," Mr. Baron remarked, with a far-away look. Then he lifted his head and announced, "Well, we shall have to be going. Come and see us sometimes."

He led Judith out of the room, down the staircase and into the street.

Clouds were gathering over the ghetto and the two figures sped through the streets towards their school. The smell of rotten turnips, red beetroot, garlic and onions accompanied them everywhere.

It was in one of the side streets, not far from their place, that Judith suddenly stopped, stared incredulously in front of her, and then, quivering, buried her face in Mr. Baron's coat.

"No, no, no!" she shouted, shaking her head.

Unshed Tears

A carriage that was nothing, else but a deep black coffin drawn by a lean horse, stopped in front of a house. It had no lid, and was so filled with bodies wrapped in white sheets, that the top layer could easily be seen. Out of the little grey house two men were carrying a dead person, wrapped in the traditional white sheet. The outlines of his head, torso and limbs were quite distinguishable. They threw the body on top of the others and the coffin-carriage went on its way to pick up yet another victim. A group of mourners emerged from the house and followed the carriage for a time, lamenting with fearful noises.

"Oi, wei, mir! Oi, wei, mir!"

The mixture of shrieks, mournful wailing, hideous cries, pierced the air as Judith, terrified, covered up her ears. The other people around gave it little attention, for it was a long established custom, and could be met with every day.

"It must be dreadful to die here," Judith said at last, having been assured that the grim scene was out of sight. She was still trembling.

"It makes no difference where we die, Judith, and how they bury us, we still go to the same place. What matters is the way we live before death," Mr. Baron tried to explain.

"If I had to die, I'd rather die somewhere else. I don't want to be put on a pile of other bodies," she argued.

"I shouldn't worry about it now," Mr. Baron remarked, quite cheerfully.

They turned another corner and found themselves once more in the main street.

★ ★ ★ ★ ★

Chapter 4

At two o'clock the courtyard of the second and third transport began to fill with people. Judith, like all the others, took her little saucepan and climbed down the stairs. She was hungry and exhausted and her knees felt weak. The soup was brought out in huge cans and shared out by the kitchen staff.

A crowd of hungry looking children stood on the other side of the fence, their black eyes eagerly watching for an approaching person whose palate still hadn't become used to the sickly taste of the red beetroot soup, or the smell of the rotten turnips.

The queues moved forward with considerable speed and at last Judith's vessel was filled with the red liquid. She stepped aside, found a corner for herself, and dipped the spoon in it. Hesitantly, she brought it to her lips and dipped the tip of her tongue into it. Something inside her shuddered, and although her stomach felt desperately empty, she couldn't make herself swallow a drop of the stuff that had been given to the pigs back home. Unhappily she looked around her and caught the wistful eyes of the Polish urchins nearby. Their hands, clutching saucepans and tin plates, were outstretched towards her, and when they saw her make her way hesitantly in their direction, they swarmed to one place, and greedily fought for her favour. A little disgusted, though not without pity, Judith emptied her saucepan into another one and walked away.

Was this all they were ever to get? She looked around her. Some people were eating their soup quite heartily. Others took theirs upstairs, while the rest did the same as she had done. What was going to happen?

"In two or three days you will eat it all right. You are not properly hungry yet," a passing friend of her mother said to her, seeing the frustrated look in her eyes.

"Do you think so?" Judith said. "I wish I could. It just makes me sick."

"It made me feel sick on the first and second day, not now!"

Judith sighed and went upstairs.

V

The ghetto was divided into two parts by a busy road running from one part of the Polish free town to another. On both sides of it were barbed wires closely watched by German guards. Along these wires on the pavement that was still a part of the Jewish quarter, its inhabitants were allowed to move freely, though always conscious of a watchful eye. The two parts of the ghetto were joined by several wooden bridges that stretched over that road, and prisoners crossing it could stop for a moment or two, and gaze wistfully at the trams, lorries and other vehicles moving underneath them, taking their normal passengers to normal homes.

The administration of the ghetto was in the hands of a few officials who felt themselves very important, and of a Jewish mayor who was a white-haired man over seventy years of age, and disliked by the ordinary dwellers who envied him his comfort and full stomach. When he rode through the streets in his own cab, people eyed his well-groomed figure with wrath, though not without respect. Perhaps in their hearts they knew that he was a kindly person who, after having satisfied his needs, did his best for his subjects. In his office, when he received the orders from the Germans, the pattern of life of the powerless inhabitants was moulded. Anything that was outside the ordinary, everyday routine had been announced by big posters in German and Yiddish, stuck to the walls of houses.

* * * * *

Two more transports from Prague arrived in the ghetto, bringing the total of Czech people up to five thousand. Seeing the anxious, inexperienced faces of the newcomers gave Judith a feeling of propriety. The terrifyingly strange impressions of the first day had gradually retreated into the background, and a new picture of her surroundings presented itself to her mind. In a way she was becoming part of it.

The newly arrived Jews totalling many thousands, formed a class of their own, and moving freely through the streets gave the atmosphere a new flavour. Nevertheless, very little had changed since the day Judith first set foot on the ghetto soil. It was inside her that the change had taken place.

Without her knowledge, the ghetto was imprinting little marks on her own person. The look in her eyes became sharper, her body more erect, always on guard, always ready to cope with any situation. In many ways she became hardened, practical and insensitive towards many things that had troubled her at first. She learned to be patient and to take things in her stride. She became accustomed to being hungry, cold, uncomfortable and surrounded by dreary ugliness. All this became part of her, and she managed to joke about her own misfortunes. A new kind of humour had descended on a great number of people, as though they had known that it was the mightiest weapon against insanity. Overcrowded conditions gradually rid them of a sense of shame and embarrassment, and in these surroundings, Judith, like many other children, matured quickly.

By the middle of December winter was in full swing. It was an exceptionally hard one. Snow lay in the streets, on roof-tops and window ledges, thus covering part of the drabness. All vegetables arrived frozen and their offensive smell dominated the place.

Every day dozens of people were found in their appalling dwellings, frozen to death. The black coffin-carriages ricketing through the cobbled streets became a sight so familiar, that passers-by stopped taking any notice of them.

* * * * *

One day, to the great amazement of everyone in the third transport, the big luggage arrived. It was a day of rejoicing and a friendly spirit based on mutual happiness filled the rooms of the school. Fresh hope entered their minds, for with the luggage arrived a piece of life. Now they would be able to sell, and to buy, and to barter.

There was no room for the suitcases in the school and they had been stored in a hut nearby. Two people at a time stood vigil in the interior of the hut, guarding the treasures against possible intruders.

Mrs. Baron and Judith wrapped scarves around their heads and, full of expectancy, made their way to the shed. The cases were arranged according to number and they had no difficulty in finding them. There they were, all three of them. The place was swarming with excited people.

Mrs. Baron opened one case after another, thoughtfully rummaging through their contents, carefully putting aside objects of luxury like silk dresses, fancy braces and scarves, which she hoped to exchange for food and money. Food was the most important thing. Seeing Judith and her husband grow thinner, wearier and paler every day had filled her heart with a painful sadness. They had long since learned to eat the soup that was given to them, and would have been grateful for more.

She was the only one of her family who couldn't share the optimism with the rest. She believed she was looking truth straight in the face without cheating herself, as the luckier majority were capable of doing. She did her best to conceal her fears and premonitions. She laughed when others laughed, said comforting words to Judith and to people around her, and bore her sufferings bravely. All the time she was desperately trying to keep up the morale of her family. She could not stop the skin of their thin cheeks becoming even sallower, and their eyes sinking deeper into their heads, forming big hollows round them, but she could do everything to prevent them losing their self-respect and human appearance as long as possible.

There were now enough clothes to pull them through this winter - and perhaps another one. The rucksack which they had left behind in the Exhibition Hall and which contained their most precious belongings, they were never to set eyes on again. However, receiving this luggage that had been collected from their homes a day before their departure, and considered as lost, was more than they had expected.

Chapter 5

Judith was following her mother's movements with eager curiosity. Answering her instincts, Mrs. Baron had packed some food among the clothes. There wasn't much of it regarded in normal terms, but in terms of ghetto values it seemed a fortune to the two hungry souls. Judith's eyes shone with excitement as she watched her mother pull out little bags filled with semolina, dried milk, sugar, peas, flour, dried onions, mushrooms and rice from sleeves, shoes and stockings. She recovered a few tins of meat, condensed milk and jam and a box of noodles and a tin of cocoa. They put all the treasures into one case and set off for their home. Then Mrs. Baron went into conference with her husband. They decided to leave a part untouched in case of emergency. The rest they were going to use for soups, for food in any other form was at that time an unheard-of luxury. Soup filled one up - for a time, anyway.

But for once that day they decided upon a feast. Mrs. Baron and Judith packed a few things into a satchel and walked down the road to the nearest gas-kitchen. It was one of many of its kind in the ghetto. They passed through a steam-covered glass door, and found themselves in a large room filled with chattering people of all kinds. The floor boards were dark, the sweating walls had a coat of brown oil paint on them. Around the walls hung shelves about a yard from the floor on which stood gasrings. These could be hired at a small rate.

Several people were sitting on a wooden bench or standing around awaiting their turn. Mrs. Baron advanced to a little desk where an old woman put down her name. The air, filled with steam, smelled of oil, garlic, onions, turnips and other ghetto foods. The meagre rations were only for Polish people who had been working in the factories, of which there were many. They bought them with their wages, which were given to them in the form of ghetto marks. Ordinary German marks had their value too, though nobody knew how they got there.

Judith passed her waiting time observing her surroundings. Women, men and children bent over their pots mixing up concoctions true to ghetto style. Lice crawled freely up and down their dark shawls and garments and criss-crossed the tangled hair that was falling into their faces. Their skinny hands clutched old spoons with which they were stirring a soup of some kind. When they finished, they wrapped the saucepan into a rag to keep it hot, paid for their time and hurried home. Then a new name was called out and another person was relieved of waiting.

The gas pressure was very low and it took a long time for a pot to boil. Eagerly Judith watched her mother prepare the meal. Her mouth was watering as the aroma of the appetising food rose into the air. She would have liked to throw herself at the half-cooked meal, and from time to time Mrs. Baron passed her a spoonful of something, bidding her taste it. It was the habit of almost everyone to taste his cooking, for every mouthful was a meal in itself. It brought about a momentary satisfaction and was hard to resist.

About six o'clock in the afternoon the Baron family settled on the floor around the pots and pans. With festive looks on their faces they concentrated on the meal, forgetting their immediate surroundings. They ate pea-soup, stewed beef from a tin and rice, and semolina pudding strewn with cocoa and sugar. They held their little saucepans between their knees, rinsing them after the main course with some of the pale coffee of which there was no shortage. They ate slowly, drawing out the bliss of the moment as long as they could.

Chapter 5

* * * * *

Towards the end of December all members of the third transport moved together into one building. There the rooms were filled with double-decker bunks bare of all mattresses save those for children, and they were sixty persons in one room. It was a slight improvement to living on the floor. There people spent their time reading, playing cards, gossiping or sleeping, for their bodies were exhausted. They dreamed of large meals and a better future. There wasn't a person in the transport now who turned up his nose at the beetroot soup or any other, for that matter. In vain did the Polish children climb fences and stretch out their arms for some. There was no surplus.

The building in which they lived had wide corridors, massive staircases and thick walls. At the back of it was a huge field on which the children played in the snow. There was also an attic, and in there young people gathered almost daily at about three o'clock, determined not to let the circumstances crush their youthful spirit. A handful of older boys and girls set up an entertainment committee. By candlelight they sang to the accompaniment of an accordion and a violin which had been rescued from the German clutches. They danced, acted, told stories and did everything that reminded them of the life outside. They were not going to be beaten. They were young; the future belonged to them and one day they would right the injustice that had been thrust upon them. The songs they sang were often patriotic, and one day they sat in a circle and jointly composed a March that was to become their anthem in time to come. It spoke of determination to go forward unafraid, of peace and friendship among the nations of the world.

On the second floor was a primitively furnished office in which the transport leader, with a group of men, managed the affairs of the third transport. They were the link between the mayor's office and his people. Mr. Baron was one of them, and although there were no advantages attached to his job, he was grateful for being able to escape the morose atmosphere of the dwellings, and to prevent his mind from becoming stale. To rot away on his bunk did not appeal to him. The feeling that he was doing a useful and important job kept his back erect and his eyes alert.

Towards the middle of January, Judith contracted gland trouble. She had a painful swelling in her neck, and a temperature. She was confined to her bunk and spent most of the time sleeping, for she felt very weak. The doctor who came on his daily round remarked, "It's the lack of vitamins. In the spring when the sun comes out, the temperature will go."

One after another went down with some disease or other, and an epidemic of dysentery swept over the transports, leaving its victims exhausted, prone to catch any infection that came their way. In many cases the lungs were affected, and any extra attack on them often proved fatal. Nevertheless, people desperately fought off the brutality of their fate with will-power, and above all, with a sense of humour. It was those who gave up who were the quickest to perish.

VI

The Germans, with all their might, were not powerful enough to keep the Spring away from the ghetto. It came at last after long, bleak, cruel months, and brought the sunshine with it. Its rays spread over the drab rooftops and grimy streets, making people wonder whether God had remembered them after all.

Those from the transports who had spent the hard winter time lying helpless and resigned on their bunks, shuffled out into the open, and leaning against the walls, turned their sunken faces toward the sky, thankful for the little source of strength and happiness.

Small, grubby, dark-eyed children appeared in the streets and courtyards, wild and eager to fend for themselves. The boys and girls from the third transport gathered in the field behind the school building, much more grown-up now than when fate had first thrown them together, organizing their time according to taste. Some played, others talked politics while the rest strolled around exploring their surroundings.

One day, after their watery lunch, Judith, her mother and father, went for a walk into the surrounding open space. They had left the grey houses behind, the bright sun was above them, in the near distance before them stretched the callous barbed wire of their prison.

Judith gazed longingly beyond it. How near the free world was, yet how unobtainable! The grey-green figures of the guards passed ruthlessly up and down their territory, determined to let nothing escape them....

Her mind filled with ideas, her imagination went to work and for a time she was behind that wire, running into freedom, away from this gruesome place, into a world without fences, filth, smelly cabbage soup. She managed to get as far as Prague with her parents, where friends looked after them and where, although in hiding, they were in close contact with normal life, away from the lousy, savage crowd.

Returning to reality, she realized the impossibility of her dreams. Even if they succeeded in getting out of the ghetto, where would they go from there, so far away from home? Anyway, were there any friends who would take them in and look after them? It was just a wild thought, but after that day, Judith often returned here on her own, seated herself where the guard couldn't see her and gazing behind the fence for hours, let her dreams govern her reason and take her away from the dark place she loathed above everything else.

They were precious hours and it was good to be so near the place where freedom ruled, for some people; actually to be able to see it and be convinced that it really existed.

Although the Spring brought new strength to withered bodies, the sun did little to influence minds which were gradually submerging in the pool of weird influences.

The ghetto, with all its strangeness, was strengthening its

hold on them. The once elegant people had lost interest in their clothes and moved about shabbily clad with no desire to clean, mend or iron their garments. The first lice made their appearance among the "newcomers", and some more followed, to the disgust of the few who were trying hard to keep up certain standards. Disagreements became more frequent and hostility wormed its way among the once cultured and civilized people. Friends ceased to be friends: members of families quarrelled, children stopped respecting their elders and hit their parents and stole their food. One's own ego became the supreme ruler of all actions.

The bad diet played havoc with their bodies and gave to many a grotesque appearance. Faces which at first were hollow, blew up like balloons, taking all character and dignity from them. Water gathered round their ankles and rose to their knees, in some cases further, making their legs look like heavy tree trunks. Many aged rapidly, some lost most of their reasoning power, their faces taking on a blunt, wrecked and helpless look.

Women, on the whole, were much tougher. They bore the discomfort and hunger more quietly and in many instances assumed the leadership of the family, mothering not only their children, but their husbands too. They went on fighting with greater determination and less self-pity and, guided by a natural common sense, faced up to the situation more readily. On the other hand they nagged and quarrelled with greater zest.

There was, however, a handful among them who, guided by their conscience and deep-rooted decency, did not let the laws of the ghetto undo their principles. They were determined not to let anything make animals of them, and they went on struggling hard.

Judith was grateful that nothing had destroyed her respect and admiration for her parents. They had not let her down and she swore that she would always try to live up to their standards. She was lucky to have their unselfish love and the security their presence bestowed upon her. Her mother, now thin and fragile and a little grey, still had her beautiful eyes with their gentle expression. Her father, though very lean, stayed erect and confident, wisely directing his family along the path of their present life.

Here, in the midst of uncanny vileness, where people's kind feelings had become prey to an all-embracing evil spirit, she needed their love and reassurance more than ever before.

★ ★ ★ ★ ★

One day a rumour found its way among the third transport, and travelling by word of mouth, managed to reach all Czech prisoners in the ghetto. It seemed too good to be true and the idea of it was dismissed with a sarcastic laugh and an incredulous look that was directed at the whole world.

"What, us? Getting out of these crowded rooms?"

"A place of our own? Nonsense."

However, the miracle happened, and each family was allocated a room in one of the battered houses that made up the drab streets of the Jewish quarters. A lot of rooms were vacant now, after the hard winter had disposed of thousands of helpless inhabitants, and the schools which the transports occupied were to be turned into new factories. Once official, the news was welcomed with great jubilation. It meant an end to all the petty friction which at times had made collective life almost intolerable.... No more sleepless nights listening to snoring and moaning, no more quarrels about lights on or off, no more noise and dirt and crawlings through the narrow passages between the tall bunks, but peace and quiet, a certain amount of freedom and, above all, privacy was in view.

At last the day arrived. It was a day full of bustle and excitement. People who for so many weeks had had to tolerate one another, relaxed and showed some goodwill toward their fellow prisoners. The tension that had held them in its grip gradually disintegrated as farewells rang through the rooms and bundles, cases and blankets were dragged into the courtyards. The rooms emptied slowly, taking on a different, unfamiliar shape.

Outside on the courtyard of the third transport, four wooden carts waited to be loaded with the luggage. Eight men, all members of that same transport, had attached themselves to each cart, ready for a bowl of soup to take the place of horses, and from morning till night helped to deliver the luggage to the appropriate places. The yard was buzzing with activity; people with worried looks ran to and fro, checking, counting, exchanging addresses, saying their last farewells and wishing each other luck.

Every cart was going in a different direction and after a lot of fuss connected with their loading, they set off, rattling, into the busy roads. Four men pushed on either side, a sight not unfamiliar in these parts where horses were almost non-existent. In every street similar vehicles were making their way to their destinations. The ghetto was full of them. It seemed as though everyone was moving.

Unshed Tears

For Mr. Baron and two other men it was a busy day. As members of the transport committee they felt it their duty to give a helping hand whenever there was need for it. There were old and ill people who had no one to look after them, and, still a gentleman at heart, Mr. Baron carried their suitcases and packages down the stairs, helped to sort things out for them, patiently assuring them that everything was going to be all right and did a hundred and one odd little jobs. He was everywhere, regardless of the pain in his leg which made itself felt after a few hours of ceaseless strain. Judith and her mother had gone ahead to their new place to get it ready for when he came home.

It was not until the afternoon that at last he had to give up, for his leg, which was now double its normal size, refused to go another step, and he also had a high temperature which took the last ounce of strength out of him. Defeated, he sat down. His eyes were aglow, his forehead hot and every movement sent daggers of pain through his leg. When at last he wanted to get up in order to make his way home, he realized that he couldn't. Some friends helped him onto a bunk and covered him up with a blanket. There, in a deserted, dark room, surrounded by thirty empty bunks, he lay waiting for help to arrive.

* * * * *

Parrot Street was busy as usual when the cart arrived in front of number thirty-five and Mrs. Baron and Judith pointed out their luggage to the men, who set about unloading it. A mob of dirty little children swarmed round them, keen not to miss an opportunity of a possible gain.

Chapter 6

"You will have to watch them," one of the men said. "They will stop at nothing."

"Yes, I should imagine so," said Mrs. Baron, organizing the removal of their luggage to the third floor of the house which could not yet be seen from the street.

They made their way along a wide dark passage that ran like a tunnel from the front through a building onto a small square cobbled courtyard surrounded on all sides by similar houses. It was in the one on the right that their new home was to be. There was an old rusty pump in the centre of the yard and a shed with latrines at the side of it. The pump was out of order, and the nearest one was a few houses away, across the road.

Nobody else from the transport stopped there, and an atmosphere of strange unfamiliarity enveloped them. The people who at first had frightened Judith and made her shrink into herself, were now all around her, and though she wasn't frightened any more, a feeling of forlornness overcame her. They had in a true sense become part of the ghetto, just single people lost in a crowd of surly, uncivil beings.

They took it in turn to climb up the dark staircase with a piece of luggage, for they were too weak to carry much, while the other kept watch over the group of cases and parcels at the entrance. The soiled walls inside the house were damp and cold. A musty smell, mingling with that of garlic, onions, rotten vegetables, dirt and latrines dominated every corner of the building. On each floor were eight brown doors leading to single rooms, each housing one family. The room on the third floor which the Barons had been allocated was fairly bright and the walls were not too dirty.

Unshed Tears

Once all their belongings were upstairs, Judith and Mrs. Baron sat down exhausted, trying to gain new strength for the task that lay ahead of them. Whilst waiting to get back their breath they peered around, planning how to make the room look most attractive. Mrs. Baron who in the past always knew how to make their home the best place to come to, was full of ambitions now, for although there was so little to manipulate with, she was determined to make it into a cosy and lovely home, where once more they could continue their family life. There was no furniture about save a small tin stove and the wooden planks that, put together, made up two simple bunks. It was really one double-decker bunk cut in half, for use as two beds. They managed to get two straw mattresses, but that was all.

First of all they had to scrub the wooden floorboards that were covered in filth and rid all the paintwork on the door and windows of the dirt that must have been accumulating there for the past few years. Mrs. Baron had bought some of the most important implements with which to set about this task.

They took it in turn to fetch the water, scrubbed and cleaned wherever there was something to clean, dusted the walls and swept away all the cobwebs. At last they were ready to put up the beds. They placed them in corners along opposite walls near the window, made them up as best as their meagre supply of covers would allow, and covered them with bright spreads which Mrs. Baron had packed in their cases. They made a table and seats out of suitcases, covering the table with a square cloth.

Judith borrowed a plank from her bed, spread out the others cunningly so as to leave small, even gaps between them,

Chapter 6

and made a shelf out of it above the tin stove which stood in the corner near the door. The two buckets, one for clean water, the other for dirty, they put by the stove - the most inconspicuous place in the room. Then they drove huge nails into the wall in the same corner, which they called the kitchen, on which they hung the pots and pans and other utensils. They hammered some nails into the other wall for clothes, washing bags and odd little things. The rest of their belongings they pushed out of sight under the beds. By the end of the afternoon the job was complete. They stood by the door looking over the accomplished task, pleased with what they had done. It was like paradise after the many months when half a bunk was a person's only living space.

"Isn't it good to be able to breathe again!" Mrs. Baron said with a contented air.

"I bet Daddy will like it," Judith remarked, joyfully. "I wonder why he is so long? Do you think he has forgotten the new address?"

"I very much doubt it," smiled Mrs. Baron. "He is probably very busy. To move a thousand people is not an easy thing to do."

They sat down on the bunks, stretching out their weary legs.

"I am terribly proud of Daddy," Judith said, speaking her thoughts aloud. "He doesn't seem at all different from what he was at home, and he is just as handsome."

Mrs. Baron looked at her gently.

"We must all try to stay as we were at home, not only in our appearance, but also in our behaviour, our deeds, and our outlook on life. We don't want to do things that we would ever have to feel ashamed of."

They rested for half an hour, then it was time to return to the old school building where they were to receive their daily soup. They had no ration cards yet and for a few days they would have to fetch their meal from its canteen.

Tired out, Judith put on her coat and mittens, removed her little saucepan from the hook on the wall, got hold of a spoon and followed her mother into the street. The prospect of a ladle full of warm soup brightened their spirits and forced their legs to move forward.

The Polish folk were coming home from work, and the streets were busy with people shuffling in all directions.

It was about six o'clock when they arrived at the forecourt of the school building. The last cart with its load of luggage was pushing off, and familiar figures were making their way about, stopping here and there, telling each other their newly acquired experiences. It had been such a busy day for all of them.

The two women looked around for Mr. Baron but he was nowhere in sight. They walked up to Mr. Alexander who was giving some instructions concerning the last cartload. When he saw them he came to meet them and explained about Mr. Baron.

"I would have arranged for him to be taken to his new home straight away, but I thought it would be wiser to keep him here in peace before the room was ready. I'll see to it that he is taken there now on one of the carts; perhaps it would be a good idea if you called a doctor."

They went into the darkened room where Mr. Baron lay all alone on his top bunk. Something within Judith gave a little cry when she saw her father, a small figure in a huge place,

Chapter 6

obviously suffering so much. When he saw their worried looks, he smiled and said, quietly: "It's nothing, it will probably be all right tomorrow."

One look at him told Mrs. Baron that it would not be all right tomorrow, and her heart filled with anxiety.

"We must get you home at once," she said, and then turning to Judith; "Try and get the doctor. Try to get him tonight."

* * * * *

Judith searched the ghetto for their doctor. (Knowing her way about certain places and people, she at last reached her new home.) He came back with her and examined Mr. Baron very carefully.

"Your leg is overstrained," he said, seriously. "You have forgotten that half a year of starvation didn't exactly leave you with much resistance. You may be able to order your mind about, but not your body. It was not a very wise thing to do, what you were doing today. You should be more considerate towards yourself."

"This is what he gets for helping people," Judith thought, quietly.

The doctor touched the swollen leg once more.

"On no account must you get up before I tell you. The calf is inflamed near the bone and it needs complete rest."

He prescribed an ointment and bandages, and left, promising to call again.

Suddenly all the joy of having their own place had shrunk to an insignificant size, and anxiety and worry took its place.

Unshed Tears

Mrs. Baron was calm and gentle, trying hard to appear untroubled. Judith didn't quite know what to make of the whole thing, but she found it impossible to rid herself of the heavy burden that had settled upon her. From her corner she watched his tormented face, the perspiration on his brow, the body that trembled with fever and she turned her mind to God, begging Him to help them.

She walked over to the window. It was getting dark. The houses that, during the day, lay surrounded by a cloak of peace, had in the course of the evening come to life. The clatter of pots and pans filled the air, the smell of garlic and rotten vegetable became more prominent. The courtyard and staircases livened up with exhausted people dragging buckets of water. Voices and shrieks mingled with the cries and laughter of children, but mostly cries.

Somewhere someone sang an old, melancholy Yiddish tune and at one of the windows opposite an old, bearded man was bowing up and down in prayer.

After a day's work at the factory there wasn't much time, strength or desire left for hygiene, patience and tolerance. Work was voluntary, but at the end of each day there was an extra portion of soup and a thick slice of bread, and some money every Saturday - enough to buy the rations when they came along. Many of the ghetto children worked, too, carrying goods from one department to another, sewing buttons on military garments or placing the finished products on neat piles. The very old people worked or looked after the babies and of course there were the hundreds of invalids who never left their grubby beds. This was the ghetto.

VII

The days came one after another, cheerless and tiring, filled with sadness, hope, worry and expectation.

Many days had passed since Mr. Baron had been taken ill. His face had grown thinner and paler and the look in his eyes took on a strange far-away look. Judith and her mother attended to him tenderly, each keeping her secret fears to herself. Judith found it hard to concentrate on anything else. Filled with compassion and sad thoughts, she found it difficult to bring a smile to her face. The burden that was weighing upon her heart accompanied her wherever she went. A hundred times a day she said to herself: "It's only an overstrained leg," but this argument brought no relief. She spent long hours by the window, watching the children at play in the yard, envying them for their carefree laughter. Some of them hardly remembered any other kind of life, and although their experiences made their dark, wide eyes fill with wisdom, they were not particularly worried by their environment.

It was by the window that Judith prayed: "Please God, make him well again ... I will always be good, but please make him well."

Unshed Tears

Sometimes the realization of her own thoughts startled her.

"What am I talking about?" She would say to herself. "Of course he is going to get well. After all, it's only an overstrained leg."

Mrs. Baron knew that there was only one thing that could help him to get better, and that was food. At last the day of the first ration arrived. Judith picked up the shopping bag and strolled down the road to the shop where she joined the long rank of yelling, fighting, quarrelling, dirty men, women and children. The children were alert, squeezing between people's legs, cunningly worming their way to the front. Most of the ghetto folk had baskets tucked under their grimy rags on which pale grey lice were parading in all directions.

Unhappily, Judith mingled with them. There was no other way out. She stayed on the outer edge, and though not fighting, managed to hold her own place.

After several hours of this new experience, she pushed her way through the oncoming stream, tightly clutching her newly acquired treasures. There was a little flour, some oats, a bit of sugar, coffee substitute, a small dish of treacle and a few kilos of tiny red beetroots with the leaves on them. But best of all there were three round beautifully smelling loaves of rye bread, one for each person. With a little lighter heart, Judith took it all home. She too knew what the value of food was for an ill, weak person.

She had intended to keep at least half a loaf for the next day, but its presence gave her no peace. The smell was too tantalizing. By the end of the day it was gone.

The doctor called several times. Some complications had arisen and the flesh along his shin bone began to fester. He

Chapter 7

made out a new prescription and ordered Mr. Baron to keep his leg still.

With the winter gone, Mrs. Baron took her winter clothes one piece after another, and parading down Parrot Street watched for the highest bidder. A life had to be saved, she knew it, and there was no point in worrying about the next winter, when summer wasn't here yet.

With the money she bought some oats or barley. Sometimes she would barter a skirt for half a kilo of bread - a quarter of a loaf. She bought a pair of clogs for herself and with the money for her best shoes she bought half a kilo of sugar. Sugar was very important, it gave strength to the body. Without Mr. Baron knowing it, he had eaten most of her own sugar, which was too inadequate for her anyway.

Mrs. Baron was thinner than ever now. Her clothes that had so carefully been made to measure, hung carelessly from her shoulders. Her hair was becoming greyer every day, her step was heavy and strained, and her back that had once been so beautiful and elegant, was slightly bent.

It came to Judith quite suddenly, in the middle of the night, how much her mother had changed. She was worn out and weak, her body was starved. She looked an elderly woman. She thought for a while. How obvious it all was to her now. Her mother was giving most of her food away, as if she didn't care what was going to happen to her. Everyone needed food.

Judith's heart filled with compassion, remorse and new anxiety.

"No, nothing must happen to her, not to her. I must do something before it is too late."

She thought again. Only last night Mr. Alexander, who was

a frequent and welcome visitor, told them that the non-Polish people were now at last allowed to seek work.

"Yes, that's what I will do! I will find work. That will be some soup and a bit of extra bread, and I shall manage to get it to her somehow."

This seemed a good idea and she turned round more peacefully to continue her sleep.

It was quite early still when Judith left home in search of a job. She had told her parents where she was going, though she did not disclose the true reason for this decision. Filled with a new warm sensation she climbed down the stairs. How grateful she was for this idea.

* * * * *

Work started at seven in the morning. The factory was in a large building about twenty-five minutes' walk from her home. The rooms were full of sewing machines and the grey-green cloth of the German uniform. Eighteen machines made up a group, and the ready-cut material travelled from one to another, until the last one parted with a finished pair of trousers.

It was there that Judith's work started.

The trousers had to be trimmed up, rid of all thread-ends, turned right side out and folded ready for the presser.

Although it was not a skilled job, the trousers were heavy and she had to handle them all the time, turning them over and over on her lap until her weak arms ached, holding them high in the air when folding them ready for the creases to be put in, which was the most painful job of all because a boil under her

Chapter 7

arm had made itself felt in a most agonizing manner.

From time to time a machinist in her room would burst out with a well-known Yiddish song and the rest would join in the sometimes jolly, sometimes melancholy tune.

Little children with piles of materials and finished garments on their shoulders were coming in and out of the door, taking the goods from department to department, thus earning their bit of food.

Almost all of the men and women working there were Polish, and it was here that Judith penetrated deeper into the mentality of these people and learned their two languages - Polish and Yiddish.

The factory was run by Jewish overseers, and only once in a while a German would come round to inspect the place.

At twelve o'clock there was a half-hour's break, and it was then that the workers lined up with their saucepans or tins for their soup and ten decagrams of bread.

It was at five o'clock that at last they could put down their work and with their last bit of strength drag themselves home. What news would there be today, she wondered as, with a tremendous effort she hastened along the way.

However, her steps did not lead straight to Parrot Street. There was a little job to be done first. In one of the narrow side streets, down in a basement there was a tiny shop. There Judith called daily to exchange her bread, which she had received, for some sugar.

On the first day at work she had brought the bread home to her mother, but she wouldn't accept it. Crushed by the failure, Judith called daily to exchange her bread which she had received determined to set her plan in motion by some other means. She couldn't let her mother go on like this. There was always a moment when she could manage to pour the newly bartered product into her mother's sugar bag.

For everyone's convenience they kept some of the rations separately. It worked out better that way, for each of them was free to do with it as he wished, without fear that he was depriving anyone of his life-giving treasure. Every crumb was food, every grain mattered, every slice of bread was a priceless gem....

VIII

It seemed as though reward would come at last to the two devoted women for the loving care with which they had surrounded Mr. Baron.

Towards the middle of June his leg became better and his temperature fell to normal. A great weight fell from Judith's heart and after a long time a smile of relief appeared on her face.

The doctor came and said, seriously: "You must be very careful. Don't go out for a few weeks. Get up every day for a little while and then go back to bed. You may increase the time gradually and don't do anything foolish."

Step by step, with the aid of tremendous will-power, Mr. Baron gained a little strength. He was very thin and when he walked he had to support himself with a stick. A slight limp was noticeable to those who watched him closely. It is incredible how much the human body can endure, or how little it can live on and still recover from an illness. But although it seems one has recovered, something must suffer as the result of the heavy strain. With some people it is the nerves, the mind; with others it is the heart that becomes weakened. One might not even notice it at once, but it is there.

Unshed Tears

Mrs. Baron decided to go to work, too. She got a job as a machinist in a factory making military jackets. Many of the newcomers began work because it meant getting the soup and a piece of bread and some money for buying the rations. It was Mrs. Baron now, who tried to deceive the other two members of her family by pouring sugar into their bags, or adding a little margarine or syrup to their dishes. Although Mr. Baron was better, it hurt her to see him so weak and in consequence, rather helpless.

One day, two weeks later, Judith stayed at home from the factory. There was so much housework to be done, and although she felt exhausted, the change seemed quite attractive to her. She knew she would lose her daily ration of bread and soup, but the work had to be done sometimes, and in the evening she was too exhausted to do anything except throw herself onto her bed.

Under her bunk stood a sack with dirty linen. It had been standing there for some time and it had been getting bigger from day to day. Judith bent down and pulled it into the middle of the room. She untied the top and began to sort out the various garments, getting them ready to be washed. When she had finished that, she picked up the bucket and turned smilingly to her father.

"I won't be long."

It was hot outside and Judith felt very weak. The bucket of water seemed heavier to her than at any time she could remember, but the job had to be done!

Mr. Baron was sitting on the edge of his bed watching his daughter toiling in the heat. She had to warm up some water, but there was no fuel. She took a plank from underneath her

Chapter 8

straw stack, one of the eight planks that had formed the bottom of the bed. Although it was forbidden, she had done it once before, and was therefore now left with only six. Then she covered them up with her utility straw mattress again. She chopped up the wood and lit the fire in the little stove. She had a big basin in which she did the washing, resting it upon a pile of suitcases. When she had used up one lot of water from the pump in the yard, she went and fetched another pailful. And then another one.

As Judith stood bending over the basin with her back to her father, tears suddenly came to his eyes. He felt desperate and helpless. It was too much for him to watch his daughter toiling and sweating for him, for her family.

"No: I can't go on like this any longer. It's time I did something for my family."

Thought after thought crossed his mind. Then suddenly he got up, picked up his stick that hung from the back of his bed, put his cap on his head to protect himself against the sun and said determinedly, but with a quiver in his voice: "Judith, I am going to look for some work."

She looked up at him with fear and sorrow in her eyes. "You mustn't go out, the doctor said so," she said anxiously.

"I shall be all right, you'll see."

"Please don't go, please! We are managing all right as we are," Judith pleaded. As she looked at him she suddenly realized how much older he had grown in these last few weeks. His face was sallow, with a yellow tinge; there were wrinkles around his eyes and forehead, and his cheeks and temples were hollow. She became aware of his greying hair. Under the monumental determination that showed in his eyes, weakness lurked and disclosed the loss of his former confidence.

"You can wait another three or four weeks," she insisted.

But Mr. Baron had made up his mind.

"No, Judith. I am going!"

Judith could hear the tapping of his stick on the stone staircase. She left the washing for a while and walked toward the window. Her heart was overflowing with compassion. Through her tears she watched the bent figure of her father.

"This must all be a dream," she said to herself. "This can't be my father."

In her mind she saw a picture of a distinguished looking man, young and strong, upright and smiling and very sure of himself. She felt so sorry for him, and desperate almost beyond endurance. Now slowly he was making his way forward. He turned and looked up at her, waved his stick and smiled gently as if to say: "Don't worry, I will be all right."

As he did that he lost his balance, stumbled a few steps backward and fell. Tears began to run down Judith's face.

"Daddy!" she shouted and flew down the stairs. He had got up meanwhile, and when Judith reached him, she embraced him and kissed him and begged: "Please don't go, not today, please Daddy."

"I am all right, it's just that I am not used to it," he replied, and limped away.

* * * * *

The hours seemed endless. And all the time Judith kept wondering about her father. He came back in the afternoon. With one hand he was leaning on the stick; in the other be carried a shopping bag half-filled with leaves of red beets.

"Make some spinach of it, and make as much as you can!" he ordered sternly.

Judith glanced at him in surprise. There was a strange look in his eyes. Deep rings and shadows under them only emphasised it. An expression of fright was mingled there with hostility. He could scarcely walk. His feet were swollen. Utterly exhausted, he dragged himself to his bed and threw himself upon it, letting the stick drop onto the floor. He had changed since he had left in the morning. Something new was going on in his mind. Judith knew that instinctively.

With a tender look in her eyes she approached him. She felt he was very unhappy. "Something must have happened this morning. Perhaps he discovered he was not strong enough and the defeat upset him," she thought. She did not want to ask him in order not to discourage him further. She stroked his cheek and temple and said:

"It is such a hot day today, everyone feels so weak and exhausted."

A spark of hope lit up his eyes. "Then it is not only me," he said, raising his head a little.

Judith had guessed rightly. He could not take the defeat. She took off his shoes, helped him out of the jacket and placed a pillow under his head.

"Have a little rest. I am going to make some coffee."

She prepared the coffee substitute and passed it to him in the cracked mug, the only one they possessed. With a vigorous movement he smashed it out of her hand. For a moment she stood there motionless, not able to grasp it all. Then she picked up the fragments, wiped the floor and began to prepare the spinach. She felt very uneasy. Somehow it was not her father who lay on the bed, but an entirely strange person.

"Pass me some water. I want to wash my hands!" he ordered.

Judith filled the small basin with the last of the water and took it to her father. He raised himself to a sitting position and pointing at a tiny stain on the rim said, angrily: "Can't you see it's dirty? Clean it and get me some fresh water!"

"Couldn't you make this do?" Judith said, meekly. "I would have to fetch some more water and there will be a long queue there at this time of the day."

"Didn't you hear what I said? Don't answer me back," he shouted.

Judith's nerves gave way. She replied, irritably: "You do it just for spite. It is a waste of water and energy. I have worked enough today. It's not my fault that you ..."

With a sudden effort, Mr. Baron forced himself up. Annoyed, he jumped onto his feet and picking up his stick and waving it in front of him, he headed towards Judith. Frightened, she moved forward. She heard him limping behind her. She turned round once and met the tense sadistic expression on his face. His eyes were bulging out, his lips were tight. Terrified, she threw open the door - and fell into the arms of her mother.

"Mummy, Mummy," she sobbed, clinging to her tightly.

Mr. Baron came after her.

"Go on, protect her, because she has been cheeky to me," he burst out. "I know - you are both against me. And I know why. You think I am a good-for-nothing. I am in your way. I have been good enough for you for fifteen years. I don't need that food of yours; you can keep it. You can have mine, too, if you want it. I don't need your water, either. I can be dirty, what does it matter? What does anything matter, anyway?"

His face grew purple, he was on the verge of collapse. Mrs. Baron took him by the arm and leading him to his bed, said: "You know that whatever we do is because we love you very much...." She turned towards Judith, and with an encouraging smile said: "Would you please get some water now? I will get the food ready."

"I know you are sorry for me. I don't want your pity," Mr. Baron retorted. "Just wait. I will show you that there is no need to be sorry for me."

* * * * *

There was very little Mrs. Baron could do now except be patient and ask Judith to be the same. They became the victims of violent insults.

"Judith darling, you must let him talk, and try to please him always. Don't answer back, even if you know that he is wrong. He is ill and it does him great harm to get excited. We want him to get better, don't we? We must be sensible," she said quietly, stroking Judith's hair.

"Mummy, do you think that he will ever be as he used to be before?"

"It's possible," Mrs. Baron said, quietly. "It depends very much upon us. We must never fail to show him that we love him."

Judith tried hard to swallow all the insults and injustices imposed upon her by her father. Sometimes, however, she could not keep control over herself any longer and burst out into fits of temper.

"When I'm dead you will be sorry for how you have treated me," Mr. Baron threatened.

He seemed to take a pleasure in this statement. He knew he could hurt them by it. The world had defeated him, he couldn't fight it any longer, and he took revenge on anybody who came near him. His mind was not quite clear and it was becoming visibly worse. Subconsciously he tried to hide his weakness by making himself superior to his family and people who came his way. And then again he had moments when he felt sorry for his behaviour and tears came to his eyes. He had little control over his feelings. He was also hiding even from himself a great fear - a fear of death.

The water in his legs that made them look shapeless and clumsy was rising gradually. It was the result of a weak heart and lack of solid food. Most people in the ghetto were suffering from swollen ankles due to the presence of water there. Eventually the water in Mr. Baron's legs rose to his knees. It rose in the direction of his heart. The doctor ordered him to go to hospital.

It was a cloudy morning when the wooden ambulance cart pulled up at number thirty-five Parrot Street. Mr. Baron was sitting silently on the edge of his bed when the attendant, dressed in white, knocked heavily on the door. For a moment he looked helplessly at his wife and Judith, then, supporting himself on his clenched fists, he rose to his feet. A sudden determination changed the expression on his face. Refusing all assistance he stepped forward and, holding on to the walls, he walked down the stairs. A smile of triumph penetrated through the sadness in his eyes.

Chapter 8

"You see, I am not really all that ill. I managed to walk down the stairs without any help. I will soon get better. I am sure I will," his eyes were saying.

Mrs. Baron put her arms around him, stroked his head for a moment and kissed him very affectionately. He then bent down and kissed Judith on her forehead.

"Goodbye. I will be seeing you soon," he said, and stepped into the dark cart.

Seven other people, looking more dead than alive, were already seated there on the wooden benches, covered with blankets. They were sighing and moaning without taking much notice of their surroundings.

The door closed behind Mr. Baron and the cart, driven by a lean horse, moved slowly forward along the cobbled street, rocking from side to side.

When at last Mrs. Baron turned her eyes away from it, they were filled with tears.

"I am so much afraid we shall never see him again," she said very quietly.

* * * * *

That sentence haunted Judith wherever she went. A desperate forlornness enshrouded her and when she was away from her mother she didn't know where to turn. Only the nearness and the touch of her mother's gentle hand brought a little relief to her.

With a pain in her heart Mrs. Baron sold her wedding ring and bought a loaf of bread for the money.

"I am sure God will forgive me ... it might save his life," she said to Judith when she came home from work.

Unshed Tears

Judith looked at her triumphantly and said, "I have sold my ring too, and produced a bag of sugar."

Mrs. Baron looked gently into the distance and said, "Maybe we shall manage to pull him through, it is food he needs." She pressed Judith towards her.

Suddenly a voice on the courtyard called, "Baron! Baron!"

They leaned out of the window and saw a man standing there.

"Maybe someone has sent us money from Prague," Judith exclaimed.

At that time people were allowed to receive small cheques from friends outside the ghetto and when the postman arrived he called out the names in the courtyard or the street in front of their house and they sent down to collect it. Once before the Barons had received a cheque for ten marks.

"Perhaps it is a lucky day for us today," Mrs. Baron said, more cheerfully.

Judith ran down the stairs and out of the door into the yard. There she stopped for a moment, for it was not the postman standing there, as she had expected.

"Baron?" he asked.

"Yes," Judith stammered.

"Sign this," he said, expressionlessly, pointing at a piece of paper that he held in his hand. It bore the stamp of the hospital.

A terrible suspicion set her trembling. Frightened, she looked at the man, not finding the courage to read on. She felt she knew what was coming but she wanted to postpone the moment when she would have to face the naked truth. There was still hope....

Chapter 8

"Sign this," the man repeated, impatiently.

"Dead?" she breathed out.

"Yes," he said.

For a moment Judith's senses were benumbed. She stood as though paralyzed in the middle of the yard. Then suddenly she dropped the pencil and rushed like an insane person up the stairs.

"Baron! Baron!" The children in the yard shouted after her.

At that moment Judith had one aim - to be with her mother. Breathlessly she threw herself upon her. She embraced her impetuously. She couldn't talk, she couldn't cry, she couldn't quite grasp the reality of the moment.

Mrs. Baron guessed right. She pressed Judith to her and stroked her head fondly. She also did not cry; only her sad eyes searched the distance, and many thoughts crossed her mind. She felt quite helpless, alone, without a support, but she knew she had to appear to be strong for her daughter's sake. She had to be brave.

At last Judith tore herself away from her mother and began to walk desperately around the room.

"I can't believe it, I can't imagine that I shall never, never in my life see him again. I know I shall never be happy again, even if the war should come to an end. I will never be able to laugh again...." Incidents from the past came to her mind and tormented her. She saw her father laughing happily, their holidays together, the jokes they played on each other, the way he always tried to help others. It was her first great sorrow, and her heart felt as if it would burst into pieces.

"I wish I could die too," she said, and at that moment she

meant it. Mrs. Baron looked at her gently, "Judith, I am still here with you. I need you so much. We have to live for each other now."

IX

It was late September. The greyness of the autumn was darkened even more by events that were hard to comprehend. They came in succession, one by one, leaving the inhabitants of the ghetto almost senseless. For several days the air was filled with rumours; tension hung over the ghetto; something was about to happen, but nobody knew exactly what. Then one dark night lorries arrived at the two hospitals. One hour later they drove out of the gates of the ghetto again. In the morning both hospitals were found to be empty. It filled the hearts of the majority with horror. Many people had had relations there. They never heard of them again.

Somehow it seemed that that was only an overture to the events to come. The Germans were seen more often in the ghetto. Something was brewing; everyone knew it. The atmosphere was becoming more and more tense. People were making guesses, but nobody knew anything for certain.

Then one afternoon posters appeared in the street.

They read: FROM TODAY THE 20th OF SEPTEMBER 1942, 7 O'CLOCK P.M. EVERYBODY IS ORDERED TO STAY IN HIS OR HER HOME UNTIL FURTHER ORDERS.

ANYONE BREAKING THE CURFEW WILL BE SHOT IMMEDIATELY. ALL WINDOWS MUST REMAIN SHUT.

Men and women coming from work crowded around the posters, talked excitedly, made guesses about the meaning of the announcement and went home. There they were expecting the happenings to come with fear and curiosity. For the first two days everything was quiet. It was the silence before the storm.

The town was deserted. Only here and there the gallop of horses could be heard as the German police rode through the streets.

One afternoon two open lorries arrived in front of number thirty-five Parrot Street. Harsh commands began to echo through the yard.

"All the children under ten out!"

The Germans in the military police uniform invaded the three adjacent houses. Everyone was terror-stricken. What would the next minutes bring about?

For several moments Mrs. Baron and Judith held their breath. It was not long before the first desperate cries rang out. They were heartbreaking cries and came from all parts of the houses, echoing along the various staircases and eventually in the yard.

"No, no! Leave me my child!"

"Don't take my child away from me!"

"Let me go with him!"

The women became almost hysterical. They hardly knew what they were doing. Their motherly love and instinct which, during the past years had often lain hidden beneath a savage exterior, rose to the surface. There was nothing they were afraid of. They defended their children with hands, feet and teeth. After all, what could they lose by it?

Like wild animals protecting their young, the mothers clutched their most precious possessions with cramped hands and fought till their strength was utterly exhausted. They hit and kicked the German officers; they did not care about the consequences, for what did life mean to them, when the only thing left to them was torn out of their arms, taken away from them?

But what chance did the poor women, weakened by years of starvation, stand against the gigantic armed brutes in uniform? The fathers, weaker than the women, came crawling out of the houses, following their wives into the yard. They beat their heads against the walls or knelt down on the cobbled yard and knocked their heads against the stones. At the same time they tore their hair and howled in loud, lamenting voices.

When at last the little boys and girls had been torn away from their mothers, the latter ran after the Germans, begging them to let them go, too. But they were only brutally pushed back.

The terrified children were thrown onto the lorries and driven away, leaving behind them their frantic parents. It was all worse than the most horrible nightmare. The cries and wailing of the stricken parents were heard for many nights and days to come.

"Never in my life, as long as I live, will I forget that scene," said Judith, in a trembling voice.

Mrs. Baron embraced her tenderly, thanking God that she did not have to share the fate of so many mothers in the ghetto....

Unshed Tears

For a long while they sat in silence, each with her own thoughts.

At last Judith got up, she was starving! She wanted to eat. That was the thing that mattered most of all! She could scarcely control herself. Her knees felt as if they could not support her body, but she forced herself up and began to search the room in the hope of finding a crumb somewhere which might give the feeling of food to the tip of her tongue for a second or two.

She had done the same yesterday; she knew there was nothing left anywhere. Perhaps she believed in a miracle.

She looked into all the cases, took the lids off all the saucepans, turned the linen sugar-bags inside out and then, in one corner of the shelf she discovered two or three tiny breadcrumbs, no bigger than pins' heads. She moistened her forefinger and hastily picked up the crumbs with it.

The feel of food on the tip of her tongue only made her craving for it stronger. Irritated, she looked round. Her eyes caught sight of a piece of wood under the stove. She picked it up and tried to gnaw it. At least her teeth had some work to do, but it only irritated her more. She threw it back under the stove.

She approached her mother. "What would happen if we made soup of ashes instead of flour? I am going to try it."

New hope rose in her. "Perhaps I have invented something new," she thought. She never left anything untried. With her last shred of strength she chopped up some wood and lit the fire in the stove. She put some ashes in the frying pan and fried them for a little while, just as she used to do with flour. Then with a small saucepan she took some water out of the bucket

Chapter 9

and poured it on the hot ashes. After a moment of sizzling the ashes dissolved, leaving the water as thin as before, only a little grey.

She gave up. "I mustn't think of it," she said to herself, and lay down on her bunk.

★ ★ ★ ★ ★

On the following day towards midday, lorries arrived again in front of number thirty-five Parrot Street.

"What do they want this time?" everyone was thinking. Some mothers were hoping that they might be sent to the same place as their children.

Once again German police officers jumped off the lorries as they had done all through the ghetto in the past few days, and their boots echoed on the stony pavement, yard, and staircase.

"Everybody down! Everybody down!" they shouted.

From all three houses people came crawling out for the first time in many days. There were old people and young people, men and women dressed in rags, dragging their heavy feet along the floor. All of them were weak, many were ill, resigned to their fate.

Mrs. Baron and Judith wore their best clothes. They looked clean, tidy and civilized.

"Keep your chin up and show them that you are not afraid. Show them with your eyes that your conscience is clear." Mrs. Baron gave this last minute advice to Judith. They both looked quite sure of themselves as they joined the crowd downstairs.

Unshed Tears

The Germans broke into every room, making sure that nobody was left behind.

The ghetto policemen co-operated with the Germans. Their method of handling people was very similar to theirs. They became merciless. It paid them best that way. It kept their stomachs full, anyway.

Two tall German officers stood in the street with their legs, encased in shiny boots, apart. Their arms were folded and each held a cane under his arm. Their faces expressed superiority and sarcasm. With sadistic satisfaction they watched the half-dead people crawling in front of them.

"Get into line," ordered one of them, eventually.

With his cane he pointed to the edge of the pavement along which he wanted the line of people to be formed.

The ghetto police helped to establish order. They pushed the people into their places and shouted at them in voices filled with self-importance.

Judith and her mother had one aim, and that was, to stay together. It was not always easy, as others pushed between them, but they always managed to smuggle themselves back into their original places.

Several minutes later dead silence reigned in Parrot Street. Only the heavy steps of the chief police officer could be heard as he made his way slowly down the line. All eyes were fastened on him. The rest of the German Schu-Po (Schutz-Polizei) and the ghetto police, stood in their appointed places.

The chief Schu-Po with the shining eagle on his helmet looked searchingly at every person he passed and with his stick he pushed the people he chose to the rear of the line. There the other policemen took over. They chased the bewildered people

Chapter 9

up the stairs of the house facing the street. They ordered them not to go near any window.

Everyone soon gathered that the rumours that had been spreading across the ghetto in the last few days were based on truth. All ill, old and unfit for work persons were to be sent to an unknown destination. The rest were to stay behind. They were those at whom the officer had pointed his cane, and who were now driven back, out of the way. It was the policy of the Germans to get rid of everyone who looked unable to slave for them. They were not going to feed useless persons. That was why they had taken away those who were ill in the hospital, and the little children.

The German officer slowly approached the place where Judith and her mother stood. He came nearer ... nearer. They could scarcely breathe with apprehension. What were the next few seconds going to bring to them? But they tried to appear composed.

And then it happened! He pointed his cane at Judith. Anxiously she turned round to see whether her mother was behind her, but she saw only the German walking away, leaving Mrs. Baron where she was.

Judith wanted to say something, to run back into the line, but she was seized by two policemen and forced up the stairs with the rest.

For a moment Judith couldn't quite comprehend what it all meant to her. Then suddenly she became panic-stricken. Hundreds of visions crossed her mind. She realized what had happened. She knew she would never see her mother again. She felt that she was no longer the master of her senses. She pushed her way through the masses of people that thronged the staircase and fought her way up to the first floor. She headed for the window that looked onto the street, but they drew her back.

"Get away, you fool! They'll shoot you," they shouted, "and us too!"

"Let them shoot me! I don't care!" Judith cried. A supernatural power took possession of her and she fought with her legs and fists, crying hysterically: "Give me my mother! I want my mother!"

At last she managed to wriggle herself loose. She reached the window just in time to see the lorries laden with the prisoners depart. The street became silent and deserted as if nothing had happened. The crowd began slowly to move down the stairs to their houses. Some were talking, expressing their happiness that they had got through. Some were even glad to have got rid of their old or ill relations who had only been a burden to them. Several were lamenting aloud.

Judith felt that everything had come to an end. The people she knew and loved meant everything to her. Now they were gone. As long as she was with them she could endure anything with a smile on her face and even a glance of mischief in her eyes. But the last one, perhaps the most precious one had gone so suddenly that Judith had had no time to prepare herself for it. She could not quite grasp everything; she only knew that everything was over and that she could not possibly go on living alone among these indifferent strangers without a soul to turn to. At once the whole world took on a different aspect. The burden of it lay so heavily upon her heart that she felt it was being squeezed by someone's hand, and breathing became difficult for her.

Chapter 9

Suddenly her expression changed. An idea struck her. She had found a way out. She felt thankful for that idea and a little smile of relief entered her eyes. She began to force her way forward through the crowd, overtook the slowly moving procession and ran as fast as she could.

"Another half an hour, perhaps, and then I will be happy. The tube of aspirins should be enough - everything will be peaceful then ... the pain from my heart will be gone ... and perhaps I shall meet my father and then my mother ..." she thought as she ran across the yard to their building. From somewhere strength came to her and she took the steps two at a time.

First floor ... second floor ... and there she was.

She ran along the corridor and fell into the doorway, her eyes looking in the direction of the little first-aid box that stood upon the shelf ... and then - !

Her heart missed a beat. She uttered a cry.

"Judith, my darling," she heard a voice say.

For a moment she stood, transfixed.

"No! This must be a dream! I must be mad!" Judith cried. She was frightened, she couldn't grasp it all, and then she collapsed - into the arms of her mother.

She could not laugh and she could not cry; only her body trembled as she tried to control herself. And then after a while, suddenly she began to sob violently, unable to stop herself for a long time.

Mrs. Baron put her gently on her bed. Exhausted, Judith fell asleep.

When she awoke, she smiled, happily conscious of the fact that something wonderful had happened. She sat up on the bed, leaning on her elbows, touching Mrs. Baron's hand.

"How did you manage to get here? How did it happen?" she asked.

Mrs. Baron smiled and explained: "All the people who were left behind in the street were put into a row again. That big brute began to inspect us again. Then his eyes caught mine. I looked at him, not showing any fear. I tried to make him understand what I thought of him. I was not afraid for I knew nothing worse would now happen. He looked me up and down, from head to foot, and I knew he thought I looked a bit more civilized than the rest. Then suddenly I said: "How can you take me away from my child!" Perhaps it was my good German that made him take notice of me. He slapped my face then ordered in his military voice: 'Disappear at once!' and he let me go! It really sounds like a miracle. I still find it hard to believe that I am the only one who got away with it."

Judith put her arms fiercely around her mother, and smiling happily, she said: "It has been the most unhappy and the most happy day in all my life. But nobody will ever separate us again!"

X

The curfew was over. The winter was approaching. Life in the ghetto went on as before. Only the young and comparatively strong were left there to slave for the Germans. Uncle Richard and his family had disappeared and with them many of the Barons' friends.

One evening Mrs. Baron came home from work with a headache. She felt weak and her face was flushed. It was not the first time she had felt like that. Judith made her lie down and she herself cooked the soup.

During the night Judith was suddenly woken up by a bump. She called her mother, but there was no answer. Frightened, she jumped up and switched on the light. Mrs. Baron was lying on the floor in the middle of the room. She did not move. Her face was white, her lips blue. Terrified, Judith felt for her pulse. It was there, but very weak. Judith wished someone was with her. She thought for a moment and then began to drag her mother to the bed. She was heavy and stiff. When at last she had succeeded in placing her comfortably on the bed she remembered a small bottle of Eau de Cologne which Mrs. Baron kept in her case. Quickly she found it and, having opened it, she held it near her mother's nose. It did not seem to have any effect on her. Judith was scared. She rubbed some vinegar on her temples and patted her cheeks, as she had seen others do it.

Nothing helped.

She became desperate. It seemed as if her mother scarcely breathed. There was nothing else she could think of doing.

For a while she stood at the side of the bed, watching with wide open eyes for the slightest movement that would indicate some life in her. The minutes seemed like hours to her.

"No! I mustn't let her die! I mustn't let her die!" she told herself. Then she began to shake her mother vigorously, and cried aloud: "Mummy! Mummy! Mummy!"

In between the cries, Mrs. Baron opened her eyes and smiled slightly at her daughter. A little colour came back to her face. Relieved, Judith thanked God.

"What is the matter?" Mrs. Baron asked.

Judith explained everything. "Oh Mummy, I was so frightened," she added.

"I remember now. I was very cold. I wanted to fetch something to put on. But I feel better now than I have felt for a long time."

* * * * *

For days Judith believed that her mother was better. Only Mrs. Baron knew where she was heading for. A depression had settled on her which she felt she could not fight. Somehow she did not mind. She was even glad that she had reconciled herself to the idea. She longed for peace and rest. She looked

Chapter 10

at the world with different eyes. Her only worry was Judith. "But she is young. Time will heal the wound; she will forget. She has the chance of being happy again. There is nothing left for me. Judith, you must forgive me, but I can't go on any more," she said to herself. And so, like thousands of others, Mrs. Baron gave up the fight. She lost the will to live.

One evening she was walking sadly through the narrow streets of the ghetto, recalling moments from her past life. "It was short, but beautiful. Now it has finished. It is a pity in a way, but I must be thankful for what I have had. I did not really ask for very much. I did not crave for luxury. All I wanted was to have a modest home in which I could make my family happy. It was taken away from me, and it will never come back."

She went out on a special mission. She visited several friends. She knew she could not really rely upon them as friends, but she hoped that perhaps one of them would take notice of her wish. "When I have gone, please take a little care of my Judith," she pleaded.

"You must not talk like this, of course you will live," they all told her. But Mrs. Baron was calm. She did not even wish to believe them.

★ ★ ★ ★ ★

Not caring about herself anymore, she drank the water which was full of typhoid germs, without boiling it first. And so one day she came home ill. She had a very high temperature, her face was flushed, her eyes were glowing and her whole body was trembling. She refused to eat anything and did not want a doctor.

Unshed Tears

Judith put her to bed. She felt the whole burden of responsibility on her shoulders. She was alone with her fears. "If only there were someone who would share it all with me, perhaps I could bear it better." But nobody cared. There was nobody to give her a few words of hope. Everyone had his own troubles to cope with. In a way the responsibility made her feel years older and then again she felt lost, like a little child. Whatever was going to happen, Judith made up her mind not to lose her head.

She attended to her mother tenderly, scarcely finding time to eat, herself. Against Mrs. Baron's will she called the doctor. He came in the evening and found symptoms of typhoid, and ordered her to hospital. The next morning Judith had to go to several offices to get her mother fixed up in hospital. The officials were unkind and put as many obstacles in her way as possible, but Judith was determined not to let herself be beaten. When she came out again she met their doctor, stopped him, and asked anxiously: "Doctor, tell me, is my mother very ill?"

He looked at her gravely, and stated: "Yes, she is very ill."

"But ... but she will get better again, won't she?"

Judith tried to force the doctor to give her the answer she wanted to hear.

"Yes, of course, let's hope so," he said. "Did you fix the hospital?"

"Yes."

"Good girl. Goodbye now."

"Goodbye," Judith said, absentmindedly and walked away. In her mind she was repeating his words - "Yes, of course - yes of course -" She tried to make herself believe this part of the

Chapter 10

sentence. Only from somewhere far away she heard the end of it - "let's hope so."

★ ★ ★ ★ ★

Sadly Judith packed a few things for her mother. She was very depressed. She had a fear of the hospital because her father had died there, and because recently all the people had been taken away from there. On the other hand, she knew that the Germans never repeated their tricks. They always thought of new ones.

She realised she would be alone now, alone in the room, alone with her thoughts, alone with her worries.

"Alone! Alone! I shan't be able to bear it. It is too much for me!... Alone." The thought of it tormented her. Then she tried to pull herself together. "I have to bear it. I have to. I must do everything to make her well again ... but how?"

Suddenly her train of thought was interrupted by her mother's feeble voice: "Judith, come here. Sit here beside me." She pushed her blanket to one side to make room for Judith to sit there. She smiled tenderly but sadly. It was a strain for her to talk. She took hold of Judith's hand and said slowly: "Judith, you are young, your life has only just begun. The whole future lies in front of you. You must not let these times break you.... Stay honest and brave as you have been until now and you will see that life will give you much happiness and pleasure yet ... once you are able to go back."

"Oh Mummy, don't talk like this," Judith interrupted, "we shall both go back ... and if not ... I don't want to live, either."

"Judith, you must not say that. You are very young. Time

will make you forget this horrible place with all its misery. Life is like that ... one does forget eventually ... perhaps not quite forget, but the wounds get healed and new joys take their place. You have a strong will, it will help you through. You are intelligent - you will know what to do. As a matter of fact," she said, with a gleam in her eyes, "you are a real gentleman! Once you come out of this, there is some work waiting for you. Your experience will always help you along. You will have known what misery is and with that you could do a lot of good work. Don't forget about the hundreds of little children who are unhappy, even in the normal world. When you grow up, remember my words and you will understand what I mean. I know you will do something worthwhile one day. I know you can do it."

For a while she looked into Judith's face, and then continued: "Judith, you must not forget that you were born a girl and that you will grow up into a woman. It is beautiful to be a woman, if you make the most of it. Nothing brings more happiness to a woman than to occupy her real place in life and fulfil her duties - to live as a woman. Don't think that power, fame and money offer the greatest happiness. When you get married and have children, it is very much up to you to make a success of it. You must try to understand people, to forgive them, and above all, don't see their faults alone, try to see their good points. They are there, in everybody, if you only look for them. But you will find out for yourself."

★ ★ ★ ★ ★

The same ambulance cart that had fetched Mr. Baron,

Chapter 10

stopped again at number thirty-five Parrot Street. Mrs. Baron
was too weak to walk down the stairs. She had to be carried
down on a stretcher. Judith felt heartbroken when she looked
at the slim, helpless figure being put into the cart. She stared
at her as long as she was given the chance to. She did not quite
realize why, but somewhere in her subconscious mind a voice
was saying, "Perhaps for the last time."

The door of the cart closed at last. The horse moved
forward. Judith could not let it go. She began to walk beside
it. It moved slowly enough. Sadly she was dragging her feet
along the cobbled streets, following the cart wherever it went.
Every time it stopped in order to collect another patient, Judith
waited for the wooden door to open hoping to get another
glimpse of her mother. But it was dark inside and Mrs. Baron
was at the very back, covered up with a blanket.

At last they were out of the maze of shabby streets and
making their way along a narrow lane in the meadows. It was
very uneven and the patients inside the cart suffered from the
many bumps. The hospital was in Baretin. It stood on a little
hill and consisted of small one-storeyed houses. Altogether
there were eight of them, four and four, opposite each other.
They were yellow with red roofs.

At last the cart arrived in front of one of the houses. The
attendant opened the door and one by one the patients were led
or carried into the building. Once more Judith took an eager
glimpse of the thin face of her mother. "How can anyone's
appearance change so much," she thought.

Mrs. Baron gave her a kind smile and then Judith was left
alone in the middle of the street.

For a long while she stood there gazing into the windows

trying to guess behind which one her mother would be. She felt completely lost. Nurses were dashing from one hospital building to another, but nobody took any notice of her. She stood there for a very long time, not finding the courage to tear herself away and go to her empty home.

It became dark, and only then, with bowed head and a heavy heart, did she decide to make her way home through the barren fields.

When she woke up next morning, it was still dark. The time was four o'clock. She got up, put on her clothes and half an hour later she was on her way to Baretin again.

"I must go and see how she is before I go to work. Perhaps she needs something," Judith said to herself.

She was not quite conscious of the real purpose of her journey. The streets were dark and empty. She had to be back at work by seven o'clock. She hurried. It was only when she was nearing the hospital itself that her steps slowed down. "Come on, Judith. Your mother is in hospital now under expert care. Of course she is better, of course you will have good news," she encouraged herself. She was afraid, she would not admit to herself why, but she lingered for a long time before she plucked up the courage to approach a nurse and ask after her mother. As long as she had no news, there was hope.

The nurse who descended the three or four steps that led from the main door was young and quite pretty. She listened to Judith rather impatiently.

"Yes, she is better," the nurse answered, hardly looking at Judith. Her voice did not sound very convincing, but Judith was at least sure of one thing - her mother was alive. That was what she really came here for. As long as she lived, there was hope of her recovery.

Chapter 10

On her way to work she drew mental pictures of the day when her mother would come back from hospital. She imagined the end of the war and the wonderful time they would have afterwards.

As soon as she finished work in the afternoon, weak and exhausted she was on her way to Baretin again. Somehow the journey did not seem so very long anymore. She wrote a little letter and sent it to her mother by a nurse. She spotted the doctor and tried to speak to him. But he did not realize or perhaps did not care to understand that in front of him stood an unhappy girl for whom his answer was the most important thing in life, who took in eagerly every detail of what he said and analysed every word. He did not bother to understand her and give her a few words of comfort. It would have been so easy for him. But he just told her the plain truth and left her standing in the middle of the street.

"She is seriously ill. She has typhoid, but there is no power of resistance. She is undernourished, overworked, and her heart is weak. She doesn't seem to want to fight."

For a moment Judith remained standing with a blank expression in her eyes.

"No! No! It is not true. She has a strong constitution. She can overcome everything. Food! That can save her," she tried to convince herself.

The next morning she cooked some porridge, put a lot of sugar into it, prepared some bread and margarine and took it to the hospital. She knew now in which room her mother lay. She was not allowed to go inside; nobody was allowed to enter the hospital, as only patients with infectious diseases were admitted there. The room into which they had put her mother was on the first floor. The huge window faced the quiet street. There were eight patients in one room. Next to the window lay a woman who was recovering from her illness. She got to know Judith by sight and was able to give her some information through the window about Mrs. Baron. Judith was very grateful to her as she was the only person who took some interest in her. She told Judith that Mrs. Baron refused to eat anything, but that she was craving for an impossibility - fruit juice.

Judith had not seen fruit since she had left her home in Prague.

"Fruit juice ... where am I going to get it? It is impossible, but I must get it!" she thought.

On her way from work that evening, Judith entered a secret shop in the basement.

"Do you sell fruit?" she asked.

The man looked at her cunningly and said, "We have some apples and pears. They are six marks each."

She went home, opened her suitcase, selected a few of the better articles, put them over her arm and went down the road. The sly buyers swarmed around her, but Judith was determined not to be taken advantage of. She sold a blouse for six marks, and a summer dress for six marks, and then she went back to the shop and bought one apple and one pear.

She boiled the apple in a lot of water, added her last bit of sugar to make it nourishing and took it to the hospital. The next day she exchanged her last piece of bread for some sugar, made juice from the pear, filled a huge bottle and went on her usual journey to Baretin.

Sometimes in the morning, when it was still dark, and

Chapter 10

every evening after work, Judith made the same pilgrimage. And every evening she managed somehow to take a bottle of fruit juice along. She fought desperately for her mother's life. She did not find much time to look after herself and care for her appearance. When she came home late in the evening after having spent hours gazing into the same window, she found neither the strength nor the desire to do otherwise than throw herself into her bed. She did not bother to cook, she ate raw cabbage or turnips when she was lucky enough to have some. Otherwise she made the soup and a piece of bread, which she got at work, do for the whole day. She sold one thing after another, until there was nothing left and she had to sell her bread, her only nourishing food. She exchanged her last pair of shoes for clogs, and with the difference she bought sugar for the fruit juice. "It will strengthen her heart," she thought. Her mother's health was the only thing that mattered.

Day after day passed. Three weeks had elapsed since Mrs. Baron had been taken to hospital. For those three weeks Judith lived in the exhausting uncertainty of doubt about her mother's recovery, without being able to get any proper information. Every day was the same except that it was becoming much colder and the days were getting very short. She felt oppressed all the time, finding relief only in sleep and prayers. She prayed quite hard for her mother's health, for freedom, and for peace.

The strain was too much for her. She spent too long a time in front of the hospital, breathing in the infected air. One day she went home from work early, shivering. She felt hot and cold and exceptionally weak. She took her own temperature. It was very high.

"What am I going to do?" she thought, desperately. "I mustn't be ill now. Not just now.... Whatever happens, I must go to the hospital today. Mummy knows I am coming every day. She would be worried and it might make her worse." She decided to take two aspirins. After about two hours she felt better. The temperature fell to almost normal. It was only temporary, but Judith did not care. She was all right for the moment. She made the juice and went on her way. By the time she reached Baretin she felt quite giddy and feverish again. She knew she might not be able to go to work the next day. On a scrap of paper she wrote a little message: "Dear Mummy, I might not be able to come tomorrow as I shall be very busy at work. We might all have to work overtime. Lots of love, your Judith."

When Judith woke up the next morning everything around her seemed like a dream. A high temperature made her shiver violently. Every movement was too great an effort. Her face was burning, her tongue was dry, her lips were cracked in several places.

"Water ... water ..." she called, but nobody could hear her. "Water ..." she whispered again through burning lips. Then, with a last effort she raised her fist and banged it a few times against the wall. Nothing happened. It seemed as if her effort had been in vain. After a while she repeated the knock and at last a scruffy-looking, worn-out woman appeared in the doorway. Judith felt relieved to see a human being. The woman stopped a few yards away from her and asked impatiently, "What is it you want?"

Judith looked at her through her feverish eyes and pleaded in a trembling voice.

Chapter 10

"Please help me ... help me ... I don't know what to do ... the doctor ... get a doctor please ... and some water - water!"

"I will bring you some water and call the doctor - if I find the time," said the woman, and re-arranging her dark shawl on her head she left the room.

Judith was grateful that there was someone who knew about her. She spent the rest of the morning tossing about from side to side impatiently waiting for the reappearance of her neighbour. But nobody came.

Evening arrived and everything was dark again. Night followed - a night full of terror, and then another day dawned.

Shutting her eyes she lay motionlessly on her back. She was thinking what a relief it would be to fall asleep and never wake up again.

Suddenly she jumped up and with horror in her eyes she gazed in front of her:

"No! I don't want to die, I want to live! ... and I will live!" she panted. "I must not give in! ... I must do something. I can't lie here and wait for death to get me. I must do something! I must! ... I must! I must!"

Holding on to the end of the bed she tried to push herself up. Two or three times she fell back. At last by sheer force of will she succeeded in pushing herself onto her feet. The whole room was spinning around her, the floor was rocking beneath her. She was holding on to the chair with tortured movements. Her heart was pounding inside her chest, tears of strain streaked out of her eyes. Then a little smile spread across her face. "I have done it. I got up," she whispered. "I have to do some more!"

A sudden idea struck her.

Unshed Tears

"Mr. Alexander - I will go and see him. He will know what to do. He always knows what to do."

She dressed into the first thing she could find and straightening her hair casually with her hands she set out. It was the most gruelling journey in her life. Holding on to the landing, she let herself down step after step until she emerged in the dark street. The first rays of light were appearing in the sky. With all her willpower, supporting herself on the walls she made her limbs work, moving unsteadily along the streets. There was nobody about. Approaching the building where Mr. Alexander lived, she could see with relief that the shutters leading onto his balcony were pulled aside. Mr. Alexander was awake.

She pulled herself up the dark staircase, then took a long rest. At last breathlessly she dragged herself to his door and knocked slightly.

A beautiful girl of about thirteen came to the door. She smiled kindly,

"Do come in," she said.

Judith had met her there before. Her name was Tania and she lived with her mother and sister in the same flat. Judith entered the little well kept hall. It was square and had a wardrobe with a huge mirror on one side of it. A chair with a dark green leather seat stood on the opposite side. The floor boards were well scrubbed and there was a small landscape picture hanging on the wall. A door leading into the hall opened and Mr. Alexander stood there facing her. For a little while he stood there, motionless, looking intently into her face, then he came quite close, put his arm round her and said quietly, "You needn't tell me anything. I know. I thought you would come."

Chapter 10

Judith gaped at him in a bewildered astonishment.

"Wwwhat!?"

"O? O, my God! Didn't you hear?... I thought you knew, that's why you came. O my dear Judith." His tone and eyes were full of compassion.

A terrible premonition, which gradually changed into a fearful certainty gripped her heart. Petrified, speechless she looked in front of herself. Suddenly she knew it all, her mother was dead. It was as if she had known it all the time.

"When ... how ... when did she die?"

"Last night. I met the doctor who was treating her, I know him, he told me. I was coming to see you, but it was very late after curfew so I left it till today.... Apparently she was too weak to take the illness," he added softly. "They should have informed you by now ... however it's better this way.... Now come in and have some hot coffee." Supporting her under her arms he led her into his room. It was really only half a room, separated from the other half by a huge wardrobe and a curtain. It looked neglected. The wooden floor-boards were black, the walls and furniture were shabby and the bed was untidily made. And in that gloom the handsome figure of Mr. Alexander stood out even more. Nothing has changed him, as yet.

Judith wished she could cry, but the tears didn't come. "Everything is over now," she thought. "There is nothing more to worry about, nothing." Desperately she tried to put two and two together. She realized now how she had been kidding herself all this time. Only she had been afraid to admit it to herself. Looking at it now she wondered how she dared ever to hope otherwise.

Unshed Tears

The uncertainty had lasted too long. Suddenly she seemed to have lost all feelings.

"It's all over ... it's all over," she muttered under her breath. "I wish I was dead."

Mr. Alexander took both her hands into his and said gently, "Judith I know how you feel."

He paused for a moment then seating her on the bed, he placed himself next to her.

"Listen - you are not a child any more. You have been very brave until now, you have to go on being brave. I know how much you loved your parents. They were very fine people. I have lost my parents, too, when I was very young. One day you will realize how lucky you were to have had the kind of parents you did, although for such a short time."

"But why did they have to die so young? Why?"

"One day, perhaps, you will know. God may have his reasons for it."

"I don't believe in God! There is no God! There couldn't be! I prayed to Him every day, but it made no difference."

He looked at her tenderly and stroked her head.

"I know," he said softly, "one day we may understand." Then he looked at her significantly.

"Judith, if there is ever anything I can do for you, you can always come to me. You know that, don't you?"

Then his hand stopped still upon her forehead.

"Your head is very hot. Have you got a temperature?"

"Yes I think so," she whispered, "I have been in bed for some time. I couldn't make that long journey to the hospital so I came here ... now, I don't think I can face going back to that room of ours. " Her voice quivered.

Chapter 10

He held her hand.

"As a matter of fact I had thought of that. Last night when the doctor told me, I bumped into Mr. and Mrs. White who live in the same street as you. Do you know them?"

"A little."

"They are very nice people. I knew them at home. They have a spare bunk and they said you could go to stay with them. What about it?"

"Thank you! I don't know what I would have done without you."

"I am going to make some coffee now. We shall have some breakfast together," he said more cheerfully.

"Thank you - thank you very much - but I can't eat anything."

"You are jolly well going to eat something now, and no monkey business. How do you expect to carry on without food?" he said firmly.

Judith was not quite sure that she wanted to carry on at all, but she sat by the table without saying any more.

Michael Alexander removed a small electric cooker from a hiding place and put on a saucepan with water for the coffee. Then, out of a suitcase that stood on top of two other cases, he took some bread wrapped in a cloth, and a jar with a little jam in it. He cut two slices of bread, spread some of the jam on them and placed them on the small square table that stood in front of his bed. When the coffee was ready he poured it into two mugs and putting some saccharin into them, handed the less chipped one to Judith.

"This will do you good," he said with a smile. "Now eat this...."

Unshed Tears

When at last she had to take her leave, Mr. Alexander took both her hands and said, "I hope you will be happy with the Whites. Go to bed and get the doctor. I will come and see you sometimes."

★ ★ ★ ★ ★

The streets were busy with people hurrying to work. As if in a dream, Judith made her way through the crowds. Slowly and sadly she walked on, an unknown strength preventing her from collapsing. She wished she could cry, but the tears would not come. In her mind she tried to sort everything out, but found it a difficult task. The only thing she seemed to be able to grasp was that she was alone, alone in a hostile world.

Judith looked for the numbers of the houses. Twenty-two, twenty-four. At last she reached her destination - twenty-six Parrot Street.

It was a tiny old house, painted light green. She stretched out her hand and touched the lower edge of the roof. She entered the main door which was open and found herself in a dark passage. Stopping for a while in order to become accustomed to the darkness, she began to look around her.

There were four doors in the passage, one in each corner. Judith looked out for the one which Mr. Alexander had described to her, and knocked lightly. Nobody answered and Judith knocked again.

At last she heard a shuffling of feet. The door opened and she found herself face to face with Mrs. White who was dressed fairly well in a skirt and a grey pullover. Her hair was almost white, although she was not more than fifty-five. She wore grey

Chapter 10

suede boots and thick stocking. There were big pouches beneath her eyes and her whole face was slightly puffy, a condition common in the ghetto where food consisted mostly of water. Her lips were large, but flat and her back was a little bent. She had long, bony hands.

The moment she saw Judith she showered her with sweet words of pity and sympathy. At last she led her into the "kitchen". It was a large room with a small window looking out onto the yard. The bare dirty walls, the neglected floor and the wooden ceiling made it look still darker. In one corner near the door was a long table. Near the adjacent wall stood an old rusty stove and exactly opposite the entrance was a hole in the wall which at one time was a door. It led into the bedroom.

Here there were two wooden bunks along the walls, left and right of the door, and along the wall opposite the door stood another bare bunk. In the middle of the filthy floor stood three suitcases piled up one on top of the other, serving as a table.

Judith hardly noticed all these details. The only thing she knew was that it was a very dark and gloomy place. It had a musty smell about it, but on the other hand, people lived here. She would not have to be alone in the room where everything reminded her painfully of things that would never come back again. She could not bear it.

With a blind expression in her eyes she listened to the expressions of sympathy and assurance.

"My poor child," Mrs. White said. "We shall treat you like a daughter. Of course it is a little difficult to put you up here, but my heart said 'Here is a child who needs a little motherly care,' and I could not refuse. I was born with an instinct to help others. All my life I have sacrificed myself for other people's happiness. My heart bled when I heard about your misfortune. But you won't be alone any more.... Now go and fetch your things. And when you have a little time to spare, you can give us a hand. You know we are two elderly people. I am sure you understand."

Judith saw through her instantly. But she had no choice. She was glad to have been given the chance to stay here, in human company.

"Thank you ... thank you very much," she said, at last, without a spark of emotion.

★ ★ ★ ★ ★

For the last time Judith glanced at the room in which she had experienced so much misery. It was in this room that she had waited for nightmares to come true. In this room she had lain helpless, without anyone caring for her. Here she had daily prayed to God in vain. Everything reminded her of her parents in a way she found almost impossible to endure.

When finally she closed the door behind her and began to walk down the stairs, dragging a heavy case in one hand and her bedding in the other, tears at last filled her eyes and rolled down her cheeks, and she said quietly to herself: "I will never forget them ... never!"

In a way she felt relieved. There was no more dreading bad news, no more uncertainty. It seemed as though the worst thing that could have happened to her, had come her way. She had nothing to fear any more. She had no special wish to die, but she did not care to live, either. She did not care about anything and she could not imagine that she ever would.

Chapter 10

When she came back into her new home, nobody was there. She pushed her case carelessly under her bed and then sat down, resting after the exhausting task.

In thought, she was far away. Subconsciously she began to walk round the room. Her eyes searched it for details, but her mind could not take them in. They saw the cobwebs and the spiders on the wall, the tiny window obscured by dirt, from which panes were missing. They saw the wood rotting in the ceiling, the old, unused tiled stove in the bedroom with the iron parts turned rusty. They spotted the cracks in the ceiling, the dark walls and the dirty floor.

Judith felt very shivery.

She prepared her bunk and, dressed as she was, lay upon it, pulling the feather bed over her head.

XI

The last few weeks had been too much of a strain for Judith. Her powers of resistance had become very low. She had a slight temperature all the time.

She felt shivery and very weak and spent most of her time in bed, dozing. Her appetite had not returned and there was nothing that really mattered to her.

Mrs. White kept on giving her tasks which Judith did without saying anything.

"I know they want to take advantage of me, but I must stay on good terms with them. It's all for the best at the moment," she thought, and picked up the bucket and fetched the water. Then she cleaned the room.

When a new ration was announced, Judith was asked to fetch it, and she queued for hours to get it. She did not go to work, she knew she could not cope with it, and besides, she did not care for the bread or for the soup.

Every evening when Mrs. White came home she glanced across the room at Judith's bed and thinking that she was asleep, she began to weigh her bread and other provisions on the old-fashioned scales that stood upon the table in the kitchen checking whether she had not been robbed of a crumb or two. Judith knew everything and had she been capable of any feelings at all, would have felt very hurt. But she did not want a row, she did not even have the will to stand up for herself and defend her pride and honour. All she wanted was rest and peace. She grew to dislike Mrs. White, and her husband who let her domineer him, every day more and more. But in spite of that fact, she was looking forward to the moment when they came home in the evening and life returned to the grim place.

Judith stopped doing anything for herself. She began to look poor and shabby. She hardly ever bothered to wash herself, it was too much of an effort for her and, besides, the room and the water were icy cold. The only thing she forced herself to eat was her bread.

One day, when conditions weighed upon her more heavily than usual, she lay for hours in bed, dozing, not being able to get really warm. The day dragged on endlessly. At last, evening came and Judith listened for the kitchen door to creak and Mrs. White to enter and begin her usual evening routine.

At last she came, and Judith pretended to be asleep. She did not feel like talking.

From the kitchen came the sound of the clinking of dishes as Mrs. White prepared to cook the meal. Then she made a fire in the kitchen stove. A little while later her footsteps approached as she came to fetch something from the bedroom, and then again Judith heard her bustling from one end of the kitchen to the other. Suddenly there was silence. Judith listened for a while and then she opened her eyelids slightly and peeped through her lashes.

Chapter II

She saw Mrs. White, who wasn't really very clever, or she would have got out of the range of Judith's vision. She stood at the kitchen table near the hole in the wall. In one hand she held a tin of meat; with the other she helped herself hastily to its contents. Her movements were swift, her eyes were eager. She did not seem able to stop herself. But at last she put down the tin, which had been a special Christmas bonus for two people. Then the door creaked again. Mr. White came in and at once approached the stove and warmed his hands above it.

"Is she asleep again?" he asked his wife, glancing at Judith.

"Sure. She is always asleep. Lazy, I call it. Who wouldn't like to lie about in bed these days!"

Mr. White was starving, as usual. He entered the bedroom, threw Judith another glance to make sure that she was asleep, then looked into the kitchen and satisfied himself that his wife was busy. This was his usual daily routine. Eventually he opened the little rusty door of the unused stove and recovered his bread. It was his secret hiding place. He used to keep the bread in his suitcase, but as any key might have fitted it, he decided to be on the safe side. Having cut himself a slice of bread he placed the rest back in the stove. He always cut himself only a single slice, one in the morning and one in the evening. He was one of the few people who still had a slice left when the next ration came.

Biting into the dry bread he suddenly remembered the tin of meat and with heavy steps he walked into the kitchen. Having prepared the scales in order to divide the contents of the tin into equal parts, he stretched his hand out for it and then held it under his nose. He examined it from all sides with the eye of a scientist, then shrugged his shoulders and nodded his head in disbelief. Mrs. White watched slyly through the corner of her eyes. Then with a face of innocence itself, she walked over to her husband and asked: "Is anything the matter?" Then she looked at the tin and said, "Oh!"

Mr. White looked at her enquiringly but without a trace of suspicion. She shrugged her shoulders and cast a meaningful eye at the girl inside the other room.

"I wouldn't be surprised -" she said, at last.

"Do you really think so?" Mr. White asked, reluctantly.

Mrs. White made an expansive gesture with her hand and remarked: "Well, here you are. This is the reward for our kindness. Of course we couldn't have expected anything else."

Before Judith had moved in, Mrs. White had not dared to do anything wrong because she knew she would come under instant suspicion. That was why her husband did not doubt her innocence now.

Judith heard everything. Her blood was boiling. She felt like jumping up and screaming and stamping her feet and telling them what she thought of them. But something prevented her from making a scene. She hated scenes.

"How can you be so mean! I loathe you! I loathe you!" she thought, angrily. But then once more she swallowed the bitter dose of injustice. She preferred peace. She thought of all the consequences of her revealing the truth. "It might wreck the marriage and turn the place into an even greater hell." She tried to console herself by thinking that a clear conscience was the only thing that mattered and that she did not care what others thought of her.

Similar incidents occurred again and again. The words "dear" and "darling" addressed to her made her angry: so did

Chapter II

Mrs. White's motherly advice. She wished she had someone to turn to in her distress; someone who would understand her and believe her innocence. Even Mr. Alexander seemed to have forgotten about her. Judith learned gradually that words alone have no meaning unless they are accompanied by deeds. She also gradually resigned herself to the idea that she was quite alone in the world.

Mrs. White kept sending her on errands, and every time she returned her portion of bread seemed to have shrunk. Judith was not quite sure and disliked the idea of condemning anyone without actual proof. She thought that perhaps the hatred she had for Mrs. White made her imagine it.

Then one day she laid a trap. She did not like the idea very much, she did not want to occupy her mind with tricks and cunning, but she saw no other way of effecting a cure.

It was a very cold day. Purposely, Judith left the water bucket empty. She knew it would make Mrs. White angry, and she also knew that she would be sent to fetch the water in the evening.

She climbed from her bed, brought her suit-case from underneath the bunk and took out her bread. Then she made a few marks with a knife on the crust that surrounded the part of the bread to be cut next. She kept her loaf wrapped in a cloth and as she was putting it back into the case she tried to memorise the shape of the folds into which the cloth had formed. She pushed the case back under the bed and put a little bundle of dirt beside the right hand corner of the case at the back. Then she waited.

Mrs. White came home at her usual time. It was dark outside. She turned on the light and searched around. As

Unshed Tears

Judith had anticipated, she noticed the empty bucket and immediately reproached her for not having fetched the water. Wearily, Judith climbed out of bed, put on her coat and, without saying a word, lifted the bucket and walked out of the room.

When she returned Mrs. White received her with a sweet face and kind thanks. Judith knew at once what had happened. She was sure now. She had proof. She could not help feeling a real hatred towards Mrs. White. It was the last straw. She could not go on pretending any longer. She thought: "I ought to be thankful to her because she took me in, but I am not. I can't! I can't! I can't! I hate her!"

She could not be courteous to someone for whom she had not the least respect, someone she despised.   Mrs. White suddenly knew by Judith's behaviour that instead of fooling the girl, she had been fooled by her, although she had kept silent for such a long time.

She became afraid that her reputation might suffer, that Judith would talk. She tried to think of a way in which her good name would not be tarnished. There was only one way and that was by challenging Judith.

It did not take long before everyone knew that Judith was "too clever" and the most ungrateful being in the whole ghetto who repaid kindness by insolence.

"Never mind that sometimes she is so hungry that she can't control herself and 'borrows' from my rations while I am at work. I could forgive her that, but the way she sometimes looks at me, one would think that I have taken something away from her!"

Mrs. White was very clever and soon a wide circle of

Chapter II

friends were sympathising with her and admiring her for her patience and good heart.

Judith had reached the point where nothing could make her more unhappy any more. She sought comfort within her heart, in her memories and occasionally in thoughts about her future. "Perhaps one day when all this is over I shall find a little happiness again."

She stopped caring about the world around her. She got used to being unpopular; the hostile looks brought forth a hostile feeling within her, in return. She despised everybody. She was convinced that all people were bad and not worth bothering about. They looked at her with suspicion and in return Judith showed a cold and proud mask. She tried to convince herself that all this did not make any difference to her. It was only somewhere deep in her heart that she longed for a little sincere understanding.

XII

It was New Year's Eve. The air was bitterly cold. The big white clouds hanging over the town at last released their burden and huge snowflakes descended towards the dark ground of the ghetto. People in the Jewish quarter did not give them a friendly welcome. They never did, especially those whose feet were covered with old rags, and whose bodies were not clad in anything more luxurious. Their noses were red, their limbs stiff and their stomachs empty.

It was morning. Judith lay curled up in her bed as usual. She felt cold and stiff and depressed, without any plans, without any aim to live. She lived because she had not yet died. But it did not make much difference to her. Subconsciously her eyes gazed around the room which seemed more gloomy than it had ever looked before. The frosty air penetrated through many gaps in the roof and windows. Thick clouds of vapour ascended towards the rotten ceiling every time Judith breathed out.

As her eyes moved expressionlessly from object to object, she remembered suddenly that it was New Year's Eve. She cast her eyes in the direction of a little heap of white snow which lay on the floor. It had come in through the faulty roof and was still crisp.

"Snow ... the same snow that used to make me so happy," she thought. "How long ago it seems. It is just like a dream that has gone. Was it really ever true?... Five years ago, yes just five years ago today ... I can see it all so clearly in my mind ... the ball on ice, the performance, the triumph of the ice hockey match, the music and the laughter - no, that will never, never come again ... David was there, too. I wonder how he is now. He was seventeen then, a young man. Perhaps he is not even alive any more ..."

She sighed loudly. Her face was pale, her dark eyes and hair made a great contrast against the whiteness of her skin.

There was a sudden knock at the kitchen door. Without waiting for an answer, Mr. Alexander entered and made his way across the kitchen toward the room in which she lay. Her cheeks flushed slightly as he approached her bed, tall and upright, as usual. Perhaps she knew that if there was anyone in the ghetto who mattered to her a little, who might have any influence on her at all, it was he alone.

He looked around and within a few seconds had noticed all the peculiarities of the place. He stopped at her bed and it did not take Judith long to recognize that there was a glance of disapproval in his eye.

They talked about general things, and all the time Judith wondered what were the thoughts behind that set face. "Does he also believe the gossip? Has he heard about me from Mrs. White?" she asked herself, anxiously. Suddenly she realized that there was no other explanation. "So he also, the only person I had a little faith in ... But of course, how can he

Chapter 12

know the truth? He despises the sort of person he believes me to be. What made me think that he would not believe Mrs. White, who was a good friend of his?" she thought, bitterly. "Now he thinks himself noble because he still speaks to me, because he is forgiving me. He thinks I have done this out of desperation."

At last Mr. Alexander came to the point. He looked at her with straightforward eyes and said firmly, but still in a friendly manner: "Judith, I didn't think you would let yourself go like this. We all have our troubles here but we have to control ourselves. You are grown up enough to understand that. You must pull yourself together."

The pain in Judith's heart was swelling. She was incapable of words. Her very last hope had faded away. She looked at him with disillusioned eyes which seemed dark and large in her pale thin face. They were pleading for help and understanding. Mr. Alexander searched in that face for a moment, then he remembered his own worry - the operation that was to take place in two or three days' time. Suddenly he turned round and walked towards the main door. He was almost outside when he heard Judith's desperate voice: "Do you believe that grown-ups are always right in whatever they say about younger people?"

He closed the door behind him and walked out into the snow-clad streets.

Judith sat up on her bed and with numbed feelings stared at the door through which he had disappeared. A strangling pain gripped her throat and tears filled her eyes. She threw herself on the bed and buried her face in the pillow. She cried loudly, bitterly and desperately. Gradually the wet patch from her tears spread over a large area of the pillow.

Unshed Tears

Michael Alexander was making his way towards his office. There were many things he had to attend to before the year was out and the forthcoming operation was still another worry. As he walked along a pair of pleading eyes remained in his memory. He could not get them from his thoughts. Those eyes had expressed full confidence in him and he had let her down. They had expressed the owner's innate truthfulness. "Do you believe that grown-ups are always right in whatever they say?" The sentence haunted him. Doubts began to assail him. Had he made a mistake?

Gradually his steps began to falter. He stopped, hesitated for a moment and then, with an energetic gesture he turned and began to walk back.

Judith did not hear him enter. She found it hard to quieten down. For a while he stood at the door before walking toward her. He sat on the bed.

"It's me, Judith. I am back," he said, warmly.

On hearing his voice Judith tried to stop sobbing, but she was not altogether successful.

For a while he stroked her hair and hand and then with gentle movements he took her head between his palms and placed it on his chest. Tenderly he put his arms round her and tried to comfort her.

A warm feeling spread over her, taking the place, gradually, of the suffocating pain in her heart.

"Judith, we all make mistakes sometimes ... I am sorry I hurt you," he said.

Judith lifted her head and looked at him through red, swollen eyes. He helped her to wipe away the tears. She could not quite understand what was happening. She could not grasp

Chapter 12

that he, one of the most distinguished and respected of men in the ghetto, came to her, an ordinary girl, to apologise.

"Why did you come back?" she asked.

"Judith, there are a lot of things you must tell me, and a lot of things I want to tell you. There isn't enough time now. I shall have to go in a few minutes. It's New Year's Eve today, do you know that?"

"Yes, I know," Judith whispered, between two sobs.

"What about having a little celebration - together? Would you like that?" he asked.

Judith looked at him for a moment. At last she said quietly: "Yes," and a gleam of joy entered her eyes that had been so desperately sad a little while ago. She smiled at him.

"Do you think you can manage to walk to my place without any help?"

"Yes, I am sure I can," Judith answered hastily.

"All right then. Come about seven and I will take you home later. Now cheer up."

"I ... I am all right."

With one hand he pulled up the pillow and put it back with the dry side up. Then he placed Judith's head gently upon it, covered her up and said: "I'll be seeing you tonight. Take care of yourself."

Judith smiled at him gratefully and said: "Thank you ... thank you for everything."

"It's all right, Judith. Everything will be all right, you will see."

He turned round and in a moment Judith was alone again.

Suddenly she felt a little stronger. Although she had told herself many times before that she would never trust anyone again, that she would not believe in sweet words or promises, she could not help giving herself another chance, perhaps because she wanted nothing more than to be able to trust someone.

"He came back to apologise to me. He must be kind and human. I know he understands me and he is sincere and just and honest. There is nothing sham about him, I know it."

Her little inward voice was saying: "There is nobody in the whole ghetto who isn't sly and selfish, who doesn't do everything for his own profit." But Judith was trying hard to disregard it. "But Mr. Alexander is different. I know he is. Perhaps he is the only person in the whole ghetto who can hold his head up, because he is a person with principles and because he has never yet let himself down. Whatever mistakes he has made, he is honest, with others and with himself. I don't want anything from him, only to see him from time to time. It makes me feel less lost to know that there is a person like he is about. He is a real gentleman."

For the first time in many weeks Judith felt hungry. She bent down from her bed, took her bread from the suitcase and, without cutting it, began to bite bits of the big lump as she held it between her hands. Then she threw the remainder into the case. A little while later she stepped out of bed, walked towards the unused stove on which stood a mirror, picked it up and gazed into it.

"What has become of me?" she thought.

With her fingertips she touched her face and then began to finger her hair that was all tangled. She wetted one fingertip and rubbed her initials into her dirty forehead. Then she examined her clothes. They suddenly seemed comical to her,

Chapter 12

and she smiled. She walked over to the water bucket but found it was full of solid ice. Although she felt weak there was a force in her that made her do things which she hadn't thought she would ever wish to do again. She took a plank from her bed, chopped it up and made a fire in the kitchen stove. Then she placed the bucket on it and heated the water. She found a few pieces of coke that belonged to her and added them to the fire. Pouring the warm water into a bowl she took off all her clothes and began to scrub herself briskly. When she had finished the water was quite black.

Looking around for something to put on she found Mr. White's warm dressing gown and slippers. Judith hesitated for a moment and then put them on. She stood over the stove, warming her hands and thinking what to do next. At last she fetched a hairbrush, sat down beside the stove and began to brush out her hair. It was not an easy task and it took her almost an hour before she was able to run through it with a comb without any hindrance. She felt very relieved when she had finished.

Then she walked over to the other room, opened her suitcase and examined the contents. There was nothing much to choose from. At last she took out a red pullover with a polo neck and her only skirt, which was navy blue. She went back to the kitchen where, with the remainder of the warm water, she made an attempt to get her skirt and overcoat clean. She put on a pair of warm stockings and socks and her last set of clean underwear.

It was her favourite pullover and when she had finished dressing she picked up the mirror and examined herself in it. It was another person who stood there now, a totally different person from the one who had looked into the same mirror not very long ago. She was very pale and thin but she was clean and fairly neat. She felt quite different.

She combed her hair again carefully and then with a pair of scissors cut off the odd ends.

It was about two o'clock when she had finished. She felt quite exhausted and decided to lie down for a while. She lay on the bed carefully lest her skirt should get creased. The fire was out and the room was very cold again. She pulled the cover over herself and closed her eyes. When she woke up it was five o'clock.

* * * * *

When Judith arrived at Mr. Alexander's place he helped her out of her coat. It was the first time in her life that anyone had done so and Judith liked it. Suddenly she felt conscious that she was not a child any more and that he treated her like a lady, and she blushed slightly. Mr. Alexander smiled a little but did not say anything. Perhaps it was his charm and knowing what to do at the right moment that made him so lovable. When she saw him smile she smiled back at him, a little shyly, and then said: "It was nice of you to invite me."

"Oh, not at all. It's a pleasure to have such a smart young lady here," he said. He examined her face and clothes with his eyes and winked at her approvingly.

Judith guessed what was on his mind and burst out suddenly: "I have had a good wash today."

"Oh, have you?" he asked, with a twinkle. "That was quite an event, I guess."

Chapter 12

"It was," she replied, quietly. "I know what you must think of me...."

"Hm! I'll tell you what I think. I think it's a shame that a girl like you should walk about like a tramp when she can look so nice," he said, and ran his eyes over her once more.

"What does it matter what I look like? Nobody cares here. Everybody looks scruffy in this place."

"I beg your pardon!" he said, laughing into her eyes.

"Yes, I know, but then perhaps you are the only one. You are different from the rest," she said.

"There is no reason why there shouldn't be two of us. It's no good dressing up suddenly when you come here. You must always try to look your best, like a civilized human being. Keep your head up and say to yourself that in spite of the fact that you are here you are as good as you were before, as good as anybody outside this place, and you will see how much better you will feel. And there is one more thing - smile. You look nice when you smile and don't bend your head. Try to find things you can smile at and you will be much happier. But that's enough of preaching. I am starving, aren't you?"

"A little."

The only illumination in the room was from a lamp that burned on the wall near Mr. Alexander's bed. The shutters were closed and the room was fairly warm. In the other half of the room, separated from Mr. Alexander's part by a long wardrobe and a curtain, life went on in its usual way. Neither he nor Judith took any notice of it.

"Sit down here; it's nearer the stove. And make yourself comfortable," he said.

Judith sat down at the small square table. It was laid for

two. There were knives and forks and two aluminium plates. He brought the pot from the stove and placed it on the table.

"No soup," he emphasised. "We are going to use our teeth today!"

"How posh," smiled Judith.

She picked up her knife and fork and said, "I have almost forgotten how to use them."

Mr. Alexander began to dish out the stew that was mainly potatoes. Bits of horse meat and turnips were floating among them. Judith inhaled some air and remarked: "It smells delicious."

"Next year perhaps we'll have roast goose and dumplings."

"Do you really think we might?"

"Perhaps yes ... perhaps no. But one day we'll have everything again, you'll see.... By the way, that butler of mine forgot to bring the wine in again. I told him I wanted it at seven o'clock," he said, cheerfully.

Judith laughed and replied: "Call him."

Mr. Alexander looked round the room and suddenly exclaimed: "Oh, here it is!"

From the shelf he brought two mugs filled with cold red beetroot juice.

"I forgot, I gave him permission to go to the ball at the Ritz Hotel."

Judith ate everything she was given. For the first time in many months she was able to relax and forget her troubles and live for the moment.

Michael Alexander was watching her. He was glad when he succeeded in making her laugh. He guessed that she had not laughed for a long time. There was a warm and pleasant atmosphere about the place. A feeling of well-being spread over Judith, marred only by the thought that the moment would come when she would have to go back to the place which she loathed so much.

After they had finished the meal, Mr. Alexander cut each of them a slice of bread, put jam on it, made some ersatz coffee, sweetened it with saccharin and filled the mugs. He pushed the table away so that the heat from the stove could reach them and they sat on his bed, which was more comfortable.

"This is a real feast," Judith remarked, "but you should not give me your bread. One does not give bread away in the ghetto."

"I am going to do just as I please with my bread," he remarked stubbornly. "And you," he said, tapping Judith's nose with his forefinger, "are not going to teach me what one does and does not do in the ghetto."

Judith gave him a smile of surprise, but did not say anything. His manner of putting things pleased her.

Mr. Alexander was watching her while she drank her coffee. He looked at the delicate white skin and her lovely eyes bordered by dark lashes. They were filled with sadness and although she was more mature than most girls of her age, they revealed from time to time a child's helplessness. He knew her better at that moment than she knew herself. He wanted to help her, but he had to be careful lest she should become too attached to him. He did not want her to get hurt.

"How old are you?" he asked.

"I was fifteen a month ago," she replied.

He thought there was nothing adolescent or awkward about her. She was a mixture of a grown-up girl and a little child. Her face was full of thought and although she was very thin, her movements were gentle and graceful.

"Would you still rather be a boy?" he inquired.

"I don't know ... I don't really mind. My mother said it is lovely to be a woman if one tries to make the most of it. I have been thinking about it. I wish I could be like her. She was so beautiful, kind and gentle, and so clever. She always knew how to comfort anybody who needed it.... But to be quite honest, for the past few months I have hardly bothered to wish anything ... except ... except perhaps ..."

"Except what?"

"Oh, I don't quite know how to say it ..."

"I know, Judith. You were very lonely and you wanted someone to understand you. Especially when you felt you were being wronged," Mr. Alexander said, calmly.

"Look at me," he said, suddenly.

Judith looked up into his eyes. Her conscience was clear and he could see it.

He took her hand in his two, and said: "I feel very much ashamed of myself, Judith. I knew Mr. and Mrs. White for a long time. I used to visit them in Prague and I was quite fond of them. They were always very charming. I thought it was very nice of them to take you in, especially as you were not very fit. When they told me, reproachfully, how ungrateful you were and how you took advantage of their absence during the day, I believed them and I was rather cross with you as I had asked them to put you up. I don't quite know yet what had happened, but I do believe that you are honest and I hope that you will forgive me for hurting you so much."

Judith looked at him for a long while. She found no words

Chapter 12

with which to express her feelings or perhaps she was too shy to say what was on her mind; only her eyes gave her away. She smiled in an attempt to chase away the tears that were so near the surface. At last she pressed his hand firmly and whispered, "Thank you."

"Now you must tell me what is going on in that place of yours."

Judith hesitated for a while.

"I know you don't like to tell tales, especially behind their backs, but I think I ought to know something about it. I want to help you."

At last Mr. Alexander persuaded her to tell him everything she knew. She talked quietly without any hatred in her voice. He was watching her carefully as she spoke. When she finished he said calmly: "When I come out of hospital I will do something about it. Meanwhile be patient and brave. Whatever people say I believe you are a decent, honest girl and you know that God sees us all as we really are."

"Oh, I don't believe in God."

"We are not going to discuss that now."

"When will you come out of hospital?"

"I don't know. It might take quite a time. This sort of operation is quite a tricky business, especially in this place. But I have heard they have a good surgeon in the hospital."

"It's in the other hospital, isn't it? Not the one my mother was in."

"No, she was in Baretin. That's for infectious illnesses only. I will be in the new hospital."

"May I come and visit you sometimes?" Judith asked slowly.

Unshed Tears

"If you don't mind looking at all the sick people who will be in the same ward with me ... I'll look forward to seeing you."

"I shall come then."

"I think it's time we started to celebrate. It's New Year's Eve. It might be a good year for us. Let's ask the Friedmans in ... shall we?"

Tania and her mother and sister came. They sat around the room and did their best to make it into a gay occasion. They sang and told jokes and treated everything with a sense of humour. Tania performed a Polish national dance while the others sang and clapped their hands. Later, a friend of Mr. Alexander's came and joined in the merrymaking. He made them laugh quite often with his manner of speech, and throughout the evening everyone felt the warmth of the atmosphere. They imagined themselves to be in places they would have liked to be in, and imitated the behaviour appropriate to those places. It was then that Judith realized that perhaps she was capable of being happy again.

About ten o'clock the party broke up. Most of them had to get up early the next day.

Mr. Alexander helped Judith into her coat, wrapped the shawl around her head and led her down the dark steps. It was so dark there that Judith could not see. He got hold of her hand and guided her step after step and Judith suddenly wished the stairs would never come to an end.

For a split second the idea of taking his hand, pressing it against her cheek and kissing it, flashed across her mind. It was only an idea and the next moment she dismissed it as ridiculous.

She tried to prolong the journey home as much as she

could. He probably noticed it but did not show it. Only sometimes he laughed to himself when he saw Judith trying to find excuses for stopping or walking slower.

The air was sharp, the ground was covered with crisp snow and there wasn't a soul in the street. When they were about half way, he put his arm through hers and they walked along for quite a while without saying anything. It was the first time in her life that a man had put his arm through hers. The sensation brought about was spoiled a little by the pressure in the pit of her stomach. She was glad that she did not say anything because in answering she might have given herself away by the slight tremor in her voice.

When they were approaching her house he took hold of her hand again, pressed it firmly, and said: "A happy New Year."

Judith suddenly realized that this was the end of the magic interlude. In a little while she would be back in the world of ugly reality and the happy hours would be just a memory. She tried to think how she could prolong the last minutes, but nothing came to her mind.

"A happy New Year," she said, at last. "I hope you will soon be quite well again."

She felt the swelling in her throat but managed to suppress her tears.

He gave her a caressing smile, one that said: "You are all right. There are a lot of nice things about you and I can see them."

When Judith thought about it later, she knew it was a smile that had comforted many people before and given them encouragement, especially as it came from someone they respected so much, but that night, Judith forgot about all the other people and made herself believe it was a smile he had for her only.

For a long while she looked at him. "Does he really believe in me?" she asked herself. His warm gaze reassured her and she was filled with gratitude and tenderness for him. She felt at the moment that there was nothing in the world she wouldn't do for him. At last she whispered, her voice trembling a little: "Thank you very much. It has been a wonderful evening."

Then, suddenly, against her will, she turned and disappeared in the dark passage of the house.

XIII

The next day Judith got up and went to fetch her winter ration of potatoes and vegetables. Most people had collected it two months ago and by now had very little or nothing left.

The vegetable place was very near and Judith dragged the full sack along the snow-covered street. There was a whole wealth in that sack and Judith was aware how rich she was. Now that she had made up her mind to free herself from the horrible past and face the future, to stand on her own feet and look at the brighter side of life, her appetite returned.

It was the first time since she came to the ghetto that she had been in possession of so much food. She was hungry and she could eat as much as she wanted. Others were hungry, too, but they had nothing to eat. Judith was conscious of that. It gave her a certain satisfaction, a feeling of superiority. She felt as everyone felt who had something that the others were crying out for.

There is something magic in suddenly being the possessor of riches like food in a prison, while others are starving. There is a certain primitive instinct that is satisfied by such a position. Although Judith never took anything from anyone and condemned all the crooks and people who behaved like animals, she had not yet reached that kind of maturity where, with understanding, she could penetrate so deeply into the minds of people, and into her own mind, as to see them and herself in a true light and so, with the help of her intellect, conquer the lower instincts and raise herself above them. She had not yet learned to understand them fully, to understand the reasons for their behaviour, and so to forgive them.

She laid out the cabbages on the floor in the kitchen and left the potatoes in the sack. After cutting a raw cabbage and eating it, she went out again to fetch her ration of fuel. She emptied the sack of coke into the corner of the kitchen, went to the stove and put a few wet planks on top of it. Having lit the fire with some old wood she cooked a potful of potatoes. They were frozen and stayed quite hard, even after being cooked.

Judith had grown used to frozen potatoes during the last winter and did not take much notice of it. She fried an onion in a drop of oil and poured it into the pot where the potatoes were boiling. Some were sound and fell into pieces and formed a thick gravy.

After her meal, Judith went to the works office. Because of her long illness she was offered a job in the children's factory where the working hours were from seven to one. She started the next day.

She got up at six o'clock. The water was frozen and she couldn't wash herself. She put on her skiing suit which she had cleaned the previous day and had placed under the mattress to press it. She ate a few cold potatoes, cut herself a slice of bread and put it into her pocket. With a saucepan in her hand she set out on her journey.

Chapter 13

She arrived before seven o'clock and queued up for the hot coffee which she drank from her saucepan, sitting on the stairs. It was still and dark outside and the electric light was rather dim.

An instructor showed her into the beginners' room which was on the first floor of the massive building that once was a school.

The room was small and lofty with wooden forms around the four walls. Boys and girls from ten to eighteen were sitting silently around the cold, empty room, each toiling with a heavy military jacket.

Most of the children were thin and undersized with large heads, often cropped, and dark sad eyes that looked into the world with hurt and the understanding of a grown-up. Their legs were like sticks, their cheeks hollow and it was obvious that many suffered from tuberculosis. With their skinny hands they were sewing on badges or making buttonholes.

The supervisor handed Judith a jacket, showed her where the badge went and told her to hurry with her job as the children were not allowed to go home until a certain amount of work was accomplished.

This supervisor, a Polish woman, was one of the few who were not in rags. She was very efficient, strict, but not unkind. The children respected her and liked her because she was not a bully, and they felt she was on their side.

Most of the instructors in the children's factory were intelligent people and fairly human in comparison with the general population. They knew how to keep the children in order and make them work hard without being cruel.

When the bell went at one o'clock, door after door opened

and a mob of starved children rushed down to the basement to get their soup. They sat on the floor or on the stairs and eagerly spooned the turnip water from their little pots.

Judith went home, made a fire, heated up some of the potatoes left over from the previous day and cooked a new pot of cabbage and potatoes cut up in small cubes. When she had finished her meal she heated up some water, washed the dishes and washed her hands, face and neck. The rest she left for the next day. A good wash twice a week was enough, especially in the winter. She fetched a pail of water and then, exhausted, went to bed. She slept until the next morning, waking up only once or twice in the evening when Mr. and Mrs. White came home.

The next day she had a lesson on the machine, and afterwards spent the rest of the time doing buttonholes.

Judith found a relief in work. Sewing on the machine was quite new to her and it required a lot of concentration, thus leaving her with little time to think of anything else. She became quite absorbed in her work and tried to prove to herself that she could do any job well if she really made up her mind to it. "What others can do, I can do too," she used to say to herself, and within a week she became one of the eighteen machinists who worked in a chain producing thirty-five jackets or trousers in one morning.

The group she worked with consisted of girls only and Judith became quite friendly with all of them. There was among these girls, who were in the charge of a well-educated, broadminded man, a kind of comradeship that could not be found among the grown-ups in other factories. They sang for hours while they worked and if they finished before time, they talked to each other or sat around while the instructor talked to them about Jewish history, literature or great men. It was then that Judith realized that she was no longer an isolated stranger in the ghetto but was gradually becoming part of it.

The days were hard but she knew that each one of them was bringing her nearer to the end of suffering. There was Mr. Alexander, who had awakened her from the terrible nightmare to which there had seemed no end, whose way of living was an example to her and who was always there when she needed encouragement. He was her friend.

She went to see him three days after the operation. When she asked for him at the reception desk, everyone knew at once who he was. Readily a nurse showed her the way.

"He is a nice man, isn't he?" the nurse said, with respect in her voice.

"Yes, a very nice man," Judith answered, proud that she knew him.

The hospital was bright and modern, built just before the war. The floor was clean, the walls and doors white. Nurses in uniform and doctors in white overalls were hurrying along the corridors.

"He is a very good patient; all the nurses like him."

"How is he?"

"He is as well as you can expect him to be. These things take time. He will probably spend a little while here."

"Is it serious?"

"It was quite a serious operation, but he is not so easily overcome. He has a great force in him that doesn't let him give in to anything.... Are you a relation of his?"

"No ... just a friend."

Unshed Tears

"Here we are."

Mr. Alexander looked very cheerful and welcomed Judith with a friendly smile.

"You have come!" he said.

"Yes. I said I would. How are you?"

He stretched out his hand for hers and drew her nearer.

"You may sit down here," he said, and showed her the edge of the bed.

Judith felt very shy, suddenly, but did as he asked. She smiled at him and asked again: "How are you?"

"Oh, not too bad, really. I mustn't complain. The nurses are doing their best. They are spoiling me!"

"How is the food?"

"Just the same. Soup and some bread. Sometimes I get a little extra. It's quite a help."

"Was the operation bad?"

"No," he replied, with emphasis.

"I am glad.... By the way, I am working now ... in the children's factory," she announced, proudly.

"Good for you! It's the best place you could be in. I know some of the teachers. They are quite decent types.... It's nice of you to have come. You must be very tired after your work."

"I like to come and see you," Judith admitted timidly. "I have brought you something; it's not very much."

She passed him a little parcel wrapped in a serviette.

"You are a naughty girl. You shouldn't bring me anything," he said.

"Oh take it, please ... you must."

He unfolded the serviette, uncovering a few potato scones. She watched him. He picked one up and took a bite.

Chapter 13

"Mmm ... they are delicious," he said. "But you shouldn't give me your food."

"I can do what I like with my food," she grinned.

"Oh ... I see," he said, with a meaningful glance, and then they both laughed.

Judith went to see Michael Alexander about twice a week. On these days she woke up with a feeling of well-being, at first not quite aware of what had brought it about. Later, smiling to herself, she remembered that only a few hours divided her from the moment that had become so important in her life.

Although she was determined now to carry on hopefully, to leave behind the nightmare and look into the future with courage, the loss of her parents had left her with a feeling of gloom which hardly ever left her. On the days when she visited the hospital, however, it receded to the back of her mind and for a while happier feelings prevailed. She even managed to laugh sometimes, which was something she had never expected to happen again.

Every time Judith went to the hospital she brought something with her, in spite of Mr. Alexander's protests. She sat on his bed for about half an hour and they talked about anything that came to their minds.

Judith treasured every minute of it. She never quite got rid of her shyness, but she managed to talk more freely and more happily about everyday events and after a time confided all her problems to him. He always managed to give her a satisfactory solution.

Often they just chatted light-heartedly, making fun of each other. Judith often felt that he was watching her carefully without saying anything and she wondered whether he ever thought about her between the times of her visits.

Unshed Tears

A few weeks of eating comparatively well had brought about a change in her appearance. It was slight at first, but became increasingly more visible. She filled out in places, developed a little, and although she was still pale, the greyish sallowness had gone. Only once did Mr. Alexander remark on her appearance. After examining her from head to toe, he said approvingly, "You have changed, you know. You look much nicer now." She blushed slightly, and he saw by the gleam in her eye that his compliment pleased her more than she would admit.

Had he been other than the person he was, someone else would have taken the place he occupied in the ward; but the doctors and nurses insisted that he stayed in hospital until he was quite fit again. They fussed round him and gave him the best possible care. He was comfortable there, and it soon became apparent in his face. He was not keen to stay in hospital but knowing that it was his only chance of recovering, he did not protest.

Towards the end of February the snow still lay on the ground but the days were getting considerably longer. Spring and summer lay ahead of them. Judith stopped caring about Mrs. White and her gossip. She stayed calm whenever there was an outburst of temper and ignored the whole matter, which infuriated Mrs. White even more. Judith did what she considered to be her duty and then had nothing more to do with her. Now that she had a friend, she saw everything in a different light.

One day, when she was leaving the hospital, after having chatted to Michael Alexander for longer than usual he shook her hand, pressed it firmly and said with warmth, looking into her eyes: "Come again ... soon ... I want you to...."

Chapter 13

Judith looked up at him in surprise, trying to guess whether he really meant it. She had realized that it was a treat for her to be in his company and thought it good of him to have her there. A little bewildered, she cast her gaze away from him for a moment, and then looked at him again.

He wanted her to come again! She knew it now. A deep feeling stirred within her; suddenly the whole world took on a different aspect.

She left the hospital noticing the sun. A little song was upon her lips. She felt a warm happiness flow through her veins and the people around her seemed less wicked than usual.

★ ★ ★ ★ ★

Judith climbed up the dark staircase of Michael Alexander's house. In her hand she was clutching the key of his room. It was a large old-fashioned key and it gave her a pleasurable feeling of possession.

It was about two o'clock in the afternoon and the early spring sunshine was spreading across the shabby rooftops and cobbled streets of the ghetto.

She held on to the wall as she made her way up to the first floor, for she was blinded by the sudden change from the bright streets to the dark interior of the house.

Michael Alexander had asked her to go to his room and fetch his brief-case that contained some important papers.

Judith unlocked the door and shut it behind her. To get to the main room she had to cross the hall. She enjoyed this little excursion into his kingdom and with slightly trembling hands she let herself in.

Unshed Tears

The shutters were closed as usual and she turned on the electric switch, for the light penetrating through the other half of the room was inadequate for her to find her way about.

For a moment she stood between the two "rooms" searching them with her eyes. Then, making her way along the narrow space between the table, chairs and bed, she approached a pile of suitcases that stood against the wall near the balcony door. She buried her hand in her coat pocket and fished out a handkerchief which was tied in a knot, in one corner. Placing her gloves on the table she undid it and with concentrated movements, took from the handkerchief a tiny key.

"He said the middle one," Judith muttered to herself, looking at the shiny black case bordered with yellow pigskin. Carefully she placed the top case on the bed beside her. Her heart beating a little quicker than usual, she tried the little flat key in the special lock. She turned it and something clicked.

Judith enjoyed the confidence Michael Alexander had shown in her by asking her to do this for him. The case was the only one that had a special lock and his most private possessions were in it.

Judith opened it. The brief case lay on top. She took it out, closed the lid, locked the case and put the other one on top of it. She was glad that she had so easily overcome the temptation to look through its "treasures". Her hand automatically smoothed the blanket on the bed, which had become rumpled under the heavy load.

A layer of dust had gathered on the bed and looking around, Judith noticed that it covered every object in the room. She tried to find something to remove the worst of it but

Chapter 13

without success. Her scarf seemed to be the only thing and she decided to use it and wash it when she got home. She was filled with a desire to tidy up the room.

She wiped all the dust off the furniture and cases until the scarf could absorb no more. It was not much good trying to shake it out into the coal bucket. She went over to the windows and wrestled for a long while with the shutters without success. They were stuck. So was that covering the balcony window. She stood upon a chair which she pulled toward the window and after several attempts with a knife she saw lying on the table, it gradually gave way.

It was the only one that had ever been opened since he had lived there. Judith was pleased with the achievement and went out onto the balcony to shake out the scarf. Coming back she switched off the electricity and watched the strip of daylight and the rays of the sun mingle with the particles of dust. For a moment she stood there gazing into space. Suddenly she was overcome by a desire to throw open all the shutters and let the spring sun and air in.

She did not know how long she stood there with new thoughts flowing into her mind. When, eventually, she came to the end of them she was so overwhelmed by the new idea that her heart began to race within her at the thought of the final outcome of it. "Wouldn't it be lovely? How would he receive it?" she said to herself.

She finished dusting the room, shook out the scarf again, switched on the light and closed the balcony door and shutters. Before she left she paused once more between the two rooms and searched around her with her eyes. She saw it all just as it would be when she had finished the job: daylight, bright walls and furniture, clean floorboards, little personal touches. "Yes, it should be nice ... but perhaps I haven't got the right to touch anything without his permission ... but if I asked him it wouldn't be a surprise ... and that wouldn't be the same any more."

She decided to risk it. She didn't quite know where she would get all the materials necessary for carrying out her plan but she was determined to get them somehow. All she really needed was paint and a brush and some nails and a few other little things.

She closed the door behind her.

All the way to the hospital she smiled to herself, delighted with the new idea, and delight shone forth from her face.

"I do hope he will like it!" she prayed.

★ ★ ★ ★ ★

Judith wandered through the ghetto in search of some paint and the implements necessary for redecorating Mr. Alexander's room. She had a list of everything she needed.

It was in a small dark shop at the back of a house that she found what she required. When she entered there was nobody there, but a small greasy man emerged from the room behind the shop, letting a smell of garlic emerge with him.

"Do you sell paints and brushes?" Judith enquired.

"We haven't got any here just now but I know where to get some; that is, if you can wait a day or two."

"How much will they be?"

"What exactly is it you want?" asked the man, looking at her with a speculative eye and breathing out some more garlic.

Chapter 13

"I am not really particular but I should prefer something bright: cream, yellow, pale blue or so. Do you think you can manage that?"

"It all depends ... hm ... you know what I mean.... These things are hard to get ... but if you call here the day after tomorrow ..."

"I want to know how much they will be."

"Well, how can I tell you now if I don't even know what I am going to get? How much do you want?"

"I want enough for a small room. If possible, two colours. One for the walls, the other for the furniture. And some whitewash please. I want to make it look bright. And two brushes and some nails and some wire. I've put it down on this piece of paper. You may have it if you like."

"Now let me see ..." he mumbled, stroking his unshaven cheeks and looking through the list.... "I tell you what - you come here the day after tomorrow and we make a bargain. I'll do my best for a pretty girl."

At this point Judith found it wiser to say no more. She knew that once he had the paint and other things he would want to get rid of them. Nobody bought luxuries in the ghetto.

She smiled at his compliment as she turned towards the door.

"Goodbye, young lady. I shall be expecting you."

Judith left the shop. As soon as she had gone the little man walked to the other side of the room where there was another door, opened it, let himself down some winding stairs and came into a dark cellar. Here the floor was covered with goods new and old, half forgotten. They lay covered with dust and cobwebs. He rummaged through them for a while, mumbling to himself while pointing his torch at one thing after another. Here and there he buried his hand in the heap of unused objects and fished out a tin or a tool and by the end of his search he had set aside a group of things that included a tin of cream oil paint, a tin of cornflower-blue powder paint for walls, and a little sack of whitewash, two old brushes, some old rusty wire and a few long nails. Pleased with himself, he climbed up the stairs, wheezing at every step.

Heating up some soup, he sat down to it with a satisfied mind. He lived alone in this place, did business, ate well and spent most of his spare time dozing on his bed or in the summer sitting on the threshold, basking in the sun.

★ ★ ★ ★ ★

Judith let the sack of coke slide down her back onto the floor next to the cases and dropped down, exhausted, on the bed. She shut her eyes, put her feet on the chair nearby, and relaxed. It occurred to her that she was lying on Mr. Alexander's bed and that her head was probably touching the same place as his must have done on many previous occasions. It made her feel happy.

She was glad the coke was indoors.

Thoughts began to chase each other through her mind and the sound of a key in the lock disturbed her. She jumped up and took a few steps forward.

"It's all right. I am in here," she shouted, trying to avoid giving anyone a shock.

It was Tania. She came in smiling gently as usual, her fair hair hanging gracefully onto her shoulders, making a contrast with her blue coat.

Chapter 13

"I've brought Mr. Alexander's coke ration," Judith explained.

"Is he coming home soon? I went to see him last week. He didn't know then."

"He is coming in two or three weeks' time."

Judith had liked Tania from the first time they had met. She felt that Tania liked her, too, though they had never had any conversation before. Tania looked dignified and thoughtful and Judith believed she could trust her.

They went back inside and Tania asked her into her part of the room.

Judith sat on the chair while the other put her coat away and began to make preparations for the fire for the evening. She helped her chop the wood and placed it neatly on a small heap on the floor. They chatted in Polish.

"We are moving soon," Tania remarked suddenly.

Judith looked at her in astonishment.

"What do you mean ... where to?"

"The old woman who lived across the passage died last week in hospital. We are moving into her room. It's a sort of flat and it will give us all more room."

"Does Mr. Alexander know about it?"

"Not yet, but I am sure he will be pleased to have more breathing space."

Judith sat silently for a long while, her eyes moving from place to place while her mind coped with all the thoughts and plans that were gathering in it. Then she lifted her head suddenly:

"I say ..." she said, confidentially. "There is something I thought of, but promise you won't tell anyone?"

"I promise I won't ... cross my heart!"

"Good. Come and sit over here."

Tania did as she was told, watching Judith as she spoke.

"I want to surprise Mr. Alexander when he comes home. I want to brighten up his room. Someone has promised to get me some paint, and I shall try to open the shutters and ... well ... yes, and build some shelves so that all the things needn't lie about ... and a picture or two perhaps.... What do you think of it?"

"It's a wonderful idea! But will you be able to do it all, though?"

"I have never done anything of that sort before, but I have seen others do it. I think I know how to use a brush. Anyway, even if it isn't so professional, it should still look better than it does now. And look at the floor! I am going to scrub it every day until it's white.... Do you think he will be pleased?"

"He jolly well ought to be.... You like Mr. Alexander, don't you?"

"Yes ... I think he is very nice."

"He is."

"Not a word to anyone. It's a surprise!"

"Of course." Tania got up and began to busy herself with odd jobs around the room. They were both silent for a few minutes, occupied as they were with different thoughts. Then Tania stopped with the broom in her hand: "What do you intend to do with this half of the room?"

"When are you moving?"

"In a day or two. We have to clean the other room first. It's in quite a shocking state."

"I don't really know what to do. Are you taking all the furniture?"

Chapter 13

"I think we are leaving this wardrobe behind and the stove. There is some furniture in the other room."

Judith sat quietly for a while. Suddenly she had it all worked out. Her cheeks flushed slightly at the idea, and a little spark appeared in her eyes. It all seemed far away as yet. She had not set her mind upon it; it was just an idea worth trying.

She said, casually: "I think we could leave the wardrobe as it is; perhaps we'll just shift it a little bit more towards here. It would make the other room easier to move about in and this one could be converted into a kitchen. The shelves and some of the suitcases could be in here and so could the fuel and cabbages, and all the messy work could be done here, too."

Tania lifted her eyes, looked at Judith for a moment, and a tiny smile appeared in them.

They were friends.

★ ★ ★ ★ ★

Judith stood on the floor looking at what she had accomplished so far. An old piece of rag was tied around her body to protect her clothes. She had shifted all the furniture into the next room to give herself enough space to work in. Only the table that had taken the place of a ladder stood in one corner where she had left it, after finishing the job. She was rather pleased with herself. It was her first attempt at whitewashing a ceiling.

The most difficult job was to get the shutters open. She tried with a hammer and a knife and in the end this proved successful. With a creaking noise they slid aside, letting in the light. When Judith managed to throw open the other pair a feeling of joy and achievement overcame her. For the first time the room was filled with daylight and sunshine and she went to fetch Tania to show her the result.

After that day she did not see much of her, as Tania worked on an afternoon shift and she herself tried to get out before people came home from work.

She scraped off all the old paint from the table and chairs and shutters. Having whitewashed the ceiling, she decided to paint the woodwork first, otherwise the paint on the walls might merge into the wet edge of the ceiling.

Having painted the table and chairs she put them into the other room and went home, leaving them to dry. She left the brush dipped in the paint, sprinkled a few drops of oil on top and covered the tin with a damp cloth. Turps was unknown in the ghetto.

It took Judith a whole week to get all the painting done. She came every day after work and stayed until five o'clock except on the afternoons when she went to see Mr. Alexander. The work was tiresome as the whole of her vegetable supply was now exhausted and she lived on the meagre portion of bread and soup, of which there was very little. At the factory five more pairs of trousers or jackets had to be finished each day.

The following week Judith scrubbed the floor every day, thought out the best way to place the furniture, arranged the kitchen, transformed the bed into a divan and added a few personal touches. She sang quietly to herself, pleased with her achievement. Although it was hard work she enjoyed every minute of it.

XIV

The sun was shining gently through the large windows. Judith went out onto the balcony and scanned the road for the rickety ambulance cart.

It was early; she knew it and went back into the room where everything was ready for Mr. Alexander's arrival.

For some unknown reason the Germans had not ransacked every home in the ghetto and Mr. Alexander's had not been touched.

Judith looked around making sure that everything was in its place. She felt happily excited and walked up and down the room onto the balcony and back again. She approached the table and re-arranged the few twigs which she had found in Baretin on the previous day. They looked nice in the tin which was painted blue and cream like the rest of the room.

Everything looked cheerful with cornflower-blue walls and white ceiling. Judith had put on the shelves the crockery for which there was no room in the wardrobe. The latter she had painted cream, like the rest of the furniture, and had shifted it two yards towards the other part of the room. She had put the bed along the back of it and transformed it into a divan by getting rid of the wooden poles on the corners and covering it with a huge tartan rug which Mr. Alexander had once used in his car.

Over the bed she had hung two primitively framed photographs of Prague.

The square table stood not far from the divan with two cream-painted chairs on two adjacent sides of it.

Judith had found a dark blue flowered square cotton scarf and used it for a tablecloth. It looked very gay. The tin stove that used to stand in the middle of the room she had put along the wall and covered it up with a piece of cloth, for the days were now warm enough to make the "kitchen" stove adequate for the next six months.

She had managed to get hold of a small picture of a charming country scene and hung it on the wall opposite the balcony. The cream-painted shutters made a pleasant contrast with the blue walls. The windows were clean and the floor boards were almost white with repeated scrubbing.

The kitchen did not look quite so attractive as there wasn't enough paint with which to decorate it. But it was as tidy as possible with all the odd bowls, buckets and sacks lying about.

There was an empty space near the window which Judith liked to think looked as if it had been left free because other places were more suitable for the things lying about the room.

She was dressed in a white blouse with short sleeves and her navy blue skirt. The sports shoes for which she had given a few pounds of potatoes two months ago, were not very glamorous but they looked better than clumsy clogs. Her hair was tidy, her face was full of anticipation.

Chapter I4

Soup was cooking on the kitchen stove. It smelt delicious. Judith went over to stir it. She had saved up for it for a long time. It was made of vegetables, potatoes and barley and was luxuriously thick.

She replaced the lid and wiped a drop that had fallen from it onto her shoe. As she bent down her hair fell onto her forehead and she quickly picked up Mr. Alexander's shaving mirror and rearranged it. She looked at herself for a moment, wiped the corner of her eye and put the mirror back in its place on top of his cases which she had not dared to move from their original position.

Her skirt was a little short and somewhat tight. It revealed the roundness of her hips. She was slim but having eaten comparatively well for a few weeks after a year of starvation her bones had become covered and her arms were graceful and round and so was the rest of her body.

She held herself erect. Self-confidence had returned to her after long weeks of indifference and helplessness. Her mind was made up - she could face everything and fight back.

She went out onto the balcony again and there, at the bend of the road she saw it, rocking in its usual way on the large cobbles.

With her heart pounding she ran out of the flat, down the dark staircase and into the sunlit street. Suddenly her hair did not matter. She ran to meet the cart, eagerly watching its windowless sides, and walked back beside it toward the house. At last the hospital attendant jumped from his seat in the front and went over to the back to open the doors.

Mr. Alexander came out, a little shaky, and smiled when he saw Judith. He stood for a moment at the corner, trying to get used to the light. The cart turned round and went back down the road.

"It's dark in there," he explained with a smile.

"I know ... how does it feel to be out in the air, to walk again after all that time?" Judith asked, cheerfully.

"Not bad. I had a little practice in walking yesterday. I felt quite helpless at first."

"If you feel very weak ... you can hold on to me," Judith said with a little uncertainty, and Mr. Alexander looked at her happily, patted her cheek, got hold of her hand and said: "Come on, let's go in."

When they were on the stairs he remarked, "It's nice to have someone waiting for you when you come home after such a long time."

They walked up slowly, step by step, resting now and again.

"I have made some thick soup. That will make you stronger," said Judith.

For the rest of the climb Mr. Alexander put his hand at the back of Judith's neck and they walked through the corridor toward the flat. There Judith freed herself, opened the door and walked before him across the little hall. At the door she stopped and hesitated for a moment. She was happy and excited and her face shone with these emotions mixed with a little apprehension. She looked up into his face, put on a gay smile and said: "Well, here we are."

She opened the door proudly and walked in. He followed.

For a long while he stood there without saying anything. His eyes wandered round the room and at last stopped on Judith. He looked at her and the cheerful smile suddenly disappeared from her face. She watched him, trying to

Chapter 14

overcome a feeling of uneasiness. After a while he said: "Did you do all this?"

"Yes."

"You have made it into a lovely place to come back to, Judith."

"I enjoyed doing it."

He looked at her searchingly for a moment, then said: "I really believe you did."

He took her hand in his and held it for a while. Then he brushed back her hair from her forehead and said: "You are a nice girl, Judith."

His face grew brighter and he took her by the hand and led her through the place while she explained everything about it. She felt more at ease now and answered many of his questions in fun, joking all the time and laughing happily. When they came to the "kitchen" he looked around and remarked: "I shall be the poshest person in the ghetto. I am sure nobody else has a separate kitchen, like this. It smells wonderful here."

He walked over to the stove on which stood the soup and whispered in a conspiratorial manner: "May I have a look?"

"Of course!" she laughed.

He removed the lid and sniffed. Then he stirred it with a spoon that lay nearby.

"I am really looking forward to this," he said.

"Let's have it then. I am starved, too."

"Have you eaten anything today?"

"I had my soup at the factory, but it was only water. Cabbage water."

"Come on then, let's have a feast."

Judith removed the twigs and laid the table while he

washed his hands in a bowl in the kitchen. When he sat down she brought in the hot soup and they each had two platefuls.

"You seem to be a very good cook," Mr. Alexander remarked. "In hospital when they put these things into soup it tastes like nothing on earth."

"I learned some of my cooking from mother...." When they had finished, Judith jumped up and said, "You must go to bed now."

"Oh?" he queried in a surprised tone.

"You know the doctor said so. You are to get up for a short time first."

"I guess you are right. I really feel quite exhausted."

"I am going to wash up while you get into bed."

★ ★ ★ ★ ★

It was getting dark outside and Judith went to close the shutters. Mr. Alexander watched her from his bed as she climbed up onto the deep window sill and stretched out to bolt the top part of it. Blackout regulations were very strict and night watchmen paraded the ghetto in search of chinks of light. There was a fine for every one they found.

When she came down he stretched out his hand toward her and she took it and sat down on his bed beside him. He looked at her.

"Judith, why have you done all this for me?"

She tried to avoid his look and said, a little bewildered: "I had nothing to do and I thought you might like it ... men usually don't bother doing things for themselves."

"You wanted to do something nice for me, didn't you?"

Chapter 14

"Perhaps," she whispered.

His eyes watched hers in which the whole truth was written and he lifted his hands toward her face, touched her eyelids lightly with his thumbs and stroked them gently for a moment.

"I don't know what I am going to do with you," he said at last, smiling cheerfully and gently.

She smiled back at him, a little, embarrassed smile mingled with happiness.

"I shall have to go now," she said, at last. "But you shouldn't really be left alone here."

"I shall be all right. You go and have a good sleep. You have done enough for today."

"I wouldn't mind staying tonight ... you might need something."

"Where would you sleep?"

"I could sleep on a chair or on the floor.... There - there is a spare bed out in the corridor ... from the room the Friedmans moved into."

He looked at her in sudden surprise and Judith blushed slightly.

"Where would you put it?"

"Oh, anywhere. I ... I am not quite sure, but I think there might be enough space in the kitchen under the window."

It suddenly dawned upon him.

"It might not be worthwhile dragging it there for one night."

"Perhaps not ... just as you like.... I'd better be going then," Judith said quietly. She raised herself and without saying anything more put on her coat and moved toward the door. He called her back.

"Sit down for a moment," he said.

"Yes?"

"Judith, do you realise what it would mean if you lived here? I am not always easy to get on with. I have my moods. You would probably want to do all the work around here and you need time for yourself. Sometimes I have to get up at night and put the light on or go to bed very early and ask for peace; can you see it all?"

"Yes."

"Well?"

"I think I'd better go." There was a slight tremor in Judith's voice and she turned her head so that he could not see her. He touched her chin and turned it to him and looked into her swimming eyes.

"Judith, I am not trying to discourage you because I don't want you here; I just want the best for you. I am not a healthy person yet," he said gently.

"I want to look after you," she said quietly.

"Do you really want to?"

"Yes...."

He thought for a minute or two, then his face brightened and he said cheerfully: "Come on, let's get the bed in...."

XV

Days and weeks passed by. Mr. Alexander was back at work and Judith, who came home early, tried to get all the housework done before he came back. They had only a small meal a day besides the soup at work, but she managed to stretch out the ration so that there was never a day without any food at all.

Judith enjoyed cooking and thinking out new dishes, especially as Mr. Alexander never failed to notice anything she did and always showed his appreciation.

Slowly she began to know him better and to understand when he wanted her company and when he preferred to be left alone. She got used to his moods and learned to meet them sensibly.

She often wondered whether there was a home like theirs anywhere in the ghetto. They learned to tackle together the everyday difficulties with common sense and humour, taking everything in their stride.

Throughout the whole day of hard work Judith looked forward to the evening. When Mr. Alexander came home tired, she helped him take off his coat and boots and filled a bowl with water for his hands.

Unshed Tears

After the meal they would go down together into the courtyard, wash the dishes, empty the bucket of dirty water and bring some clean water back in the white pail.

He also helped her to do the washing on Sundays. When she then ironed his shirts, she took special care with the collars.

"I want you to look smart," she would say gaily, when he praised her work.

One day, after having finished all the work, they sat together on his couch and talked as they so often did. He played with her hair and looking at her gently, said, "Judith, I could always stand on my own feet and do things for myself. I managed on my own for a long time and was quite happy. But you have made this place into a home, a real home. I look forward to coming here in the evenings because I know I will find you here."

He stroked her cheeks and then took her hand on which there were blisters from holding the heavy iron at work, and kissed her palm.

Sometimes when they sat on the couch or on the balcony after the work was finished, Tania or her whole family joined them. Mr. Alexander smoked his pipe, using a special kind of Ersatz tea-leaves for tobacco. He spent hours telling them about foreign countries he had visited, all he had seen, the customs of the various people who lived there, thus trying to bring them nearer to the outer world. He managed to get hold of an old torn atlas and pointed out the various places on the maps. The girls kept asking questions and he managed to answer them all. He seemed to know everything.

On Sundays when they did not go to work Mr. Alexander often read to Judith from a Czech book he had borrowed from

someone and made her read aloud, too. Sometimes they read
poetry and he would talk to her about the various poets or
writers, their lives, ambitions and disappointments.

XVI

Life on the whole was passing very quickly in the Ghetto. People counted the hour to the next meal, which was the most important event of the day. Next came bedtime when they could stretch their weary legs and in their sleep find oblivion. Life was a bit easier in the summer. Although the toil in the work factories made sweat run down the workers' faces, they preferred it to the cruel winter, when their limbs were stiff; food was even more scarce and hundreds of people were daily carried out of their homes, frozen to death. They were still dying, even in the summer, of tuberculosis, exhaustion, weakened hearts, typhoid and many other illnesses that were so typical of places of misery like the Ghetto.

People were walking about in the streets hardly recognizable because of their puffed-up faces and shapeless legs filled with fluid, which they dragged along the pavement unable to lift them off the ground. Their brains became dulled. Once intelligent, confident men in smart suits, who held high positions before the war and carried themselves with an air of superiority - what was left of them? A disfigured body with a big face and two little eyes that revealed fear and helplessness. Their movements were uncertain and their mental power was that of a small child. There were others whose cheeks and temples were hollow and their jaws big. Death looked out of their eyes.

There were some, however, who having overcome the crisis, seemed to adapt themselves to the place with their minds made up not to give in. Usually they were those with a strong constitution and a sense of humour that helped them to look hopefully into the future. Some even made an attempt to smarten themselves up and invented fashions that could be put into practice, like decorating their clogs, wearing scarves in various ways and setting their hair in a new style.

The ghetto consisted of various types, but most of them had one thing in common - selfishness. The animal instinct had got hold of almost everyone and gripped him tightly, squeezing humanity out of him. Self-preservation took the upper hand in almost every person, and with some there was no limit to how far they would go in order to keep alive and satisfy their basic needs. Other people didn't matter.

One day something happened which Judith had never thought possible. Even months later she could not grasp the fact that she was the victim of something stronger than her own will, that the baseness of the ghetto would get so close to her.

It was towards the end of August. Judith was alone at home. The heat seemed almost unbearable. The sun scorched the pavements and the walls of the houses. The whole morning she had sweated at the pressing table without having had any breakfast. Her feet were swollen, her stomach was empty and her hands were shaking with exhaustion.

Chapter 16

The little soup she had had for lunch had only whetted her appetite and now she was sitting on Mr. Alexander's divan, resting, before tidying up the room and getting the meagre supper ready.

The ration had been delayed and there were hardly any provisions in the house. Judith had finished her loaf of bread three days ago and the watery soup twice a day was not enough to keep anyone going.

Several times she had made an attempt to get up, but her knees gave way under her and she fell back onto the divan. At last she managed to get up but her head began to spin round and she became angry. The acute emptiness in her stomach kept nagging at her and at moments she felt near desperation.

She wiped her face with her arm, staggered into the kitchen and searched all the corners for a crumb of bread. But the crumbs had gone days ago.

Morosely she dragged herself back into the room and sat down again. There was nothing else she could think of save bread, nothing else seemed to matter at that moment. Was she going mad? Her nerves seemed to be giving way to something stronger, to something she tried to fight but couldn't.

Bread! Bread! Bread!

Her brain began to work rapidly; two thoughts were battling with each other. Desperately she wrestled with her conscience. It must have been the devil himself that got into her. A look crept into her eyes that had never been there before. She was confused and she hated herself.

Bread! Bread! Bread!

One little piece; only one tiny little piece!

The thought of the crumbs melting on her tongue brought

a keen expression to her face. Then, suddenly, she made up her mind. As she crept towards his case she began automatically to think of an excuse for herself to ease her conscience. She succeeded. Probably everyone succeeds in justifying himself when it comes to clearing one's conscience, for a while, anyway.

"I have given him so much of mine when he was still in hospital. I only take one little piece back."

She hesitated for a while. "This is an ugly thought," something inside her was saying. But Mr. Alexander's case seemed to have a magnetic power. On tiptoe she crept across the room, stopping several times, looking round as if to make sure that no one was watching her. For a moment she looked hesitantly at the suitcase and then with trembling fingers she opened it.

The bread lay there: about a quarter of a loaf, wrapped in a tea cloth, a knife beside it.

Her conscience made her take every precaution. She remembered the time when she used to lay traps for Mrs. White and now she studied the positions of the bread and the knife and the folds in the cloth.

She made a mental picture of everything and then she lifted the bread from its place and unwrapped it eagerly. The smell of it seemed to make the hole in her stomach even bigger.

Carefully she cut off a slice and put everything back as it was. Then she seated herself on the bed and started to nibble at the precious piece of bread she was clutching between her fingers. She tried to make it last as long as possible, tasting every little bite to the fullest.

For a while she was happy and nothing else seemed to matter. But at last the interlude came to an end and she swallowed the last precious crumb.

Chapter 16

When it was all over she felt suddenly numb. Her hunger was worse than before as her digestive system became irritated. She stared in front of herself, trying to grasp everything and then it gradually came to her. She was a thief! She had stolen bread, of all things! What was she to do?

"But I had given him a lot of mine. It does not matter if I took a little piece back," she said to herself again.

She forced herself up and began to tidy the place. Somehow the room did not look as friendly as usual. Every bit of furniture was a witness to her theft and she became angry and a hostile expression came into her eyes.

Thief! Thief! Thief! She seemed to hear the cry everywhere, but she made up her mind to resist.

She tightened her lips and went on with her work. She was fighting against the weakness that had spread to every part of her body.

While she struggled with what she was doing, she pictured in her mind Mr. Alexander's homecoming, and decided how she would behave. She would act as if nothing had happened, carry on as usual. After all she did only take back a little bit of what she had given. There was nothing so bad in that, she kept on repeating to herself.

When she had finished with the room, Judith went to the cupboard and found a solitary red beetroot with the leaves on it and took it over to the table. She cleaned it and cut it up in little pieces including the leaves and getting a few ingredients together she put them into a shopping bag with the saucepan and went over to the gas-kitchen to cook their supper.

The air there was thick to suffocation and she had to make several excursions into the open to prevent herself from collapsing.

Unshed Tears

Some other people were hanging around the door while their food was cooking on the ring.

When the bits of vegetables floating in the pot-full of water were tender, Judith added some saccharin and crystallized lemon ersatz to them, which gave it a piquant taste and helped the water to become an attractive red. Then she took it off the flame and went home.

★ ★ ★ ★ ★

Judith did not go to meet Mr. Alexander that night. When he entered the room she tried to greet him cheerfully, but avoided his eyes.

"Everyone in our office got a coupon with which he can collect two pounds of potato peelings," he said, triumphantly handing the ticket over to Judith. "Those little cakes you made last time we had the peelings were really delicious. Hm ... what about it?" he said, lifting Judith's chin.

She tried to smile.

"Yes, it's lovely," she said.

"You don't sound very happy," he commented.

"This heat really gets me down," she said, wiping her moist forehead.

All through supper Judith was very quiet. She tried to think of something to say and when at last she succeeded, she found it hard to speak naturally. The strain began to show on her face. The more she tried to be herself, the more irritated she became.

Mr. Alexander observed at once that something was the matter with her but decided to pretend not to have noticed

Chapter 16

anything, for the time being, anyway. During the course of the evening he made a few attempts at finding out what was wrong, but she resented his questions and he did not persist. He had become used to her coming to him with all her troubles and now he began to wonder whether her strange behaviour had anything to do with him.

They sat on the balcony and each read a book. Through the corners of his eyes he watched her and saw that several times she gazed into space without turning over a page, and then again she stared nervously into the street in front of her without taking in the bustle that was going on there.

The air was beginning to get refreshingly cool and towards ten o'clock they turned indoors. Judith said goodnight and went into her part of the room.

"Perhaps hunger has overcome her," he thought, and opening his suitcase he called her in.

She appeared at the partition and seeing him standing at the case stretching out his hand for the bread, her eyes filled with fright and anticipation. In a second she had succeeded in concealing her feelings, but it was too late. Their eyes had met at the crucial moment and he had recognized her fear at once but decided not to show her that he had noticed anything.

He took out the bread, unwrapped it, cut two slices and began to smear them with the remainder of the jam which he scraped off the sides of the jar.

"He has not noticed anything," she thought with relief.

He smiled at her encouragingly as he passed her one slice and Judith looked into his kind eyes. Something stirred within her. As if she had suddenly woken from a trance she thought, with anguish: "What have I done? I have stolen bread from him, the one who is so good to me! Who else would offer bread to someone at a critical time like this?"

Her hand was shaking as she stretched it out for the slice and then it suddenly dropped.

"I ... I am not hungry," she said.

The expression in her eyes was different, now. She was desperately unhappy. Although he had by now guessed the reason for her strange behaviour, he was aware of her feelings.

Not knowing what to do with herself she walked onto the balcony. He followed. It was almost dark outside and the streets were empty.

He touched her shoulders lightly and turned her round to face him, looking into her eyes that were filled with frustration.

"Judith," he said at last, "do you realize that there are few things that we do which are wrong and that can't be put right again?"

She raised her eyes in amazement toward him. They were filled with thought and eventually a little gleam of relief appeared in them.

"Do you really think so?" she asked.

"Yes, of course."

It was as if suddenly she had become fully conscious of all that had happened. His kindness only seemed to deepen the wound in her heart. The lump in her throat was strangling her and then, suddenly, she threw her arms around him and buried her head on his chest and cried. He comforted her with his hands and in between her sobs she took hold of them and kissed them.

When she had calmed down a little she lifted her head and looking at him through swollen eyes, muttered: "I have ... I have taken a piece of bread ... from you ... I suppose you won't talk to me any more now. I shall be very unhappy but I won't blame you."

"Why should I stop talking to you?"

"I have stolen bread from you."

"I gathered that a while ago," Mr. Alexander answered calmly.

"But - but you were so nice to me! You gave me some more bread!"

"You were hungry, weren't you? Judith, we all make mistakes. We all slip up sometimes. The main thing is that we know it was wrong and make up our minds not to do it again. I know you won't take anything from anyone again. It makes you too miserable."

"No, I won't, I promise! I will give back to you what I have taken, I will give you twice as much ... but still, it won't be the same any more. You could never really forget it," she said, feelingly.

"Don't be silly Judith. You took a piece of bread, you told me about it, you want to give it back to me, so what's all the fuss about? I shall have forgotten it by tomorrow. We are all tempted sometimes."

"You would never do a thing like that."

"One never knows. Besides you are growing, you feel hunger more strongly. And believe me, in the course of my life I have sometimes done worse things. Sometimes one just can't help it. Now forget about it."

Judith looked at him gratefully and whispered: "Thank you. You are so wonderful."

He smiled with a twinkle and said cheerfully, trying to

change the subject: "I haven't heard a woman say that to me for a long time!"

"I expect you miss all those smart women making a fuss of you," she smiled.

"No, not really. I have had a very good time. I miss the freedom and comfort, but surprisingly I don't miss those smart women as much as I thought I would. Perhaps it is because ... well, never mind. You go to bed now."

Judith searched his face, wondering what he had intended to say.

They went into the room which was now almost dark. He picked up the piece of bread which he had prepared for her and passing it to her said, in a comforting voice: "Good night, and sleep well."

Then he bent down and kissed her forehead.

For a moment she lingered. Then she said: "Thank you.... Goodnight," and walked slowly toward her room.

As she lay on her bed she was saying to herself: "There are very few things we do wrong that we can't put right again. It really is a wonderful sentence." And then again she remembered that he had kissed her for the first time. "It is a funny world," she thought, just before falling asleep.

★ ★ ★ ★ ★

On the anniversary of her mother's death Judith went to the cemetery to visit both her parents' graves. Autumn was well advanced; it was quite cold and the skies were cheerless.

It was two years since they had come to the ghetto. It seemed a lifetime. The outer world was something beyond her

Chapter 16

reach. The horror of the place had vanished, but the hunger and discomfort remained.

The whole two years appeared before her inward vision as she made her way through the muddy fields. There were no flowers to take to the graves. It was the first time that she had visited the cemetery. She had been on the way once before but had returned before reaching it. Something had gripped her heart and choked her and she could not go through with it. The thought of seeing the heaps of earth under which lay the bare bodies of her parents, without coffins, without flowers, drove her to desperation.

Mr. Alexander had offered to accompany her but she had insisted on going alone. She could not quite explain why she did not want anyone with her on that first visit to the graves of her parents, but she knew she wanted to be alone.

There was no one at the cemetery when she arrived. Walking over to the building near the gate she enquired at the office for the numbers of the graves. In the doorway she met an old Jew with a covered head who, on hearing her request, told her to follow him.

He led her through a hall in which lay two rows of dead people, covered with white sheets. At this sight, Judith's body stiffened. It frightened her, but just the same she couldn't help peering at them and visualizing their faces and bodies under the wrappings, thinking of them as they were, walking through the streets, laughing and crying and quarrelling.

The man took Judith to a little room where, after asking her for details, he began to search in a huge book. He found what he wanted and handed Judith a piece of paper with two numbers on it.

Unshed Tears

She sped through the hall looking neither to right nor left. Outside, she looked around trying to get herself orientated on that vast area of ground.

The graves were nothing more than heaps of earth with numbered plates instead of a tombstone. They were arranged in long rows. It was not too difficult to find the right number.

Judith went to her mother's grave first. She was not quite sure what she ought to do. It did not really matter, she thought. Her body grew rigid as she looked down at the piece of ground under which her mother lay.

She spent a quarter of an hour beside her father's grave and went home, wondering whether it would be possible to put the two bodies into one grave, so that at least they could be together. Then again she thought of how, after the war, if she had enough money, she would have them transferred to the Jewish cemetery in Prague. There they would have a beautiful grave with flowers and a tombstone. "But who can guarantee that they did not get mixed up? How could anyone recognise them and make sure?"

The gloom of that afternoon stayed with Judith for many days and only gradually did she succeed in centring her mind fully on other things.

For that she was grateful to Mr. Alexander, who was always there when she needed him.

XVII

Judith woke up with a faint awareness that this day was a little different from others, apart from the fact that it was Sunday. She opened her eyes and then suddenly realised that it was her birthday. She was sixteen.

For a while she lay on her back letting her eyes wander aimlessly through the semi-darkened room. Thoughts flitted in and out of her mind. She knew Mr. Alexander was awake for the black-out in his part of the room had been removed and she heard him turn the pages of a book.

At last, deciding to begin the day, she stood up on her bed and removed the black-out frames from the window above her. Daylight penetrated into the room. It was the grey daylight of a drizzly, late autumn morning.

She looked into the street which was empty save for a solitary figure wrapped in a shawl, making her way to the gas-kitchen.

It was with mixed feelings that she lay back in her bed. A little while later she heard movements. Mr. Alexander was putting on his dressing-gown. Reaching for her hair-brush she began swiftly to tidy her hair, anticipation mounting within her. There was a knock on the partition. Hiding her brush beneath the bedclothes she called out: "Come in!"

Mr. Alexander strode in with a dignified air, stopped about two yards in front of her bed and said solemnly: "Good morning, madam. Breakfast will be served in twenty minutes!"

Judith looked up at him with amused curiosity.

"Breakfast? What is that?"

With unchanged serenity he answered: "It is something people occasionally eat in the morning."

"Oh ... oh yes ... I vaguely remember now."

"Would madam prefer it in bed or in the parlour?"

Judith was filled with inward happiness and gratitude, feelings that were mirrored in her eyes. She stretched out her arm. He came forward, smiled, and sat on her bed.

"Happy birthday, Judith," he said, warmly.

"Thank you," she answered, quietly.

"You are sixteen today," he said, after a pause, looking at her intently.

"Does that mean anything special?" she asked with a provocative tone in her voice.

"Well," he said, frowning a little and pursing his lips, "it means something - yes - it means that you are growing up." Looking her up and down he continued: "You have become quite a young lady."

Judith smoothed the covers, sat up properly in the bed and leaned her head against the wall. Her face still flushed a little, she asked: "Is that a good thing?"

"Oh," he said with a twinkle. "It depends ..."

She opened her mouth with the intention of replying, but refrained. He examined her face for a while, looked at the dark

Chapter 17

hair that reached to her shoulders and said quietly: "Judith, you have grown up very nicely."

He touched her delicate skin with the back of his fingers, stroked her forehead and smoothed her hair. All the time there was a soft glow in his eyes which filled her with a strange emotion. He noticed it and closing her lids gently, leant towards her and kissed them very lightly as if afraid he would harm them, stroking her cheeks and hair and neck, meanwhile. She raised her arms, feeling for his shoulders and put them round him. He covered her forehead with tender kisses and then, leaning his cheek against her for a few seconds murmured: "Judith, I am so thankful to have you here with me."

He released her and sat up straight on the bed. Seeing the wonder in her eyes he assured her: "I really mean that. The ghetto doesn't seem such a terrible place with you in it. I'd rather that you needn't be here at all, but considering all things, I am grateful to have you with me.... Why do you look so surprised?"

"Well ... it sounds somehow funny coming from you. It's the sort of thing I might say ... but ..."

"Judith - I am a human being," he remarked, very quietly.

"Yes ... I know." She was staring in front of her, thoughtfully, trying to sort everything out in her mind. "He needs me a little bit," she said to herself, "He is not keeping me here only out of kindness." Suddenly she looked up at him gaily and remarked: "I think it's nice being sixteen."

He grinned understandingly, presented her with another swift kiss on her cheek and got up.

"The day has only just started," he announced, and

meeting her interrogative expression with an impish smile, added: "What I mean is that for a whole day I shall be at your service. You are not to touch a thing. You shall have breakfast, lunch and tea and a day of leisure. Does it appeal to you?"

Judith found it difficult to reply. He had as little as she had; how could she accept such luxury as he suggested?

But he wanted to give her a little happiness and she knew she must on no account hurt him.

"May I know what you meant by 'You shall have breakfast, lunch and tea'?"

"Exactly what I said."

"And what about you?"

"That's none of your business."

"Oh. So you are going to sit down and watch me eat - is that it?"

"Will you kindly answer the question! Do you want breakfast in bed or in the other room?"

"I want breakfast sitting down properly, served on two plates and with two cups placed at opposite ends of the table. Is that clear?"

"All right, we shall have breakfast together. Is that better?"

"Yes.... I wouldn't really enjoy it otherwise," she replied quietly.

He looked at her seriously. She returned his gaze. Then he went into the other room again.

Judith took care with her appearance. When she entered the other room it was tidy, the table was laid and everything was ready. They ate dry rye bread which tasted like the finest cake, and drank black ersatz coffee sweetened with saccharin. The silence between them was a happy one. The atmosphere of

Chapter 17

joy that had been with her since the early morning brought a song to Judith's heart. It enriched the day and brought new thoughts and feelings into her mind. She was happy, happy in spite of all the dread and misery around her.

After they had washed the dishes and put them away he sat on the couch, stretched out his hand for the book that lay on the case near his bed and said: "I want to read something to you."

While he looked for the right page Judith knelt on the corner of the couch, resting on her heels and propping herself up looked straight at him with a questioning smile.

"I am so happy today!"

He looked at her, his thumb between the pages.

Putting his free hand on hers he asked: "Do you know why that is?"

Her eyes avoided his.

"I think so ..." she faltered.

"Look at me!" he pleaded.

She did so, and between them there flowed the acknowledgement of their feelings for each other.

Judith said, lightly touching her left side, "Do you have a funny feeling here?"

He looked amused and replied: "You know, men don't like to confess to such things!"

"Oh!" Then, after a pause, she said: "But you have it, haven't you?"

Instead of answering he beckoned her to come nearer, pulled her down close beside him, put his arm around her and finding the page he had been seeking, began to read to her.

The day passed happily in the new atmosphere of

contentment and affection. They had two more meals, once a concoction of turnips, cabbage and spices, and a clear soup in the evening with the remnant of the bread. Jokes flew between them.

Tania brought Judith three scones made of potatoes and flour. In the evening the whole family came over and everyone joined in to make it happy. The little room was filled with noise and laughter and song.

Judith felt proud and grateful that she belonged to this close little community. It was like an oasis in the middle of a dreadful desert. Tania was a loyal friend who had never let her down. They had started the library, she remembered, with anxious hearts, watching it grow and become a success, and the fulfilment of their joint ambition had brought them even closer together. Now that it was well established and in full swing they had appointed a few helpers to run the library on alternate days, thus releasing the two girls from too much work.

Both of them were fully alive to their environment, aware of their predicament, treasuring their mutual confidence. There were hardly any secrets between them. They spent many hours together, sewing, mending or knitting old wool, and chattering as young girls do, about their past, the present and the problematical future, sometimes light-heartedly, sometimes seriously.

* * * * *

The winter came bringing with it a piercing frost and howling winds that drove the dancing snowflakes through the faulty windows into the doomed dwellings.

Chapter 17

The coffin-carts, busier than ever, driven by lean horses, were filled to the brim, revealing under the white cover serving as a lid, the outlines of two or three corpses.

Men, women and children, having discarded the remnants of what once were shoes, bandaged their feet and legs with many layers of old rags or strips of blanket.

A deathly hunger fell upon the place, driving hundreds of people to insanity, to death, or to both.

Very few goods came to the ghetto owing partly to the shortage and partly to the railway tracks being blocked by snow. Nevertheless there was always enough material to keep the victims busy at their work.

There was a group of people in the ghetto who held on to their lives and sanity, determined and supported by a supernatural strength not to give in. They went their usual way, shutting their minds against suffering, hoping that one day the sun would shine for them again and that they could look back upon the present and the past as a dreadful nightmare. They never acknowledged the fact that they might be the victims. Most of them went on living.

Tania was the only person with whom Judith shared her feelings. Being together for hours after work, they told each other how hungry and weak they were; they grumbled to each other about the trouble the Germans brought upon them and being on the verge of desperation they began to joke about the whole situation. Remarkably they always ended up laughing. They found swearing quite useful at times. Often they lay in bed together, keeping each other warm and making up vivid and fantastic accounts of their future as they visualized it.

XVIII

It was long past bedtime and the ghetto lay asleep under the dark still skies. When Judith woke it was about one o'clock. She thought she heard movements. Light was coming through from Mr. Alexander's room. She was now fully conscious and propping herself up on her elbows, listened intently. She couldn't hear much, only from time to time a slight movement of the chair, a rustling of paper and a tiny clearing of his throat. Quietly she got up, put on the old sandals that served as slippers and walked toward the partition.

The last bits of wood in the small tin stove had long since crumbled into ashes and the room was filled with cold air. With curiosity in her eyes she stood at the partition studying Mr. Alexander who was seated at the table busy writing. He looked up at her, not too pleased, and remarked: "You should be fast asleep."

"What are you doing?" she asked, calmly. "It is very late."

She saw the nervous tension in his face as he looked at her, searching for an answer.

For quite a time he said nothing, then with an expression

of resolution on his face he told her: "Judith, you shall know. I can trust you."

She took her coat from the hook on the door and put it over her long night-dress, approached the table and stood in front of him.

"Sit down," he said.

She did so and let her eyes slide over the sheets of paper that covered the small square table.

"This is a great secret and except for one other man, you are the only person to know about it."

Judith looked serious, proud to have his confidence.

"No one will ever know anything from me," she replied, quietly.

"I know.... These are letters, important letters, telling about the conditions in the ghetto. We are going to smuggle them across the wires. They have to be delivered tomorrow night. If we succeed in getting them into the proper hands we might be able to get a transmitter. Not all together. Bit by bit. We could put it together and then ... then we could listen to the outside world and tell them something about us. It's all very vague yet, but if the Germans should find out about our activities - that would be the end of us!"

Astonishment and wonder crept into Judith's face.

"Are you going to have the transmitter here?"

"No, it's too dangerous and besides, I would never drag you into it."

"I am not afraid, really I am not."

"I know, but it's better like this."

Judith was very serious. She realized what it all meant.

For a long while she looked at the wall opposite her. At last her gaze settled upon his and she said quietly, in a solemn tone: "If there is anything I can do to help I shall be happy to do so."

He thought for a moment.

"Do you really want to help?"

"Yes, of course."

"These letters have to be finished by the morning.... Put on your gloves and start copying this one. Do it in block letters. We don't want any fingerprints nor anything that could help them to trace us."

"How are you going to deliver them?"

"They have to be dropped through the wires opposite no. 105 Wilhelm Strasse at 8.20 tomorrow night. It's the safest spot and it will be easy for the others to pick them up."

"Let me do it."

"No!"

"Why not?"

"It's too dangerous."

"I will be all right. They will never suspect me. They are much more likely to take notice of you."

"We can talk about it tomorrow. Now let's get on with the writing."

He gave her further instructions about the codes. Her eager mind absorbed all the details quickly and she began to work quietly, aware of her responsibility. He had spoken to her as to a grown-up, making her do the same work as he was doing. They wrote in silence, linked by a common aim. It was as though they got to know each other much better.

The air became colder and their fingers began to stiffen. But they had to go on; they knew it. This was a way of letting the world know about their sufferings; perhaps a way of getting into contact with the outer world! It was enough to stimulate them to go on in spite of the odds against them.

In the silence of the night Judith became aware of the harmony that settled upon the room. Their minds were set on one and the same thing: they were united by a secret. At this moment she felt years older, perhaps because he had let her into the secret as an equal, because he had treated her like a grown-up person.

At about three o'clock Judith finished her part of the work and there was nothing more for her to do. Her limbs were stiff with cold. She got up from the chair and began to rub her feet and hands. She went into the kitchen and made sure there was no more fuel left. From behind a loose brick she took the small electric ring, made some hot coffee, filled two mugs and took them into the other room.

"Here," she said, placing his drink in front of him, "to warm you up a little."

"Thank you; that's jolly nice of you," he declared, putting down his pen and giving her an appreciative smile. He took the hot mug between his hands, trying to warm them.

"I wish we could use the electric ring for heating the room," Judith said.

"No, we mustn't. They would wonder how we used up so much electricity. Besides, it wouldn't make any difference in this damp place."

"I know."

"Judith, you should be going to bed now; it's cold and you must be very tired."

"I am not," she declared.

She sat down on the chair, sipping the hot dark drink. He

resumed his work and Judith watched him, proud and happy to be in his company. She did not wish to leave him. She sat very still for a long while, conscious of the secret bond between them. Although his thoughts were concentrated on his work he was aware of the current of strong feeling between them, of her nearness and her loyalty and he was grateful for her calm understanding.

Eventually she rose, went into the other room and came back with a blanket. She walked towards the table, knelt down and slowly took off his slippers. She touched his feet. They were ice cold. She took them between her palms, in turn, and rubbed them, trying to bring circulation back into them. Then she wrapped them gently in the blanket and crawled out from under the table. Without pausing in his work, his hand went to her head and stroked it once or twice.

"Thank you, darling," he said without taking his eyes from the papers in front of him.

He looked up at her then for a moment and she answered with a fond smile.

She was thinking of something she might be doing, but there was nothing and she sat quietly down on the couch beside his chair, watching him. She had an urge to make a fuss of him, to show him the depth of her feelings. Suddenly she knew that she was able to do things which she had felt too shy to do before. Somehow it did not matter now. This night had changed something for them and she knew it.

Her gaze fell on his left hand, resting on the table, its fingers rubbing against each other in an effort to get warm. Stretching out her hands, she drew it nearer to her, took off the glove, rubbed it for a while and brought it quite close to her mouth, warming it with the heat of her breath. After a few minutes she kissed it and put it back into the glove and laid it on the table.

He had not interrupted his work, but she felt pleasure surge through him.

Conscious of her closeness he said, faltering a little: "Judith, go to bed. You have to get up early in the morning."

"I don't mind.... I'd rather stay here with you.... I'll be all right."

"I know.... but ..."

Seeing the nervous intensity in his gaze she hesitated for a moment, got up and walked towards the partition. There she turned, smiled and said: "Goodnight."

He stretched out his hand and beckoned her to come to him. She returned and he put his arm round her waist and kissed her cheek.

"Thank you for all the help, darling," he said, quietly.

"Have you much more to do?" she asked.

"No, not very much."

"Are you sure there is nothing more I can do?"

"No - now off to bed. Goodnight."

Judith went to her room and took off her coat. The air was really frosty now. Coming to a sudden decision she walked over to the door, took Mr. Alexander's coat from the hook and crept once more into the room where he was sitting. She stood behind him, placed his overcoat about his shoulders and clasped her hands in front of his neck. He put both his hands on hers and held them firmly, drawing her slightly nearer to him. There was a moment of silent suspense, then she lowered her head and touched his cheek with her own. She kissed his

Chapter 18

temple and cheek and chin and he turned and kissed her. She rubbed her cheek against his and felt the warmth the contact brought about.

Their breathing became agitated. Overcome by a wave of tenderness he drew her quite close to him and showered her with kisses and caresses, which she returned. Their feelings grew more intense every minute until, stirred into passion, they became lost in each other. Finally he picked her up, took her to the couch, got a cushion and lowered her head upon it. Then he drew over them the overcoat she had brought to him. They lay together, crouched under the heavy garment, his arms around her, their faces pressed against each other. Judith felt a quiet happiness flow through her veins. Every part of her body relaxed, and with the awareness of the precious feeling, she fell into a sweet slumber.

He placed her head more comfortably on his shoulder, smoothed a stray lock of hair from her forehead, and spread the blanket over them both. For a few moments he watched her calm face with a protective air, then, switching off the light above him, he settled down to a short sleep.

$$\star \quad \star \quad \star \quad \star \quad \star$$

Judith woke up before her usual time. Realising at once where she was, she lay quietly reflecting on what had happened. She wished that time would stop still and that she could go on lying enclosed in his arms. She had never thought she could be so happy in the ghetto.

Recognising that time was slipping by, from the various sounds coming from other rooms, she stirred a little, lifted her head and kissed him lightly on his forehead.

Unshed Tears

"We shall have to get up soon," she whispered.

He blinked and opened his eyes. In the darkness she could only see them dimly. Remembering everything, he locked her closer in his arms and said: "Good morning, darling."

"Good morning," she answered, quietly.

"Are you very tired?" he asked.

"No, not really," she lied. "And you?"

"No."

They lay in silence for a few minutes, conscious of their nearness. Then, smoothing her hair, he asked gently: "Are you happy?"

"Yes ... very happy." After a pause she added: "You know ... I never thought I would ever be happy again." Then she put her arms tightly around him and went on, a little hesitantly: "There was a time when I didn't care to live. And then you came along and everything changed. "You know -" she paused, "I love you so very, very much."

She couldn't see the expression on his face, but she sensed it as he said: "I know, Judy. I love you, too, very much."

"Do you really mean it?"

"Of course darling ... I am only a human being.... I want to love, and I want to be loved, by someone like you, here more than anywhere else.... You are very dear to me."

He stroked her face, kissed her eyes and cheeks and found her lips with his. For a few minutes their mouths were joined and a strange, pleasurable sensation invaded Judith's body. At last he released her, stretched out his hand for the light switch, turned it and with an apologetic smile announced: "We have to get up now."

It was a quarter past six. The air was bitingly cold. The

water in the bucket was frozen and there was no fuel.

Judith dressed quietly in her warmest clothes while he tried to remove a piece of ice from the bucket. He put it into the saucepan which he placed on the electric ring. The pressure was so low that they only just managed to thaw the ice and wash their hands and faces in it.

There was no breakfast.

He hid the secret papers and a little while later they were plodding through the snow on their way to work. At the corner they parted with a secret smile on their lips.

The factory was brightly lit and in every room a fire was burning in a cylindrical stove. The bell had not yet gone and the children were standing around it, warming their numb limbs. The heat did not spread much through the room. However, the temperature was a bearable 48° and in five hours' time they were going to get hot soup.

Some of the children were miserably dressed. Their bones stuck out and there was a pitiful expression on their faces. Judith herself had got much thinner during the past few weeks. As she looked round at the group of little figures, some of them not more than ten or eleven years old, a protective feeling gripped her. She was one of the oldest and strongest in that room and several months ago had been appointed their group leader. If the instructor was out of the room, she was responsible for order and work.

There were eighteen of them altogether, eighteen individuals, each with a story to tell. Judith looked about her, wondering who was the next one to go. Some of them coughed badly, death looking out of their huge, deeply-set eyes. Four children had already died since the winter set in. One day they were at work; the next day they were dead. New children took their places and life went on as before.

One teacher had died last week after having been ill for a fortnight. Another was in hospital with meningitis.

Tuberculosis in the ghetto did not take long to kill the victim, sometimes several months, usually a few weeks, and very often a few days. It was caused more by conditions than by infection.

Judith knew every child in her group, together with its background. Genia, Sala and David each lived on their own in some dark, dirty hole. Their families had died, one after another. They took their wretched life for granted, having seen hardly anything better, struggling for existence. Their cunning and necessity had taught them to be physically independent.

There were others whose families constantly fought and quarrelled, snatched each other's food away and taught their children to steal.

Two brothers, Joseph and Mendel, lived together. Joseph was the elder, taking pride in his smaller brother. They were alone in the world and very devoted to each other. Judith had never seen their home, but judging by the way the children turned out for work, she had a good idea.

Several girls and a very few boys came to the factory clean, with tidy hair and washed faces. They were the lucky ones who had someone to look after them, or enough instinct to look after themselves.

With the newly acquired happiness flooding her mind, her heart went out to these little creatures. From Michael Alexander she had learned to understand their minds and behaviour. She admired the courage with which they stood up

Chapter 18

to their fate. After her parents had died she had taken up a passive attitude towards everything. These children fought bravely, without complaining, taking everything in their stride. Only their sensitive eyes disclosed the sadness in their hearts.

As she sat at her machine this morning, Judith thought of the excitement of delivering the secret letters, the transmitter, her love for Michael Alexander, the will to do something for the children. It all played upon her mind and she was determined to do something about it. If only she felt a little stronger!

* * * * *

The snow lay frozen upon the ground when Judith and Michael set out on their mission.

Everything was planned. With no lights burning in the streets and the blacked-out windows, the darkness was hard to penetrate. The streets were almost empty.

Judith had wanted to go alone but he had insisted on accompanying her to the corner from which he could observe her and the guard. In case something went wrong he could step in and take the blame on himself.

It was quite a distance from their home. The frost was biting, their cheeks and noses were red.

Judith had arranged her hair in plaits, thinking it gave her a more innocent appearance. She wore a blanket around her shoulders in the Polish fashion.

They met very few people. Those who were about were hurrying home from a late visit. They sped through the narrow smelly streets, past the ancient unromantic houses and ruins towards the wooden bridge that joined the two parts of the ghetto. Underneath it the main road ran from one part of the Polish town to another, and was cut off from the Jewish quarters by barbed wires.

It lay quietly between the two rows of houses that were inhabited by Jews, only here and there a lorry or a rickety tram breaking the silence.

Under the bridge the guard was parading up and down, stopping from time to time, stamping his feet against the cold and throwing his arms about him with great vigour.

On a corner, about thirty yards away from him, they stopped. With a reassuring smile Judith detached herself from Michael Alexander and walked, apparently unconcerned, past the sentry box and along the pavement between the houses and the wires. Her cheeks were burning with frost and apprehension.

She found no. 105. A deep porch enclosed the gate-like door. With a natural movement she entered and leant for a moment against the corner of the porch. Mr. Alexander's watch which was fastened on her wrist, showed a quarter past eight.

A tram approached and Judith flattened herself against the little wall. It hummed past, its little blue lights burning. The noise decreased and then died in the distance.

Everything was silent again.

Judith glanced across the road. She faced a gap between two bare shells of houses. She realized why this spot had been chosen. Then she heard the tinkling of a little cow bell. She forced herself to peep out of her hiding place.

There it was!

Her heart stood still for a moment as she spied the small sledge-cart laden with logs, drawn by an ox.

Chapter 18

The big envelope with the three letters in it was pressed between her fingers. She took a deep breath, then flung the white flat object along the white snow.

With eager eyes she followed it along the pavement under the wire and down into the street. The guard, some thirty-five yards away, was stamping his feet unconcernedly.

In the street in front of no. 105, two or three logs fell off the cart. The man in the balaclava helmet and long whiskers, stopped the ox, climbed from his seat, picked them up, stuck them on the pile and proceeded on his journey. When he had gone, the envelope was gone, too.

Judith stood there until half past eight when the guards changed. She waited another five minutes, then emerged from her hiding place and with a calm face passed the new guard and walked on to meet Michael Alexander.

"He has got it!" she announced, with a radiant face.

"Yes, he has got it," he repeated thoughtfully, "but the hardest job is yet to come."

"We will manage it, you will see," she assured him, enthusiastically.

"Yes, perhaps we will, only I won't have you sticking out your neck for it."

"I will be quite safe, really - I am so sure of it," she said, eagerly.

"You can't be sure of a thing like this."

He gripped her by the arm and led her home.

XIX

They did manage it somehow, or to be exact, Mr. Alexander with his collaborators did. From time to time Judith was sent on an important errand, but that was all. Only once more did she go to the wires, this time to receive a little parcel.

A Polish peasant trotting beside his cart laden with bracken, threw it in. Judith, as arranged, hid it in a prepared place inside the house and left, intending to collect it the next day. As she passed the sentry box the soldier on guard, probably to break the monotony, called out to her: "Come here!"

Judith, a little shaky inside, appeared quite self-confident as she faced the tall figure of a fairly young man.

"What are you doing here so late?" he asked in a military tone.

"I went to visit a friend of mine who is ill," Judith lied, looking calmly into his face.

She soon realized that he had no real suspicion. Probably he wanted to tease her and frighten her a little. She was well acquainted with their mentality.

"You've received some smuggled food," he said.

"I did not, sir," Judith replied, politely.

"You know what happens to people who are caught smuggling?"

"No, sir," Judith retorted, innocently.

He gripped the front of her coat by the neck, brought his eyes quite close to hers and hissed grimly: "I shoot them!"

"Yes, sir."

"Now I must search you," he announced.

She wanted to say something, but the thing that really mattered was to get away safely and proceed with the important work. Therefore she decided to remain quiet.

He dragged her into the sentry-box, searched her outer pockets and ordered her to take off her coat. He looked for inside pockets or secret hiding places in the lining, then dropped the coat on the floor. He continued the search, flattening his hand against her woollen jumper and shirt, then underneath them, touching her bare body.

Judith's blood was at boiling point with rage. She had a strong desire to slap his face, wrench herself free and run. But there was nothing to prevent him from shooting her in cold blood. At last she said impatiently, her feelings plainly apparent in her face: "I have nothing at all."

"But we have to make sure, haven't we?" he said, with a significant smile.

All the time Judith was thanking God for the narrow escape, and all the time she wanted to hit him and call him "swine". But she refrained, with the thought that after all, it didn't really matter.

At last he set her free.

She put on her coat, arranged her woollen cap and with her

Chapter 19

head high, but not high enough to be called insolent, and without a glance at the face with its sadistic smile, she took her departure.

Speeding along the road she had a most uncomfortable feeling that any moment a bullet might swish through the air and hit her in the back.

At last she reached Michael Alexander. He gripped both her arms firmly and for a long moment they stood silently savouring the feeling of relief after the ordeal. Eventually he said firmly: "This is the last time you'll ever be mixed up in this." After a pause he added, looking deeply into her eyes: "I was praying for your safety. I swore to God that I would never let you take part in this again." He shook his head. "I don't know what I would have done if anything had happened to you."

"It wouldn't have been your fault. I asked for it."

"Did he hurt you?"

"No. He searched me. He was a bit of a swine, but what do I care about him!"

"You acted very wisely. Thank God you didn't have that parcel on you. Just imagine! I daren't even think about the consequences!"

"You know," she said, as they turned their steps towards home, "at moments like this I begin to believe in God again...."

Michael Alexander was very resolute about his decision. Except for a few errands which she performed in the afternoon, she had nothing more to do with the secret work. There were evenings when she waited for him in fearful suspense, and then one day, about three weeks after Christmas, it stopped. The job was done.

Unshed Tears

Judith knew very little about it. She didn't know what it looked like or where it was hidden. The only thing she did know was that very soon they would be able to send messages and listen to the outside world.

Michael Alexander explained: "Darling, it isn't that I don't trust you, that I think you couldn't keep a secret, but in case there should ever be any questioning about it, I want you to be genuinely innocent. I want you to be able to say truthfully that you don't know where it is, who is involved in the business, that you have had nothing to do with it.... I shall keep you informed of the latest news, you needn't worry about that."

Towards the very end of January, he came forth with the first big news. Rushing into the room, swinging his brief-case, he stopped in front of Judith and looking joyfully and triumphantly into her eyes, he announced, "British and American troops have landed on the west coast of Italy, some forty kilometres from Rome. Just imagine - they are in Europe! And Berlin is being bombed like hell. Do you know what it all means?"

Judith's eyes filled with happiness. Then she exclaimed: "It's wonderful ... everything is - the news, your machine ... and you!"

She put her arms vigorously round his neck and gave him a big kiss. Then she retreated a little, and her face grew more serious.

"To be quite honest, I am a little afraid for you. Are you sure they can't find your radio?... Is it really worth the risk you are running? I keep on being scared that one day something terrible will happen. Do you think it could?" She looked at him anxiously.

Chapter 19

"I don't think so, Judith," he said, calmly. "Everything has been planned carefully and elaborate precautions are being taken. The set is never going to stay very long in one place. The chaps who are on it with me are very clever and we have considered all the risks and taken all the steps to avoid trouble. It would be very bad luck if we were found out ... but well ... we have to take risks sometimes. It's worth it, Judith, believe me!"

* * * * *

It was a bleak afternoon at the beginning of February. There had been no snow for days and that which covered the narrow streets of the ghetto had been constantly trodden on and its colour had changed from white to pale grey and then to a grey that was darker than the cheerless skies.

Judith was making her way along the streets, away from the factory, away from her home. Her knees were shaking with weakness, but she detached her mind from the body that was trudging along the ugly slums and occupied it with thoughts of eager anticipation. The fate of the little children who were under her care in the factory had taken a prominent part in her mind. She was able to forget them once she left the factory and became engrossed in her own everyday struggles, but she could not escape their wretchedness, their sad eyes and their tattered clothes, while she was at work. Her heart softened towards these small people who were alone in the world, forsaken by all kindness, love and humanity. She might have let things go another few days had not Mendel, Joseph's brother, collapsed at work and later been sent home.

Judith found number 56, Bierstrasse. It was a three-storey

old-fashioned building, shabby like all the others. She pushed open the heavy door. It creaked, and she stood engulfed in a cold darkness and the familiar smell of garlic, onions, oil and bad air, the result of lack of hygiene and absence of lavatories.

When her eyes became accustomed to the darkness, she groped toward the staircase and went up the musty stairs. On the second floor she found room number eight, and knocking once or twice, entered without waiting for an answer. The familiar sight of poverty, untidiness and dirt was spread before her in the home of the two children.

Under a heaped feather-bed lay the tiny frame of Mendel. His head rested upon a huge pillow, his big troubled eyes were turned towards her. The place was strewn with pieces of children's clothes, utensils, and litter. One of the two windows was without its black-out and a calm, grey light filled the room. Old cobwebs hung from the walls and balls of dust rolled on the black planks.

Judith walked over to Mendel. He smiled. His cheeks were burning and his eyes glowed with fever. She touched his hot forehead.

"Where is Joseph?" she asked.

"He went out. He promised to get some food." Mendel spoke very quietly.

"Oh, I see," Judith answered, guessing where the food would come from. "I came to see you," she smiled, wiping the hair off his moist forehead. Then she added with a little spark of light-heartedness in her tone, "You know, you have a temperature. You need a doctor. When Joseph comes home I shall send him for one."

A faint smile of appreciation spread over Mendel's face.

Chapter 19

He coughed from time to time, though not very badly. He was obviously weak, too weak to wish to talk very much. Judith sat on his bed, took his hand and held it for a while. Except for his coat that was flung on a chair with the sleeves inside out and his clogs in the middle of the room, he was fully dressed.

"You can't receive the doctor like this," she said.

She found his pyjamas under the dresser and fished it out. It was black with dirt and covered with lumps of dust. With a sigh Judith relinquished the idea of changing him. Instead she went over to him and with his help got him out of all superfluous clothing.

Then the door opened and Joseph came rushing in. He paused when he saw Judith.

"What do you want here?" he asked coldly, a little perplexed.

"As a matter of fact I came to see how Mendel was," Judith answered calmly, gazing at his bulging lumberjacket, "but as I happen to be here, I would like to see to a thing or two." Looking straight at him she asked: "What have you got under your jacket?"

"Something for us to eat," he answered, shamelessly.

He opened the middle button of his jacket, thrust his hand into it and emerged with a large cabbage. He repeated his effort, bringing forth a few potatoes which he proudly placed on the table.

"Where did you get them from?" Judith asked.

"From somewhere," was his reply.

"You stole them, didn't you?"

"And if I did? They all died because they had no food when they were ill; Father and Mother and Rachel. I am not going to let Mendel die, see?"

Judith was silent for a while. What was she to tell him? Stealing was wrong and yet she sensed the terror in Joseph's heart, the fear of losing his last relation, his desperate effort to keep him alive. There was something wrong somewhere. She knew it, but she was not quite sure of the solution.

"I think we ought to get a doctor," she said at last. "I know of a very good one. You go and fetch him. Tell him I sent you. He lives at no. 63 Holzstrasse. His name is Epstein."

"But Mendel must have his soup now," Joseph argued.

He associated death with hunger and illness, and his prime thought was to make Mendel eat. Nothing else was as important.

"I shall see to it," Judith told him. "You run along now."

When he had gone Judith went over to the sick boy.

"Is there any fuel?" she asked.

"We burn the old clothes and rags from the cupboard."

"Oh, I see."

She wondered whether the smoke from burning clothes would produce more harmful effects for him than the cold air. He was well tucked in under his cover and she finally decided to go to the gas-kitchen nearby. She found an old saucepan, black from the outside and greasy inside. There was no water in the place. Reluctantly she reached out for the stolen goods, got a knife and spoon and went to the nearest pump where she washed the vegetable, rinsed the saucepan and half filled it with water. The gas-kitchen was pleasantly warm and she waited for a few minutes for her numbed fingers to regain their feeling before she commenced her task.

Joseph returned announcing that the doctor would come about five o'clock. The smell of the soup brought new energy

Chapter 19

to Mendel's body and prompted an eagerness in his glowing eyes. He propped himself up in bed and with shaking hands spooned the thick liquid and vegetables hastily from the small chipped pot. Joseph, being unable to resist the temptation, consumed the rest without feeling in the least obliged to offer a little to Judith. That was life in the ghetto. Nothing else was to be expected.

"Do you often go stealing?" she asked him.

"No, this was the first time."

"Where did you get it from?"

"I don't quite know. I tried various places. I went in from the back. There was a window. It was broken so I went in."

"Oh. Was there a lot of it there?"

Joseph looked up at her as if remembering something. He paused and then said quietly: "No."

Judith guessed that it was all the owner possessed. After trying to juggle himself out of the situation, he at last confessed to it. She was silent for a while. Then her eyes softened. She bent down to him and said quietly: "You love Mendel very much, don't you?"

He looked at her silently without answering.

"You don't want to lose him, that's why you did it ... isn't it so?"

He nodded.

"Now listen to me very carefully. There might be someone else who is very ill. More ill than Mendel perhaps. Maybe in hospital. It might be a little boy like him. His mother wants to cook him something every day and take it to him. Tonight she will come home and will find that the food with which she has fought for his life has gone. Someone has taken it. And that someone is you...."

Unshed Tears

Remorsefully he looked at the floor and a big drop detached itself from his eyes and dropped on Judith's hand.

"I didn't think about it like that ... I ... I ..."

"Yes I know. Your only thought was for Mendel, but we all get an equal ration to struggle on ... the rest we have to leave to God. Do you understand that?"

He nodded, and his little chest began to heave with sobs. Judith got up and said in a cheerful, encouraging tone, "He will get well again, you'll see. We'll pull him through together. Tonight the doctor will come. He will tell us what to do. And we are going to do many other things, too. Just you wait!"

Joseph wiped his eyes and nose on his soiled cuff, and then they set to work. They made a huge pile of clothes and rags which Joseph took on a sledge to the disinfecting station. "That will get rid of the lice," Judith thought. Meanwhile she cleared the room of litter and cobwebs and dust. Before the doctor came it looked reasonably tidy, though by no means attractive.

The doctor arrived a little before five o'clock. He examined the little boy carefully.

"Bronchitis," was the verdict. "He must not get out of bed at all." He was very firm about it. "It is important that he is in an even temperature all the time." He instructed Joseph how to apply compresses and prescribed some aspirins.

"You don't have to worry. Just do as I have told you and he will be all right. I shall call again tomorrow."

It took Mendel three weeks to get over his illness. He came out of it even thinner than he had been before. Judith had been a frequent visitor to their home. They had chopped up three chairs and a bedside table and a chest of drawers to keep the worst of the frost out....

Chapter 19

Then there was Genia aged ten, Sala - eleven and David twelve. Their homes looked very much alike: dirty, shabby and untidy. Judith managed to bring a little relief to the girls' lives, but David had a mind of his own and it was filled with cunning, harshness and insolence. It seemed that he had never known love and had no desire to meet it. He looked perfectly satisfied with his way of life. The main ghetto aim of survival had caught up with him and it suited him well. Judith shrugged her shoulders. It seemed that there was nothing she could do. She took her problem to Michael Alexander.

"You are doing your best, you are doing all right and I am very proud of you. Just go on being kind and don't give up," he said.

"David doesn't want any kindness," Judith remarked bitterly.

"David is very unhappy, you must be patient...."

They were sitting on the couch. Michael put his arm around her and drew her to him. He kissed the top of her head tenderly and said, "Judith, I have loved you for a very long time, but seeing you looking after the children and trying to give them a little happiness has made you even dearer to me."

"I would never have thought of it if you hadn't shown me first. You were the only person who tried to understand me and show me kindness. Knowing what it all feels like, I couldn't let the children down. Besides, you go on visiting people, giving them hope and the will to live."

She freed herself from his embrace and sat on her heels, facing him. She looked deeply into his eyes. Her voice was a little husky as she announced quietly, "I would like to be just a little bit like you."

XX

The following few months were filled with hope, suffering, happiness, struggle and suspense. The struggle was never-ending, but the political situation and the springtime gave rise to a new, optimistic outlook on the affairs of the ghetto. Nobody knew where the news came from, but rumours spread rapidly, were often enlarged upon until they grew to gigantic proportions, but everyone was aware that just a small part of them could be taken seriously. Although people hoped, they had trained themselves not to anticipate anything. They would rather let themselves be pleasantly surprised than suffer terrible disappointment. On the other hand they believed that in every piece of news, however fantastic, there was at least a fraction of truth.

Many people in the ghetto, fed on these hopes, would not admit it even to themselves.

The Russians were fighting their way slowly towards the west - towards them. Berlin and other German towns were suffering from heavy bombardments. In March for the first time, Germany had been bombed by U.S. planes. The Allies were slowly gaining a foothold in Italy. Something was moving, something great and important was happening in the world beyond the wires. There was the burning question, of course, would the Germans let the prisoners live to see their great moment, or would they destroy them in the last minute. The latter course seemed more likely, though the eternal strife and the desire for survival buried deep in their hearts overcame such pessimistic speculation. In any case there was nothing much they could do except stand up to the desperate internal situation with a stronger will, and wait patiently for the future.

Judith visited the children regularly at their homes. There were six of them now. Although she saw them every day at work they regarded it as a special treat to have her at their own place, and enjoy her full attention. She was patient with them and listened carefully to what they had to tell her. They clung to her with a confidence which Judith knew she must never destroy. Above all they loved listening to her long tales about life outside the ghetto. She told them about the beauty of the countryside all the year round, the mountains, forests, meadows and lakes; the flowers and butterflies and all the other contributions of wonderful nature. They got to know about the peoples and nations of the world, their way of living, their dress, homes and food. They listened as to a fairy-tale with shining eyes glued upon Judith's face.

The evenings belonged to her and Michael. She had been calling him by his first name for several weeks and it gave her a special pleasure. Quite often they spent an evening lying together on the couch, his arms about her and her head resting on his shoulder, covered with a blanket or a coat if it was cold. They talked about everything or nothing, planning, dreaming,

Chapter 20

visualising, teasing each other and laughing heartily. Sometimes they just rested silently, their eyes closed, sensing the deep harmony that lay about them....

★ ★ ★ ★ ★

One evening Judith came home shivering, her face very pale, her teeth chattering. From the glow in her eyes Michael saw that she had a high temperature. He sent her to bed and a little while later brought in the thermometer. He had been right. Now in bed, her cheeks had begun to be flushed and every movement had become a strain. He sat down beside her, stroked her cheeks and temples and asked, tenderly, "Does anything hurt you?"

" No," she answered, feebly.

He made her a hot drink. He boiled some of the few potatoes they had and made a puree with which he fed her carefully.

"If you aren't any better tomorrow morning, I shall call the doctor," he said, and gave her an aspirin. Then he turned off the light and sat by her bed until she fell asleep....

The doctor came the next day, examined her carefully and said to Michael who had stayed at home from work: "It's her glands, due to the lack of vitamins. She should have food. The temperature will probably go down a bit but not quite to normal for a good while, yet. Keep her in bed. With the spring coming and the sunshine her body might respond. I will come again."

Judith became so weak that she could hardly move. For a few days everything seemed like a dream to her. Although she was very ill, she never thought of death. It didn't occur to her that she might die.

Michael stayed with her all the time, composed, gentle, efficient. He fed her on anything he could get hold of, which was very little. He practically stopped eating himself. From the rations he made soups, gave her fresh grated vegetables for which he sold his watch, and the bread when it came. He made her bed and washed her. At first she protested, but he assured her lovingly: "It's all right, Judy. It doesn't matter. You are my little girl, aren't you?"

Suddenly it didn't matter, and he changed her pyjamas and washed them in a basin together with his own clothes.

She was grateful to him for everything, although she wasn't aware of the extent of his sacrifices. When she asked where he got the food from he persuaded her that it was the new ration.

Then one day a miracle happened - a parcel from Prague arrived. It was a new legal arrangement and Michael was among the first to receive one from a friend. It was as though all his prayers were answered. A card came first to inform him that he could collect it from the Czech office. He went at once. Excitedly he showed the card at the counter.

The parcel was the size of two shoe boxes. It was wrapped in brown paper and tied with paper string. He could hardly grasp this wonderful fact. His hands were itching with the desire to open it, but instead he tucked it under his arm and with a joyful heart headed for home. He wanted to see the sacred moment with Judith.

The excitement had given her a little energy. She propped herself up on one elbow and, sitting on her bed, he began to unwrap the paper while her eyes eagerly followed every movement.

Chapter 20

At last he removed the lid. Along one side nestled a loaf of rye bread, and beside it were four full paper bags. For a while they just stared at it. Then gently he began to open the bags in search of their treasure. In one was semolina, in one barley, in the third there was brown sugar, and in the last one there was dried milk.

"What do you say to this?" he asked, casting his shining eyes upon her.

She could say nothing, only look at it all with excitement and joy.

He threw the box down and flung his arms around her and kissed her happily. It was only when he sat up again that she remembered that she had not seen his watch for a long time.

"Where is your watch?" she asked.

For a split second he hesitated. Then he said light-heartedly, with a wave of his hand: "That old thing? Oh, never mind that. I have lost it."

She looked at him intently.

"You have sold it, haven't you?"

"What does it matter, darling? We had a parcel today and there might be many more. And we shall start to eat straight away."

She took his hand, lifted his sleeve a little and felt with her thumb for the place where the watch used to be. Then she drew him down to her and kissed him with her eyes closed, and whispered: "Thank you, darling."

She held him for a long time, then suddenly she let him go and asked innocently but with a sparkle in her eyes which gave her away: "Why did you do it?"

He took the hint and answered with an affectionate smile:

"Because I love you, of course. Didn't you know?"

Instead of answering, she smiled happily.

They began to eat.

"I wonder what made them suddenly allow us to have parcels?" she remarked.

"God knows! Probably they know they are in a stew, and think we shall judge them more lightly when all this is over."

There were more parcels, and although they could not eat as much as they would have liked, the effect on Judith's body was remarkable. She gained strength rapidly and with the sunshine giving important vitamins, her temperature returned to normal. By the end of April she was back at work. Michael's health also showed a vast improvement. Life and energy returned to him and he was able to concentrate much better on whatever he did.

The bread in the parcels was usually mouldy through and through. They had to cut it up in sections and soak it in water until the green mould separated itself and formed a layer on the surface. Then they took it from the water, wrung it out, mixed it with flour and made little scones which they fried.

They were still hungry, but now it was just a normal hunger, not one that made them see black in front of their eyes, gave a cramp to their stomachs and caused them to feel that they were floating on air.

By then the Russians had captured Odessa and Yalta.

★ ★ ★ ★ ★

The month of May was sunny and everything looked better. Some vegetables and potatoes reached the ghetto. Then came

Chapter 20

June - the sixth day of June, and with it the invasion of Normandy by Allied troops from the West. It was hardly believable.

Events began to move quickly. The Allied troops captured Rome. The Russians opened a summer offensive with an attack against the German line. They captured Vitebsk and later, at the beginning of July, Minsk and Vilna. They were advancing into Poland towards Warsaw, only eighty kilometres away from Lodz.

The news must have penetrated into the ghetto through several sources for everyone knew about the great happenings. The atmosphere was charged with apprehension. Those who had an old battered map handy, looked up the routes by which the troops would be advancing on all sides. Great Germany was shrinking. The most exciting news was the forceful approach of the Eastern armies.

Bialystok, Lublin and WARSAW!

August 1944.

Boom! Crash! Boom! Everyone's ear in the ghetto was tuned to the most wonderful music and guessing its distance. Suddenly all the grim faces brightened up with happy expectation. The air shook with explosions which were only eighty kilometres away.

Those who, until now, had taken all the news with a sceptical shrug of their shoulders, had no doubt left in their hearts. The fight for Warsaw was on! The ground trembled as in an earthquake. Two more days and everything might be over! At last all the hopes and dreams were within reach!

The last fear that the Germans might evacuate the Jewish quarters had gone. If the Russians advanced at the same speed as they had done until now, they should be in Lodz in two or three days' time. It was practically impossible to remove eighty thousand people in such a short time, unless they destroyed them by bombs, and they had to keep the bombs for more vital issues.

The place was humming with victory. People's backs straightened, the gloomy, heavy atmosphere that had oppressed them for so long, had melted, and one of joyous suspense took its place.

Except for the guards at the bridge, no German was to be seen. The everyday routine and discipline were gone. Everyone took liberty and there was no one in authority to do anything about it. People gathered in the streets, formed little groups and discussed the situation. Suddenly friendly smiles appeared on their faces. They sang quietly. All were united to welcome their liberators. The ghetto, now basking in scorching sunshine, was a different place.

Michael Alexander and his friends had to dispose of the radio, but it didn't really matter any more. Judith and Tania spent their time visualizing all the things in store for them. They had pictured it all in their minds, everything was worked out in detail. Hundreds of times they walked onto the balcony and gazed towards the wire, hoping that the guard might be gone. Every time a lorry roared past the wires they rushed out again, eagerly anticipating the arrival of the heroes.

They chatted endlessly about the first hours of liberty, the journey home, the food they were going to eat, the schools they wanted to attend and the clothes they were going to wear. They promised solemnly to write to each other regularly and visit each other in the holidays.

Chapter 20

Michael was rarely at home during the day. He was always busy. He had to attend to very important matters and although Judith was not quite sure of what he was doing, she knew by the look in his eyes that it was very urgent. He still came home with the latest news. In the evenings his friends gathered in the little room, chatting and discussing the situation.

The battle for Warsaw was taking a little longer than they had hoped, but then, what did a few days matter after years of waiting? The sounds that were bringing freedom with them were always there, and as long as they could hear them, optimism glinted in their eyes. Political jokes raced through the ghetto, the poor Germans being the victims of their humour.

One week passed and people began to get used to the idea of approaching liberty. Whereas at first it had all seemed like an incredible dream, it became more real now. The air never ceased to vibrate with the thunder of guns and within the ghetto everyone was his own master. "Perhaps tomorrow ..." was the usual phrase, accompanied by a distant gaze. "Perhaps tomorrow ..."

The atmosphere built up to a climax.

* * * * *

Then suddenly, as if a bomb had fallen into the midst of the rejoicing crowds, the dream was over. For a moment, frozen to the spot, speechless and trembling, with a hollow feeling in their stomachs, they gazed at the innumerable open lorries carrying troops of the German Police.

They watched silently, paralyzed, crushed. The sadistic

grinning faces of the Germans were like those of monsters.

They should have known!

There followed a few moments of panic. The streets were cleared of all Jews.

Petrified with horror, people peered through the windows. In the deserted streets the lorries were slowly moving up and down. Like statues of pride, the Schu-Po men stood motionless upon them, spreading an atmosphere of deathly fear. Otherwise, there was silence.

Terror crept into everyone's heart.

On each corner two or three lorries stopped, the tall men jumped off, the shining eagles on their helmets dazzling in the sun.

It was about midday.

Within minutes the blocks were surrounded by lines of men who knew no mercy.

"Nobody must leave the house!" thundered from downstairs.

Judith, like most of the people, stood hidden behind the window, stunned by the sight below. She clung to Michael who was calm, ready to face the situation.

A hush hung over the dwellings.

Neither of them spoke. Occasionally Michael moved his hand to press her arm lightly or caress her in a comforting manner. She was trembling.

At about three o'clock the first lorries arrived, overcrowded with people of all ages. They stood pressed against each other. The children were crying, the women were lamenting and some of the men were beating their fists against their heads or tearing their hair out. They passed underneath their window

Chapter 20

and headed in the direction of the railway station.

The evacuation of the ghetto had begun!

"How could we believe they would really leave us here?" Judith said bitterly.

The same words were on the lips of thousands of other disillusioned prisoners.

"If the Russians had come as soon as we expected them, the Germans wouldn't have had a chance.... Anyway, it was nice while it lasted." Then he turned to Judith and smiled. "At least we had a taste of liberty, a few happy days ... when you come to think of it, it was really quite wonderful, and besides, whatever happens, it won't take long now."

"Where do you think they will take us?"

"I don't know. Nobody knows. Probably to another old town where they will make slaves of us. They need people to work for them. But they have had a taste of defeat, anyway. The troops from the west are advancing. They have almost captured Paris. The Russians are advancing. In a little while the Germans will be squeezed dry like a lemon." Michael demonstrated the happening by pressing his clenched fists together. A satisfied gleam danced in his eyes.

"Perhaps the Russians will come before everyone is evacuated. They might come any minute," Judith tried to reason.

"Perhaps ... it seems to be a tough battle, though."

The Germans began to clear the far end of the ghetto first. It was the section across the bridge. There were eighty thousand inhabitants in the ghetto and about ten thousand could be dealt with in one day. That meant that the emptying of the Jewish quarters would take a week or so. There was still hope for some people. Eight days could be a long time in a critical situation. So many things could happen in eight days!

In the evening the Schu-Po men disappeared from the streets, but the number of guards at the wires was trebled. There was no question of escape, no chance to hide anywhere. The Germans knew their job.

All shops were closed, all rations cancelled. To succeed in hiding would mean to die of starvation in addition to other risks. It might take weeks before the Russians arrived. Nobody suspected, however, that the great leaders of a few nations had arranged for the Russian forces to stop at Warsaw for another six months.

"We have to be prepared for everything," Michael said resolutely, and he and Judith began to stuff their rucksacks with the most valuable things they possessed.

"Shall I pack my pullover and mittens and socks?" Judith asked in the middle of the process.

"Of course. It's better to have them when not needed than not to be ready if it goes on through the winter. One never knows. It's good to be optimistic, but never rely on anything that you can't be quite sure about."

They shared the little provisions they had in stock in case they got separated for a while. Into the side pocket of her rucksack Judith lovingly put the photographs of her parents.

They were free to move within the ghetto, except for those sections that were on the programme for the day. These were heavily guarded by the police force.

By the way things moved, people could work out when their turn to leave the ghetto would come. Some played cat and mouse, dodging the chosen places, leaving their homes and

Chapter 20

loitering about in the safe area of the day, although no area was really quite safe, for the Germans made surprise raids on different areas and picked up anybody they could lay their hands on.

Most people reconciled themselves to the idea, knowing that most likely one day their turn would come anyway, and handed themselves over to the clutches of fate, taking everything as it came. Nobody could know what was really the wisest thing to do.

Then one day Germans in S.S. uniform appeared on various corners of the ghetto. They built up little platforms or stood on tables, the bewildered, uncertain prisoners gathering around them.

"You have nothing to fear!" these orators cried, thrusting their fists in the air and shaking their large double chins. "We want to protect you from the Bolshevik terror! They are murderers! Plunderers! You will be safe in a town where you will work in factories making military clothes. We are going to move all the sewing machines and you will be comfortable there. Those who come first will have a better chance of finding a good job and better accommodation. Therefore pack your things and go to the station now! We advise you to take the best things with you."

As they finished and left, the crowd was wondering what it was really all about.

"It's ridiculous propaganda," some said. "They want us to stop dodging and go to the station by ourselves."

"Fancy, they want to protect us! Ha!" said others. "I like that!"

Resignedly Judith waited for things to develop.

Unshed Tears

Mendel and Joseph had come to see her, unconcerned about their fate, perhaps not quite being able to comprehend the meaning of the latest events. They were glad of the opportunity to leave the ghetto. They could not remember anything else and they were eager to see for themselves what the other parts of the world were like. Mendel was quite excited.

"We shall go by train and see many places," he exclaimed joyfully.

"Do you think we shall see all those flowers and trees and mountains you have been telling us about?" they enquired with shining eyes.

"Perhaps," Judith answered calmly, glad that they had taken the matter so lightly.

"We might be seeing your country," announced David.

They were not at all afraid. Perhaps they had forgotten the difference between fear and peace of mind.

"We would like to go with you," they pleaded.

"All right. You come tomorrow and we shall all go together," Michael Alexander said gently but cheerfully, and they were grateful to him....

* * * * *

About one o'clock at night Judith woke up, propped herself up on her elbows and turned her ear towards the window. She listened intently for a while, then put her fingers into her ears, trying to get rid of the rustling noise. But it stayed and seemed to be coming nearer. She jumped out of bed and ran barefooted towards the window.

Chapter 20

It was very dark outside and she couldn't see anything, but the sound was coming nearer and nearer and gradually grew louder and louder.

She stared into the darkness and then the murmur became more distinct, became the sound of human voices!

The street was humming with them and then the noise that was only a few yards away now, changed into a mixture of voices, rattling wheels on cobblestones, and the clatter of wooden soles on the stony road. It was like a bad dream.

Suddenly the moon came out from behind the clouds and revealed a picture that was unforgettable.

People, people, people, a never-ending procession of them, making their way forward, shuffling their leaden feet along the ground underneath the window and disappearing into the darkness.

They were going in the direction of the station.

More and more were coming - ragged mothers with bewildered babies in their arms, the bigger children walking beside them or following behind, sensible as the grown-ups, grasping the seriousness of the situation and trying to make it easier. Old grey men, leaning their bent bodies on rough sticks, struggling to keep up with their families, worn out, half dead - more and more of them all the time! Their clothes were ragged, many of them were barefooted, their feet sore and bleeding. They were tossing their luggage, which consisted mainly of bundles made of old sheets, from side to side. Here and there they stopped, sat on it and attempted to get their breath and gather a little strength.

From time to time a little rickety cart came rattling along, heaped with luggage and little children.

Unshed Tears

There was no panic, only sometimes a pitiful lamentation rang through the air. The stragglers' faces were tense, worn out, resigned.

People from neighbouring dwellings gathered at the windows watching with amazement this exodus of, apparently, a whole nation.

Michael got up and stood behind Judith. For a long time they gazed speechlessly at the spectacle. At last Judith broke the silence.

"Is it possible that so many people should suddenly volunteer to go away?"

"No, I don't think so. There must be something else behind it."

Little groups of people were forming in doorways along the route, trying to investigate the nature of this amazing sight.

Judith detached herself from the window, sped towards the door and down the stairs, joining the few neighbours on the pavement. And there she found out what it was all about. The whole section of the ghetto on the other side of the bridge had to be cleared by the morning.

"Poor things," she thought, as she walked up the stairs again. "Today is their turn ... tomorrow ours."

Suddenly a dread of the unknown clutched at her heart. She turned frightened eyes towards Michael and whispered, her lips trembling: "When will all this terror end?"

He laid her head against his shoulder and stroked it tenderly.

"It won't be long now," he said quietly. Then he closed the window against the noise and led her to the couch.

He made her lie down and he himself lay beside her,

Chapter 20

comforting her with words and little caresses. His strong presence, his gentle voice full of affection, soothed her and she fell asleep with his arms around her, and her head on his chest.

He kissed her once or twice on the forehead, then closed his eyes and himself drifted into a doze.

* * * * *

It was four o'clock in the morning when they were aroused by a knock on the door. They listened for a moment, then the knock came again.

Michael jumped to his feet, switched on the light, and Judith sat up on the couch, following his every movement with bewildered eyes.

"Who could this be?" she said, a number of visions passing through her troubled mind.

Michael entered the little hall and unlocked the door. It was a friend of his who had just come from the Czech "headquarters" where it had been decided that all Czech people should voluntarily leave the ghetto in the morning.

"At least we shall all be together. We shall have to go anyway, so we could just as well go in one body."

Michael was in favour of the idea and the man departed quickly to continue on his round.

Towards morning the clamour outside gradually ceased until the last straggler had disappeared in the distance. Tension was in the air in their little flat. The rucksacks were packed, waiting in the hall, each with a rolled-up blanket attached to it. The beds were carelessly made and the room was in disorder. There was not much for them to do but wait, for they knew it was their turn today.

Unshed Tears

The hours went by and the heat became greater all the time. The children did not arrive. From the early morning the block of houses had been surrounded by Schu-Po men and no one was allowed to enter the chosen district, just as nobody was able to leave it.

The poor children, their bundles ready, stood crushed at the border of the guarded territory, peering with hungry eyes through the lines of German giants. Once more they were left alone, dependent on themselves. At last most of them made up their minds to pick up their bundles and wander off towards the station. There they hoped to be reunited with the only friends they had.

About ten o'clock in the morning, Tania, with her mother and sister came to say farewell. They were going to join their relatives at the other end of the closed section of the ghetto. They wanted to go together.

For a long while Judith faced Tania speechlessly. There was nothing much to say. At last Tania broke the silence: "We might soon see each other again."

"Yes ... maybe we shall go to the same place ... and if not ... it will soon be all over ... then we shall meet again."

They attempted to smile, but their hearts were sad and something inside them stirred as they clasped each other's hand and kissed goodbye. "Perhaps we shall never meet again," a little inward voice said to each of them. Tania's eyes were filled with tears.

Then she was gone and with her all those long hours they had spent together.

Judith stepped over to Michael who stood at the window and slid her hand into his, seeking protection in the strength of his mind. With him she felt safe....

Chapter 20

About twelve o'clock a deathly hush spread over the street. It lasted for endless seconds. Then a chain of lorries burst into the entrance streets. Speeding along, they rocked on the rough cobbles, making the shiny eagles on the helmets of the standing Schu-Po men dazzle more brilliantly, spreading the glitter to all sides.

Brakes squeaked abruptly and for a moment everything was at a standstill. A fraction of a minute later the sound of a hundred pairs of boots echoed through the street as the uniformed men descended energetically from the lorries and hastened to raid the houses.

A commotion followed. The staircases trembled under their feet. Their shouts rang through the musty corridors. Doors were kicked open and people dragged from their homes. More men followed, attacking the furniture with their heavy boots, forcing open doors, looking under beds, cupboards and searching for secret hiding places.

"Heraus! Heraus!" they shouted, pistols in their hands, pointing constantly at the victims.

Children were screaming. Some women and old men wept silently.

Suddenly Judith and Michael found themselves on top of a lorry surrounded by a panic-stricken crowd. There was scarcely space to breathe. They were all standing, squashed, about eighty of them on one lorry. The sun was burning mercilessly upon their heads and sweat was running down their faces.

With a jerk the lorry started off towards the station.

Judith was concentrating on her luggage, determined to preserve everything of the small amount she had brought with her. As they sped along the narrow, ugly streets, she thought: "Wherever we go, it can't be worse than here."

At last they reached the railway station. It was not a real station. They had arrived at this spot almost three years ago. The train stood on the rails in the middle of a field, a little hut serving as an office.

The lorry stopped by the side of the train that consisted entirely of cattle trucks. From it Judith and Michael saw a group of about sixty Czech people, among them many friends, entering one of the trucks.

"Too late!" said Michael. Then: "Can't be helped. Anyway we shall be going to the same place."

Empty lorries were leaving the place and more, full ones were arriving. There was plenty of shouting, pushing and kicking going on, the German officers handling the crowds in a rough manner.

A procession of volunteers was pouring in and the place resembled one huge chaotic mass of people. Nevertheless things went according to plan. Within a few moments the crowd from Judith's lorry was herded into one of the cattle trucks. A man in the grey-green uniform of the German army was standing at the opening, counting them as they struggled up into the hole that was high above the ground, and disappeared into the dark box.

There were sixty to one wagon. As soon as the people got used to the darkness, the scramble for places around the walls began. Then at last they threw their luggage on the floor and sat down on their property exhausted after the nightmarish drive to the station.

In the middle of the wooden floor stood an urn filled with

Chapter 20

black coffee and a Jewish ghetto-policeman came and began to fill the little pots or mugs of the prisoners with the dark bitter liquid. Then the urn was taken out and the same policeman reappeared with a bowl of thick wedges of bread. He gave one to each. After this he jumped out and a minute later the sliding door was closed with a thump, and sealed, and the sixty victims found themselves helpless, overcrowded, enclosed by darkness and unbearable heat.

Judith wondered whether it was all a nightmare. She sat silently next to Michael. They had nothing to say to each other. She was frightfully thirsty, but did not want to touch the little amount of coffee they possessed and she could not even eat the bread, her throat was so dry.

Sweat was streaming down Michael's face. His shirt stuck to his body. In vain did he try to wipe it off. Judith's heart went out to him when she saw him suffer so much.

At last darkness began to creep in and the prisoners settled down for the night. They found places on the floor, supporting their heads on folded-up pieces of clothes, satchels, or someone's arm, leg or other part of the body. Most of them clutched their belongings with eager hands, protecting them against possible loss. With the passing hours, a cool breeze found its way into the stuffy box, bringing relief to those inside it. One by one they drifted into slumber and heavy breathing mingled with snores began to fill the place.

By midnight, hardly anything stirred within the rocking train. They were heading south-west.

For a long time Judith and Michael sat leaning against the wall. His arm was about her shoulders, his face was thoughtful. Through the darkness she tried to see the meaning in his eyes, but he looked steadily at the opposite wall, and she could see nothing. She drew nearer to him, stroked his head a few times and leant her cheek against his shoulder. Slowly, lulled by the regular rhythm of the train, she fell asleep.

When she woke up it was still quite dark inside the truck. She opened her eyes. Michael's head was leaning against hers. She stirred a little and he moved his hand.

"Aren't you asleep yet?" she whispered.

"No," he said very quietly.

He propped himself up a little and began to stroke her hair. Something was troubling him and she knew it. At last she asked him softly: "What is the matter?"

There was a long silence. Then he felt for her head and taking it between his two hands he stared gently, longingly into her eyes. At last he said quietly: "Judy, darling, you might have to be very brave in the near future. Perhaps ... perhaps tomorrow we shall not be together any more ..." Then seeing her frightened look he added: "It all won't take much longer anyway, then we shall probably meet again."

Incredulously she gazed at him and gasped: "What do you mean?"

"Well you see, I think I know where we are going. I have heard some Germans talking about it in our office. I didn't want to say anything until I was pretty sure of our destination. We followed the route yesterday on our map. It all points towards it."

"Where are we going?" she whispered, with troubled eyes.

"We are probably going to a camp where men and women are separated and the Germans don't seem to be too nice to the prisoners."

Chapter 20

"Do you - do you mean a concentration camp?"

He took her hands and pressed them tightly.

"Yes ... I didn't want to tell you at first, but then I thought it would be better to prepare you for it while we are together. It will save you the shock.... But you have nothing to worry about. You are young and quite strong, you can work hard, that's what they want.... Just be brave and don't give in whatever they might do to you.... It won't be long now...."

For a long time she gazed speechlessly in front of her. He placed her head on his chest and comforted her with little caresses. A whirlwind of thoughts invaded her mind. She tried to sort them out and grasp the meaning of his words. Eventually she realized there was only one way out - to reconcile herself with the idea and fight whatever might come.

At last she raised her head and straightened her back. Looking at him through the darkness she said faintly: "I shall do my best - I shall fight - I will try to be brave. But you must take care of yourself, too."

A very tender smile appeared in his eyes. He looked at her for a few seconds, then he drew her quite near to him and kissed her with great affection. While his cheek lay against hers he whispered: "Judy, my darling, whatever may happen, I want you to know that no one has ever meant so much to me as you do. I never believed it possible for me to love anyone like that. My love for you has kept me strong and sane. It has helped me to maintain life in the right perspective.... In that great big hell you found a corner which you turned into a lovely home, and you filled it with laughter, happiness and love for me.... Perhaps one day I shall be able to prepare a home for you and take you into it and make you happy." He lifted her chin and asked: "How would you like that?"

Unshed Tears

Overcome by emotion Judith found no answer; instead she pulled his head and his whole body towards hers and pressed it tight and kissed him as she had never kissed him before.

They drifted into a world of their own, oblivious of their surroundings. They only knew each other. The snoring, groaning people around them ceased to exist. The dusty floor on which they rested was hard; the dark air was stuffy; their throats were dry and tomorrow, with its unknown threat, lay ahead of them. At this moment they found a happiness which filled their hearts and their whole beings. Heart and mind were united. They belonged to each other.

They lay so near that they could hear each other breathe. They sought strength and encouragement in their unity, in their belief in one another.

At this intimate moment nothing lay between them; there was nothing they would not have been able to speak of. All their thoughts and feelings, needs and longings of the past broke through the little barriers that had until then stood in their way, and filled their veins with powerful desire and brought a flow of wild, short sentences to their lips. There was so much they had to tell each other now. Their thoughts came alive. It was so dark inside the waggon that they could scarcely see one another.

Their words, although filled with strong emotion, were uttered so quietly that only their greed to hear them could make sense of them. They spoke of their feelings, of their past desires, of what made them love each other so much. The whole history of little incidents that brought them so closely together unwound itself in front of them. During these moments they were storing up happiness and courage which they knew might have to last them for a long while.

Chapter 20

There was a moment of eloquent silence when only their minds communicated with each other, and then suddenly Judith broke it: "You know, Michael, whatever may happen to me I will not regret it and I will not feel sorry for myself because this night is a compensation for all suffering. I wouldn't like to change with anyone in the whole world. Knowing you, having your love, the kind of love you have given me, is more than I have ever dreamed of, and even if I should have to die I wouldn't resent it so much, because I would know that I have experienced the height of such great happiness. It will always accompany me, wherever I go. It will keep me strong."

Moved and overwhelmed by a new flood of emotion, he bent over her and looked at her through the darkness. Her body was radiating a lively heat. She caught his eye as a gleam of light came in through the little barred windows and lit up his face. She had never seen him like this before. There was a new glow in him that was infectious. Her heart began to beat violently within her. He lowered his body over hers and the kiss that followed was different from all others.

They wanted each other very much.

He unbuttoned her blouse and kissed her hot body in the dark and played with it while Judith stroked his hair and face and body passionately, kissing him wherever she found a place to kiss.

The minutes passed. At last Judith undid his shirt, threw her arms around him and pressed the bare part of his body towards hers. She clung to him wildly while their mouths kissed. They kissed for a long, long while, then suddenly he unlocked himself from her embrace and, still leaning over her, pleaded: "Please, darling, help me to be strong. Tomorrow ... tomorrow we may have to part ... and after all the lovely months we have had together I don't want you to remember me with disgust."

"I could never remember you with disgust. I would prefer you to be strong now, but whatever you do I shall always love you."

He stroked her forehead tenderly, then said: "You are so very young and I love you so much. I mustn't do it to you, not just now, and you must help me."

She smiled and kissed him gently.

He buttoned up her blouse, sat up and passed his hand over his forehead and eyes.

XXI

Towards midday the heat became unbearable. There wasn't a drop of water to be found anywhere inside the stuffy waggon. People sat still and silent, for every movement was too much of an effort. Those who had some bread left did not eat it for their tongues were too dry to munch it. They did not know how much longer they were going to be enclosed in the dark oppressive box that was throwing them from side to side, but many of those whose eyes yesterday had been shining with a resolution not to give in, were by now resigned to their fate. There was not much strength left in them to struggle.

Judith sat, leaning her head against Michael's shoulder. Like the rest of them, they did not speak much. There wasn't much to be said. There was a quiet understanding between them that didn't need any words. Judith felt wiser than the rest of the prisoners because she knew what to expect. The knowledge gave her a certain amount of confidence for the thought of what was in store for her gave her an incentive to build up a resistance. The past few hours had helped a lot.

It was about two o'clock when the train began to lose speed. Automatically people lifted themselves up from the dusty floor and gathered at the little barred windows. The shabbily clad figures pressed at each other, those at the back attempting to push their way forward with their elbows, their eager eyes looking in one direction. Was there a town which was to be their home in the future? Were they at last going to step out of the smelly waggons and find themselves in the light and air?

A complete silence fell on the prisoners as sight and mind made an attempt to take in the strange picture that unfolded itself in front of them. Their eagerness was gone, a look of meekness and surprise took its place. Judith stood on tiptoes to get a glimpse of the spectacle that had brought this sudden hush about.

"So that is it," she thought at last.

She turned back and met Michael's eyes. A shiver passed through her as she recognized the silent premonition in them.

Was this the end? It couldn't be, it couldn't! Did he really look afraid? No, not he. He was never afraid of anything.

Suddenly he bent down, dipped his fingertips in the black dust on the floor and applied it to his greying temples. Outside the barred holes a strange world was spread in front of them. The hot sun was scorching the yellow sand that stretched for miles like a desert on which stood this incredible town that was no town at all. It was enclosed in barbed wires strewn with hundreds of wooden huts placed in rows and swarming with people who resembled human beings very little. They were all dressed in a sort of striped pyjamas. Their cheeks and temples were hollow; their heads were shaved! They dragged their feet behind them as they walked, apparently aimlessly, from place to place.

There wasn't a tree or plant in sight. The air was still and a deadly threat hung over the endless place.

Chapter 21

The train stopped, and a mixture of noises composed of sharp German commands, the howling of dogs and cracking of whips, filled the immediate surroundings. Within seconds the doors flew ajar, unbolted by skilful hands that had undoubtedly done such jobs many times before.

An unearthly chaos followed. There was no time for the prisoners to think, no time to make decisions. The light that flowed into the dark interior of the waggons almost blinded them.

"Get out! Get out! Hurry up! Quicker! Quicker!"

Whips cracked, dogs barked.

"Leave your luggage behind! Hurry! Hurry!"

Those who stood at the back of the waggon managed to snatch their bread, or an object that was very precious to them and hide it in their clothes.

Young and old, helpless people, without defence, all poured out of the wide opening, hardly knowing what was happening to them. And then, suddenly, unaware of the true meaning of it, they found themselves at the crossroads. The look in the eyes of the Germans filled them with terror and foreboding. Having no other option, they followed the direction of a whip, gun, or outstretched arm.

"Left! Right! Over here! Over there!"

Brutal pushes or kicks with leather riding boots, helped the stragglers to get to their appropriate place in good time. The Germans took great pride in being good organizers, and although the procedure looked chaotic to the frightened prisoners, everything went according to plan. Within a few minutes several groups stood ready, waiting for the next move. On one side were the young and healthy-looking men, separated from the women. On the other side old men, women, and mothers with children formed three groups of their own. Seeing how reluctant some relatives and friends were to part, and trying to avoid further scenes, several Germans shouted: "Push on! You will see each other again!"

"In hell," remarked a young man in uniform, grinning to himself.

Judith who was nearby caught the remark, and a feeling of cold terror surged through her. Her scared eyes settled upon Michael who stood erect in his group many yards away, smiling encouragingly across to her. Only a few minutes ago, they had walked forward hand in hand, a secret bond between them. Their silence was eloquent. It was only when they found themselves within yards of the place of action that Michael had pressed her hand harder and uttered gently: "Never lose courage and faith."

Then they were torn apart, pushed into their places, and only the longing remained.

The sun shone mercilessly upon their heads, the still air filled with a gruesome strangeness, hung over the flat stretch of scorched sandy ground on which in the distance thousands of broken, shabby figures were moving aimlessly from place to place.

This was Auschwitz, the concentration camp.

The harsh order was given, and the groups in lines of five marched off in different directions. Anxiously, heads turned all ways trying to snatch a last look from a beloved one, and then there was nothing but the road ahead, lined with huge S.S. men on motor-cycles or marching with police dogs at their sides, nudging them on, making them walk faster and smarter.

Chapter 21

Judith was in a procession of young women, of whom about fifty were Czech. Many of them knew each other and now at the critical moment automatically huddled together. As they marched along towards a huge iron gate, always nearer to the strange world behind it, with the dogs at their sides jumping and barking madly, and the men savagely hurrying them on, they found it hard to believe in the reality of the moment.

Two guards who were on duty by the gate held it open for them, and the procession made its way through. From high above, the inscription "ARBEIT MACHT FREI," (Freedom through Work) grinned down upon them. New to the place, however, they failed to see the irony of those three words.

As they walked along the dusty camp road crowds of people gathered along the barbed wire which stretched on both sides of it. Some glared at them with an empty look; others who had any energy left, waved and shouted at them, urgently beckoning them to throw over some of their bread or other precious belongings.

"They must be crazy to think that we would part with our bread," someone in the procession said.

"As if we weren't hungry enough."

"Who do they think we are, millionaires just arrived from our palaces?"

With hostile eyes they surveyed the pleading prisoners and clutched their treasures closer to their bodies.

At equal distances along the barbed wires posters with a skull and crossbones warned that it was loaded with electricity.

At the end of the long road stood a group of buildings. Relieved to get out of the scorching heat, the women entered one of them and found themselves in a large stone hall surrounded by bellowing men and women in the S.S. uniform.

"Take your clothes off! Faster! Don't dawdle. Put it all on that heap there together with all your belongings. Clothes off! Clothes off! Put your property down! Bring jewellery to the desk! Hurry up you dirty Jewesses!"

That was the beginning of the 'bath'.

With satisfied grins the huge men with their arms folded on their chests watched the women discard one piece of their garments after another, until, naked, they stood waiting.

"Dirty swine," Judith whispered to Ruth, an old acquaintance of hers.

"Let them stare; who cares?"

"Do you think we shall get our things back?"

"I very much doubt it; they are all mixed up now."

"I wish I could hide these photographs somewhere. They are of my parents and my best friends. I want them more than anything else. Perhaps they will let me keep them."

"I don't see why not. Why should they want our photographs?"

Near the two girls stood an officer. Judith felt his glare upon her naked body and something inside her revolted.

"You there, Jewess, come here," he beckoned to her.

With her head high up Judith took a few steps forward toward him.

"What is it you have got in your hand?"

"Only some photographs."

"Weren't you told to get rid of everything?"

"But they are ..."

"No buts! There!"

Brushing his hands past her breasts he took hold of the

Chapter 2I

little bundle and threw it on the heap which was now only a sad reminiscence of personal belongings.

Looking her up and down once more he said, "Scram!" and the whip swished on her backside.

Judith went back to her group. Tears of anger and humiliation blurred her sight for a moment. "Swine," she uttered once more.

"I shouldn't bother about him or any of them. Where this is concerned they are just air for me. They can stare as much as they like ..."

Next came the hair treatment. It did not take long. Skilled hands, a pair of clippers and the women were deprived of the last thing left to them to give them a feeling of self-respect. And then the hairs of the body were removed in the same way.

"Now we all look like monkeys," Judith remarked half jokingly, half bitterly.

"It's absolutely disgusting," Ruth retorted.

The general inspection was next on the list. Every inch of the body, including the ears, mouth and the most incredible parts were searched for jewellery or other hidden treasures. With a blank look on her face Judith followed the rest into the shower-bath hall. Hundreds of showers were turned on at the same time and the officers made sure that everyone obeyed the order "Wash yourself!"

As they filed past a desk after leaving the bath, each was thrown a frock and a pair of clogs, regardless of size. A fashion parade followed.

The women crept into their new attire examining each other not without a sense of humour. Some even passed a few jokingly rude remarks while others commented on the absurdity of the situation. It was quite a pitiful sight - the bare heads, the ridiculous frocks, the large clogs and even the perverted smiles on their faces.

Judith, in her new pale blue dress which reached high above her knees and had short sleeves, kept close to the group of Czech women.

The whips cracked and the procession moved back towards the camp. Now they knew why the prisoners had the audacity to ask for their bread. A gate opened for them again and they found themselves inside a women's camp. It looked like all the others. Long huts were on either side of a narrow dusty road. There were about two dozen of them. All around were similar camps, separated from others by the same dangerous wires. At one end of the camp was an open space and on that the large group was told to stand at attention in rows of five.

It was early afternoon and the scorching sun shone upon their bare heads. The sand beneath their feet was hot and there was no plant in sight. The hours followed each other and nothing happened. The other prisoners were moving about the camp regardlessly or sitting leaning against the wall of the hut. Some even lay in the sand sleeping.

Not far away was a men's camp. All the men wore striped prisoners' garments. Some activity was going on there; huge boulders were being carried to one place and after the last piece had been placed on the heap, the work began in reverse. Another two hours, and the boulders were gone. The hours dragged endlessly. Thirst and a feeling of weakness caused by the heat tormented them.

As she stood there patiently waiting for the unknown, Judith thought of a thousand things. "Was Michael right in what he had told her? Where was he now? Were they ever to meet again? How long could it all last?"

After six o'clock the most incredible and horrifying thing happened. Down the main camp road came marching a group of prisoners, preceded by a band playing a well-known march. And then another group and another as they returned from work. The gay music made Judith's blood curdle. The endless, bare, cheerless plain, the animal-like prisoners, the cropped heads, the stillness in the air above, the whips and terror of the unknown and music made a most gruesome combination.

In a girls' camp nearby another band struck the first note and proceeded to play Mozart. Judith shrank into herself and a dreadful loneliness overcame her.

"What a perverted mind must have been behind this idea," someone remarked, nearby.

That circus lasted for about an hour after which followed a commotion in camp accompanied by shrieks, commands and within a few minutes groups of a thousand each stood in ranks in front of their barracks in a deadly hush. That was "Appell" - roll call. In front of each group three or four women were running up and down securing order with a whip.

For the eye which met the spectacle for the first time it was an unforgettable experience. All the camps, stretching under the endless skies, forming one unit, followed the same pattern. The silence was a ghostly one. All eyes were turned in one direction from which the self-satisfied figures were expected to appear and count them and thus relieve them of the tedious task of standing in one place absolutely still.

The sun was beginning to go down when four tall men in uniform strode into the particular camp. With chins up they counted the rows of five and marched on. They moved from group to group, taking their job very seriously. When at last every one in the camp was counted and recounted the "Appell" was over and the most sought-for moment was within reach. Everyone retired to his particular barrack or block - as it was called. A few moments later monitors from each block reappeared on the camp road and made their way down towards the canteen where huge cans filled with soup were waiting for them to be taken back to the hungry mob.

Judith and the rest of the group were led into an empty barrack. It was one large hall with a stone floor and very small windows by the roof. Except for two cubicles by the door and a stove whose brick pipe ran along the centre of the floor, thus dividing the hall into two parts, it was absolutely bare.

Five wild women with violent gestures and rough speech were giving orders. One was the block leader, a beautiful dark haired girl from Slovakia, the others were her helpers. All were prisoners but had managed in one way or other to gain the privilege of their status. It seemed they had forgotten that the helpless prisoners they were now bullying, and beating, and pushing around were there for the same reason - Jewish blood was flowing through their veins. But then of course, they would have never risen to their rank had their conscience allowed them to soften toward their fellow prisoners.

In files of five they were seated on the cold, hard floor. There was hardly an inch to spare between them on either side, as all thousand women had to be accommodated in the one hall. How they were to lie down and find room for sleeping, nobody knew. Several new monitors were picked, some to go and collect the soup, others to give out the basins, one for each line of five.

Chapter 21

After about half an hour the performance started. Several baskets with slices of coarse brown bread arrived, followed by the cans of soup. Everyone's interest was aroused at that moment, and a hush dominated the place. The baskets were taken round along the narrow passages and the barrack supervisors threw the slices to individual prisoners who fell upon their share with a ferocious gusto. The first in each file lined up for the soup which was being shared out by the block leader. With the ladle she reached down to the bottom of the can and brought out the solid potatoes and vegetables with which she filled a saucepan of hers and those of her fellow-helpers. Hostile eyes followed her action and rebellion rose in the minds of the prisoners.

"She is the same as we are," someone near Judith remarked.

"Why should she have all the privileges?"

"Collaborator!" hissed a spiteful voice.

"She needs to be punished more than the Germans!"

"For some food and power she sells herself to the enemies! Phew!"

"We'll get our own back one day."

One after another the women with their little basins filled returned to their places. There were no spoons and to make the distribution just, the sips which they had to take from the edge were counted. Judith's turn came and all eyes this time were fixed on her. One, two, three, four, five - and no more, for the time being anyway. Under the strictest supervision of others' stares, it was impossible to get away with an extra drop. Small and large quarrels arose in various parts of the block, for some people managed to get a larger mouthful than the others. The basins licked clean, the pilgrimage to the latrines followed. It was part of the daily routine and everybody had to participate. The latrines were housed in a barrack and there were rows and rows of them. It seemed as though the whole camp and all the others were engaged in the same sort of activity.

With that behind them, it was back to their block and time to settle down for the night. There was a certain art in this, for there wasn't half the room on the floor for everyone to lie down. The newcomers found it especially hard to puzzle out the problem. Quarrels livened up the place, which brought the block leader and the others along with whips and buckets of cold water, which they readily emptied on the helpless crowd.

"Shut up, everybody! Quiet! Or I'll send you into the chimney."

Half an hour later the floor was a mass of intermingled legs, arms and bodies.

Judith with her head resting on someone's body and her own covered up with other people's limbs, her skirt soaked with cold water, lay awake for a long, long time.

"What was it all about?" she asked herself. "Where was Michael Alexander? Why did they lie here like this on the cold, stone floor soaked with water. How could those Czech girls betray them and treat them so beastly? Where would it all end, and what did she mean by 'I'll send you into the chimney'? Who was the man who entered the block leader's cubicle? He didn't look like other prisoners, he was well fed and decently dressed. Was he a German? What were they laughing about so heartily in that cubicle now? They were certainly enjoying themselves.... The chimney ... what was the chimney?..."

Exhausted and soothed by the bromide that had been one of the soup's ingredients, she fell asleep.

XXII

"Out! Out! Into fives! Appell! Appell!"

With a start Judith opened her eyes and tried to prop herself up. This was impossible, she was weighed down by other people's limbs.

"Appell! Appell! Get up! Quicker! Appell!"

It took a second or two before she realized where she was. The block leader and her girl helpers were furiously running up and down the narrow gangway waving their whips, bellowing their orders. The time was half past three in the morning. After the process of disentangling themselves, the women got up, straightened their stiff limbs and rubbed their eyes. All this took only a few moments, for before they quite grasped what was going on, they were on their way out of the barrack.

The air was chilly and dark. Stupefied by the sudden intrusion they obeyed orders silently. From barracks all over the camp silhouettes of prisoners were pouring out, quietly arranging themselves in rows of fives on the camp road, only the commanding shrieks of the female monsters piercing the air.

Unshed Tears

How slowly the minutes went by! The women stood and froze and stamped their feet to keep the circulation going. Slowly the sun appeared from behind the horizon and spread its rays across the strange spectacle.

Six o'clock ... seven ... eight ... nine, and still they stood waiting. Several people collapsed, and were taken away, never to be seen again. Then suddenly the order was given: "Attention!"

The German officers appeared on the camp road. Moving from group to group they counted the fives as they had done on the previous day. By ten o'clock it was all over and they were dismissed, free to move anywhere within their own camp. Only the newly arrived prisoners were kept standing at attention until the order was given for them to march towards the 'bath-house'. It was a long hall with rows and rows of troughs and cold water taps, with soap smelling of antiseptic scattered here and there.

Judith was glad of the opportunity to rid herself of the dust and dirt she had gathered on the barrack floor. All around her women were taking off their clothes and dropping them onto the floor by their side, or throwing them over the water pipes above the troughs. In a few moments the hall was humming with a concentrated busyness, water was splashing on all sides, soap was the object of fights and quarrels, and here and there a song left the lips of a spirited girl.

Then suddenly all doors burst open and with bulging eyes, animal faces and cracking their whips in all directions, several German officers raided the bath-house, bellowing: "Out! Everyone out, at once!"

Streams of women, dressed, naked, or with a garment in

Chapter 22

their hands scrambled towards the door - out of the way of the whips and pointed pistols. Most of the dresses were trampled on. Some of the women managed to get hold of a piece of clothes, regardless of whose it was. Outside the barrack a few more officers with their feet astride, arms folded on their chest and a satisfied grin, watched the prearranged spectacle.

"You wait until we get you!" Judith hissed out of the corner of her mouth. "You'll have some fun then, you'll have a show!" She clutched a black dress, which she had managed to rescue from under stampeding feet, towards her body. They were all walking back to the barracks where they were told to stay in their places.

"They certainly have a sense of humour," remarked Ida.

"Yes, it's so funny, my ribs are aching with laughter," said another woman trying to cover up parts of her torso with a torn pair of flannel knickers.

Some, either overcome by a kind of hysteria or perhaps an unconquerable sanity, managed to laugh at themselves as they faced each other in their comical garments, or just parts of them, desperately trying to fasten them to various areas of their bodies.

Judith put on her new black dress which reached almost to her ankles. She grinned at Ruth who had managed to get away with a towel, which she artistically draped around herself and said quite merrily, "Nothing worse could ever happen to us. It can't last all that long, and then we'll hack them to little bits." Suddenly her face grew serious again. "I hope it won't be too late."

* * * * *

Unshed Tears

Judith strolled out into the sun. It was nearly noon. The problem of clothes had been met by the block leader, for whom the situation was nothing new. Several girls were sent to the bath-house to gather up all the remaining garments which were then distributed, in the air, to the needy. A few extras supplied the gaps. Swapping of dresses followed, and Judith exchanged hers with a middle-aged woman, who found the little red frock with a white collar most uncomfortable and a little embarrassing.

The camp was full of women, wandering apparently aimlessly to and fro. Some were resting on the ground, sleeping or dreaming of good days, or crying and lamenting, some sat in groups chatting and even laughing. There was a mixture of nationalities, though Hungarian and Polish prevailed.

Judith walked slowly down the camp road. There were sixteen barracks on either side of it. That meant almost thirty-two thousand people in this little allotment. And wherever she looked camps stretched like the sea to the horizon.

At the bottom of the camp were the canteen and the hospital. With longing eyes, she peered through the windows into the huge kitchen. Dozens of girls were busy peeling potatoes, vegetables, stirring tremendous coppers of soup, clattering dishes and gossiping. They looked cheerful and healthy. With envious eyes Judith watched them nibble at the raw vegetables, and wondered in which way one had to be privileged to get access to a post of this sort.

Her stomach felt desperately empty and her knees were weak. A dreadful loneliness took possession of her, for amid these thousands of people she was an isolated figure, alone with her fears, worries and sufferings.

Chapter 22

There was something ghastly in the atmosphere around - the rigid discipline, sadism, the barbed wires threatening death, cropped heads, monotony of scenery, and above all the constant threat of 'the chimney'.

About a mile away at the edge of the camp stood a prominent, windowless brick building, with a large rectangular chimney towering up toward the sky. From there clouds of smoke and the smell of scorching bones burst forth with ceaseless energy.

"Is this the much talked of chimney?... It must be ..." A premonition took hold of her and anxiety filled her heart. Where was all this going to end?

For the first time she asked herself, "Is Michael still alive?"

Several Hungarian-speaking girls came strolling down the road and stopping not far away from Judith, gazed around, making little comments here and there. Then they sat down on the ground in front of the barracks opposite the kitchen, leaning against its wall. Judith thought for a moment, hesitated and then with resolute steps made her way toward the little group.

"I say, have you been here long?" she asked, seating herself nearby.

They looked at her with shrewd eyes expressing neither sympathy nor hostility, and answered, "For almost a year."

"You must know a great deal about this place then. I only came yesterday."

"Where did you come from?" one of them asked.

"From the Ghetto, Lodz, but I was born in Prague."

"Oh, we come from Czechoslovakia, too, but from the Carpathian part. There was a whole Czech camp over there, on the other side of the wire, they are all gone now. There were thousands of them ..." explained a girl, her voice assuming a more friendly tone.

"And ... and what happened to them?"

"All sorts of things really. They were a good lot, and brave too."

"What do you mean?"

"Well, many thousands of them knew for six months that they were going into the chimney and when the day came they revolted. Of course it did not help, but they faced their death with songs on their lips and their heads high."

A dreadful fear gripped Judith's throat, and it was only with the greatest of effort that she asked: "What is the chimney?"

"Don't you know? Over there, look. See the smoke? That's the chimney, or the death factory, or the gas chamber. Once you go into that building you never come out again. And hundreds, sometimes thousands, of people go there every day, especially the old and incapable ones. Did you go to the shower bath after you arrived yesterday?"

"Yes."

"Well, in there it looks like a shower bath. They make you undress, give you a towel and soap and send you under the showers. Then they lock a heavy door. You expect the water to start running, but instead gas fumes fill the air and that's the end. Afterwards they take you to special kilns and burn you to ashes. They are very busy in there, they can hardly cope these days. There are several gas chambers all over the camp, and when they send you to a shower bath you never know whether water or gas will come out."

Chapter 22

"It is horrible, horrible," Judith gasped.

"You'll get used to it," said another girl.

"There are very few people who ever get out of Auschwitz. They don't call it the 'destruction camp' for nothing."

"What exactly happened to those Czechs?"

"They started coming here in September last year from Terezienstadt. For some reason or other they were chosen to be a model camp. Without being sorted out first, whole families were living in the same camp, their discipline was much less rigid, and the supervision of it was mostly in the prisoners' hands. Sanitation wasn't bad, and they slept on bunks. Sometimes delegations from outside would come to inspect it. It was all propaganda. Their hair wasn't cropped and they were allowed to send prescribed messages to Terezienstadt and sometimes home, and receive parcels. Five thousand of them, however, who arrived on the seventh of September were predestined to die in the gas chamber on the seventh of March, the birth date of Masaryk. For six long months they waited for certain death. In December another transport of three thousand arrived, chosen to die in the death factory in June 1944, in exactly six months' time."

"It must have been dreadful waiting all that time, every day bringing them nearer and nearer to death," Judith said in a little voice.

"I suppose they waited for a miracle to happen; they hoped all the time ... but the miracle didn't come and March the seventh arrived at last. The crematorium was ready. Armed guards surrounded the camp for they suspected a rebellion was being planned. In the morning we learned that the leader of the whole plot committed suicide and somehow there was no one to come forward to take the initiative and make them go through with the plan."

"Individuals revolted, but what could they do, unarmed, shut up in a space surrounded by electrically loaded wire."

"By the evening, everything was calm. The night that followed was witness to the most unforgettable scenes. The Germans always adore a spectacle; it satisfies their incredibly sadistic and perverted nature. But they were disappointed. There was no begging, lamenting or screaming. Instead the prisoners, resigned to their fate, unconcernedly took off their clothes as ordered, and with a dignified poise boarded the awaiting lorries that were to take them on their last journey.

"They took no notice of the heavily armed guards, and with proud, smiling faces they sang well known songs all the way to the crematorium. The lorries came and went and the whole night the sound of the prisoners' songs spread far and wide across the camp, making everyone crave for revenge.

"In the morning everything was still and people stood watching the smoke rise toward the sky. How empty the Czech camp looked, the five thousand prisoners were gone, and the same fate was awaiting another three thousand inhabitants."

Judith's brow was troubled. She meditated for a while.

"How do you know all this?" she asked at last.

"We often spoke to them through the wire; we were in constant touch. It was quite easy really; news spreads very fast throughout the whole camp. Messages are passed along across the wire, from one section of the camp to the other, and people who go out to work take their information with them, too. There is quite a team spirit about the place."

"What happened to the other Czech transport; did they go the same way too?"

Chapter 22

"No, a miracle happened that time. They were sorted out and those capable of work were sent out to labour camps in Germany."

"They keep the twins, though, for experiments," said a girl with dark eyes.

"I have heard they make all sorts of experiments on human beings, like injections and so on."

"Human guinea pigs, I suppose."

"Yes, and the hair, and gold teeth, and bones of the dead are used for industry."

"I was told that some Germans have lamp-shades and book-covers made of human skin, and that is a fact."

That was as much as Judith could take for the first day. She wanted to be alone and sort out the whirlwind of thoughts that invaded her mind. It all seemed so incredibly strange, so far divorced from normal life, that she began to doubt the reality of the situation. She picked herself up, said a few words to the girls and strolled off....

Suddenly there were two worlds, and she found it hard to combine one with the other. What was she doing here in this place? Was there a normal world anywhere, or was this her world from now on, and the other one just a memory which would fade with time.

Her mind found it almost impossible to grasp it all. A black cloud descended upon her and filled her with misery. She trembled a little. She was afraid, very much afraid, for she was alone with her dark thoughts. Once more her gaze fell on the tall chimney and the crematorium. How many of her friends had gone that way, and was this where her life, filled with hopes and ambitions, was going to end?...

Unshed Tears

For hours Judith sat leaning against the wall of her barrack, her eyes shut, her mind at work....

Once she came to terms with the very worst and resolved to meet it with dignity and calmness, nothing could defeat her and a feeling of relief spread over her being. The fear had suddenly gone, and now that her mind had resigned itself to the worst, the thought that she might get out of here one day after all, that there must be a normal world somewhere, full of beauty and colour, that the Germans would be defeated and the victims avenged, filled her with a new joy, and at that moment she believed that everything was going to be all right again. Having conquered her fear, she suddenly felt strong and pleased with herself. She opened her eyes and looked up toward the sun and smiled.

In front of her some men were digging the ground. They were Poles sent here from another camp to work on repairs. They were not Jews, but political prisoners who were given certain privileges and thus retained their good physique. Their cropped hair emphasized the thickness of their necks, high cheekbones, and square jaws and they wore the traditional striped overalls with sleeves rolled high up, revealing their tanned, strong arms.

There was an air of self-confidence around them, almost superiority and power, and one would sense that for some reason they enjoyed a higher status within the camp. They seemed well acquainted with the place and the run of it and in a way behaved as if they were in possession of it. There was no German supervisor with them, only a Polish one who obviously was on his charges' side.

They spoke to the girls and flirted with those who still had

Chapter 22

some spirit in them. Judith noticed one of them handing a girl whom he had obviously met before a huge chunk of bread, then whispering something to her. A little group of girls gathered round several boys, they were talking and then an air of triumph spread over their faces. That evening Judith learned that the fight for France was in full swing and the liberation of Paris was not far off.

★ ★ ★ ★ ★

It was on the next day when Judith stood gazing far beyond the camp that one of the Polish workers came up to her.

"Don't fret, it won't be long now," he remarked, patting her on the shoulder.

Judith turned her head and cast her eyes upon him.

"Do you really believe that?" she said promptly.

"Yes, of course ... how long have you been here?"

"Two days."

"Well, that's nothing."

"Seems two days too many."

"H'm ... I suppose you are very hungry," he said, looking at her.

"Yes, I must confess I am."

"Come with me, I will give you something to eat."

He took her by the shoulder and led her away. Judith's face brightened at the thought of eating. That was really good of him. She wondered where those Poles got their food from, but the main thing was that they had it and she was going to have some soon.

They went down the camp road and turned into one of the

barracks. He opened the door to a cubicle and locked it behind them. With keen eyes Judith looked about her. It wasn't very large. There was a table and two chairs in the middle, a bunk with a mattress covered with blankets by one wall, and a small stove with a shelf above it in the corner opposite the door. Two saucepans rested on the stove and half a loaf of bread lay partly uncovered on the table. By it was a knife and a pat of margarine in a little dish. At the sight of bread, Judith's mouth began to water, only one thought was prominent in her mind, and an eager look entered her face. She could hardly keep her hands still. Suddenly she felt the man's gaze upon her and something unpleasant stirred within her.

"Well, what are you waiting for?" he said harshly.

"You said you were going to give me something to eat," she said meekly.

"Now look, you don't have to act stupid with me. We are in Auschwitz, Auschwitz, do you hear? One doesn't get bread here for nothing. Hurry up," he pleaded in an uncultured voice.

"Hurry up what?" Judith asked, instinct suddenly making the position clear to her, forcing her to retreat a step or two.

"Do you want your grub? Then don't play around. I have had that one before."

He advanced toward her and Judith made resolutely for the door. It was locked.

"Let me out. I don't want your food," she said.

"If you carry on like that, I'll really let you go and that will be the end of it," he threatened.

"I really mean it. Let me go!" she said firmly.

His voice suddenly changed and a primitive, animal-like expression crept over his countenance.

Chapter 22

"That's enough of playing around." He came quite close, his tall strong figure towering over. With furious, anxious eyes Judith looked up at him.

"Don't touch me!"

His huge hands suddenly gripped her dress by the neck and with one big furious movement tore the whole front apart. Enraged and strengthened by fear and anger, Judith set up a struggle, making use of her fists, feet, teeth and her whole body. She twisted and kicked and hammered her fists against his face, but the animal had taken full possession of him now and a moment later Judith's dress lay on the floor.

"Want to run away now?" he said mockingly, inspecting her body with self-satisfied eyes. She tightened her lips and gave him a glance of hatred. At last breathlessly she shouted with a trembling voice, "You beast! You idiotic swine! You criminal!"

He laughed in her face, then ignoring her opposition carried her onto the bunk. As he touched parts of her body, his gestures were violent, and at last he locked her in his embrace making movement impossible for her. Engrossed in his own pleasure, he heard her cry, "Go away you brute, you are hurting me."

Suddenly he lifted himself up, looked into her distressed eyes and remarked in a softer tone, "You never had a man before, did you?"

"No," she sobbed.

"I am sorry ... I'll get you a new dress. Wait here." He came back, carrying a similar red dress.

"Here, put it on, I'll heat up some soup for you."

"I don't want your soup," she said defiantly.

"Don't be a fool ... I didn't know, I really didn't ... anyway nothing happened," he said apologetically in a loud voice.

"Open that door and let me out!" she ordered in a shaking voice.

On the way to the door he took the loaf from the table and put it in her arms.

Resolutely she flung it back on the table and announced, "I don't want your filthy bread!"

* * * * *

Gradually Judith learned about the life in the camp. What made her most angry was the business of corruption; for, as the man said, in Auschwitz one didn't get anything for nothing, and the worst part of it was that many wanted a lot and resolved to get it even at the expense of their own decency, pride and anybody who got in their way. Collaboration with the Germans of the block leaders and the Ca-Po (camp police consisting of prisoners), their willingness to be cruel to the helpless, and to offer their bodies to the Germans or anyone in power, called for revenge.

The days went slowly by, one like the other, with the exception of an air raid at midday, when they were all locked up in their barracks with planes roaring over their heads and explosions sounding from the distance. In spite of the dreadful feeling of being shut up in a stuffy hut with a thousand other people, with bombs flying about nearby, smiles crept to the prisoners' faces for they knew they had been seen by the Allies. It was a good feeling to know that they were near.

One day something else happened which broke the

monotony in a more unpleasant manner. As they were standing on their evening parade, the sirens began to howl and soon everyone knew that a prisoner had escaped. A terrified hush fell over the camp. Those who had been in Auschwitz long enough knew it meant standing here like this till the unfortunate run-away was recaptured and in case they didn't find him, wait for the punishment they would have to take instead of him, which usually meant death for many.

They stood Appell all that night shivering in their light clothes, almost dropping with fatigue, and all the next day without receiving any food. By the evening they brought him back and in the presence of a large crowd shot him.

New victims were arriving every day. The crematorium was busy and the camp was grossly overcrowded. Eagerly they were all awaiting fresh news which always managed to seep into the camp.

It was toward the end of August, a week after Judith had come here that a joyous spirit crept over the place. Paris had been liberated. Paris was free! The Allies were advancing from all sides.

Three days later the inmates of Block 4 were made to parade naked in front of a German committee. In fives they advanced, each row stripping for inspection. Judith knew these men. They were doctors, the same who made experiments on prisoners with injections and drugs, the same who liked their lamp-shades made of skin. A rumour surged through the files that they were being selected for work in Germany and Judith gathered her last energy, made herself as tall as possible and looked self-confidently in front of her. A new hope made her heart throb, but on the surface she stayed calm and composed. Perhaps there was a door out of here after all she thought, and watched her friends in front of her being chosen for one group or another.

It was obvious that on one side stood the younger, fitter looking girls, whereas on the other side the middle-aged women and girls whose bodies looked withered and weak, formed another group. The sorting was made at comparative speed, for what did an error matter? Only one life more or less. Judith's row at last faced the searching eyes and she squared her shoulders and took a deep breath, expanding her chest. The next minute she was putting on her frock, quietly rejoicing with the friends around her.

"Just imagine, tomorrow we might be out of here!" Her eyes shone with excitement, and the girls exchanged jubilant glances, invigorated by the unexpected, good tidings.

They didn't go back to Block 4. About a hundred and fifty of them, Czech and Polish, were led down to the bottom of their camp, and along the main longer road, past dozens of single camps, until at last, after about half an hour, they found themselves on the outskirts of Auschwitz concentration camp.

They passed through a gate and came face to face with a large brick building which they were told was the baths.

Suspicion crept into every mind; was this another of the Germans' pranks? Joy left their brows and apprehension filled their beings. What was this all about?

Judith looked up at their German escorts, trying to read in their faces the true meaning of this, but she could see only the stern, unmoved masks, which revealed nothing. Speechlessly they followed the officers into the building where they were told to get rid of their clothes. Anxiously they looked around

Chapter 22

them, eager to discover anything that would give them a clue as to the true nature of their whereabouts.

They were given soap and a towel each and sent into the shower hall. Was this the end? The hall was gradually filling up with silent prisoners, until the last one made her reluctant entry. The door closed behind her, and a little panic took possession of Judith's heart. What was it going to be - water or gas? There seemed to be no way out of there, nowhere to run. They were stupid to have come here without any protest. Then after the longest minute they had ever encountered, warm water began to trickle from above them, and Judith realized that she had known all the time that it couldn't have been anything else.

They spent the night on the gravel floor under the open sky. The train had not arrived yet and they had nowhere else to go. They all gathered close to each other like kittens, trying to keep warm. The silhouette of the crematorium towered above them in near proximity, ever reminding them of tragedy.

Through the early mist next morning they could see several processions making their way down to the brick building, unaware that in an hour's time they would be reduced to a heap of ashes. An uncanny feeling took hold of Judith, and once more she wondered whether she was dreaming or whether this monstrosity was really taking place in the twentieth century.

"If only I could see the German power scattered to bits, I wouldn't mind dying afterwards," she said to a group of girls around her.

"Don't worry, they will be made into minced meat some day," one of them assured her.

Unshed Tears

Their case, however, wasn't won yet, for the train that was to take them to Germany couldn't get through, due to bombed rails. The rumour quickly spread that if it didn't collect them within three days, the gas chamber was to be their destination.

For some reason they didn't panic. Perhaps it was the bromide that had been mixed with their soup, perhaps it was an unconquering faith, or maybe a resignation to fate that kept them calm and most of the time in good spirits. They even went as far as to look at the blazing chimney and remark humorously, "Tomorrow our bones may be sizzling in there."

And when at night the rain came down at them making them shiver with cold, someone pointed at the chimney and remarked with a strange gaiety, "In there it is warmer."

The days were as bad as the nights. The hot sun burned their weak bodies, making many faint and dried their tongues so that they were unable to eat their daily ration of bread. In spite of it all, optimism failed to leave them. They passed their time telling jokes, recollecting amusing incidents from their lives, and composing imaginary meals. The jokes and the stories weren't always clean, but they were a way of escape.

Embarrassment ceased to exist, and the true nature which so often stays buried in the depth of an individual, came shamelessly to the surface. Judith sat close by them and listened, learning quickly about many aspects of life which until then had been something of a mystery to her.

Nevertheless a great tension ruled them, especially as the hours went by without a sign of an empty train. There were moments for everyone when the naked reality would suddenly grow larger and larger, when lips would tremble and eyes would fill with fright.

Chapter 22

On the third morning the general optimism turned to doubt and an unnatural silence filled the ranks. Their eyes turned again and again in the direction of the crematorium and their ears were constantly attuned to the sound of a locomotive. They watched transports pass by without coming back. Thoughts of escape flared up in their minds only to die down again at the realisation of its impossibility. Two thoughts were struggling in their minds; they could neither imagine that they would ever get out of here, nor could they believe that in a few hours' time they might be dead.

"What will be the first thing that you will do when you get home?" Hannah broke the silence.

"Home?... oh ... I shall go and look for Michael, of course ... Michael is a friend of mine," Judith said quietly. "What will you do?"

"I shall get a comfortable white feather bed, away from everybody, and sleep and sleep and sleep ... with eating in between - that is understood."

Hannah was a Czech woman of about forty, the oldest in the group, though very youthful in her appearance and ways.

Although there was a great difference in their ages, the two had become very friendly and a certain understanding passed between them. Somehow they faced the situation in a similar manner and shared the same kind of humour. Hannah was solid and real with her feet on the ground, her mind was sharp, though not in an objectionable way, and her words made sense.

"One day we will meet in Prague and make real pigs of ourselves," Hannah continued. "What would you like to have for your feast?"

A bright gleam illuminated Judith's eyes. It was good to talk of these things.

Unshed Tears

"First of all I will have a jug full of iced water, and then a whole goose and dumplings, mountains of them."

"Well, that's a date. From today in a year's time. Remember - the 30th of August, and then we shall go dancing and have real fun."

"I have never danced in my life, I wouldn't know what to do with myself."

"You will soon learn, it comes quite naturally to a girl - a waltz, for instance, you go: one, two, three, one, two, three: left-right-left, right-left-right, like this," she wriggled her feet on the ground humming the 'Blue Danube'.

Kitty, a young woman of about thirty, who sat nearby, watched for a while and with a sparkle triumphing over her clouded face, she joined in the well-known tune. One by one the girls caught on, until the air around them filled with the sound of this universal song. They moved and swayed their bodies and arms according to the rhythm, hope, pride, determination and merriment taking for a moment the place of the gloomy silence. This was much better than engaging in fearful brooding, and an air of relief crept over them. They sat and sang one song after another, always another girl giving the lead for the next one. Sometimes the Polish women sang their traditional tunes, sometimes the Czech ones theirs, the others listening. And then suddenly as if by their merriment they had willed it, the miracle happened.

Toward midday, in the greatest heat, a goods train came slowly rattling along the rails at the top of the camp road not far away from them. The song died on their lips, and a hundred and fifty pairs of eyes turned expectantly in its direction, following its course along the route.

Chapter 22

Was this it? Hearts began to beat faster in anticipation of the approaching minutes. Many girls jumped up invigorated, making a few steps forward, biting their lips and tongues, jumping on the spot. The train slowed down, jolted and stopped still. A wave of excitement surged through the crowd.

"Is this our train?"

"Do you think this could really be it?"

"We might get out of here after all!"

"I hope we shan't be disappointed."

"Out of here at last!.. maybe ..."

"Just imagine! Just imagine! This might be our train!"

"It looks as though it's us! What would an empty train do here?"

The cries came on top of each other and intermingled, everyone shouting her own, relieving the tenseness of her emotions.

Not far away something stirred, an air of busyness came toward them. Groups of Germans appeared on the horizon, bringing their harsh voices nearer. The atmosphere was humming with activity, something was going on. Then the huge gate opened, the officers looking very important greeted the guard, shouted something at him, and surrounded the restless group.

"Into fives! Into fives!"

Everything happened very quickly. The gate opened for them again, they marched up the camp road, in the opposite direction to the crematorium, toward the waiting train. Their bodies felt suddenly strong again, the thirst and the hunger were for the moment forgotten.

Before entering the train each of them was given half a loaf of bread, some liver sausage, and churns filled with camp coffee were pushed through the openings, up into the waggons. From other parts of Auschwitz groups of prisoners came to join the transport and the train soon filled up.

There were fifty girls, all Czech, in Judith's dark waggon. As the heavy, sliding doors were pushed together on the little Czech community, the girls fell into each other's arms, and with the first sign of motion they jubilantly said farewell to the place which would always stick in their memory as the camp reigned over by terror and death and crying out for revenge.

With the little enamel mugs which had been distributed to them a short while ago, they threw themselves on the slightly coloured, lukewarm liquid, and having satisfied their thirst, they arranged themselves along the four walls, enthusiastically disposing of a great part of their provisions. It was quite dark and stuffy inside that wooden box, where four long, square, barred windows were the only source of light and air, but nobody seemed bothered by it.

"Isn't it wonderful to travel so light, nothing to carry, nothing to worry about," commented Lilly, a blue-eyed girl of eighteen, lightheartedly.

"Oh, watch out, you spilled some nectar on my new travelling outfit," mocked Doris.

"I beg your pardon! Here, I'll ring for my maid, she will get it out for you. Meanwhile put on this pink quilted dressing gown of mine," said her neighbour.

"Can someone show me the way to the W.C. please?" came from one corner.

"It's quite simple really. Make three steps forward, turn to your right, walk five steps, turn twice around yourself, walk

Chapter 22

seven times around the coffee churns, look carefully and you can't miss it."

"Watch the chain, it's rather delicate."

"Don't scratch it, it's made of marble!"

Irenka, a fourteen-year-old girl who was there with her sister Dita and her mother, got up and peered out of the window.

"It's all gone," she said.

"I wonder where our men are," someone remarked feelingly.

A little silence fell over the group, and fifty pairs of eyes filled with thoughts.

"God knows ... they could be anywhere...."

"We only got married in the Ghetto," said Inka. She was a beautiful girl of twenty-three.

"And my girl, she was eleven, they snatched her away from me...."

"My boy of six, they took him away with the other children in the ghetto," remarked Kitty sadly. "I don't suppose I shall ever set eyes on him again."

"You never know, with the Germans anything is possible."

"I wanted to go with him, but they wouldn't let me."

A general conversation followed, in which the women related experiences from their lives, introducing their families to the others....

Then pretending to curl their hair and change into flimsy nightgowns, they settled down for the night. The floor was hard, but none found difficulty in falling asleep.

The next morning found their train shuffling through a beautiful countryside bathing in the sun, interspersed by pretty, clean villages, fields and forests. They all took a turn at the window to make sure that the normal world with its green trees, pretty flowers, people going about their business, really existed. With envy they watched the coloured houses with bright red roofs, clean curtains, well-kept gardens and little innocent children, neatly dressed, with thick slices of bread in their hands, waving at them, rather startled by seeing human faces in windows where cattle's heads ought to be.

Toward midday the train entered a forest. The smell of the pines, the fresh air, the song of birds, all spoke of nature at its best, and it all looked as if nothing had ever gone wrong.

XXIII

The forest stretched for miles, and it seemed as though the whole world was bedecked with trees. Having travelled like this for a while, somebody suddenly spied a building half hidden in the ground and camouflaged so as to look as if it were part of the forest. And then another one appeared, and another, and soon everyone realized that there was a whole town of them cunningly concealed from hostile eyes. Long pipes about fifteen feet from the ground connected one building with the other, letting forth humming sounds that filled the air. The trees, whose trunks had been made bare save for a cap of branches at the top, stood in straight lines, following the military pattern of their country.

"Must be some factories."

"It couldn't be anything else," the girls guessed, pushing their way to the little windows.

At about two o'clock the train slowed down and stopped. German guards who had accompanied them jumped from the train, shouted at each other from all sides, footsteps sounded along the gravel, and a little while later the sliding doors thundered open.

Unshed Tears

"Everyone out!"

"Into fives!"

The girls looked at each other incredulously, wondering what was wanted from them in the middle of the forest.

"Probably going to work in these underground boxes," one suggested.

"Most likely."

"Porter for my luggage," Judith whispered with sparkling eyes.

"Taxi!" said Hannah, raising her thumb.

Altogether there were a hundred of them marching along the track now, fifty Polish and fifty Czech women. The rest stayed on the train and were probably being taken to another part of Germany. Curiously the girls looked around them breathing in the fresh air, wondering where they were going to end up. After about ten minutes they turned to their right and found themselves on a concrete road leading down a gentle slope. It wasn't very long and at the end of it was a gate guarded by two soldiers. Behind it, inside a border of barbed wire, nestled a tiny camp consisting of several wooden huts.

"They must be taking us to a holiday camp to recover from Auschwitz," remarked Sonia.

"If that's where we are going to end up, we must be going to paradise - pine trees, colour, fresh air, no gas chamber, and even the German monsters seem more human after the Auschwitz parasites," said Doris.

"I believe we must have all gone batty ... paradise - my foot!" said Kitty indignantly, but not without a sparkle.

"One day I am going to write a book - 'The Jews in Paradise," grinned Judith.

Chapter 23

"You might all be talking too soon, for all we know these huts might be full of electric chairs."

"Thanks for cheering us up, it's highly appreciated."

"It's quicker than gas anyway."

The gate opened and they walked through it. A woman in an S.S. uniform counted them and placed herself in charge. The German guards exchanged a few sentences with her, said something that set them off laughing hysterically, clicked their boots, ejaculated "Heil Hitler," and made their way back to the train.

The concrete road continued for a while within the camp, before reaching the huts. On both sides of it, sun-tanned girls were busy felling trees, sawing wood, chopping blocks into small pieces and carrying the former to their appropriate place. On seeing the newcomers a wave of excitement came over them and the daring ones sped to the edge in order to satisfy their curiosity. The two parties managed to throw a few sentences at each other, and the air was a jumble of laconic information.

"Yes, we are Czechs too!"

"We have been here almost two months."

"No, it's not too bad!"

"We were formerly in the Ghetto, Poland, Lodz."

"Yes, there are some Polish girls with us."

"We have a few Hungarians here!"

"There is no electric chair here!"

"Do you get any food?"

"The others will be coming home at seven, we shall be free to talk then."

"See you in the evening!"

There were nine huts altogether. They were painted green

with green shutters to fit within the pattern of the forest world. Six of these huts were inhabited by the inmates, two served as bathrooms, and one at the very front by the side of a small square as a canteen.

It was in the square that the girls spent the next half hour. They were given a blanket each and a piece of bread with jam. After that they were shown to their new homes. The huts were divided up into rooms and each of these housed about twenty women. There were bunks and a table and a stove in each room and everything was spotlessly clean.

Judith and Hannah shared the top part of a bunk and they soon made themselves at home there. Around them and underneath them the excited chatter of the Czech girls all revolved around the same subject - the new camp and what it promised. They were eager to speak with the 'old' Czech girls who were bound to have some useful information about friends and relatives for them. They even hoped they would find friends among them.

The rest of the afternoon was their own. Judith and Hannah walked out of the hut into the open. They went around exploring the surroundings, exchanging a few remarks with other girls whose curiosity brought them out for the same reason. It felt good to walk on the soft pine needles, to hear the birds sing, to sense nature at its best, after having spent three years in a terrifyingly ugly, gloomy, grey slum. There were patches of forest between the huts and behind them, on which the girls could lie about and rest after work or on Sunday afternoons. The latrines were behind the huts, near the barbed wires, which were guarded day and night by elderly soldiers. There was a road outside the camp which was for public use for

Chapter 23

the Germans, and jeeps, tanks and lorries made their way along it quite frequently. A constant hum echoed through the forest - the hidden factories at work.

Between six and seven o'clock groups of girls were arriving in the camp. Dirty from work they make their way to the shower baths, then with saucepans or tin plates in their hands lined up for the evening meal. Seeing strangers about, they looked around searching for friends or relations, at the same time keeping an eye on the Jewish servers, making sure that no differences were made between single inmates.

The dining room was a huge hall with long tables and benches. The girls, however, preferred to take their food into the open or to their rooms. From time to time people recognised each other and arranged to meet after supper outside a certain hut. The newcomers were told to join in the queue and those who had no dish were given an empty meat-tin by one of the German supervisors. They had about six medium sized potatoes in their jackets, and a slice of garlic sausage made of horse meat.

They were free until eight thirty. They settled down in groups under the trees and talked. There was much they had to say to each other, especially if they had friends in common of whom they could give information. Even the sad news did not upset the girls very much as their whole attitude to life was such as to take all these things in their stride. Their only aim was to survive themselves. They found out that they were in Silesia, not very far from Breslau. There were many men's camps strewn all over the forest, French, Italian, Dutch, Polish, Russian and others, but theirs was the only Jewish one. The girls went out in groups to work in quarries, dig roads, fell trees, lay bricks, work in factories and do any work that was required of them. They quite often came in touch with prisoners from other camps who passed on information to them and at times gave them a piece of bread or a present they had received in a parcel which their people at home were allowed to send them. Only the Jewish camp was not permitted to communicate with the outer world. All the girls who had arrived here two months ago came via Terezienstadt and the mixed camp in Auschwitz. They were the lucky ones who got out just before their six months of waiting for the gas chamber was up.

Judith learned that her grandparents had died in Terezienstadt and Eva, her best friend went to the gas chamber. Two or three of her former school-mates died in one camp or another, overcome by illness or exhaustion.

At half past eight the whistle sounded for roll-call. The German camp leader came out to count them, passed several rules onto the new inmates, gave a few words of warning and dismissed them. By nine o'clock the place lay in absolute silence.

* * * * *

It was four o' clock in the morning when Inge, one of the German girls, roused the prisoners from their sleep. She came like a storm, opening every door, blowing her whistle and shouting, "Aufstehen!"

At half past four they all stood on parade in the little square. The air was very chilly, and although it was officially forbidden, the girls had draped their blankets over their shoulders to keep themselves warm. Somehow they sensed when they could afford to disobey a rule. Perhaps there was just a fraction of humanity left in the women who had all that power over them or maybe they knew that their end wasn't far off, and it was wiser not to inflict unnecessary cruelties over their charges. It was only from time to time when one of them was in a specially ill-humour that she sent everybody back to put her blanket on her bed.

They stood in groups according to their work.

At about five o'clock the various German overseers who were to escort them arrived and counted them. There were two to each group of about thirty. One by one they were led off in different directions, having first received some camp coffee and a slice of bread.

Judith and twenty-nine other Czech girls found themselves under the supervision of two young German women in uniform whose names were Anne and Erika. They were both blonde, vivacious and over-confident. In matter of fact they were quite cheap little things, thoroughly enjoying the power that had been bestowed upon them. They flirted with the guards at the gate and were supposed to have been seen leaving their huts, on the outskirt of the camp, early in the morning.

The journey was a long one and lasted for over an hour. They marched in fives along the concrete roads through the forest, passing most weird buildings. There was something uncanny about the place with its underground city of ammunition factories, bomb-shells lying in ditches, trees keeping the light out, and other prisoners passing them silently on their way to work. A quiet, organised business ruled over the miles of carefully guarded land.

Unshed Tears

They worked from seven till five in the afternoon. There was a bare hill on top of which was situated a brick factory. They were given spades and hoes with which to dig the rich, red clay, shovel it on to little wagons, and wheel the latter on narrow rails into the building. It was hard labour, for sticky clay is more difficult to dig up than ordinary earth, and they were not used to this kind of work. There were no trees about, and by midday the sun was ruthlessly pouring its rays upon them. From the hill they could see into the valley where the little town of Kristianstadt was situated. They were fascinated by the clean houses, with pretty curtains and coloured roofs. There were no wires between them and the town, and that brought about a feeling of being once again part of the normal world. It was a good feeling, and the haunted look in their eyes that had accompanied them all through the Ghetto and Auschwitz had changed into one of relief, envy and hope.

By the evening their hands were badly blistered, and tired as they were, they had to march all the way back. One thing urged them on - their evening meal. Little as it was, they were sure of getting it.

* * * * *

Judith got hold of some paper and a pencil. She found it in the canteen cellar when she went to exchange her spade. It lay on the floor by the turnips and potatoes, left there by one of the staff who had been taking stock. She paused for a while, her eyes sweeping the piles of vegetables, her brain working frantically. No, there was nothing she could do just then, with only a frock on, and the overseer waiting for her up there in the

Chapter 23

yard, but she knew she would be back there one day. Then she spotted the sheets of paper and the pencil, and an idea struck her. Here was an opportunity to exercise her mind which she believed was going stale, and at the same time an account of the happenings in camp might stand her in good stead one day. Cheered by the novelty of the idea, she screwed up a pile of papers and the pencil and hid them under a sack near the exit door, in case she was searched on reporting back. A little while later when the girls drank their coffee and the supervisor's attention was turned on a group of girls having a quarrel, Judith slid back and recovered her treasure.

For the rest of the day she worked on her idea of writing a diary. While digging the clay, her mind was preoccupied with working out codes that would be impossible for anyone to decipher. She made up signs that stood for words and people, thought of words which she could use instead of others in order to bluff uninvited readers. When she came home in the evening she made a slit in the side of the straw mattress and squeezed the newly acquired property into it. She shared her secret with Hannah, though the code she did not dare share with anybody.

XXIV

11th September 1944.

The best news for a long time. Germany has been invaded at last. The Allies are on German soil! It is hard to believe but Francois who works at the brick factory has a reliable source of information, and anyway, in every rumour there is always a shadow of truth. Perhaps it won't last so long any more after all. When we had 'coffee' at work we pretended it was wine and drank a toast to the speedy ruin of the 'Great Empire'. Erika came over asking us what we were doing, and after a slight pause Doris proclaimed that it was her wedding anniversary. She looked at us suspiciously but there was nothing she could do. We spent the rest of our midday half hour's relaxation calculating the unpleasant feeling that must be creeping over the Germans, and forecasting their reaction and behaviour following future events.

Kitty suggested that when the great moment arrives, the Germans, men and women alike, will go down on their knees and beg us to save them and put in a good word for them. I believe she was exaggerating a little. I bet they don't feel too good inside themselves though, and I wouldn't change with any of them even if it meant roast pork and fried potatoes and no work, every day. We specially enjoyed thinking of the time when the Germans will do all the donkey work and we will drive them with a whip. I wonder where I shall be in a year's time.

16th September 1944.

Russian armies reached Czechoslovakian border and Warsaw was taken at last. This means that the Allies are coming towards us from all sides. Somehow it is the general opinion that the Germans won't destroy us all at the last minute. They will be too eager to show how well they treated us. From today onwards we shall be getting soup at work every day - that certainly means something. If they gave us proper clothes to save us freezing in the morning and evening, things wouldn't be so bad. However, the wonderful air here and our hopes compensate for most discomforts.

25th September 1944.

Life here is in full swing now. Most of the girls have established themselves somewhere, and come back from work with small parcels of food, or little objects like combs, pen-knives, cups, pencils, etc. Every night Sonia brings home a thick sandwich of coarse bread and cheese, weighing about 20 decagrams. Dita also brings food back regularly and shares some of it with her sister and mother. Most of it though she eats herself. Sonia works in a crane by the lake with a French boy. They are alone the whole day while the rest of the party work further away in the forest. Dita works in the forest. There are a lot of Italians around there, and some other girls find opportunities to be alone with the prisoners of war too.

Chapter 24

12th October 1944.

Today all pregnant women were told to report to the camp hospital. By the evening they were gone. God knows what the Germans have done to them, probably murdered them. Paula, who is expecting her baby in February, said nothing good would come of it and didn't report. I think she was wise, though how long she will be able to conceal it, nobody knows. We told her she mustn't walk about the camp alone, at roll call to stand at the back and at work to try to be surrounded by a group of other girls. Anyway, we all have tummies like tanks from all the water we are drinking and with a blanket wrapped cleverly around her, she might get away with it.

It is amazing how the body can adjust itself, if necessary. The other day we got soaked wet at work during a thunder storm, we had to go on working, and so the clothes dried on us. However none of us suffered for it. At home we would have had pneumonia twice over.

4th November 1944.

Our hair which has grown quite a bit, looks a shocking mess. We are like boys who need a haircut. We have made scarves and sleeves out of our blankets which have shrunk to such a size that we wish we could take our legs off for the night and place them level with our bodies. However as it is, we have to screw up into a knot in order to fit under the piece of rag that is left. Luckily we manage to gather some wood in the evenings and then we light a huge fire in our stove. It gets the room blissfully warm. The air-raids are continuing, and we take it in turns to sit under the hole in the roof of the shed at work, for we all hate it. It gives us a feeling that if a bomb came, it could come right through at the person underneath. The Germans run to a bunker somewhere away, and we enjoy an hour or so of good fun.

10th November 1944.

Rejoice! We received coats today. We had some fun watching each other putting them on for the first time. I have a very posh astrakhan one. It is very long, but beautifully warm. I suppose I look sixty in it, but who cares? The days are getting very chilly and the half frozen ground is difficult to dig. Yesterday I worked for a day in the sand quarry. Why, I don't know, but it was a change. It is a huge place and men and women of many nationalities work there together. There I learned that all Germans between sixteen and sixty had been mobilized for the 'Home Army'. They must be in a really sticky position to do that. The Russians have invaded Norway and the eastern part of Czechoslovakia. Things are certainly moving.

21st November 1944.

About eleven o'clock this morning we heard a tremendous explosion. There is a rumour that it was sabotage and that the French were responsible for it. Good for them! A bomb factory blew up. It was like an earthquake, the whole ground shook and for a few seconds we didn't know what was happening. I must admit I was rather frightened, so were others. When it all subsided, we guessed and rejoiced.

6th December 1944.

Today is St. Nicholas Day. Last night we had a party in Block 1. We sang and told jokes and some of the girls gave little performances. There were skits on the Germans which were very funny, especially as one of the guards was present and couldn't understand a word. Once he asked what the joke

Chapter 24

was and Janka who was in that particular spot quickly made up a story which made him rock with laughter and put us in an even better mood. There is something satisfying in fooling a German.

1st January 1945.

It is the New Year. Will this one be different from the others? Every year we hope for the same. I spent Christmas at the camp hospital. The mysterious epidemic of what seem like epileptic fits had caught up with me at last. It's revolting and I thought I would never get it. Rotten luck that it should happen just at Christmas when we had time off from work anyway. I had about ten fits in two days.

5th January 1945.

We have been working in a factory for the last few days. At present we are on night shift working from 10 p.m. till 6 a.m. With the snow making walking difficult for us, the journey there takes us almost two hours. There is something sinister about this forest by night with the humming of the factories disturbing the dark stillness. It is beautifully warm inside. We are making little hand grenades. It is the best job we have had so far for we work together with French and Dutch boys and there is a very good atmosphere about. The boys let us into their secrets of sabotage, telling us how best we could take our part in it. There is something very satisfying in that. Apparently those who mix the gunpowder use the wrong proportion whenever they are not being supervised. I myself sit under a turntable with a Dutch boy. Our job is to unscrew the little bombs when they are filled with the molten stuff. Our intuition tells us when we can afford to take them off not quite filled. Every time means an ally's life saved. We have to be on the alert all the time, though fortunately for us, there is only one German foreman and two other men about the whole factory. There are at least a hundred of us.

6th January 1945.

The boys at the factory have told us about the advances of the Allied forces. The Russians are steadily moving westward and are nearing Austria. They are also not so very far from us. Perhaps they will come quickly and the Germans won't have time to evacuate us. We hardly talk of anything else these days. Also the Western armies are proceeding in France. It looks as though things are really moving. Somehow I can't imagine that we shall really be free.

10th January 1945.

For several days now our food ration has been much smaller. The atmosphere around here has become quite tense. We can sense something in the air. Yesterday we heard a few explosions very far away. They sounded like machine guns. We were not working at the factory yesterday and today. We only cleaned the tools and the machines. We were not told why, but we believe that the transport can't get through because of damaged rails. That's why we haven't had any potatoes lately. We are all full of hope. Maybe this time it is it?

12th January 1945.

For the last two or three days we have spent our time shovelling the snow in our camp, (a useless job because it only falls again), and standing roll-call. This morning we stood Appell in the dining hall, when suddenly we heard a terrific explosion. The floor rocked beneath us for quite a few seconds and the pressure of the air almost deafened us. Glass shattered around us. The girls began to scream and made for the door.

Chapter 24

There was a few minutes of panic when people were trampled on, and everybody only thought of herself. Outside it was better, especially as the tremor had by then subsided. The windows in our huts were broken and one roof was damaged. Later in the day when a group of girls came from work we heard that some French boys had blown up a factory. They had timed it so that it would happen between the two shifts, but as bad luck would have it one group was delayed and the other one came on a little early and the boys from both shifts died. It is very tragic and we all feel very sorry for them.

14th January 1945.

We believe the Russians are approaching for we can hear shooting from time to time. All transport is blockaded and no goods can reach us. We hardly get anything to eat, but it might all be a matter of days, for if there are no trains they won't be able to take us away from here. The Germans behave queerly, I am sure they don't feel so fine, or are we imagining it? Yesterday when we were clearing the snow from the camp, I deliberately loosened the spade and asked whether I could go to the cellar to exchange it. Nobody was there so I quickly grabbed some potatoes and filled my coat lining with them. I had previously unpicked some of the stitches on the side of the lining in preparation for it. Anne must have suspected something for she inspected my pockets and felt over my body. I looked very unworried and innocent. I wonder, though, what she would have done if she had felt the bottom of my coat. In the evening we roasted the potatoes in the ashes and had a good feast. I don't feel at all guilty having stolen from the Germans.

16th January 1945.

The shooting is approaching. What is going to happen in

the near future? Is it really possible that we shall be free in a few days' time? Something is certainly going on, the air is full of it. We are all on tenterhooks, aware of every change in the situation. We sing a lot and make plans, every other sentence starts with "if".

XXV

Judith sat on top of her bunk, making a pair of slacks out of her blanket. Hannah sat next to her doing likewise. The room was filled with activity, everyone was getting ready for something, something unknown that lay in front of them. Now that the moment they had been waiting for so long was rapidly approaching, doubts crept into their minds and mingled with the expectant joy.

Last night a cart pulled by horses and laden with feather beds, boxes, utensils, pieces of furniture and a family including a bunch of blonde children came rattling along the forest road by the side of the camp. The girls spotted it as they were returning to their huts from roll call. Soon afterwards came another one and another, and before long the road became alive with a stream of moving homes. The women who sat at the front or walked beside the horses wore long peasant skirts, their heads and shoulders were wrapped in huge woollen shawls. The only men present were the old grandfathers, often wrinkled and unsmiling, looking expressionlessly in front of themselves. Most of the children were nestled in the huge feather beds, their heads covered with scarves or German peaked caps, which also protected their ears. They appeared unworried, regarding the situation as an adventure. They had fled before the Russians, hoping to save their necks in western Germany.

The prisoners eyed them with curiosity and their minds speculated. Things were certainly happening. There was something satisfying about the whole situation for it was obvious that for the Germans this was the beginning of the end. On the other hand a new way of transportation suddenly presented itself to them and they realised that a train wasn't the only means by which they could be moved before the liberators arrived. There were still two feet.

The whole night the air under their windows was alive with the clatter of pots and pans, a confusion of voices and the thumping of footsteps in the snow. It was a feast for the girls' eyes to see the people who were partly responsible for their suffering, homeless, uncomfortable and afraid.

"Look, the Germans, the big, great, powerful Germans are running. Isn't it a wonderful sight!"

"All the same, they are still free to do what they like, but I wouldn't change with them for anything."

"Nor would I."

"You don't know yet what's waiting for you."

"Never mind, it can't last very long."

"They might shoot us all at the last minute, you never know."

"They haven't got a bullet to spare, besides, somehow I feel they wouldn't do a thing like that just now."

"Perhaps tomorrow, perhaps the day after ..."

That was last night. This morning just after roll call a lorry arrived and with a lot of noise the German girl supervisors clambered into it, full of laughter and spirit. They were going home, convinced that their Führer wouldn't let them down and this was just part of his scheme. For ten minutes exclamations of "Heil Hitler" and boisterous shouts of farewell rang through the air, and then the lorry was off leaving behind the waving old soldiers and pleasantly excited prisoners. This certainly was a step forward. Would the men follow suit?

That was the end of working parties, except for three dozen girls, who were picked to do a job that set them all guessing. Everybody's coat was to be handed in in the dining hall, and the chosen girls under the men's supervision cut squares out of their frocks and replaced them with odd bits of conspicuous material. It was then that the rest of the inmates began to prepare for the worst, making slacks or odd bits of garments out of their blankets, leaving huge triangles for shawls to cover their heads or shoulders, at the same time concealing the telltale patch.

The caravan of carts had no end. Day and night they rattled past the camp, becoming almost part of the scenery. The thunderstorm from the east was coming nearer and nearer, and with every explosion the hearts of the prisoners gave a joyous leap.

"They are coming, they might be here any day," was on everyone's mind; and then one morning this dream was over.

"Appell! Into fives! Appell!"

A group of unknown German guards stood in front of the canteen. The prisoners were counted and then it was "Left turn!"

The gate of the camp opened and a few hundred women

found themselves on the road, alongside the stream of wooden carts. The new guards kept watch over them, and the children, muffled up on top of the furniture and feather beds, eyed them with great curiosity. It all happened so quickly that they had had hardly time to sum up the situation.

"We should have known better than to dream of liberation," some said bitterly.

"I shall never anticipate anything good. At least I won't be disappointed," said Judith.

"That's the best thing, when it comes, we shall know soon enough," agreed Sonia.

"You know, it doesn't feel bad to leave behind a place surrounded by barbed wire and march along a public road together with people who are not prisoners."

"There certainly is something in it. Anyway the Russians might catch up with us. On the other hand we are bound to bump into some of the Allied forces at one time or another. They are closing up upon us from all sides."

Gradually they managed to talk themselves into a good mood again. They were lucky to have thought of bringing all their belongings to roll call; at least they were fairly reasonably dressed in their self-made garments.

They passed towns and villages, like the others who were going the same way. They were all heading west - some aimlessly toward their destruction, others towards freedom. Wherever they went, the day would come when there would be nowhere to turn.

"Nobody will ever split their families and put them into gas chambers," the girls remarked resentfully.

"Perhaps it is better that way. One race with such

Chapter 25

tendencies in the world is more than enough," answered Hannah.

They sang once again. "We don't care where we go, as long as we can see the world." They pretended not to envy the German refugees who were cutting thick slices of bread off huge loaves and, topping them with jam, feeding their children and themselves on it.

In villages huge open air canteens provided the German refugees with hot soup and potatoes. The market squares were bordered with rows of people lining up with their pots to get their share of the deliciously smelling food. A lot of fuss was made of them and all the inhabitants seemed to have been mobilized into this welfare work. Homes and barns were open to those who wished to stay the night.

The optimism of the girls was soon overpowered by fatigue and hunger. The snow stuck to their wooden soles, making walking a torture. Still, they had to walk and walk, there was nothing else left to do, for inability to carry on was rewarded by a fatal shot. At least the exercise kept them warm. In inhabited parts, the thumping of their clogs brought curious eyes to the windows and doorsteps. Their weird appearance filled the onlookers' faces with an even weirder expression.

Their suffering began to reflect in their faces. A look of misery entered their eyes. In addition to the obvious discomforts new tortures cropped up and took possession of one or two of them. A nail protruding through the sole had dug a hole in Judith's heel, and as she was making an effort to keep her foot in a special position so as to counteract the pain, blisters sprang up where the canvas of her clog rubbed against the upper part of her heel. How long would she be able to endure that? An idea of taking her shoes off altogether and walking barefoot flashed through her mind, but immediately she dismissed it as impracticable. Her feet would soon get frozen and what then? One woman had already been shot because she couldn't keep up, and she wouldn't risk that happening to her, not just now when all the good things were so near.

Late in the evening their faces grew grim, the last spark had gone out of them. Was there any hope of food or a warming drink, for rest and shelter, or were they going to plod on through the night and the next day and the next until one after another would drop exhausted, unable to endure another moment of it? Even a well nourished person equipped for the ordeal couldn't go on marching without rest and sleep.

The villages they passed were full of German refugees, and although the guards who were longing for a rest themselves had attempted several times to put the women up somewhere, the answer was always the same - "There isn't enough room for our own people," or "We are full up." It wasn't until after midnight that they sighted a huge open shed storing straw in the middle of a snow-bedecked field. They turned from the road and headed towards it.

They buried themselves in the straw and found it miraculously warm. They slept in the open air unaffected by the frost around them. It was wonderful to relax, stretch one's legs and forget about tomorrow. At the moment only the present and the distant future existed and as the blanket of sleep descended upon them a flicker of a smile appeared on many a face.

At six o'clock the next morning they were on their feet

again. In the next village they received hot coffee and a few cold potatoes in their jackets.

The day wasn't very different from the previous one. It was all marching, stumbling, shaking the snow off their wooden soles, limping and trudging on speechlessly. A strange power held them and made them move forward step by step. Perhaps it was the wonderful scenery, the snow-clad forests, the clear air and hope that worked miracles; especially hope - the mighty ruler who touched the mass but deserted the few. Several women gave up and were shot; the others clenched their teeth and marched on, dragging their feet behind them.

As the hours went by, the procession spread into a long stream of about half a mile long with one guard at the front and one at the rear. They walked through lanes in the fields while the German refugees took the shortest road; sometimes they met in the villages or towns.

It was on the outskirts of one of the little towns that a group of small German boys gathered by the roadside and watched them open-mouthed. Incited by an older member of the gang they broke some rods off a nearby bush and followed the procession, crying, "Jewesses, Jewesses, dirty Jewesses," they swished their weapons among the crowd. One blow struck Hannah on her back, and Judith, filled with rage at the impudence of the little brats, stopped one, looked him straight in the eyes and asked, "How would you like someone beating your mother? You wouldn't like to watch that, would you?"

The boy hesitated for a while and his blue eyes became thoughtful. He was only very little and his mind was still elastic. The rest of the gang came crowding around him and for a moment stood in silence, looking at each other. Then suddenly as if woken up from a dream one boy shouted, "They are not people, they are Jewesses."

Provoked by the war cry, the boys picked up some snow, made hard balls and aimed at the passing ranks. There was only one thing the women could do. Silently they prayed for revenge.

Toward midday Judith was looking sternly in front of herself, her teeth clenched, her eyes hard. She was on the verge of collapse. The nail in her shoe had worked its way through the pad made of material she had torn off her scarf and carefully placed under her heel, and dug deeper into the bleeding wound. The blisters had burst, leaving the raw flesh exposed to some more rubbing. In vain did she try twisting her foot in such a way as to ease the pain. Each step was a new agony which weakened her whole person - body and mind. As time went by and there seemed to be no chance of a rest, she kept on repeating desperately to herself, "I can't go on, I really can't go on any more." And then with a last flicker of courage would whisper as in protest, "No, you mustn't give in now, you mustn't, you mustn't, you mustn't! The end of the war is approaching and you want to be here to see it." For hours the two voices inside her went on fighting each other, whilst as though in a trance, only half conscious, she dragged herself along with the crowd. And then when it seemed that courage had at last submitted to the strength of its opponent, a third strange voice emerged from the depth of Judith's being, commanding "Judith, don't think, close your mind, kill all your thoughts, but walk, for goodness' sake walk, walk, walk!"

Miraculously her legs obeyed. She suddenly discovered a new sensation, the one of the separation of the mind from the

Chapter 25

body, from the senses. Everything inside her concentrated on one thing - on the movement of her legs.

So the hours went by and darkness embraced the ghostly procession. They came to a crossroads; a signpost indicated that it was seven kilometres to the next village.

"If they will put us up, we shall stay the night there," said one of the guards.

Some faces brightened at the prospect of it, for everyone suffered, some more and some less. They were all starved, weak and overstrained.

"Seven kilometres," said Judith to Hannah who dragged herself along beside her, "is as much as I can manage, and not a step more."

"Me too."

Seeing the end of the day's torture gave her a new incentive to carry on.

Five kilometres ... three kilometres ... one kilometre....

The silhouettes of houses appeared in front of them. From another road German refugees were pouring into the village. Anxiety spread over the marching ranks.

"That's that," someone said, and it was just that.

The guard who went to investigate came back with the news that there was another village only three kilometres away. Judith felt like crying with desperation, but the tears did not come.

"One hour, and the whole night is yours," she persuaded herself. And again trying to kill her senses, she concentrated on her legs. Indescribable suffering glared out of everybody's eyes. Once more the silhouettes of houses appeared in front of them and hope and fear mingled in their minds. Half dead they arrived at the outskirts of the place. There was a church with a tall spire surrounded by a few dozen little buildings. This time the other guard went to investigate. With eager eyes they waited for his return. After about a quarter of an hour they saw him coming back and their hearts leapt with anticipation. Then he waved his hand and shrugged his shoulders and their spirits sank again. He pointed beyond the field and his fingers indicated 'nine'.

"Nine more kilometres," breathed out Judith, "and after that another five and another six and another ten!" Every nerve trembled with anger and desperation.

"Nine kilometres, that's impossible!" They exchanged glances, silently. Several women sat down in the snow and refused to move. The guards gave them a warning. Some made a new, superhuman effort, the others reconciled themselves to their fate and several even smiled as the thought of final peace entered their minds.

Four shots echoed in the dark air, four women fell to the ground, and the procession set on its way again.

Eleven o'clock found the stream of stumbling people, stretched disorderly along half a mile of road. Even the two guards who were not happy themselves made allowances for the unfavourable conditions. Their harsh, threatening voices died down. Calmly they marched in front and behind the prisoners. A quiet call pierced the air, "Hannah."

"Yes, Judith?" came from slightly behind her.

Judith slowed down and waited for Hannah to come in line with her. She pointed in the direction of the field on her right and whispered, "See that stack of straw over there?"

"Yes." Hannah threw Judith a curious glance.

Chapter 25

"Listen. I can't carry on any more. I am going to run away and hide in there," she said in an exhausted trembling voice.

"But ... but what if one of them catches you?"

"I am going to risk it. I would have to give up anyway. I just can't go on any more." She was breathing heavily.

For a while Hannah was silent, her mind at work, her eyes calculating.

"What will you do then?"

"Get this darned shoe off and sleep. Tomorrow is another day, then I shall think about the rest. I might pretend I am a German refugee," and simulating the typical German accent she spoke. "Those Russians have destroyed my home, but our Führer will show them, yet."

Hannah smiled and suddenly decided.

"Judith, I am coming with you."

"Good. We must move toward the beginning of the transport, and disappear when the front guard isn't looking and the one at the back is too far away to see us."

They were both quietly excited.

"But what about the others?"

"They will be all right. They won't give us away. We must dive into the ditch and bury ourselves in the snow. All right?"

"O.K.... Judith, can you imagine that perhaps in a little while we shall be free, for the first time after over three years ... no guard, no anything?"

She pressed her hand. They looked at each other with a glance of enthusiasm and wormed their way down toward the front of the rank.

Trying to hide their burning emotions they looked around for the last time. Everything seemed in order. They gave each other an approving look. A quiet, "Now!" and two figures separated themselves from the rest. Three seconds later they were on their backs frantically covering themselves with snow which was quite hard. Several heads turned round in amazement, there was a slight commotion among the immediate crowd, and then everything was as before.

Motionlessly they listened to the thumping of the clogs as the procession made its way along the snow-covered road. There seemed to be no end to it. After what seemed an eternity they could at last hear a steady step accompanied by the creaking of leather riding boots. They held their breath. The step was coming nearer and nearer - and passed them.

The familiar sound of a few hundred women marching along the snow-covered road was subsiding in the distance, till at last it died down completely. Only then something stirred in the ditch and two faces looked at each other. As if suddenly remembering their situation they glanced around them carefully, but everything was still. They began to free themselves from the cold snow that was starting to melt on their warm bodies. Sitting up and listening to the silence around, Judith breathed out, "We are free."

"We are free," Hannah repeated after her.

They agreed to crawl to the stack of straw which was about a hundred yards away. The snow was hard enough not to leave obvious marks on it.

Making herself a comfortable seat from straw, Judith washed her wound with clean snow dug from underneath the surface and bandaged her foot with a piece of her dress.

"Somehow I still can't imagine it. No wires, no guards, no ugliness," she was saying.

Chapter 25

Then they buried themselves blissfully in the straw. It was warm and comfortable. They stretched their legs and a wonderful feeling of relaxation spread over their bodies and reflected in their faces.

"Do you realize what we have done?" Hannah spoke suddenly and a spark of laughter entered her eyes.

"Yes, I do, and I am enjoying every minute of it," Judith said, with mischief in her voice.

"So am I, except that I could do with a big meal."

"Me too."

After that they were quiet, their minds trying to comprehend the full meaning of the situation. Appreciating every second of this delightful moment, they fell asleep.

XXVI

"I say, if we had something to eat we could stay here until the end of the war," suggested Judith after they had had a good look all around. It was daylight now but they had no idea of the time. There was no sign of civilization anywhere.

"How would you know that it's the end of the war anyway?"

"I guess you are right. I think we ought to stay here until dusk though, and hide our untrained countenances under the blanket of darkness, don't you think?"

"Yes, I suppose that's the only thing we can do. Looking like scarecrows as we do they would detect us from behind that mountain over there," she chuckled.

"And what then, when the time comes?"

"Food!"

"We shall have to think it all out very carefully and predict the various snags, so that we are prepared for any circumstance."

"We'd better start talking in German now and get really used to it."

"And practise our phrases and expressions to make them appear convincing," and Judith put on the most pitiful grimace she could muster. "We are poor refugees from Grünberg and we ..."

"You won't find it so funny when you are confronted with the situation; just you wait -" threatened Hannah.

"I hope I won't get the giggles."

"Giggles, did you say? I hope you won't be paralyzed with fear, your teeth chattering, your chin trembling, your knees giving way ... giggles! Ha!"

"I am going to be very bold, as if nothing was wrong; you'll see. It's the only way. You mustn't show a flicker of fear. I am going to live it all," Judith said determinedly.

"That's true, we shall have to live it, we shall have to convince ourselves that we are German refugees from ... from ..."

"What's wrong with Grünberg?"

"I suppose it's all right.... We are German refugees from Grünberg...."

"You could be my mother and I your daughter."

"Müller is our name."

"O.K. Müller.... I am Gretchen Müller and you are my mother and we have fled before the Russians and ... and ..."

"We burnt our house so that they shouldn't get it and we forgot our documents were there."

"Well done. My father was killed in action ... he loved the Führer so much, he must have been proud to give his life for him."

"Our family is scattered all over the country, we don't know where they are.... I say, I hope we don't bump into anybody who is from Grünberg - anyway if we do we'd better say we come from Kristianstadt, one of those cottages in the fields."

Chapter 26

"And how is it that we possess nothing at all - a coat, a rucksack - nothing?"

"Oh, why don't we?..." hesitated Hannah.

"I know. We didn't burn our house, but we went away for the day to a neighbouring town, say Neusalz, because an aunt of yours was dying, an old woman you know. When we were coming home, we were advised to flee as quickly as we could, to save our skins, for the Russians had made a sudden quick advance. It was either our possessions, or our lives, we chose the latter," Judith explained, grimly.

"That should do us for a start. All we have to do is to make ourselves believe that we really are those characters, keep on talking in German and use our brains all the time. Anyway, things always turn out different from what one expects, so it's no good planning too much ahead. Just be on your guard, always. Use your eyes, use your ears, your imagination, everything, and keep on living your part, so that you yourself are convinced of being Gretchen Müller."

"Yes, mother."

"When it gets dark, we'll join the stream of refugees going into the village we came from last night. Meanwhile I think we could do with some more sleep."

★ ★ ★ ★ ★

As darkness began to descend upon the vast countryside, huge snowflakes came fluttering down from the evening sky and settled upon the straw stack.

"I think that's our signal. Let's go," said Hannah.

The two got up cautiously, rid themselves of the bits of

straw that clung to their clothes and tied their scarves so as to conceal the treacherous patch on their back. Judith had squeezed her bandaged foot into the shoe and found walking rather difficult. Both were weak and hungry but full of zest and the anticipation of coming events.

"Come on, we must walk as if there was nothing wrong. Once we get across this open field the worst will be over," speculated Hannah. "You see, we come from that village, this field is ours and we are going home. Just say that to yourself. Get it?"

They straightened their backs, lifted their chins and with self-confident strides set out.

Nobody crossed their path. They walked for a while along the road on which they had come yesterday and then turned left in the direction of the oncoming stream of Germans. Unnoticed they added themselves to the crowd walking unconcernedly along with them.

They concentrated on their rôles, adapting themselves to the atmosphere. They watched and listened, making mental notes on anything that might stand them in good stead. Their faces took on the look of the people around them, pitiful, sad, uncertain of the future, yet undefeated. It wasn't all lost yet, it couldn't be, their Führer knew what he was doing. Judith was surprised how easy this game of make-believe was, and had anybody tried to convince her that she was not Gretchen Müller, she would have felt hurt.

Most of the refugees were on carts, or were attached to one of them. A certain bustle and excitement mixed with a kind of monotony was ever present. As they walked on the edge of the road side by side a cart overtook them and an old man, filled

Chapter 26

with pity at the sight of the two weary figures, shouted down at them, "Want a lift?"

"Oh, that is very kind of you, sir. Thanks a lot," they said humbly, approaching the vehicle.

He beckoned them to sit at the back. They gratefully accepted this offer. As they sat there, their feet dangling to and fro, they laughed inwardly. On the outskirts of the village they thanked the old man once more and separated themselves from the crowd.

The village lay still in the darkness except for the main road along which the caravan of carts was making its way forward. The villagers had become accustomed to it and took no more notice of this mass migration; only here and there they wondered when their turn would come.

Judith and Hannah walked expectantly through the deserted, irregular streets. Their steps were slow, their eyes were taking in every detail of this quaint little place. Each house and cottage was different. They were all pretty, painted in shades of blue, green, yellow and pink with bright red roofs, now covered with a blanket of snow. They were all blacked out, but the clatter of dishes, the delicious smell escaping from the kitchens, here and there music from a wireless, told of life inside.

"Real houses, Hannah," Judith said emphatically, her eyes staring at the windows, her mind making them see through the locked shutters into the bright, warm, and cosy interiors.

"No bunks and suitcases, but normal furniture, a fire, soft beds, chairs, a table set for supper, a real kitchen ..."

With longing eyes they set their imagination to work.

They had planned to go into a house and see what could be

got out of it anyway, but now that they were within arm's length of it, the thought of sitting at a table in a warm, pretty room and eating to one's capacity, filled them with a desire to carry out their scheme more irresistably than ever before. At the same time they found that when it came to actually knocking at the door and reciting the rehearsed lines, it wasn't as simple as they had believed it to be.

"It really is a bloody cheek on our part to do this ... here we are, dirty Jewesses; and there the Germans, and we, going straight into their house."

They wandered around examining one house after another trying to visualise the characters behind their walls. There was nothing to go by. Then suddenly without any waiting Judith took a deep breath, made a few determined steps toward the little house on the left, and knocked at the door.

There was no way back, they had to face what was coming. Their faces and poise were set, their brains were wide awake. As she stood on the threshold Judith became aware of several voices, mainly men's, involved in a lively discussion. With a few gestures she let Hannah know about it, and then she heard footsteps approaching the door. Expectation took possession of them.

The woman who answered their call came face to face with a young, innocent girl whose brow was distorted by pity and anxiety. A few steps behind her stood a suffering elderly woman, too modest and shy to come forward. Her gestures disclosed that she was disagreeing with the young girl's action.

"Heil Hitler," Judith said calmly, half turning toward the woman by the gate.

"Heil Hitler," answered the German woman. She was

Chapter 26

about fifty. A long black peasant skirt embraced her stout figure; her hair was tied in a knot. Her eyes looked at the girl questioningly.

"Please would you let my mother dry her feet at your stove?" she pleaded, drawing her attention to the stooping figure behind her. "We have walked many kilometres today, she is very weak and exhausted after the long journey."

"Come in, come in!" The woman beckoned them to step inside.

"I am so sorry, I have told Gretchen not to bother anybody," Mrs. Müller said apologetically. There was a slight hint of a quiver in her voice.

"But of course she must look after you. She was quite right. One can't go on walking in wet shoes. Come right in."

Shyly, gratefully they entered the strange house, following the woman into a warm clean room. The furniture was bright, the blue lino on the floor was well polished. The walls were whitewashed and on one of them hung a huge map of the German Reich.

A special excitement surged through Judith's veins; adventure was in the air, but her face spoke only of one longing - that of getting near the stove. Once there, she and Hannah stretched their arms out in front of them, expressing sheer delight at the radiating heat. They seemed quite oblivious of their surroundings, there was only one thing in the world that mattered to them - warmth.

From the corners of their eyes they tried to sum up the situation. In the middle of the room stood a large carved table, with chairs around it. There were some more chairs scattered about the place and on five of these were settled young officers in uniform, all taking part in an animated conversation. In a rocking chair on one side an elderly man was smoking a long pipe from which came the smell of burnt tea-leaf substitute.

Not even the entrance of two women seemed to have disturbed the discussion. The men, who gave the impression of being here on a visit themselves, must have been used to people popping into this place, for they did not regard it as anything worth breaking off their argument for; theirs seemed to be a world widely divorced from that of the rest of the household.

The woman of the house drew two chairs near the stove and came out with the obvious question.

"Where do you come from?"

"From Grünberg," started Hannah. "Everything is gone, everything. We went away for several days to visit a dying aunt of mine in Neusalz, but we never saw our home again. The Russians had advanced so quickly, they were almost at our backs ... we had to run ..." she continued in a broken voice, desperately trying to shed a few tears. "We made forty kilometres today. It breaks my heart to see my poor child suffer so. She is homeless now ..." and she stroked Judith's hair, throwing her the tenderest of glances.

"I am young, but my mother ..." the 'child' protested.

"You must stay the night here. I couldn't let you go on."

"But, but we couldn't inconvenience you like this, we only want to get a little warm," Mrs. Müller protested vehemently.

"Nonsense. I shall make a fire in the room upstairs, it is my sons' room, they are both in the Air Force." For a moment her eyes took on a faraway look. Then she turned round and soon after her footsteps could be heard on the staircase.

Chapter 26

Hannah's and Judith's eyes met and the apparently empty gaze had a shade in it which was more eloquent than a hundred words. They never stopped observing what was happening.

Some more men came in, others left and from the activity around them and from the conversation, they at last gathered that out of all houses in the village they had chosen to knock at no other than the local post office where young officers stationed in the neighbourhood came to collect their mail. This certainly was something. The knowledge of their whereabouts gave Judith a tingling sensation in her spine. What was going to be the outcome of it all? What if the men suddenly became aware of their presence?

There was nothing to be done except preserve an innocent countenance. Once more the two looked at each other, and in both pairs of eyes there seemed to flare up a spark of mischief which in the next second died down as quickly as it appeared.

The woman came back.

"Go upstairs and make yourselves comfortable. There is some hot water in the jug and a towel. When you come down, I'll get you something to eat."

"Oh really," protested Mrs. Müller, "we can't accept all this kindness, we didn't come here to eat your food, we only..."

"Go on, and don't be long," ordered the former. "It is the door on the right as you go upstairs."

A blazing fire was burning in the stove. The room was fairly austere, floorboards, two beds, a wardrobe and a wash-stand, but it was clean and civilized.

"Look, real beds," breathed Judith.

For a moment they tried the springs with their hands, then they threw themselves upon them and for a whole minute they tasted the wonderful sensation of lying on genuine beds.

"Almost as good as bunks," murmured Hannah.

"But not as good as a straw stack," reflected Judith. "What are we going to do?"

"We have to go down there and stick to our story."

"With all those men about?"

"Yes, we must, we would draw more attention to ourselves if we didn't," answered Hannah. "Besides, you want to eat, don't you?"

Judith looked in front of herself. The thought of food tantalized her empty interior. They hadn't eaten for two days. Were they really going to sit down to a proper meal? She jumped up and sped to the wash-stand. Hannah followed.

"We'd better leave our coats here, she might insist on our taking them off. I think next time we invade a house we'd better leave these coats buried somewhere. They might give us poor things new ones," suggested Judith with a sparkle.

"I admire your optimism. So you believe that after this there will be a next time? Of course we might be luckier then, we might find our way into a police station or such-like instead of a post office," Hannah remarked sarcastically. "All the same, this is quite funny," she added.

Their minds were in harmony.

Unobtrusively they entered the post office sitting-room again.

"I hope the bedroom wasn't too cold. Tomorrow you can have a bath. By the way, my name is Mrs. Schultz," said the woman, placing glasses of hot milk in front of them.

"I am Mrs. Müller: this, as you know, is Gretchen." Hannah followed the formality. Judith smiled modestly.

Chapter 26

Mrs. Schultz cut thick slices off a round loaf of rye bread and covered them with generous layers of fresh butter and home-made black-currant jam. A happy excitement came over Judith, it seemed almost incredible that she was being treated as a human being. She had to work hard to suppress the urge to grab the whole loaf and bite into it eagerly. Instead she tried to remember how normal people consumed bread and butter. Although she could have eaten five times as much, intuition told her when to stop. Hannah followed suit.

The men were talking politics now. Some were rather sceptical, while others were filled with a definite optimism. They spoke enthusiastically, never doubting their own words. Having such a Führer, they considered themselves safe. As blindly as they had ever followed him, they now listened to his last outburst of lies. With fists crashing against the table and a loud voice he had promised them victory and glory, and victory and glory it was going to be. Even if doubts ever dared to creep into a German's heart, he either kept them to himself or did his best to dismiss the idea as ridiculous.

Again Judith and Hannah exchanged apparently blank glances, but both understood what the other meant to say. "You will soon have your glory," was written in them; and then again, "How marvellously we are fooling them. If they only knew they are sheltering Jewish deserters," and "The others might be marching somewhere along the road while we sit here in a warm room and eat, and a soft bed is awaiting us."

Hoping the woman would send them to bed, they both made an attempt to look desperately tired. Their endeavour was not without consequences.

"You look worn out. I hope you will be comfortable in your

room," she said, rising from her chair. Judith and Hannah did likewise.

"I am sure we will; we are so grateful to you."

Suddenly a voice which came to them from across the room brought all their wits to attention.

"What do you think about the situation?" it said.

Judith looked round. Several pairs of eyes were turned in their direction. However, their expressions were unsuspecting. They were used to people passing through this house and didn't give it an extra thought. Judith pulled herself up and with a face showing calm self-confidence mingled with sauciness she proclaimed, "We have our Adolf Hitler, our Führer. Nothing can happen to us. He will never let us down!"

And Hannah added, deadly serious: "Everything that is happening now is just part of his plan. He knows what he is doing. Soon we shall be marching 'Nach Engeland'."

A chorus of "Heil Hitler!" filled the air followed by the well-known song "Heute gehört uns Deutschland, morgen die ganze Welt".

Judith and Hannah sang lustily, wished them all a hearty good night, and took themselves upstairs.

It was a quarter of an hour later when two heads were poking out from underneath two snow-white, huge feather beds. Their eyes were sparkling with mischief, triumph and delight.

"If they only knew they have Jewish visitors in their house!" Judith laughed, and once more rocked her body so as to try out the springs. She was delighted with the outcome of her effort.

"This is absolutely absurd," Hannah remarked.

Chapter 26

"What is?"

"All this."

"Isn't it?" laughed Judith. "But it's fun."

"Let's hope it lasts."

Then they tried to sleep but after an hour's effort a small voice asked, "Are you asleep?" It was Judith.

"No."

"The beds are too comfortable."

"I think that's what it is," agreed Hannah.

"What about getting down on the floor?"

"I think that's a rotten idea. This might be our last bit of luxury on earth."

"There is a lot in that; let's try again."

It was about half an hour later when a queer feeling invaded Judith's stomach. On hearing Hannah tossing restlessly about her bed she announced: "I feel sick."

Hannah lifted her head, so did Judith and for a moment they gazed at each other with a grim expression.

"I don't feel too good either. We have eaten and we are not used to it."

"It might be the milk. What are we going to do?" asked Judith, a flicker of amusement penetrating the half-desperate tone.

"On no account must the people here know," whispered Hannah, getting up and groping in the darkness for the light. As quietly as they could, they searched the room for something into which they could afford to be sick. Their efforts were fruitless.

"I can't keep it any longer," Judith groaned.

"Lie down quietly on your back and breathe deeply."

Unshed Tears

Judith followed her advice, and once more they engaged in a last attempt to sink into oblivion. This time they succeeded.

★ ★ ★ ★ ★

In the morning they were each presented with a pair of old but strong boots, socks and a headscarf, and after having enjoyed the luxuries of a bath and breakfast, they took leave of their hostess. They had thanked her cheerfully and gratefully for everything including the two shopping bags which held bread and milk for the journey.

The snow glittered brightly in the sunshine. They walked to the end of the village. There they stopped for a while and looked around, making up their minds which way to go.

"A pity she didn't give us new coats. Looking as we do, anybody trying to trace us would spot us immediately."

"Whatever we do, let's get away from the village," advised Hannah.

They took a path leading to the forest. There they sat down and after careful consideration Judith decided: "There are only three possibilities. Either we try to get home to Prague and seek shelter with one of our friends, or walk towards the Russian front, or drift about until the end of the war."

"H'm ..."

They meditated for a while.

"If we walked towards the Russians, in the opposite direction from the others, they would at once become suspicious. I think that's out," contemplated Hannah. "I don't think we can really trust our old friends either. We might find that they have turned traitors. People do all sorts of things for money, you can't rely on anybody's help these days."

Chapter 26

"Yes, you are right, it wouldn't be easy to make our way through to Prague anyway. Here at least people are used to unknown characters crossing their paths. I think we ought to stick to our story, not keep far away from the refugees, and perhaps it would be wise not to stray too far away from our transport either. We could always insist that we couldn't keep up and were left behind."

"Now we are trying to catch up with them," advised Hannah.

"Yes, that's the only thing we can do. In this way we shall be approaching the Czech border anyway, it might be worth something when we get there. One never knows," agreed Judith.

They picked up their bags and set out.

★ ★ ★ ★ ★

The air was clear, the scenery beautiful, they had decent boots on and they were free. They tried to avoid people as much as possible. They made their way past a village and into the forests and fields again, and when they found themselves miles away from all civilization, they felt happy and light-hearted. Long before mid-day they found it impossible to possess bread without touching it. At last they decided that it was time to terminate the tantalizing feeling, sat down on a heap of snow and let their appetite be the judge of the quantity to be eaten. After all, there were other villages which surely housed some kind-hearted people, and there was no reason why the stunt which had proved so successful once should not prove successful again.

Unshed Tears

They had given up the idea of keeping close to their transport as firstly people who had seen the procession pass might become suspicious about them and secondly it was more comfortable and enjoyable this way. They were masters of their time, there was no need to hurry, they could go where in their opinion it was best, do as they fancied as long as they were heading westward and entered the villages in the company of German refugees. After years of rigid routine and discipline it was wonderful to drift about at will, feel the excitement of adventure and anticipation of the great day which couldn't be very far off.

It was getting dark when they spotted the silhouette of a little town in the distance. The thought of food and a bed, the warmth and homeliness of the villagers, gave them an incentive to speed up their steps. They buried their coats before they entered the streets and encouraged by last night's success they knocked at a white door.

With the same story they acquired access to the picturesque blue cottage. The young woman who opened the door for them led them into the kitchen where two little blonde girls looked at them with great curiosity. She drew up two chairs near the cooking stove which occupied one corner of the room, and disappeared. She came back later and almost without taking any notice of them, went about her jobs.

After a talking game executed with their eyes behind the housewife's back, Hannah raised herself from her seat, thanked her for the favour she had bestowed upon them and beckoned Judith to go.

"There is some soup going if you care to have it," she said coldly.

Chapter 26

"It is your children's supper, I suppose, we mustn't take it away from them," Hannah protested cautiously.

"It is all right, there is enough."

She laid the kitchen table and they all ate soup. After that the woman made ready to put the children to bed and did not try to stop the two refugees when they proclaimed it was time for them to go. Once in the street they looked at each other in baffled amazement.

"We didn't reckon with that," remarked Judith.

"No, we certainly didn't."

"What next?"

"We must try again."

Once more they knocked at a door. They managed to get themselves a proper supper and after wondering for a time what the outcome of this venture would be they found out that their benefactress had no more intention of putting them up for the night than the previous one had. They were in the street again.

"Not very hospitable in this village, are they?"

"No. What are we going to do? We haven't even managed to get ourselves civilized coats," grumbled Judith, though not quite disheartened. It was all a part of the game.

"We'd better get our coats. It looks as though people in these parts are not very generous, nor favourably inclined towards visitors."

"Shall we try another village?"

"God knows where that is. It might be miles away. I don't particularly feel like walking for another few hours, do you?"

"No, not exactly.... What about trying one of the farms? We could ask them to let us sleep in a cow-shed on straw. If they are decent enough they will ask us in; if not, the straw will do for once."

"O.K., there is no harm in trying."

The cow-shed was warm and the straw soft. The animals were breathing peacefully and everything around was quiet.

"This is more like us," grinned Judith, and this time they had no difficulty in falling asleep.

On opening her eyes the next morning, Judith met the glassy gaze of a cow whose head had been uncomfortably near her own. For a moment she made an attempt to return the animal's idiotic stare, then she wakened Hannah and together they crossed the yard towards the building in order to thank the peasants for their hospitality, secretly hoping to be invited for breakfast.

Their hopes were fulfilled, though they almost wished they hadn't. They didn't like the look on the old man's face, who was peering at them with suspicious curiosity. Though he didn't say a word, his presence disquieted them.

At last they took leave and found themselves in the street again. As they were walking toward a nearby field they encountered a woman with a basket of faggots on her back. She looked at them curiously and when Hannah turned round after a while she could see her talking to another woman. Both were looking in their direction and it seemed pretty certain that the two queer looking strangers were the subject of their conversation.

"We'd better get away from here as fast as possible. There is something in the air I don't like," said Hannah after having reported to Judith what she had seen.

"Let's get somewhere right away from here. Somewhere

Chapter 26

where they would not expect us to go. We mustn't be seen in any of the neighbouring villages, they might be waiting for us there," declared Judith.

"Yes, let's go over those hills there, and straight on, let's get lost in the mountains," suggested Hannah.

"And what about food?"

"We have been without food before. If we walk the whole day we might be safely out of reach of these suspicious people."

"Perhaps it's just our guilty conscience that makes us imagine all sorts of things. For all we know the man on the farm might have had stomach ache, and the two women might have been looking at the forest beyond us, saying how difficult it was to gather wood these days."

"We must always be prepared for the worst," reflected Hannah.

"Those women saw us walk in this direction. We ought to go into the forest and through it and that field over there to the forest on the opposite side of the village and then make our escape over the mountains that way. They will never look for us in those parts."

They reached the top of the mountain, which had been their immediate target, by eleven o'clock. For the last time they looked down into the valley at the village which would never bring happy memories to them.

"There is that blue cottage, can you see it?" Judith pointed it out to Hannah.

"Yes, and the farm is over there. It is a very pretty village, really."

Like most German villages, this one was situated around a church. It was a white church with an unusually long spire, which was blue and was crowned by an originally carved cross.

They descended the mountain, walked through a valley and then up a hill again. Toward mid-day, as if fate was favouring them, fog began to descend upon the countryside. It wasn't a very thick fog and they could see about two hundred yards in front of them but it gave them a feeling of security.

About noon they stumbled upon a little cottage upon a mountain side which they endeavoured to enter. They had come just in time for a good milk soup and a dish of barley with peas. The elderly couple who lived there welcomed them most kindly and it was not difficult to tell them their story. They even managed to get a glimpse of a newspaper, several days old. In it people were being encouraged to have faith and promised a whole lot of lies. "Are they really all so blind or do they pretend to be?" Judith thought. Somehow it seemed to her that this couple knew what was awaiting them, but they didn't talk about it.

And so they went on - up the forested hills, down them, through meadows and glades. At times they would joyfully run down a snow-covered slope, or sit down and eat from their bags which the old woman had filled with wedges of bread and jam. Toward evening visibility became poorer and there was no sign of civilization.

"We must have walked at least twenty kilometres," mused Hannah.

"At least! We must be out of danger here. I only hope we shall stumble across some sort of a village or hut where we shall be able to put to rest our weary limbs."

It was quite dark now. They were lost in a maze of hills and passes, and the prospect of carrying on like that for many more

Chapter 26

hours or all through the night took on an uncanny reality. Following the valley they walked on for another few kilometres. Their feet were tired and progress was slow for they could hardly see on their way.

And then suddenly they heard the barking of a dog. They stopped and listened where it came from. It seemed a long way off, but what did that matter? There was food and a rest and a new adventure in front of them, and in high spirits they quickened their steps. The very faint outlines of houses were visible through the fog and darkness, and they knew that a village was quite near.

"I hope the people here are a bit more sociable than those we met yesterday," said Judith.

Suddenly a brook about four yards wide and not quite frozen over crossed their path. For a while they walked along it searching for a bridge, but without success.

"Looks as though we have had it," pondered Hannah. Then her gaze fell upon a fallen tree several yards away from them. A new idea took shape in her mind.

Together they brushed down the snow from the tree trunk and with a united effort managed to move it a few yards at a time. Breathless and red in the face they looked at their accomplished task. Their new slippery bridge lay across the wide gap, ready to be made use of. Judith made the first step. Gingerly she sat astride the trunk and with tiny vaults managed to get to the other side. Hannah followed her.

"I must say, we are clever," she announced, pleased with herself.

They stopped in front of the first building they came across. It was a small farm. "It's as good as any place. It all depends on luck," said Hannah.

Unshed Tears

It was as good as any place. Their approach had by now become a routine, and their story came readily to their lips. Although they only came to warm their feet, they always succeeded in getting themselves something to eat without the slightest suggestion of asking for it. Food was still something of a miracle to them, and in spite of eating large quantities they were never quite satisfied. This was their fourth night at large, and the two days they had spent wandering and meeting people had made them more experienced. They penetrated deeper into the mentality of the Germans which helped them to deal better with every new situation.

They slept on straw again, this time in the barn. The farm was full of people and apparently there was no bed vacant for them anywhere. Grateful to be able to stretch out their legs and rest in the warm straw, they fell asleep almost immediately.

The next morning a young boy of about fifteen brought them a jug of coffee and some dry bread. They were not asked to come into the building, but having learned by now that there are all types of people they decided to get on their way without worrying about it.

They walked along a road toward a meadow. There was something strange about this place and the fields and hills around. Judith was suddenly overcome by the feeling that she had been here before. She had experienced it once or twice before in her life, and now with nothing else to think of she casually remarked upon it. There followed a moment of silence in which Hannah gave her an odd look and finally said: "You know that's funny. That's exactly how I feel!"

They stared at each other, at the countryside around them, and then at each other again, suspicion and incredulity

Chapter 26

mingled in their looks, and suddenly, simultaneously they turned round to face the village. And there it was - the white church with the tall blue spire and that peculiar cross on top of it - there was no mistake about it.

"Look - after all our efforts yesterday ..." Hannah stuttered.

Judith stared pensively in front of her and after a long while, shaking her head slowly, declared, "If you read this in a book you would say things like this only happen in fiction."

"Confounded fog."

"We have probably walked right round the world to find ourselves here again," Judith said with a little spark in her eyes.

"This isn't funny."

"I know it isn't," and then they both laughed.

Pointing at the sun-bathed hills Hannah mapped out the route they must have taken on the previous day, three quarters round the village, sometimes as far as two or three ranges of hills away from it.

"This is the first time I've lost my sense of direction, it has never happened to me before," pondered Judith.

"No wonder this place looked familiar to us," laughed Hannah.

"Come on, let's go," Judith suggested energetically. "Perhaps it would be best if we walked toward the crossroads where the refugees branched off. It might be wiser to get lost in the crowd for a while. It is only a few hundred yards down the road."

It was more than that, and having walked for about half an hour they could spy the caravan of carts in the distance.

A tall Schu-Po man on a bicycle appeared from nowhere. He pulled up by the two women who were looking unconcernedly in front of them and without asking for an explanation beckoned them to come with him. Fooling was out of place and they knew it. He only had to tear their scarves off their shoulders to reveal the tell-tale striped patch.

He looked neither surprised nor furious. His tall well-fed figure marched in front. The two followed him silently. A dreadful emptiness took possession of them. As if they had suddenly woken up from a dream, they realized that it had been too good to be true, too good to last. All of a sudden they were prisoners again and somehow it seemed quite natural to them, as if they couldn't really expect to be free for ever. Obvious thoughts crossed their minds and they began to wonder what was going to happen to them. Was he going to shoot them as calmly as he now walked two or three yards in front of them or would they end up in another Auschwitz with a gas-chamber and tall chimneys?

The police station stood on the market square of a little town about three miles away from the village that had brought them such ill-luck. The commandant sat behind a desk and without much fuss opened up a huge black book and entered their names in it. Then he called for an elderly man who came with a bunch of enormous keys and made them follow him. In the middle of the cobbled square stood a solitary tower with several tiny barred windows. With empty eyes they observed their surrounding and guessed that the tower was their immediate destiny. The wonderful interlude seemed far in the past; being a prisoner once more seemed much more akin to reality. Everyone had a place in life, and this was theirs.

The warder separated one key from the rest, unlocked the iron door, and commanded them to enter. Then the door shut

Chapter 26

behind them and in the semi-darkness they came face to face with five well-known figures sitting leaning against the walls. One of the figures bowed her head and said, "You are heartily welcomed in our midst."

Not one bothered to get up. Judith and Hannah stared at them in amazement, not knowing whether to laugh or to cry. Then a flicker of humour entered their eyes.

"Well, we were not the only courageous ones," said Hannah, "like sheep that went astray, they are bringing us together."

"You may be seated," said Sonia.

The cell was long and narrow and there was not a single piece of furniture about. In the corner by the door stood a bucket for satisfying their needs. Consciously now the newcomers took note of their companions. There was Paula, the pregnant woman; Kitty, Sonia, Dita without her mother or sister, and Margot the nurse.

Once reconciled to their bad luck they stopped brooding and decided to make the most of it. Leaning against the damp walls they all recounted their adventures from the time of their escape, throwing in some amusing details, realizing that in many ways they had come up against very similar experiences. The prison became a lively place, all contributing to the entertaining of the others.

Then the key rattled in the door once more and in quiet apprehension they turned their heads to see the new addition to their company. They were Ida and Miriam, two Dutch girls who had also been to Kristranstads with them. There had only been a handful of those in the labour camp, as for some reason they managed to attach themselves to the Czechs when they left Auschwitz. When it was getting dark two more arrived, Zdena and Inka. Now there were eleven altogether.

It had been dark for quite a while when the door rattled open again, and they were ordered to come out.

"Stand against the wall!" a harsh voice bellowed, and a hand pointed at one of the longer tower walls. He took a few steps back and his hand rested upon his pistol. Judith, like all the others, knew what it meant to stand against a wall in a row.

"That's the end," something whispered within her and the full realization of that statement suddenly came to her. The end! Panic invaded every inch of her body, sending all other feeling into the background.

"I don't want to die, I don't want this to be the end of everything," screamed a thousand voices inside her.

She had often in the past thought how she would face a situation of this kind. She was convinced she would be proud and self-composed, but now, confronted with that situation, matters took on different proportions and in vain she searched for her pride and composure. It was gone, and the craving to stay alive at all costs took the upper hand. In a fraction of a second thousands of thoughts of the past and future flashed through her mind. She couldn't reconcile herself to the idea that that future, as she had so often planned it, was never to be. Giving way to a sudden impulse she took a few steps forward and pleaded aloud: "Please don't shoot us, we are young, we want to live!"

Instantly the others came forward and joined in the plea. A confusion of voices which lasted for a few seconds came suddenly to an end when the German commandant doubled up with laughter, and continued his roaring until his belly shook and tears appeared in his amused eyes.

Chapter 26

"I certainly gave you a fright!" his face said.

A man in civilian clothes but with a gun across his shoulder was coming toward them across the square. In his hand he held a piece of paper. When he came quite near, he showed the paper to the commandant and read out the address which was written on it.

"There is another transport there, Polish women," he added.

"There are eleven of them; if they are any trouble to you, don't hesitate to use this weapon of yours," the commandant said and once more his face lit up with merriment, then he added, "They'd love it!"

Within the women the world and everything in it took on normal proportions again, and they were capable of logical thought once more.

Judith took a last look at the red, fat, sadistic face, and her craving for revenge on all Germans reached its height.

XXVII

The night was frosty and little snowflakes came fluttering through the air and settled upon the eleven women prisoners and the man who walked behind them bidding them here and there to quicken their steps. Their journey took them along a deserted country road, past fields and forests lying peacefully under the wintry sky. They had walked for about two hours and still there was no sign of life in sight. Paula, whose baby lay heavily within her gave no indication of discomfort but bravely made her way forward with the others.

Toward ten o'clock a town appeared in the distance and after another half an hour's walk their journey came to an end. They stopped in front of a factory gate where an elderly officer in uniform took charge of them. Quietly they followed him into the building and along a dark narrow passage where a babel of voices met their ears. As they were approaching a huge door, the humming and twittering grew louder. At last their leader opened the door and they found themselves in a large hall, face to face with a sight that sent a shiver up and down their backs and filled their stomachs with disgust.

Slouched on the concrete floor between some machines

were hundreds of starved, ghost-like women, devoid of all humanity, their long bony fingers hunting for lice in the unkempt, tousled hair and under the torn, dirty garments which hung loosely upon their withered, skeleton-like bodies. Wild hatred shone forth from their eyes. There were groups fighting for space and screaming and swearing filthily.

Without saying a word the officer disappeared leaving them to their fate. For a while they stood pressed against the locked door without saying a word. Some of the women threw them a glance as if saying: "Blimey, some more to squeeze into here," and "I suppose they think they are something better, just because their clothes look tidier."

"What are we going to do?" Inka was the first one to speak. They looked at each other thoughtfully, a strong aversion to this uncouth crowd reflecting in their faces.

"What can we do?" asked Zdena.

"The lice are crawling all over them, I couldn't possibly lie down among them," shuddered Judith.

"Nor could I, but ..."

"Wait a minute," Sonia said suddenly, her beautiful black eyes looking meaningfully in the direction of a German in overalls who was checking something on the machine not far away from them.

Giving them one more calculating glance, Sonia detached herself from the little group and edged her way toward the man. Curiously they followed her with their eyes, wondering where this would get them. As she spoke, the German who was about forty-five and gave the impression of being the foreman in this factory looked in her direction, obviously conscious of her beauty and refinement, and listened to what she had to tell

Chapter 27

him. His eyes were calm and not unsympathetic; hers were pleading but confident. She stood upright as she explained the situation to him and several times he looked in the direction of the group by the door and the girls imagined that they could read a flicker of friendliness in his face.

"What on earth is she up to?" Kitty wondered aloud.

"I think she is trying to persuade him that we are clean and civilized and that we can't possibly lie down among this lousy mob," guessed Hannah.

"She is crazy to go and beg a German for a favour," said Zdena.

"Why not get out of them whatever we can?" contradicted Kitty.

"Well, we shall see ..."

"If he is going to do something in our favour, the political situation must be catastrophic for them," guessed Judith.

The German leant back over the machine, turned a few handles and then followed Sonia to the door. Without speaking he beckoned them to come with him.

Having walked down the hall some six yards they came to another door which he opened and with a sign told them to go in. With curiosity lurking in their minds they did as they were told, and found themselves in an empty brick-walled room about eight yards long and five yards wide with a whitewashed ceiling and a huge boiler in one corner.

"We'll make a blazing fire, and it will soon get warm in here," the man explained.

He was quite tall, with dark eyes and thin hair, and a little moustache under his straight nose. The fuel was all there. He lit the fire and they crowded round the boiler, pleased with the heat.

Unshed Tears

"Make yourselves comfortable," the German said, "I shall be back," and he left the room.

There was something very satisfying in being different from the others and enjoying certain privileges.

From outside, the noise of the quarrelling, starving crowd came to them, and here they were comfortable and clean, with no reason to fight. There was plenty of room for everybody and warmth as well. The heat spread to all corners of the room and they started to make their beds on the floor on their coats, for they were longing to stretch out their weary legs and relax.

"How did you do it?" Hannah asked Sonia.

"I just told him the truth, I didn't humble myself at all. As an equal to an equal I told him that as a civilized, cultured human being he is bound to understand that we can't mix with those lousy people, that we managed to stay clean for so many years and that we would like to go on staying clean. You know, there is something odd about this man ... somehow he is different from other Germans."

"He probably thinks he will save his skin when the war is over by being a bit friendly to us now," argued Paula.

"You may be right, but somehow I feel that he is genuinely interested in helping us."

"He is only a man, and probably seeing a pretty young face he weakened a little," remarked Margot.

The door opened and the man returned with a whole bucket of raw potatoes in their skins in one hand, and a small tin box in the other hand. He filled the bucket with water from the tap and placed it upon the boiler. Then he grinned.

"I hope this will be enough. If not I'll get some more."

He sat on the floor with the others and opened the box. It contained a first aid kit.

Chapter 27

"I know some of you need this for your feet. Who wants a dressing?" he asked and then he examined everybody's feet. He tended to them all without saying much, cleaned the wounds caused by bad shoes and a lot of walking, dressed them with ointment, elastoplast and bandages, saw to the blisters and then looked at the shoes causing the trouble. He promised to repair them or bring others. When his job was finished and the potatoes were ready, they all sat around the bucket and ate heartily.

"You must never tell anybody that I helped you," he said. "If anybody knew, they would kill me. You see ... I am not a fascist. I am a communist. As a boy I read Marx and studied his ideals and ideas. I am a great follower of his doctrine and that of Engels and other true, great communists. Their ideals are my ideals and it would be against my principles to be dictated to by one man as to what I should do and what I should not do. I can see Hitler and his people with open eyes. I, like you, can see what they are and what they do and how wrong it all is. That's why I am here now. It makes me happy to help you. You may call me Kurt."

A silence followed, in which their minds went to work.

At last Judith asked: "Are there many of you in Germany?"

"It is very difficult to assess that - everyone keeping it secret; it is too dangerous to trust anybody, but I believe there is quite a group of us ..."

* * * * *

For a long time Judith lay in the dark, unable to fall asleep. The fire was still blazing in the stove, and a bucket of potatoes stood on the floor ready to be cooked in the morning. Each of them had a blanket to cover herself with. It was highly improbable but not impossible that a German would come and look them up. And somewhere not far away a man slept who might be dead tomorrow if it was discovered that he was the one who had brought this little comfort upon them.

How much Kurt trusted them! What was to become of him when the war was ended? Would they believe that he was anti-fascist? How many had already died standing by their convictions? There was so much Judith had to think about. There were some people in Germany who had their own convictions after all, and who knew how bad and cowardly blind the rest were. They must have had a lot of courage to go through the war not betraying their ideas, when even thoughts and opinions were punishable....

Were they wrong to have stayed here and risked that man's life? He had given them clear instructions as to what to do if someone came and knocked at the door, and had assured them that there wasn't much risk attached to this venture; but all the same they shouldn't have taken advantage of his decency.

Judith looked around. Everyone seemed to be asleep and there was no point in waking them. Why should anybody bother to come here in the middle of the night, she tried to convince herself. Anyway Kurt was the only one who had a key and in the morning they would sort things out.... Was it true what he had told them about the political situation - that Allied troops were advancing from all sides?... How was Sonia getting on for she had gone with Kurt.

★ ★ ★ ★ ★

Once more they were on the snow-covered road. The white

Chapter 27

fields, forests, villages, had no significant names. Hunger and fatigue together made up their daily lives. Step by step they were marching - about three hundred of them - forward toward the west, often making great detours in order to find a resting place for the night or merely for no other reason than that it pleased their German guard.

He was an elderly man, calm, rather fed-up with the whole situation, just obeying orders. Sometimes he would talk to the women explaining what he was doing and why, and they soon stopped fearing him. Apparently he himself did not know where they were going. It looked as though nobody knew that. They had a few guesses: some said it might be Oranienburg, a concentration camp near Berlin - another death camp; others thought they might end up at Terezienstadt as they were gradually approaching the Bohemian border. There were some other wild guesses, but nobody knew for certain.

Whenever they reached a larger town the officer would report to the authority and get further instructions like reporting at a certain place not later than in a week's time. In between it was up to him to make decisions. Although he was the only one in charge and the discipline was not at all rigid, very few tried to escape.

He seemed to have made a point of keeping away from the German refugees, and the people in the villages on the route and nearby appeared to have been warned about them and as none of them liked Jews, their ventures ended up in police stations and a humiliating return under German escort, who threatened to shoot the next person who disobeyed the rules.

So far, nobody had been shot, due perhaps to the political situation, but on the other hand there was little point in taking the risk just now when there was hope in the air; after all they didn't know the exact German rulings and one day the threat might be carried out.

The inculcated hatred of the Jews was obvious wherever they went. The German people watched with disgust the pitiful procession, their hearts remaining cold toward the suffering which looked forth from every starved, hollow, face. The women with their children came out of their houses to watch the spectacle, for they had never seen anything of that sort before. It was obvious that they were convinced that nothing was bad enough to be imposed upon this wicked, inferior race. Tight-lipped, with scorn and satisfaction on their faces, they spoke to each other over the hedges and in front of the garden gates, nodding their heads, agreeing that this bad lot deserved nothing better.

The sadistic opposition of the German folk brought the Czech women and the Polish prisoners closer together. There was no real affection between them, as there was no affection among any of the prisoners but they had grown accustomed to each other and the special hostilities between the two parties gradually ceased.

The ten girls whose fate brought them together and who had had a taste of civilization and the good things for a few days, fought hard not to let their environment and hardship take possession of their souls. Spending the nights in barns in close contact with the others, their clothes had become very shabby and lice invaded this new breeding ground with great fervour.

One thing saved them from sinking really low - it was Paula's baby whose birth they expected any day now. They

Chapter 27

made it their job to look after her. Her quiet thoughts had become their concern, it was almost as if the baby belonged to all ten of them. They were not quite sure whether the guard had noticed her, they believed he must have done, but he never mentioned the matter. What would become of this little innocent babe? Would it be able to survive the conditions under which it would be brought into this world, and if so what were they going to do with it? It was impossible to keep its existence secret from the Germans, but what was the guard going to do about it?...

The names of villages had very little meaning in them. They went from one to another, looked at the picturesque church and pretty houses and forgot about it. It was only when they passed through larger, well-known towns that their minds registered their existence. Görlitz and Bautzen were two of them. The towns were usually crowded with German refugees, outdoor canteens in the market squares were busy and the inhabitants were going about restlessly, aware of the unsatisfactory situation.

It was in one of these towns that a great many prisoners, seeing all the strangers about, were overcome by the same temptation to get lost among them, and on that day the transport was about twenty short.

"It's no good," said Judith to her friends. "They are bound to get caught - their appearance is too conspicuous and there are too many of them. I have a feeling this is not the end of it yet." They could see the usually calm face of the guard calculating grimly and they decided to "be good" on that day.

"They are fools, those girls, they are not using their brains. They can't even speak German properly. How do they expect to get away with it?" argued Hannah.

"Fools," said Zdena.

The guard reported to the commandant as usual in a town, then he led them to a farm not very far away. Another officer in uniform was with him. Something was going to happen before long, they could feel the tension in the air. They were put into the barn and the door shut behind them. It was about four o'clock in the afternoon and it was gradually getting dark.

Inside the barn it was almost dark already, for there were only a very few tiny windows near the roof. As usual they rushed forward to secure a place in the straw and, grateful to be able to rest, most of them lay down and stretched out their legs. Judith and her friends settled along the wooden wall near the entrance.

It was about an hour later that the first shot sounded through the air. Automatically Judith sat up and peered through the narrow gap between the planks. Others followed.

They could see nothing except the upright figure of the unknown guard staring attentively at the entrance to the farm about thirty yards away.

With their eyes glued to the gaps they watched the officer and the gate, suspecting the nature of the shot. Girls from other parts of the barn came forward, curiously waiting for what was to come. And then it happened. Two figures wrapped in the familiar looking blankets appeared at the gate which was in one corner of the wooden fencing that went all round the farm. They walked for about ten yards, then the shots pierced the air and the two figures fell to the ground. It was their own guard who made sure that they were dead.

About ten minutes later a similar incident occurred.

"Looks as though there are going to be some twenty bodies lying about before long," remarked Margot.

Chapter 27

"I wonder how they got here? There don't seem to be any Germans with them," said Hannah.

"Perhaps they take them as far as the gate and make them go in," suggested Zdena.

"They couldn't shoot them in town of course, not in front of the Germans, and besides, it would scare the others away," reasoned Judith.

"Probably. They would have to hunt for them all over the place. Like this they can catch them quite easily and bring them up here at long enough intervals for them not to know what's cooking."

"I know!" Kitty said suddenly. She detached herself from the group and treading between the girls who were lying on the floor she made her way to the ladder which led to a loft above them. She climbed up and disappeared. After a few minutes she returned.

"They are coming on their own," she told the others breathlessly. "Up there I could see the road and one of them was coming up on her own, there was no German."

A moment of silence followed.

"Perhaps they catch them down in town and send them here, threatening them with something if they don't arrive," said Paula.

"They must be combing the place for refugees," reasoned Zdena.

"I guess it's not too difficult for them to find them, the way they look," mused Margot.

"Silly lot."

"I wish we could give them some sort of a sign from the loft window as they come up the road, or do something," Kitty suggested.

Unshed Tears

"We have no light here, they wouldn't see us, and besides they wouldn't know what we are trying to say, it's so far away," said Judith.

"Anyway the Germans would discover us there, and that would be the end of us," said Margot.

"We ought to do something, there are too many lives involved in this," insisted Kitty.

"Yes, we ought to do something, we ought to give them a warning somehow," Judith agreed determinedly.

Miriam and Ida, the two Dutch girls who stayed with them in the group, seemed to have got the meaning of all that was going on. They had picked up quite a lot of the Czech language in Terezienstadt and in the labour camp, and understood almost everything, though they couldn't speak the language.

After some thought Ida came to a conclusion that she expressed in German: "If the girls are coming up the road on their own there should be a way in which we could give them a warning other than from the window."

It was Kitty who came out with the final idea.

"From up there, I can see everything. There is a wooden fence running all round the farm. From the other side of this barn, it is only a few yards to the fence. If one of us could get out of here that way and get outside the fence, which might not be so difficult as there is a gate, she could then make her way toward the main gate and warn anyone who comes there. She could then come into the barn through the back."

"Say we could manage all that, what will the Germans do? They are bound to find out sooner or later."

"They won't shoot three hundred of us and about the rest we can worry when it comes along."

Chapter 27

"And who is going to be the one to go?" asked Dita.

"I will go," said Kitty.

"I shall come with you," determined Judith.

The others looked at them silently.

"I don't mind coming," said Ida.

"Its all right, we shall do it somehow."

"Good luck."

Then they went - Kitty and Judith.

Stepping over the sleeping girls they made their way to the other side of the barn. The others followed them with their eyes, and some of the Polish girls who felt that something was cooking, looked on with interest.

They tried the wooden gate which was firmly shut. For a while they speculated and experimented with it, with no positive result. At last Judith hit upon an idea. Bending down she began to remove the straw which filled up a narrow gap between the lower edge of the gate and the ground. They dug a hole big enough to crawl underneath the gate and once out, made immediately for the fence. The door that led into the street was open and cautiously they crept out and pressed themselves against the wooden planks. There didn't seem to be anyone around and they decided to act quickly. Keeping to the fence they ran along one side of it to the corner which brought them to the edge of the road.

"The gate is down there, at the other corner," informed Kitty.

"Yes. A good thing the snow is so bad. We are not leaving any footprints."

"Let's go."

There was a ditch between the fence and the road and

through it they ran, half bent, to the vital point. The gate was on their left, now, a few yards in front of them, and lying hidden in the ditch they had a good view of the road before them.

"We must be crazy doing this," remarked Judith.

Kitty had no time to answer. They both saw the desolate figure coming up toward them, at the same moment. Judging by her clothes, there was no doubt that she was one of them.

"Look," was the only thing Kitty could say at first.

"Here we go!"

They waited breathlessly, their keen eyes never letting the approaching figure out of sight. At first they whispered a hundred little things to each other, then they lay motionless waiting to carry out the operation. What would be the outcome of it all?

"It must work, you'll see, it will," assured Judith, determined to make a good job of it.

The Polish girl was only a short distance away from them now. Unconcernedly she was shuffling her heavy feet along the ground. For her it was just another little chapter in her life, not a very significant one at that. Soon she would be where she belonged - in the barn with the mass of others like her, lying crowded in the straw, searching for lice and hoping for liberation.

"PSST ... you there!"

A little taken aback, the girl turned in the direction of the sound. She saw two faces and two hands beckoning her to come over.

"Come here, quickly," Judith called at her quietly.

Suspecting something unusual, the girl caught onto the

Chapter 27

idea, and her eyes sharp and questioning, she took a few hasty steps toward the two women. Automatically she bent down and then lowered her body into the ditch. With a burning gaze she inquired: "What's the matter?"

"The guard shoots anyone who enters that gate. Some have already had it. You understand?" said Judith.

"Yes. There are a lot more out there in town. You have come here to save us?"

"We couldn't just sit there and listen to the shots, could we? But never mind that now. Listen carefully. Run along this fence and round the next corner. There is a little door. Get through that and you will find a hole under the gate of the barn. It's just big enough for you to squeeze through. Just push the straw against the hole, in case the German goes into the barn. That's all."

The girl left. Ten minutes later she was back.

"I say," she whispered. "I just had an idea. You go back to the barn and I'll wait here for the next one. She then can take my place until someone else comes along."

They looked at each other. At last Kitty said: "You go back, Judith. I'll wait here until the next one comes. It's better to watch in twos. As soon as someone arrives I'll join you. I think it's fair enough."

That night, one after another made their way through the secret entrance into the barn. Every time another head appeared in the hole a triumphant murmur surged through the shabby crowd. For once their hearts were united.

Late in the evening the guard, tired of his vigil, made for the farm. To the great amazement of everyone - they heard nothing more about it. There were neither inspections nor interrogations and the next morning they set off on the next lap of their journey.

"He must have thought that they did away with them in town."

"Perhaps."

"Maybe he doesn't really care."

* * * * *

They had been on their way for three weeks. Their march to the west had taken them across a great part of Germany and the Czech border lay not far ahead of them.

"We must be going to a camp in Bohemia somewhere."

"To think of it - after all the ugly years we are so near home again."

The spirit of the Czech girls rose with every day that passed. They did not receive much food but together with the fresh air it was sufficient to keep them alive. From time to time when they sensed they could afford to take chances, one or two of them would deviate from the normal route and return to it later in the day with bags filled with bread, potatoes and milk. This would be shared out among the little group who in their way helped to make the venture a safe and successful one.

Once they came upon a heap of raw onions. Those who spotted them first made a dash at them and in two minutes the ground was cleared. For the rest of the day, raw onions were eaten like apples and enjoyed more than the best fruit in normal times.

For some prisoners, dustbins were a favourite hunting ground. It was surprising how many delicacies could be

Chapter 27

retrieved from a dustbin. Judith didn't fancy them. A certain pride prevented her from rummaging through the dirty, smelly garbage....

"Tomorrow we shall be in Dresden," the guard told them one day.

It was toward the evening of the next day when the large town appeared in front of them. It wasn't as they expected to see it. The whole area was one mass of flames and smoke. Dresden was on fire. The prisoners looked at each other and their hearts jumped with joy. Evening came, and the sky was red with the reflection of the burning city below. One more German town was crumbling to its ruin. The Allied planes had been there and had made a good job of their mission.

It meant walking all through the night for their destination existed no more, but the sight of the flames eating up the famous and important place, was a good enough compensation for a few hours' sleep.

They headed south, away from Dresden and toward the Bohemian border. In the morning they found themselves on a road leading through a wide forest. There on that road they met with a stream of Czech men who, having taken advantage of the chaos in Dresden, had deserted from the labour camps and were now on their way south to join the partisans.

Being carefully watched the Czech girls did not have much chance to talk to their compatriots. For a long time they walked side by side, some men overtaking them and others catching up from behind.

"We must show them that we are Czechs," urged Judith.

"Yes, we must let them know somehow," they all agreed.

It was a wonderful feeling to walk in the same direction of

those men, who like them had been prisoners and were now free. How different the world looked from that of a year ago. The German Reich was falling to pieces and they knew it. These Czech men were really free and nobody worried about it.

At last the ranks of the refugees widened and they were now quite close to the untidy procession.

"Hullo," Judith said quietly in Czech.

The man who walked beside her turned his head curiously. Soon the whole group of men and all the Czech girls were in quiet communication. They showed great concern for each other for they had all been victims of the same tyrant and both were ready to fight for the same cause.

"Where do you come from?" the men asked.

"We were in Poland and Auschwitz and we have walked across a great part of Germany."

"Auschwitz doesn't exist any more."

They had to interrupt their conversation several times for the German was very much on guard. However, they managed to snatch a few quiet remarks.

"Don't worry, it will soon be over."

"President Beneš spoke over the wireless last night. He is with his government in Slovakia."

"In Slovakia itself?"

"Yes, it is only a matter of days now."

Optimism and enthusiasm filled the air. Suddenly freedom was so near and all the discomfort was forgotten.

"Where are you going?" Hannah asked.

"We are going to join the partisans, we have been waiting for this moment for a long time."

"Just imagine, a real fight for our country!"

Chapter 27

"Couldn't we come with you? We are used to hardship."

The men looked at each other and held a conference. At last they decided.

"Later on this forest becomes very thick. We shall wait for you there. It should not be too difficult to escape."

A great excitement seized the girls.

"We must make it," they decided.

★ ★ ★ ★ ★

Fate was against them. The day being Sunday the guard decided to make an early break. By two o'clock they were locked in the barn and watched on all sides by German youths from the village. There was no chance of escape.

"Looks as though we've had it," Hannah said.

"H'm... perhaps it's better like this, one never knows."

The next morning they were off again. The roads were clear by this time, all the Czech deserters had gone. They marched in a tidy procession, carefully guarded by the German who sensed that certain plans were hatching in the prisoners' minds. Yesterday's experience had filled them with a new adventurous and happy spirit and he knew they were ready to break away, this time for a definite goal, at the next possible opportunity. He was not going to have it. At last he assembled them all on the road and presented them with a firm warning speech. He counted them in files of five and announced: "I shall be counting you three times a day. If someone should be missing I shall raise an alarm and you will all go without food until the person is found."

They knew he meant it, not so much because he cared what

they did, but because his own safety was at stake. He was expected to deliver a certain number of prisoners and failing this nobody knew what the result would be. He wasn't taking any chances.

Toward the evening something else took the Czech girls' mind off the subject of escape. Paula's baby showed the determined intention of making its first appearance in this world in the very near future. A new surge of quiet excitement and concern swept over the little group and they made plans how to deal with the situation. Paula was calm and composed, her face had taken on an almost saintly expression as, tormented by pain, she walked forward trying to keep up with the rest. An unquenchable faith brought peace to her mind. She was very quiet. Perhaps she was praying.

The girls never left her side hoping that in this difficult moment they could be of some comfort to the woman for whom this experience must have been a strange ordeal. Quietly they shared that experience with her.

Judith made sure that she was among the first to burst into the barn, which at last they reached after a few hours of agonizing worry. For a split second she looked round, then she made for a huge pile of straw towering in a dark corner. This she reserved for her friend and no one else was allowed to go up there. They helped Paula up, Margot the nurse came with her, so did Hannah, Kitty, Lotte and Zdena. The rest settled themselves at the foot of the pile.

The barn door shut and at last everyone was settled. The light of a candle which Kitty had carried on her for a special occasion, flickered in the darkness. Quietly the prisoners waited. Their hearts were united.

Chapter 27

On the heap of straw Paula lay panting, her fists clenched, her head moving from side to side in search of relief from the pain. Margot sat by her, holding her hand and comforting her with quiet sentences. The word spread that a pair of scissors was wanted and at last a Polish girl produced them. The deeply concealed spark of humanity burst forth from every soul, and all the prisoners, though not watching, lay awake, constantly attentive, hoping that everything would be all right. Judith lay almost beside Paula, but her back was turned to her and she could only hear the heavy breathing and the suppressed screams.

It was after midnight when the thin cry of a baby suddenly echoed throughout the barn. Three hundred people turned their heads and looked toward the place, their hearts warm with feeling, their faces illuminated with a tender smile. Some eyes moistened with tears, and the fate of this little newcomer among their midst became everybody's concern.

"It is a boy," was the general cry.

"It is a miracle that he lives at all."

"I wonder what will become of him."

"Poor, innocent child."

Margot wrapped him in a blanket and showed him to his mother. All the Czech girls crowded around and with gentle feelings admired the little boy. Paula took him in her arms and smiled lovingly. All the wrath against the father and the child who had brought so much discomfort to her and who might even be the cause of her death, were gone. She spoke to him tenderly, quietly.

"I won't leave you, I won't desert you.... Either we shall both live or die, but we shall stay together.... Perhaps they will let us live, and one day you will become a big boy and I will tell you how you were born in a barn and how much I loved you and how much I wanted to keep you.... Perhaps God will help us...."

Then everybody went to sleep and only Margot kept watch over both of them.

In the morning the gates of the barn were thrown open and everyone held her breath. Paula knew she couldn't keep the presence of her baby a secret and when the guard appeared in the gate, she picked up the little bundle with the boy and walked toward him. Without saying a word she showed him the baby. The guard looked down at the tiny face which looked quite well and contented and a big grin appeared on his face. He looked at the loving and pleading face of the mother and then he said: "I too have children. I love them very much." Then he added, "You can't go on like this, you must go to hospital. I shall see what I can do."

They all passed the hospital and waved Paula good bye and wished her luck.

"He is not a bad bloke, the guard I mean," someone said.

"No, he has a bit of heart left after all."

"I wonder whether we shall ever see them again," said Hannah.

"Perhaps we shall meet in Prague," said Judith.

XXVIII

Mile followed mile. The feet tramping the ground day after day were sore no more as the skin on them had hardened and they marched forward with a regular shuffle, taking the country roads, town pavements and all the rest of it in their stride.

By the end of February all the snow had melted and blocks of ice were rushing down the swelling rivers. Spring wasn't far off and the rays of the sun were getting increasingly stronger. The blinding snowstorms and biting icy wind were over.

The mountains along the Bohemian border showed themselves up in all their splendour.

"It is good to be so near home," remarked Kitty.

"A walking holiday in our beloved mountains for nothing," grinned Hannah. "The last time I was in Marienbad, was on my honeymoon."

They marched through familiar places and holiday resorts, famous industrial towns. They passed important coal mines and the names of the places were no more meaningless to Judith and the handful of Czech girls around her.

Usti on the Elbe, Teplice, Jachymov, Karlsbad, Cheb,

Marienbad - all those brought memories to someone or other and they passed their time recalling their experiences tied up with the various places. No one knew where they were going, not even the guard was sure what his next orders would be.

"Looks as though we are going to drift like this until the end of the war."

As their feet shuffled along the stony pavements of some of the towns, the Czech people looked at them with curiosity and an urge for sensation, but their doors were shut even against the Czech girls themselves. Once Judith and Kitty tried their luck with a local family, but were turned out.

"We are Czech too," Judith said.

"Go away, we don't want to get into trouble."

The door slammed.

"Swine! I am not going to beg them again," said Kitty.

"Nor will I," agreed Judith.

Then they entered Bavaria. It was March and spring was truly in the air. The little villages surrounded by mountains were very pretty and they drifted on from one to the other, and once again their names meant nothing to them. Only the behaviour of the people they met on the way showed that something was in the air and although big and confident phrases came from the Germans' lips, there was meekness and uncertainty in their eyes.

"They know they've had it."

"I bet they do."

"They can just as well keep their 'Our Führer knows what he is doing'; they are just bluffing themselves."

"Soon their Führer will roast in hell."

"It may be a matter of days now, the Allies seem to be closing in from all sides."

Chapter 28

★ ★ ★ ★ ★

It came quite out of the blue. Suddenly there was a train standing in front of them - a cattle truck, and before they quite realised what was happening they were on it. Judith, her friends and some Polish girls, sixty in all, found themselves in a coal waggon. They were given some bread and watery coffee and a bucket for each waggon.

"The food has to last you two days," the German in charge told them.

Then the sliding doors were sealed and they were shut off from the sun-drenched world.

"I wonder what this is all about," said Hannah.

"What difference does it make where we spend the last few days of our captivity?"

"Aren't we posh? This is really travelling in style," remarked Judith.

"Yes, no walking, no marching through the night. I say, we have really been promoted."

It was very dark and stuffy inside. Two grates were the only connection with the world outside and only a little air had a chance of getting in. The sun warmed the walls of the waggon and it soon became very hot. A layer of coal dust covered the wooden floor and they had no option but to sit in it. The dust and heat soon dried their throats and thirst overcame them. At night they stretched out on the hard planks, pressed against each other like sardines in a tin.

The air raids came one after another and for hours they stood still in the desolate countryside, while bombs played havoc around them. Several times they had to turn back onto different rails, as those they had been on had been wrecked. Silently the girls in the coal waggon listened to the explosions around them, hoping for a miraculous liberation.

"If a shell hit the officers' coach or if they ran away, we might be all right."

"The British and Americans might be quite near. All sorts of things might happen, you never know."

"Perhaps the bombs will destroy all rails around us and we won't be able to move and the liberators will come. They can't be so far off. In that case the Germans would run away any minute."

Schemes and ideas and dreams took possession of them and held them in suspense. They had worked out all possibilities and they had an answer for each one of them. All they were waiting for was the opportunity and they hoped breathlessly it would come soon. An air of anticipation was ever present. They dreamed and shared their hopes.

On the fourth day they quietened down. They had been without food and water for two days. Thirst made talking almost impossible. It was obvious that the constant raids were delaying them. The sanitary conditions and the stench resulting from them were abominable. The hours began to drag. One after another they sank into silence and, lying stretched out on the black, dusty floor, they wondered when relief would come. The heat and the thirst became almost unbearable and hunger made them weak and wretched.

On the fifth day a Polish girl died and gloom descended upon them. Was this the beginning of the end? How long could they go on without food and water? Was one after another going to fade away? Was this a journey of death?

Chapter 28

Perhaps this was how the Germans wanted to get rid of them.

"If we are to die, please God do it quickly, so that we need not suffer so long," a woman murmured in one corner.

"Water ... water ..." uttered the cracked lips of an ill girl.

With half-opened eyes Judith watched Hannah lift herself up and drag herself to the grate. She thought how strange she looked. Her body was all bones, the long dress hung loosely about her, her chin was long and pointed and her deep sunken eyes looked longingly at the world outside. Suddenly it occurred to Judith that Hannah's appearance reminded her of the statues of the suffering figure of Christ on the cross she had seen.

"If Christ really existed and suffered, at least he knew that there was a purpose behind his life and death. Did he suffer as much and long as we did?" she thought.

Hannah's bony fingers wound themselves around the little bars and she tried their resistance. Then she examined the walls desperately, searching for a means of escape which she knew she would never find. Utterly exhausted she slid down on the floor.

The nights were better, because they were cool and they managed to get a few hours' sleep.

On the sixth day another woman died.

"How long can we go on like this?" whispered Lilly.

"This is the fourth day without food."

"It is amazing though how much a body can endure," said Judith.

The train was at a standstill again. The tortured bodies lay lifelessly on the floor; most of the prisoners were reconciled to their obvious fate. Groans and quiet swearing were the only sounds.

Unshed Tears

The Germans were parading in front of the waggons, shouting at each other along the line. A lorry arrived and soon afterwards the clinking of pots and spoons sounded in the air. Incited by the strong odour which tantalized their nostrils, women throughout the train began to pick themselves up and press their faces against the barred windows, eagerly hoping for salvation. Only food and water could save them and their eyes dwelled desperately on the lorry which held cans of delicious smelling soup. The German officers lined up for it, and their containers filled, they spread themselves along the train, eating. With a sadistic satisfaction, aware of their audience, they praised the tasty food and smacked their lips.

This was too much for the ravenous mob. The odour of the soup and the tinny sound of the spoon against the vessels drove them almost to insanity. Wild and filled with new energy they fought for the places at the window. Then one waggon started it. Bashing their fists against the walls all sixty prisoners chanted: "We are hungry! We are thirsty! We are hungry! We are thirsty!"

The next one joined in and then the next one, and before long the whole train was alive with the united voices of protest.

"Shut up you savage mob! Shut up!" the Germans bellowed.

"We-are-hun-gry! We-are-thir-sty!"

A gun fired in the air and everything was suddenly still. Crushed to hopelessness they returned to their places on the floor. There was nothing they could do. The last spark of strength had left them and their spirit sank to nothingness.

Toward the evening a rattling on the wall brought their minds to attention. The creaking doors slid open and they saw

Chapter 28

an officer lifting a bucket full of water to their floor level. A glimpse of the water awakened a new strength in them and they shot up from their places and savagely threw themselves on the bucket. Devoid of all humanity they shrieked and fought and pushed and a few moments later half paralyzed they watched the liquid disappear from the upturned bucket. Several women threw themselves on the floor and licked it and then it was all over. The German roared with laughter, and satisfied with the entertainment shut the door on them.

"I bet he only did it to amuse himself," said Judith.

"I bet."

"Let's get some sleep."

That night another Polish girl died and many of them knew their last moment wasn't far off. The last particles of flesh had disappeared from underneath their dirty skin and every bone in the body took on a prominent shape.

Judith lay silently in her place, thin, her skin black from coal dust. Her body was sore from the hard floor, but the pain of the hunger had passed, only a desperate weakness remained making it impossible for her to move her limbs from side to side. She did not get up any more from her place to get a glimpse from the window, nobody did. Her senses were numb. She had no strength left to fight. Everything was like a dream. Only somewhere deep inside her a tiny spark ordered her to hold on to life. Her conscious mind was hardly aware of it.

In the middle of the night once more a bucket of water was passed up to them. This time there was no energy left to fight. The mug was passed around and the trembling lips sucked in the miraculous liquid, not being able to get enough. For a moment a little bit of life came back into the waggon and then everything was quiet again. The engine was rattling along at greater speed. Inside, the prisoners prayed for salvation. They were neither alive nor dead.

★ ★ ★ ★ ★

On the following afternoon - it was the seventh day - the train came to a standstill, and within seconds the track was alive with feet running along the gravel and harsh German voices shouting orders. Bolts crashed to the sides of the waggons and the sliding doors thundered open. A dazzling light invaded the interior, blinding the prisoners for a few moments.

"Out! Everyone out! At once!"

The prisoners lifted their heads and attempted to move, but their attempts were in vain. They had no strength left to crawl out.

"Out, I am telling you, or I'll shoot! Out! Out!"

The commands were loud and brutal.

With desperate eyes they looked into the bright sunshine and then at each other as if asking: "How can we? It is the fifth day that we haven't eaten, and before that we weren't too strong either. How can they demand such a thing of us?"

Judith tried to move. Her elbows and her knees gave way underneath her.

"No, I can't make it ... I can't," she mumbled to herself. "Well, it doesn't matter...." Then in the next few seconds the whole future as she had planned it flashed through her mind, and an inner voice protested: "It does really matter, it does!"

Whips cracked and heavy boots were on top of them.

Chapter 28

Without realising how, guided by a supernatural force, she made her way out of the dark waggon and found herself on the crackling gravel. Like ghosts, one after another followed her out, their legs collapsing underneath them. Slouching on the ground they saw the same thing happening all along the line. Around them were fields and meadows, there wasn't a building in sight. Half dead, they made no effort to think. The sun was burning upon their heads.

"Up! Up at once!" the German officers yelled.

Once more a wave of utter desperation swept through the crowd. From somewhere the news spread that they had to walk five miles to a camp. Once more they attempted to get up. Their limbs felt lifeless, the ground was rocking beneath them and everything was like a dream.

"Get into fives!"

Hardly aware of how they moved, the prisoners shuffled into fives.

"Forward march!"

There was no option for those who wanted to live. At the end of the journey there might be food and water. As in a trance the ghostly procession moved forward. And again a superhuman power took possession of their legs and made them move forward one after another. The clogs shuffled along the concrete road, the rest of their bodies and their minds were dead. They freed themselves of all burdens, throwing away their coats and shoes and anything that would enable them to travel lighter. Soon the road was littered with odd bits of garments, clogs and other objects. They arrived at a green forest. Spring had arrived there, the birds were singing and nature was showing itself in all its glory, but they didn't see it.

There was only one thing that mattered, "Left, right, left, right."

They passed some military barracks. In a pool soldiers were bathing. It was only the middle of March but the air was filled with summer heat.

Toward the evening they emerged from the forest and in the distance in front of them appeared a huge iron gate, and behind that, enclosed in a frame of barbed wire, were scattered dozens and dozens of wooden huts.

"Freedom through work", read the letters above the gate.

With contempt they looked at it. It was a familiar sight - another concentration camp. This one was called BERGEN-BELSEN.

They had never heard of Bergen-Belsen and at the moment they didn't care much what it was like. All that mattered was that they seemed at the end of the incredible journey.

They passed through the guarded gate and found themselves on a dusty camp road. The Czech girls walked closely together. Neither Judith nor anyone else uttered a word.

On both sides of the road were barbed wires separating the various sub-camps. Strange looking people of many nationalities sat leaning against the plain huts or rested in the dust. On spotting the procession they picked themselves up and dragged themselves to the wires. Their expressionless faces spied them with a certain curiosity; this procession seemed different from the usual newcomers. On seeing their skin blackened from the coal dust they asked each other: "Do you think they are niggers?"

Some of the prisoners were clad in convict's uniform,

others were dressed in rags. Their hair was either shaved off or cut very short. Through their sallow skin protruded the shape of their bare skulls. There was hardly any flesh left on their bodies. Only subconsciously did the women take in the ghastly sight. The staring eyes sunken deep in their faces did not disturb them, nor did the filth and the rotten smell which dominated this camp. All they wanted was to sit down.

On the bumpy, dusty road lay a bone, bare, covered in dirt. As the prisoners feet dragged along the ground the bone was thrown from one end of the road to the other. Hannah's keen eyes followed it for a moment, then she picked it up and eagerly began to chew it. Nothing could stop the desire of her wild hunger.

On the way they passed men's, women's and mixed camps. Everywhere was dirt and ugliness. On and on they marched until they reached the other end of the camp. From somewhere came a cry: "They are going to the gypsy camp."

A big waste ground opened up in front of them. It was grey and withered and surrounded by barbed wire. Two rows of huts stood on one side and a hut with latrines was about a hundred yards away from them. To their astonishment they saw that all over the place were scattered dead bodies. Sometimes a few of them lay on top of each other. The camp had originally been assigned to gypsies only, but now that new victims were pouring into Belsen every day, other prisoners had to share the limited accommodation.

Beneath the undisturbed gaze of the occupants who sat crumpled on the filthy ground hunting for lice, the women were taken in front of one of the huts. There, three Jewish block leaders took over from the Germans. Robust and good looking with whips in their hands they went about their business.

"In there, in there!" they shouted.

The stream of women poured into the hut.

"Looks as though we are not going to be alone here," remarked Judith.

"Yes, gypsies," retorted Doris. "What difference does it make anyway?"

The floor was made of concrete, it was hard and cold, but it was a place on which they could deposit their desperately worn-out bodies.

Little gypsy children seemed to be everywhere, worming their way swiftly through the crowd of newcomers, their huge black eyes keenly spying for loot. A blockleader came in to secure order among the women fighting for space.

"Are we going to get something to eat or drink?" asked Hannah.

"Not today. Supper is over," was the harsh reply.

"But we haven't drunk or eaten for five days. We shall die."

"That's what you came here for." The answer was a familiar one. The Czech girls kept in a group. Too exhausted to talk or do anything else, they settled themselves upon the cold floor and slept.

* * * * *

Roll call was at four in the morning. Like mad beasts the blockleader and two or three of her helpers were running about in the huts chasing out the weak, near-dead prisoners. Judith gathered her weak limbs and dragged herself out into the open.

Chapter 28

All over the place accompanied by the yells of "Appell", groups were assembling in front of their own barracks. Whips were swishing and the prisoners shuffled into rows of fives. Two girls on duty in each barrack carried out the newly dead bodies and threw them on the piles between the silent ranks of prisoners. Those who were still alive but couldn't move, were taken somewhere, never to be seen again. The early morning was bitterly cold and many of them began to regret that they had thrown away their shoes and other garments on the journey here on the previous day. They stood shivering close together until the first rays of sunlight brought a new comfort to them.

At nine-thirty a deadly hush spread over the camp and two S.S. women marched through the gate. With their chins high in the air they inspected the lines, counted them and marched on to another group. At ten o'clock all were dismissed.

Throughout roll-call, Judith's eyes had dwelt upon a trough with water taps some distance away on the bumpy wasteland.

"They are out of order," the women who had been here some time told her.

"Perhaps there will just be a drop of water somewhere around them," Judith said to herself. "Perhaps they are in order again and nobody bothers to find out." Silently she hoped for a miracle and made her way toward it. Several of her group followed her, with the same idea in their minds.

They were almost there. Incited by new hope they staggered along, quickening their pace, not looking anywhere except in front of them.

Suddenly a hard blow sent Judith flying to the ground.

Unshed Tears

"Where do you think you are going?"

Surprised, Judith looked up. A pretty Jewish face filled with sadism and authority was looking sternly back at her. The band on her arm told that she was a Ca-Po, a camp police woman, a prisoner herself. Her accent disclosed that she was Czech. Something inside Judith stirred. Humiliated and seized by fury which gave her new strength she picked herself up and slapped the girl's face.

"Aren't you ashamed of yourself? You are a Czech prisoner the same as I am!"

For a moment the girl gazed at her with a staggered look, then she seized Judith by her collar and dragged her along toward the huts.

"You wait until I tell the Germans," the girl threatened, "unless you are prepared to go down on your knees and apologise."

All reason gone, only pride raging within her, Judith ejaculated: "You filthy monster! You are worse than the Germans, they only harm their enemies." Her voice was quivering with anger.

The German overseers looked at her sternly.

"She was rude to me. Please send her to the bunker."

Judith stiffened within herself. She knew what the bunker was: a little dark hole with rats running about where one stayed without food until one died.

"I only tried to get some water and she pushed me over," she said.

"You see, she is rude again."

The two women looked at her contemptuously. They saw more than Judith knew herself. Her face was only skin and

Chapter 28

hollows, her body was skeleton-like, black from the coal dust, her knees were crumpling beneath her.

"Don't bother about the bunker, she won't last long anyway," one of the German women said. Then she looked at her sternly and pointed at a small pile of bricks a few yards away.

"See those?" she said.

"Yes."

"Get two and bring them here."

With all the will power she could muster, Judith silently obeyed.

"Now kneel on the ground, take a brick in each hand and lift them high above your head. You will stay like this for the rest of the day!"

Not knowing how she managed it, Judith lifted first one hand, then the other. The German women and the Jewish Ca-Po looked at her with satisfaction in their faces. Not a word left Judith's lips now, only her eyes spoke: "You can't make me feel small by your monstrosities. If there is anyone to be looked down upon, it's you!"

She watched the German women walk away in one direction, the Ca-Po in the other. The minute their eyes were turned she rested her hands on the ground. Watching sharply she managed to hold them up in their intended position the moment one of them turned round. Then suddenly all three of them were out of sight. Judith knew they would return and she decided to act swiftly. Quickly she threw the bricks on the pile and disappeared. She knew that none of them would recognise her again. Of course, they could always think of something else, but she was prepared to risk it, ready to cope with the situation when it came along. As she expected, there were no consequences but she made a point of staying away from the Ca-Po.

Fleeing from the punishment ground she made toward her hut, glad to see the familiar faces again. A few moments later, cans with golden coloured water called coffee were brought in by monitors. Seeing some liquid, the newcomers hurried into the queue. Something to wet their cracked lips at last. It seemed as though they would never have enough to drink. They stood in groups grateful for every drop with which to satisfy their dried-up bodies.

A little refreshed Judith decided to have a look round.

Hannah went with her. They staggered through the dusty place admiring the energy of the little gypsy children who chased about quite happily. They had never known a better life, never seen the normal world. Their skill in stealing was admirable. They had already proved it in the short time the new transport had been there.

Judith clutched her little saucepan and spoon which were definitely more valuable than the empty tins which most of the prisoners used for the same purpose. There were people from all over Europe in this camp. It seemed as though the Germans, seeing their enemies close up on them from all sides, made this camp the assembly place for all their prisoners.

"Looks as though there isn't any gas chamber here," remarked Hannah.

"No, there used to be some kind of a crematorium over there, but they have no coal left to burn the dead," said Judith. "Do you think they will do something to us, to finish us off? I can't imagine that they brought us all here so that we are nice and handy for the liberators, all nicely together."

Chapter 28

"I don't think they will gas us or shoot us, they have no spare bullets anyway. They will just starve us. As you see, they are being very successful."

Dead bodies were scattered all over the place. They lay on the ground in twisted positions, their eyes mostly open, their teeth protruding, their limbs like hollow sticks. The prisoners took no more notice of them than of boulders lying inconveniently in their way.

"Those yapping women over there are French," pointed out Judith.

"Yes, and those we just passed were Italian."

They walked from hut to hut encountering women from almost all European countries. The place was swarming with them and they all looked very much alike - colourless, pitiful, skeleton-like, weak. Although Auschwitz was a place ruled by terror, this camp seemed to be cursed with human misery, filth and hopelessness.

"Look!" Judith said suddenly, pointing in the direction of hut number 9.

"Well bless my soul, it's them."

"Come on, let's talk to them."

It was the transport from Christianstadt which they had escaped from on the road. Kitty and Zdena were already there. Somehow it was good to see familiar faces and old friends. As they approached the hut a little group of Czech girls gathered around them.

"How long have you been here?" asked Hannah.

"About two weeks. I suppose you came yesterday."

"Yes."

They had a lot to tell each other about their adventures on the way.

"Milena and Marta went with the partisans, some ran away and we haven't heard from them since."

"Paula had her baby, a boy, she went to hospital."

"What do you do the whole day here?"

"We mostly sleep. It's the bromide in the food that makes us so sleepy."

"There is a mixed camp over there, how is that?"

"They call it the family camp. They are all Dutch Jews. We don't know why they have the privilege of being together. They came here straight from Holland a very long time ago. We spoke to them over the wires, they say Belsen was not a bad place as camps go. It used to be clean, prisoners went out to work and had comparatively enough to eat. Now of course it's just chaos. Nobody cares about anything. You just come here to die."

Judith caught sight of Janka, an old school-mate of hers. Death shone out of her face. She knew it was a matter of days for she had learned to recognise when the end was really near. There was something in the expression, the grin of the protruding teeth, the black hollow from which the eyes looked out with a drawn stupefaction, all senses and life gone out of them.

"It is a good thing they give you the bromide, otherwise you'd go potty," said one of the girls.

"Somehow you really stop caring about everything. Death is quite a salvation. The sooner it comes, the better. No food, the lice are eating you, you feel too ill, too hungry, too depressed, to do anything about it. Most of us have a temperature and no strength left to go on. You lie here in the dirt feeling sick, watching one after another die, the heaps of

Chapter 28

corpses growing every day, you just wait for the afternoon for the drop of soup, and when it's over you feel more hungry than before. And you know you can't go on like this much longer."

On the way back to their barrack, they were both very quiet. They had been to the latrine and to get there and back they had to step on top of the bodies as the area of wasteland approaching it was covered with them and there was no room between them to put one's foot.

"You know Hannah, I don't want to die here. I shall go on and on fighting against death. Perhaps one day a miracle will happen after all."

"No, I don't want to die either. We may talk differently though in a week's time."

They went back into the hut which was almost empty as most prisoners preferred to lie outside in the sun.

"It's good not to see them," said Hannah.

"These confounded lice. They get everywhere. The best place to catch them is behind your ears. It's those tiny baby ones which are so difficult to catch."

"I can distinguish now between the hair lice and the body lice."

"Don't boast, I could do that ages ago," grinned Judith.

"Once I thought I wouldn't survive even as much as seeing a louse," said Hannah.

"You get used to anything, even corpses around you."

"I suppose so."

"The Allies can't be so far off," Judith contemplated aloud.

"We just must wait and see."

"Isn't it fantastic how much you can survive?"

"Yes, it's almost unbelievable."

Unshed Tears

Then they lay down and slept.

Eventually soup time arrived. It was an incredible moment, one they had been waiting for, for so many days. Again monitors brought large cans and it was for the blockleader to distribute the long sought for liquid. Everything was set, the ranks of women were pushing impatiently, violent quarrels broke out. With a ladle the blockleader dived to the bottom of the can and brought out the buried treasure - the solid pieces of turnips. With these she filled her own little basin and those of her helper. Then at last she began to deal with the roaring mob. The helpers made attempts to keep order with their whips but succeeded only to a certain degree.

Then Judith's turn came. Her saucepan half-filled, she retreated to a place of her own where she could concentrate on the divine sensation of eating. Slowly she sipped from the spoon, one drop after another, desperately trying to avoid finishing the precious treat. She left the squares of turnip to the last. There were seven altogether.

Hannah came over.

"It's disgusting the way the blockleaders have a belly-full of solid turnips while we have to be contented with a bit of clear warm water.... How many bits of turnips did you have?"

"Seven."

"I had only six. I think the Germans ought to know what goes on here. I bet they don't know that the precious little food allocated to us is being stolen by those greedy pigs."

"I bet they don't care either."

"For the good of everybody, I think they should be told. Perhaps it will help."

Chapter 28

Hannah, desperate with hunger, did tell a German officer. He was a young, strong man of about twenty-two. He listened to her carefully, then quite suddenly he flew into a rage and with his right foot encased in a black leather boot he knocked Hannah to the ground. For about five minutes he amused himself by kicking her around on the rough ground until she bled from many wounds. Her face was grazed in two places, her expression was pitiful. She could hardly understand what was going on. Judith looked on, compassion tearing her heart and from somewhere a little tear found its way onto her cheek.

"Into the bunker!" the German shouted.

Dumbfounded Hannah stared at him, not quite being able to grasp what was happening. Then it was all over. Hannah was led away and disappeared for ever.

* * * * *

New transports were arriving every day. From all over Germany they came; dressed in rags, utterly exhausted and completely indifferent as regards their fate. They were too weak to care. The numbers in each hut increased daily and at night the prisoners lay squashed and twisted on top of each other with hardly enough room to breathe. Many coughed desperately and spat blood, others were almost delirious with high temperatures. Typhus was gradually getting a grip on the camp. Other diseases like typhoid, bowel disorders and tuberculosis were spreading rapidly and there was none to attend to the sick, and nobody cared. There was no more room in the former hospital and not enough staff to cope with the thousands of ill and dying. The conditions became more and more desperate and the heaps of corpses grew and multiplied with every new day.

Drowsy and overcome by fever Judith, like the rest of them, slept most of the day and counted the squares of turnip pieces in her soup. Roll call was the greatest ordeal and every day it was somebody else's turn to drop and to be carried away, not to be seen again.

"I must not fall, not today anyway, perhaps tomorrow a miracle will happen," Judith kept telling herself every morning. Afterwards it was all right. She could lie down and sleep in peace except for the lice which had made her body almost raw. Prisoners stumbling over her and a kick from a Ca-Po from time to time did not bother her. Everything around was like a dream and through that dream she knew that there was only one thing that really mattered. "Keep on going, keep on just for a little longer, don't give in, don't give in!"

In her trance she watched life around her and saw people who in the evening were still able to nod their heads and moan about their misery, lie dead in the morning, usually discovered by a neighbour who happened to rest her head on her during the night. Their glassy eyes stared toward the ceiling. Nobody bothered to shut them. Nobody mourned, nobody cried for the deceased. Like a stone she was picked up and thrown on one of the piles in front of the hut, with the others. When the time came and transports stopped pouring in, this was one way of gaining more room on the overcrowded floor. With every dead one, there was just a bit more breathing space. And tomorrow there would be even more.

Some people had no strength or will left to go to the latrines and sanitary conditions became abominable. The

Chapter 28

stench was beyond description but all was just part of the place.

But in spite of it all, those who cared just a little bit about going on, who had a spark of hope left in them, could notice that not everything was all right with the Germans. As the days passed, the brutal S.S. men and women grew more and more restless. Their reaction was two-fold. Some strode through the camp with an air of superiority, whipping anyone who came their way; others calmed down and even showed signs of friendliness.

"I am telling you Kitty, they are scared stiff," Judith said.

"I hope they won't do away with us in some drastic way. Two or three bombs would be enough. I bet they won't leave us here for the liberators."

"We must keep on hoping."

As April advanced, the growing tension among the Germans was unmistakable, something was happening. Sirens howled more frequently, and every time a British plane droned high in the sky above the camp, Judith blinked, opened her eyes and watched it take its course through the sun-drenched air. At times like these a slight feeling of joy swept over the prisoners. But these were only moments and for many the hopelessness went on.

It was a warm evening. The women in block 6 were as usual fighting and quarrelling over their places. Suddenly, quite suddenly, a bright light spread over the whole camp. Flabbergasted the women stopped their quarrels and stared out of the window. It was almost like daylight. British planes roared above their heads and disappeared.

"The British have seen us! They have seen us! Our friends know we are here!"

Unshed Tears

They could hardly comprehend the meaning of this. For the first time joy illuminated the faces of the prisoners who had forgotten how to laugh. And then the light came once more. Like a magic carpet it unfolded above them and once again it was daylight. Excitement surged through the whole of the Belsen camp and thousands of little sparks of hope sprang up in the hearts of the condemned prisoners.

Next day there was no food, nor the day after and thousands more were carried out of the huts.

"Something is going on, we just must hold on for a bit longer," Judith told the little group of Czech friends. Miraculously most of them had survived so far. The whole camp was waiting, waiting every minute of the day. Tension was in the air, everyone felt it, and the entire atmosphere in the camp had changed.

After four days without food, the Germans suddenly decided to give them the soup again and a slice of bread to go with it.

"How long is it since we have seen any bread?" asked Kitty.

"I can't remember," said Judith.

It seemed that more people were dying now than before and thousands became violently ill with dysentery. But nobody suspected that the precious piece of bread was the cause of the new trouble. The Germans had mixed ground glass with the flour. It was one way of killing off more prisoners, without using ammunition or fuel. Besides nobody would ever know. It wasn't their fault that the inmates were dying of starvation. There wasn't even enough food to go round for all the Germans; how could they be expected to feed the prisoners! They didn't really ill-treat them. They never shot anyone in

Belsen nor gassed anyone. Surely if the British came, they would see they weren't really bad, that they did their best. They even gave them bread when there was barely enough to go round their own people. As a matter of fact, they were really quite good!

★ ★ ★ ★ ★

Appell was over. Judith went to find a warm place in the sun and lay down. Several of her friends came and lay down beside her. Without any warning thunder shook the air. The sky was blue and quite clear. Then it came again, a little bit nearer. Judith propped herself up on her elbow and turned her ear in the direction of the noise. It came from the forest behind the camp. Breathlessly the girls looked at each other.

"It's shooting!"

"Yes, it's shooting, they are fighting in the forest!"

"I can't believe it! I can't believe it!" said Kitty.

"You don't want to believe anything yet, they can still drop some bombs on us or cut our heads off. They won't give us up like that," said Zdena.

"Seeing is believing," muttered Lilly.

"If they haven't done anything to us until now, they won't bother any more. Can't you realise, they are fighting in the forest! They are almost here! There will be no time for them to do anything to us," said Judith.

"Judith is right, besides, they wouldn't dare to do anything to us now. I bet they are too scared to touch us," said Kitty.

"Anyway, how do you know that the Germans won't fight them off? The war isn't over yet."

"Dopey!"

Unshed Tears

The shooting continued throughout the day. The sound of battle came from all sides. Sometimes the huts shook and the glass panes trembled under the pressure. Throughout the camp prisoners held hands, listening to the most wonderful symphony of Allied guns. They were coming closer and closer and an unusual mixture of hope and fear took possession of all the inmates. They did not dare to be happy yet, though with every new shot a little energy and joy surged through their veins. For days the camp was in a state of expectation.

XXIX

It was a cold misty morning. Quiet rows of half-dead human beings stood on parade in front of their huts, waiting to be counted. Only an occasional sigh broke the silence. One hour followed another. The strain of it was becoming too much, many collapsed and were taken away. As in a dream Judith stood on the spot swaying from side to side hardly aware of her surroundings. Fever shook her body, she felt sick and the last ounce of energy and will power seemed to have deserted her.

"I can't any more," she whispered to Kitty.

"Try, you must try!"

"Everything is going round and round, I can't stand, I can't." Her voice quivered.

"Hold on to me."

"No, it's no use. I don't really care. I want to lie down and be sick and not know anything."

"By the sun it must be about eleven o'clock. I wonder why they are so long, they must be here any minute now. Just try to wait a bit longer."

"Kitty, I can't."

Unshed Tears

Suddenly the noise of a thousand voices rang in the air. It was approaching and was becoming louder and louder.

"What is this?" everyone was asking. An air of suspense hung over the waiting ranks.

Judith's heart stood still for a moment, she didn't dare to breathe.

Speechlessly the prisoners looked at each other and then turned in the direction of the noise which was quite deafening by now. Then they saw for themselves. Along the camp road an endless mob of tattered men and women cane running, shouting madly.

"The Germans have run away! They have gone! We are free!"

It was too difficult to grasp all at once.

"Free? Do they mean we are really free, the Germans have gone?"

Their exhausted minds were too confused to take it all in at the first moment. Then a sudden wave of recognition swept over the ranks and prisoners began to fall into each other's arms and rejoice.

For Judith it meant one thing - she could lie down. She was too ill to think; all that was happening came to her as if from a distance. Only from time to time her mind cleared a little and then suddenly she realised that the moment she had been picturing in her mind every minute of her imprisonment was actually here. She had imagined they would all dance and run and go mad. Instead ... well, there would be no more roll calls anyway, no whips, no orders.

"I can't imagine that I shall ever feel well and strong again, can you?" she asked Kitty.

Chapter 29

"No, not really, but it will come one day."

The gates between the various sub-camps lay open for people to wander in and out, but the main gates were guarded by Hungarian soldiers who had shared the military barracks with the Germans not far away. Nobody was allowed to leave the camp. Several prisoners were shot in the attempts to break through. The fighting in the forest behind the camp was still going on, and some people were afraid that the Germans might come back.

The four days which followed were full of unrest, expectation and chaos. Those who had a little strength left wandered in and out of the various camps in search of relatives and friends. Everybody seemed to be looking for someone. In parts little groups gathered, accordions played and people sang and clapped their hands to the rhythm. They were mostly non-Jewish men and women who had been treated like prisoners of war and had escaped the worst treatment. The store-huts were looted; those who could, brought away with them as much as they could manage to carry.

As though in a trance Judith made an expedition to the nearest storeroom. It was like a dream to see a mountain of prisoners' dresses. She didn't get any further. Gratefully she threw away her louse-ridden clothes and put on the clean dress. It was a good feeling.

Once more she left her camp and crawled to a pond at the bottom of which lay dozens of dead bodies. Around the edge stood hundreds of people. Someone passed Judith a newly filled cup. Gratefully she threw herself at it. Then she went back to the hut and waited....

* * * * *

Unshed Tears

It was the 15th of April 1945. After a few hours of silence, the shooting started again, this time quite near. Tension in the camp rose. The prisoners' ears were constantly tuned to the bangs echoing in the vicinity. All this, however, didn't stop hundreds more people from dying.

Judith lay helplessly in the hut hardly knowing what was going on around her. Kitty was next to her also very ill and silent and some of the Czech girls lay scattered around them. They felt too wretched to really care for anything and grateful to be left alone.

In the afternoon they dragged themselves out into the sunshine and sat against the barrack wall. Suddenly the huge entrance gate to the camp not far away from them flew open and a British tank rolled in. Another one followed and another until a whole file of them crawled along the camp road. In spite of her illness Judith gasped and stared and her heart stood still for a moment.

"Look, the British, they are here!"

"The British are here! The British are here!"

"The British," breathed Kitty.

"They are here! They have come! We are safe at last," rang throughout the camp, and those who were able, ran to welcome the liberators, jumped onto the tanks and embraced and kissed the strong smiling men, who were a little confused and horrified at the spectacle that confronted them.

Judith staggered to the wires. Holding on to the fence she gazed at the passing tanks, at the healthy looking men, wondering whether it was all a dream. Then she knew nothing more.

* * * * *

Chapter 29

"Here, have some water."

Judith opened her eyes. A soldier was kneeling by her side.

"We have got tanks full of water out there," he smiled.

Judith attempted a smile too. She looked around her. She was in the hut and near her lay other prisoners attended to by many soldiers.

"Soon you will get something to eat," the soldier whispered in a broken German.

"You have come," Judith uttered.

"Yes, we have come, you are safe now.... What is your name?"

"Judith."

"Mine is Steve."

"Steve," Judith whispered and smiled. Her face burned.

"You are ill. Soon you will go to hospital and get well, and then you will go home."

"Home ... perhaps Michael will be there ..." she whispered.

"Who is Michael?"

"Michael Alexander ... a friend of mine ... if you come across him, tell him I am here."

"Yes, of course I will."

"Is the war over?"

"No, not yet, but it won't take long. You sleep quietly now and later I will bring you some food...."

For the next few days they ate portions which were distributed among the prisoners: tinned pork, chicken soup, beef, rice and other things. Raw potatoes appeared from somewhere, and little bonfires sprang up all over the wasteland behind the huts. There the men and women baked the potatoes, heated up the tins, burned their filthy clothes when they had taken new ones from the store, and stayed there sometimes throughout the night in preference to the crowded barracks.

One morning Judith crawled out of the hut and sat on the little steps. A tank full of water stood waiting for anyone who wanted some. A cart arrived and on it were German prisoners still in their uniform. An English guard ordered them out and made them pick up the dead, distorted bodies until the cart was full of them. Then back they went, sat on top of the heap of corpses, and drove away ready to unload in the crematorium.

"Serves them bloody well right," someone said.

The smoke was belching from the crematorium chimney and the smell of scorching bones dominated the camp. It was a ghastly smell and together with the dozens of bonfires fouled the air completely. But what did it matter?

Feeling a little stronger after having eaten, many prisoners took a new interest in their surroundings and made friends with the soldiers. Although the rather rich food to which they had not been accustomed upset many stomachs, their owners did not care and went on eating. Nothing could make them resist consuming anything they managed to lay their hands on.

Kitty got hold of a lot of sugar and tins of pork and taking no notice of anybody ate greedily without stopping. Sugar was something they had not seen in this camp and Judith wondered where she got it from. However she refrained from saying anything and quietly moved away from her.

"It would be good to have some sugar," she thought, "but I am not going to beg for some."

The days rolled by. The camp was cleared of all corpses. People were still dying but were taken away on the same day.

Chapter 29

Misery, filth and hunger were still about, but the prisoners were patient, knowing that their liberators were doing their best. After all there was nobody to bully them, to push them around. They were treated with kindness and respect, the rest would sort itself out.

Kitty died early one morning. Her digestive system could not cope with all the food. She had not been used to it and her body was too weak to fight the illness.

"If she had shared some of that foodstuff with us, it wouldn't have happened to her," remarked Zdena.

"They say she had made friends with a British officer down at the food stores. She could speak English and that made all the difference."

"Poor Kitty."

Judith didn't say anything. What was the use of talking?

* * * * *

At last, early on a dull morning the evacuation of the camp began. The whole day lorries went backward and forward taking the men and women to nearby military barracks. Flags of different nationalities adorned the various buildings and Judith was glad to see the Czech one inviting her to move into what seemed nearest to home. The barracks were clean and modern with comfortable bunks and shower baths. The soldiers came every day, and sprayed them with disinfectant - their hair, their clothes and blankets, slowly winning the battle with the lice.

Still trembling with fever, Judith was taken to hospital. She had typhus. Almost half the camp was turned into typhus wards.

Unshed Tears

It was good to lie in a soft bed covered with white sheets free from lice and dirt. She knew she would be all right now. Outside the sun was shining, flower-bushes were blooming in front of the window and everything was beautiful and peaceful.

The war was over. Europe was at peace and life seemed almost perfect.

As she was getting better, her thoughts began to turn towards home. Until now she had been incapable of any continuous thinking, but with her mind clearing, the future opened out in front of her.

Stumbling to the white painted window she would gaze out at the green lawn, at the flowers and the blue sky and dream. It was only then that she fully realised that the war and suffering was over, that the normal world was ready to receive her into its arms, that all the exciting things she had so often pictured, in what at the time seemed mad fantasy, were all hers. Her face and eyes laughed with joy as she thought of it all.

It was good to be alive, it was good to think of Prague and Michael and freedom and all the rest of it! The happiness seemed too great to comprehend.

XXX

Judith left the barrack above which flew the Czech flag and made her way down to the hospital part of the camp. On the way she met gay and healthy looking men and women, their bodies strong and filled out, walking to and from the forest nearby where they had spent many hours convalescing after their illnesses. It was the middle of July.

Quietly she slipped into the white, cheerful looking ward.

"Judith," Tania said quietly.

"Hullo, Tania," she sat down on the edge of the bed.

"I hear you are going home tomorrow."

"Yes, home...."

"You lucky devil," Tania said, her eyes gazing longingly into the distance. She was pale, and sad. Judith had found her here by accident several weeks before when she was recovering after typhus. She went to see Zdena in another ward, and there she was, her dear old friend from the Ghetto, her eyes aglow with excitement, happy to see her again. She had tuberculosis and was coughing very badly. Nobody knew how her weak body would cope with the disease.

"Any news?" Tania asked quietly.

"No, I went to the office yesterday again, but they haven't heard of any of the people I had asked about."

"Not even my sister? She was young and healthy."

"No, Tania, nor Michael, they know nothing about him either." Then she forced a cheerful smile into her face. "After all, they have mostly people who were actually in Belsen on the register. Only a few other lists have come from different places. They might all be there when we get back."

"Judith ... perhaps I shall never get back," she whispered.

"It all depends on you, Tania. You must fight and want to go back, you know that that is at least as important as all the medicines they can give you. Besides the Red Cross is sending you to Sweden. The mountain air will do you a world of good."

"I know.... I want to go home ... but you see, there comes a time when you can't fight any longer ... somehow you just can't...."

"You wait until you see the beautiful countryside, the pine forests, the mountains. You will feel stronger again."

"Are there still many people in the camp?" Tania asked.

"Quite a few have gone already but there are still a lot left. Many won't be going for some time yet. They don't want to go back home, they want to go to Palestine, or to relatives in England or America."

"I see," Tania said quietly.

"I shall write to you as soon as I get to Prague and then you can write to me. I will tell you all the news, and I will try to find out about your people too."

"Thanks. Judith ... you won't forget to write ... will you ... even if I don't answer."

"No, of course not."

Chapter 30

"It's funny, you go on fighting and struggling all through the war waiting and dreaming about the moment you will be liberated, and when at last it comes, it's too late."

"You -"

"Psst ... it's no good telling me anything."

"Tania ..."

"It's all right, somehow you get used to the idea.... There are moments when I think a miracle might happen and I might get well again ... sometimes I dream and I wish I could have five years to enjoy the freedom in, five years in which I would feel well enough to enjoy the sunshine, the food and water, the feeling that I can go where I like and when I like and perhaps experience just once what it is like to be happily in love ... I wouldn't mind dying then."

The tears Judith had been forcing back filled her eyes suddenly.

"It will all come, you will see."

"I will try my best ... I shall miss you, Judith."

"I shall miss you too, perhaps I will come to Sweden for a holiday. I must go now," her voice quivered.

They held hands. Judith wanted to say something but couldn't. Then through their tears they both attempted a brave smile.

"Goodbye Tania."

"Goodbye."

She got up and walked out of the room.

* * * * *

Judith shielded her eyes with her hand against the sun.

Unshed Tears

"There it is!" She said suddenly, pointing into the distance.

The friends who were riding on the open lorry with her looked curiously in the direction.

"But it is a cattle train again," exclaimed Zdena.

"What does it matter? We are going home," Judith said, her eyes sparkling with excitement.

The train stood in the middle of the meadows, the same place where four months ago they had arrived, more dead than alive.

"Remember?" said Lilly.

"You bet I do."

The men and women who had arrived here before them were busy picking flowers, making long chains and bunches out of them, decorating the train with them. The twenty on the lorry were allocated one of the waggons, and soon they too did the same. They picked all the colourful flowers they could find and garnished their waggon with them until all the drabness had disappeared and it looked gay and inviting.

Fifteen hundred of them were making ready to go on the most wonderful journey of their lives - the journey home, towards freedom. At last the train set off. The sliding doors were wide open, there was plenty to eat and to drink, everyone was bubbling over with happiness and excitement. They were going home! Like a colourful stream of flowers the train was winding its way through the countryside.

Sitting on the floor in clean suits and dresses, the men and women sang gay songs, played games. There was plenty of room to move about and when the train stopped they jumped out and replaced the faded flowers with new ones.

Chapter 30

Hanover appeared in the distance.

"There seem to be no houses left," remarked Doris.

"No, it's just a mass of ruins," Judith cried.

"Let my eyes dwell upon this heavenly sight," said Zdena, her face alight with satisfaction.

Then they were off again. Night came and the train stopped in the station of a small town. They all jumped out and roamed about the platform. Not long afterwards another train pulled upon the opposite side and with much noise a crowd of homeward bound Italian prisoners of war invaded the platform. Boisterous, with fancy hats, they came over to the Czechs and in spite of their little knowledge of German, but with much gesturing they all managed to understand each other. An accordion struck up and moments later happy pairs were hopping along the platform. One Czech boy borrowed the accordion and led his people into a round of famous folk songs. The Italians hummed to the tunes, clapped their hands and clowned about.

An Italian boy, Guido, came over to Judith and they danced and stayed together until it was time to go. He gave her a big kiss and placed his huge panama hat on her head.

"From me to you," his forefinger said.

Judith laughed and kissed him, and then it was back to the train again.

After midnight it puffed out of the station. The Italians stood on the platform waving madly and shouting messages which none of them could understand but which they acknowledged cheerfully all the same.

It was laughter and shouting all the way. They passed many trains every day with young people from all countries making their way home from various camps, and every time it was riotous waving and cheering, incited by their common, overbrimming happiness of having found freedom and beauty once more. It was the most glorious journey of their lives. Every new day was bringing them nearer home, and with every new day the excitement and tension was mounting.

Then one evening they reached the Czech border. The train stopped and fifteen hundred voices sang the national anthem. Touched, with tears of joy rolling down their cheeks, they continued on the last lap of their journey. They were on Czech soil now, and soon they would be in Prague. "One more night and then tomorrow morning ..."

Judith lay down on the floor, her bright shining eyes looking out at the darkening sky. Tomorrow morning she would be in Prague. It was so hard to comprehend. After all the years, the moment was really approaching now. She would have liked to jump up and dance with joy, but everyone around her was quiet and most of them were asleep. Prague ... with all its spires and beauty, a liberated Prague with the Germans and tyranny gone, able to breathe under the free skies once more!

Her joyful heart was dancing within her. Tomorrow the world would belong to her, a thousand and one things she had been dreaming about would become true. Was it really possible? She had never known that such intense happiness existed and now it was all here, only a few hours separated her from it.

She closed her eyes, her lips still smiling as she drifted into a sleep.

* * * * *

Chapter 30

The sun was rising behind the castle when the train slowly drove into the station. All the men and women rose, and overwhelmed with feelings, stood silently looking at the wonder in front of them. Filled with the miracle of the moment, some prayed, some cried, others just stared. The national anthem broke out once more and they stood reverently, singing, watching the city waking in front of them.

Then they jumped out on the platform where men from the repatriation office welcomed them. They took everyone's name and gave addresses of hostels to those who had nowhere to go. There was hot coffee and rolls for all of them. They learned the address of the repatriation office where they could receive an identity card, some money, and enquire about their friends and relatives. Then a little commotion followed, people said farewells, made dates, gave each other addresses and then it was all over. The normal world was ready to receive them.

Judith took her little bundle and walked out of the station. She stopped in the morning sunshine on the pavement and gazed at the life around her.

Trams were buzzing past her, people were going to work, early shoppers were on their way. She had been here many times before, but now it all seemed new to her, she felt like a visitor stepping onto unknown magic soil. She wanted to smile at everybody, tell all the passers-by that she had come back, but they were all busy with their own little thoughts. She had imagined they would all crowd around her and welcome her and show her how happy they were to have her back ... but then, they were strangers, they didn't know her.

Slowly she strolled down the road, looking at the shop

windows, filling her eyes with all the wondrous sights. She was walking among the crowd in the city with nobody to look for her to arrest her, with nobody minding where she was going. With a new lust for life she was taking it all in, always looking for some more to add to the many marvels.

She came onto St. Wenceslas Square, the hotels, the shops, the museum and the statue were all there, just as she had remembered them. Only one house was damaged by a bomb.

"A pity Mummy and Daddy can't see it all," she thought, and her brow clouded for a moment. Then she stopped to look at the shop window of a well known store. She walked down the hill and looked up at St. Wenceslas on his horse and the famous museum building behind it. Even the sky seemed different today. "I am really here," she whispered to herself.

With the repatriation office in front of her, she quickened her step. Michael - was he back yet? And all her other friends, but most of all Michael. What would their meeting be like? Perhaps she would even see him today.

Overcome by this idea she sped along through the crowds, always faster and faster. Her eyes shone with anticipation. Could it really be that she would see him today, maybe in a few hours' time, maybe quite soon? Impatiently she entered the cool building, looked around her and followed a direction sign into a large hall swarming with people. There on the wall hung lists of names of returned prisoners, arranged in alphabetical order.

Her heart pounding violently within her, and breathing heavily, she pushed her way through the mob.

A few steps in front of the list marked 'A' she suddenly stopped, overcome by doubt, then, the pit of her stomach tight

Chapter 30

with expectation, she moved forward, her wide open eyes scaling the list. Then she tried once more.

Taken aback, she gazed silently in front of her. His name wasn't on it.

"Perhaps the new list isn't out yet," she said to herself eventually, and pushed out to the office.

"All the names we have got are on there," the official said.

"Do you have the names of all the people?" she asked, "all those who came back?"

"We take them down as soon as the train arrives."

"Thank you," she murmured quietly and walked out into the sunshine. Then she strolled back in to look up other friends, but could find none.

Instinctively she made her way toward the house Michael used to live in. She climbed up a steep hill on top of which stood a tall modern block of flats. Her face wet with perspiration and soiled with dust, her dress clinging to her body, she knocked on the caretaker's door. She heard his heavy footsteps behind the closed door and anxiously waited for the figure to appear.

"Mr. Alexander - do you know Mr. Alexander - has he come back yet?"

"I very much doubt it, Miss. I am sure he would have called. There are some things of his down in the cellar."

"Oh, I see, thank you."

She walked out into the sunshine again. A little burden was weighing down upon her heart. She tried to dismiss it.

"There will be many more trains coming into Prague every day, he may turn up any moment."

She went to the hostel which wasn't far away, got a bed in a large dormitory, washed, had her first three-course lunch and went out again.

Once more she went to the repatriation office, got a little identity card and some money. Then she made her way through the well known streets, across the bridge, through some side streets, turned several corners and then she was there. She stood on the pavement opposite the house gazing at the third floor windows behind which was her former home. At this moment thousands of little memories flashed through her mind and for a while she lived in the enchanted world of recollection. Once again the children she used to play with were scampering around the pavements, and windows were alive with well known faces. In front of that house over there the blind man used to sit in the sun. The warmth and cosiness of her childhood days seemed quite near, and she stood there for a long while lost in the past, living those days all over again.

And then the magic was gone. She gazed around her at the strange figures in the street, at the houses, the stones in the pavement, the lamp-post which used to be part of her life, all of them were gazing at her with a cold unfamiliar dignity.

Once more she looked up at the windows on the third floor. She could almost see her parents, their smiling, unsuspecting faces looking back at her. Tears welled up in her eyes and suddenly she didn't know what to do, where to turn to. For a long while she stood there, a lonely figure in the big world, her lips quivering, her flooded eyes gazing helplessly at the house opposite her. Was this what she had been waiting for for so long, a life without all those she had loved, in a city where every spot and corner would bring painful memories to her.

She turned and walked slowly down the road and into the

Chapter 30

park on the hill from where the panorama of the "golden" city opened up in front of her. She leaned on the parapet and looked down at the calm flowing river, the row of bridges, the quaint colourful houses, the thousand steps leading up to the castle. A desperate forlornness gripped her. How different it all was from what she had been imagining. She brushed away her tears with the back of her hand.

"I mustn't cry. I didn't come all this way to be unhappy."

Endlessly she stared at the life beneath, at the sight she had so often seen in her dreams.

"I am really here, I have lived to see it all, I can breathe freely once more, and tomorrow I shall go and meet the train; perhaps Michael will come back."

Aware of the novelty and wonder of her newly acquired freedom and filled with hope about Michael's return she made her way back to the hostel. There among the lively women who for so many years had shared her fate she felt better. They had a real meal on a neatly laid table and for half an hour everything else ceased to exist while they concentrated on the miracle of eating.

"I had almost forgotten how to use a knife and fork."

"Fancy eating from a china plate."

"And sitting on a chair ..."

Every little thing was a new experience. Her eyes gleaming with delight, Judith tackled each one of these with great enthusiasm. It was wonderful to walk on a carpet, eat from a table, switch on a radio, see an egg, have flowers on the table, brush one's teeth, read a book, touch money, wash one's hands before a meal, iron one's clothes, have a bath, and above all do exactly as one pleased.

Unshed Tears

She was much happier here among her own people. For the first time she realised that the outer world was a little frightening. There was no more drifting with the crowd and obeying orders. From now on she had to make her own decisions. She was seventeen, she had lived a lifetime. She knew how to fend for herself in the camp, but how did one cope with a normal life? How did one set about it? Suddenly there was a future, a real future in a real world, not one dream born of empty stomachs and blistered feet. The future which did not consist of comfortable shoes, food, a bed and clean clothes. She was very tired. Her thoughts were a mixture of joy, loneliness, confusion and hope. Her bed was inviting and she dropped into it, leaving all her worries for tomorrow.

* * * * *

Judith got up early the next morning and made for the station. There was hardly anybody about. She stood at the end of the platform waiting for the first signs of a train coming in. Again and again she lived through the moment when she would spot him among the crowd of people and rush toward him and hold him and know that everything was going to be all right. She saw his face radiantly happy at seeing her, she felt his arms around her and the warm security of his presence. She thought of life shared with him, of all the things they would do together and every part of life seemed to take on a different meaning. Could this really come true?

At last the train came puffing into the station. Judith held her breath and waited. Eventually the stream of homecomers started pouring towards her. Full of expectation she combed

Chapter 30

the crowd with her eyes, quickly looking from one to another until the last one came filing past, and she remained standing there alone. Choking with disappointment she realised that she wasn't at all surprised. Somehow she hadn't really expected him to come today.

What now?

She drifted out of the station and for the rest of the day haunted the streets, always looking for something she couldn't find.

"Perhaps he will come tomorrow," she kept on saying to herself, and then she tried to think of how lucky she was. She put a meaning to every step she made of her own free will, the trains, food shops, singing birds, houses, the sky and sunshine. She almost managed to convince herself that she was really happy....

She went to meet the train every morning. With new hope she watched the crowd come toward her until she was the last one left on the platform and there was nothing else for her to do but to go on her usual round of the repatriation office to look at lists, homes of old friends and streets which were filled with painful memories. David was dead. He had been killed in action fighting in the Czech army, and all her other friends had not returned yet....

"There will be no train tomorrow," said the porter to her one day. He had been watching her every morning.

"No train?" She gazed at him with petrified amazement. "There will be no train tomorrow?"

"No, Miss. The next train will be on Thursday."

"On Thursday," she whispered, "that's a very long time."

Oppressed with loneliness and disappointment, hardly

knowing what she was doing, she strolled out into the street. "He may never come back," she whispered at last. She recollected all the moments they had had together and then again tortured herself by imagining him suddenly appearing in front of her and telling her all the things she wanted to hear, and taking her round Prague admiring the wonder of freedom with her.

* * * * *

It was an evening toward the end of August. The day had been very hot, and she made her way down to the quiet embankment from where she could watch the silver flowing river and enjoy the refreshing breeze. Everything was peaceful, it was gradually getting dark and the twilight was giving the bridges and the castle a new, magic shape.

She leaned against the parapet and gazed sadly into the water. Down here she suddenly knew it.

"He will never come back." She was sure of it now and the realisation startled her. "No, he will never come back."

For a long, long time she just gazed, trying to get the full meaning of it. What was she going to do? She was alone and the whole future lay in front of her. She had to find a solution. The thoughts came to her slowly, one after another, arguing within her, gradually taking a definite shape.

"I mustn't go on like this. I mustn't cry anymore. I must find a way out somehow ... I am young; the whole of life lies in front of me. I mustn't build my happiness on something I know will never come. I shall try to forget the past, I will break away from it, stop torturing myself with memories and waiting endlessly for people who will never come. I must look toward the future. I will work and make something of myself, do

Chapter 30

something really worth while. Out of all my family and friends I am the only one to survive. I mustn't let them down ... I shall make myself useful ... somehow.... Whatever I do, I mustn't cry anymore. I mustn't feel sorry for myself.... The world is full of wonderful things and I will go and find them ..."

As if a new world had suddenly opened up in front of her, Judith felt relief surging through her being, the burden on her heart was slipping away and for the first time since she had set foot in Prague she breathed freely. A newly discovered happiness began to run through her veins. At last she was free, really free. Tomorrow she would go and enquire about the possibilities of study and think of a way to make new friends.

A smile of happiness spread over her face. She was going to be all right now, she knew it. Suddenly filled with joyful energy, she detached herself from the railings and began to speed along the embankment. The nearer she came to the Old Charles bridge the quicker her feet carried her forward, until she started to run across the bridge and towards the steps that led up to the castle. She ran all the way up, breathlessly reaching the top.

From there she could see the city in all its glory. Her eyes filled with wonder and excitement, she stood on the hill looking at the first stars, and the silhouettes of the rooftops and spires beneath her. The evening breeze was playing with her hair and her cotton frock. She remained like this for a long time. Eventually filled with the magic of the world she whispered: "I am alive! I am free! Tomorrow a new life will start for me.

"Tomorrow will be the beginning of my happiness and I shall fight for it until the very end."